RISING WIND

DICK COUCH

AVON BOOKS  NEW YORK

AVON BOOKS
A division of
The Hearst Corporation
1350 Avenue of the Americas
New York, New York 10019

Copyright © 1996 by Dick Couch
Published by arrangement with Naval Institute Press
Visit our website at **http://www.AvonBooks.com**
Library of Congress Catalog Card Number: 95-49583
ISBN: 0-380-72978-4

First Avon Books Printing: January 1998

AVON TRADEMARK REG. U.S. PAT. OFF. AND IN OTHER COUNTRIES, MARCA
REGISTRADA, HECHO EN U.S.A.

Printed in the U.S.A.

WCD   10 9 8 7 6 5 4 3 2 1

DAY OF VENGEANCE

"Then we will attack on the morning of December seventh—December eighth in Japan?"

Tadao nodded. "Precisely. We will storm ashore at the same time Admiral Yamamoto's air group swooped down on the American ships in Pearl Harbor. And we will see if the Americans are any better prepared than they were in 1941. Are you with me?"

Taiyo leaned forward bowing, his forehead a few centimeters from the mat. "I am honored to serve Tadao-sama. It will be victory or death."

"So be it," said Tadao. He placed a hand squarely on the man's knee, then bowed deeply before rising again to meet his eyes. "Victory or death."

And this one's for Alice

Acknowledgments

Writing a book is always a learning experience for the author. That was particularly true with *Rising Wind*. As I sought to understand the character of the Japanese people, and specifically the nature and attributes of the samurai, I was awed by the discipline and passion of these magnificent warriors. There is much to be admired in their absolute dedication to duty, and much to be learned from the difficulties that can arise out of blind devotion. But that can be said of elite warriors in our own military. My special thanks to David Keller, Earl Kishida, Mark Olshacker, George "Digger" O'Dell, Jana Marck, Al Marmelstein, Clark Presswood, Bob Ratcliff, Mike Sullivan, Gary Stubblefield, and Anne Collier Rehill—editor extraordinaire—for their help with this work. And for those of you who made me promise not to mention your names, thank you too!

The Japanese people forever renounce war as a soverign right of the nation or the threat or use of force a means of settling international disputes.

—Article 9 of the Constitution of Japan

The point isn't to be friends but to maintain peace and prosperity in Asia, which is possible only with U.S.–Japanese cooperation. For this reason, the U.S. can't afford "Japan bashing." Nor can it afford to remove its troops [from Asia] and risk Japan's arming to defend itself against a historically aggressive Russia and a more assertive China.

—Richard Nixon, June 1993

Contents

PART ONE

THE DAY
OF THE
RONIN

Sunday, 20 November, 11:35 P.M.
TOKYO, JAPAN

The room was powerful, one worthy of serious deliberations and important decisions. Its casual elegance and understated dignity were clearly the influence of a Western design consultant. The conference room's location on the top floor of the Sasasone Building, in the heart of the city's financial district, ranked the facility among some of the most expensive real estate in Tokyo, and therefore in the world. Straight-backed leather chairs surrounded the plain, massive oak conference table. A plush Oriental carpet overlaid the rich, polished mahogany flooring. From a large, heavily framed etching on one of the walls, two mounted samurai with thick eyebrows glowered into the room. They were from the Sengoku Period and particularly fierce. Behind the chairman's seat, the building's namesake, Hiro Sasasone himself, peered down on the proceedings. Three large sections of window afforded the conferees an unobstructed view of the city and Tokyo Bay to the south. One could clearly make out the subcity areas of Jimbo-cho, Ningyo-cho, and the Ginza. A million lights from the vast city shimmered clear to the water's edge while the mooring lights of ships at anchor dotted the harbor like tiny beacons on a velvet plain. Occasionally, a moving strobe marked the passing of a helicopter or light plane.

Shortly before midnight, the two huge raised-panel doors swung open and several men began to file into the room. They moved in groups of twos and threes, smiling and talk-

3

ing quietly. In keeping with Japanese corporate culture, they all wore white shirts and dark ties, young men in gray suits and older men in blue. Many carried briefcases. Only the time of the meeting and the two hard-looking individuals who stationed themselves at either side of the door suggested this was anything but another meeting of senior and mid-level executives. An imposing figure wearing an immaculately tailored Savile Row silk suit and thick white hair stepped behind the seat at the head of the table. The others quieted down and found places behind their own chairs.

"Gentlemen, I believe it is time we began our work." Formal bows were exchanged and they took their seats.

Directly above this gathering, on the roof of the building, a solitary black-clothed form stood on the ledge with his back to the harbor. A maintenance floor devoted to heating and air-conditioning equipment separated his perch from the meeting room. He stood some fifteen feet above the lighted bank of windows, visible to him only by their glow. Shintaro Nakajima wore black coveralls with heavy knee and elbow pads and stout, steel-toed boots. Fiberglass guards were strapped to his shins and forearms, and he had a plastic helmet with a thick plexiglass face shield. A precise length of half-inch braided nylon line joined an I-beam that supported the window-washing equipment to a snap link secured to the D-ring of his torso harness. Nakajima tested the line again with a sharp tug and looked at his watch. He decided to give them a few more minutes.

The November wind felt sharp and damp as it came off the bay and found the opening between his collar and the base of his helmet. Directly above, stars littered the clear sky. Nakajima again pictured the inside of the conference room, the location of the door, and the arrangement of the furnishings. Visually, he placed each of the somber-faced men around the table. He could see the vibrant colors and ornate design of the hand-woven rug, and he appreciated the quality of the paintings. He knew the bodyguards, no doubt handpicked for their loyalty and deadly skills, would by now occupy their traditional positions by the door.

His left hand unconsciously found the selector lever of his Heckler & Koch MP-5A submachine gun to ensure it was in the "fire" position. His breathing quickened, and the lower edge of his face shield began to fog. Then he smiled. Relax, he told himself as he closed his eyes and took several slow, deep breaths. He recalled his own advice to his men during training: It is reasonable to experience fear, for dangerous tasks are very much a part of what we do. But you must learn to manage it. The fear may never go away, but your management skills will improve.

For Nakajima, it was as much excitement and anticipation as fear. That, too, had to be managed.

A magnificent half moon took a low position in the southern sky and combined with the lights of the city to extinguish the stars just above the horizon. To his right, the Ara River sliced into the northern part of the city and just to his left, beyond the corner of the building, was a dark oasis in the glitter that marked the Imperial Palace. Behind him, down the western shore of the bay, the cities of Kawasaki and Yokohama twinkled like clusters of gem-stones. It was all so vast, but he took it all in with a glance, missing nothing.

Sensing the time had come, he tapped the button on the pistol grip of his weapon. Then he spoke quietly into a communications probe that hooked down from his helmet to the corner of his mouth.

"Kinichi, are you ready?"

"Yes, Captain."

"Very well, stand by. Break, Spotter Two-seven, are you in position?"

"This is Two-seven—affirmative."

"Understood, Two-seven. Give us a pass."

The command was acknowledged. Moments later, an American-made HH-60 helicopter made a single pass a quarter mile from the building and slightly above it. Inside the helo, one of Nakajima's men studied the conference room with a pair of stabilized Nikkon binoculars.

"The vultures have gathered. Gotoda is there, and I can see documents on the table."

"Very well. Kinichi, forty seconds...stand by... mark!"

Nakajima heard two clicks in his headphones as his assault element acknowledged the transmission. Inside the building, four black-clad forms slipped from the women's restroom. In single file, they glided down the hall to a corner near the conference-room door. By the time the guard posted outside the entrance saw them, a 9mm Browning High Power already rested on his temple. He carefully removed his hand from the inside of his suit jacket. One of the men in black took him silently away while another placed a light breaching charge on the double doors.

Outside and above, Nakajima stood on the ledge in a half-crouch and studied his watch. Suddenly he rolled backward, using the full spring in his legs to distance himself from the building. His body was fully horizontal when the rope came taut and began to swing him back in and down toward the windows of the meeting room. He was at the six-o'clock position of his arc and accelerating through the cold night air when he came through the window. With a tremendous crash he tore through the plate glass, sending crystal shards across the long table and those seated around it. The tension of the rope pulled him upright as, with one hand, he leveled his weapon on the two men at the door. His other hand slapped the quick-release on the tether to free himself. His feet had barely touched the floor when a second crash brought in the doors along with a cloud of sulfurous smoke. One of them clung to a single hinge while the second door fell flat on the carpet.

The men in the room froze amid the glass and smoke. Had they been legitimate corporate executives, they would have thought, Earthquake! and a few of them did, for a moment. But these men were *yakuza*, representatives of a powerful cartel in the Japanese underworld. They wished it had been an earthquake. One of the guards at the door, shaking off his surprise, reached for the pistol inside his jacket. For him it was a spontaneous reaction. Just as instinctively, Nakajima killed him as the automatic cleared the guard's lapel. He assumed the man would be wearing kevlar body armor, as he himself was, so took him with a head shot. The suppressed MP-5 rapidly coughed three times and the man's face exploded.

"Remain seated! Hands flat on the table! Now!" shouted Nakajima. Two men in black popped through the entryway. One of them put the remaining guard on the floor while the other joined Nakajima in sweeping the table with his submachine gun. Just then the helicopter made a slow pass fifty meters outside the window, only this time the passenger in the open door held a sniper rifle rather than binoculars. With the distraction of the helo, a younger man at the far end of the table tried to palm one of the documents. Two 9mm rounds ripped into the table inches from his fingertips.

"No one is to move. There will not be another warning!"

The offender's hands trembled as he pressed them to the table. Nakajima then turned to the head of the table and imperceptibly inclined his head. "Gotoda-san?"

The older man bowed slightly but surrendered none of his authority. "We will all do as we are told—for now."

Nakajima again bowed and quickly fingered the transmission button on his weapon. "We are secure; get them up here."

For the better part of ten minutes they waited, disturbed only by the whine of the helicopter that hovered outside. Periodically, one or another of those seated gave way to a mild spasm of shivering, not entirely from the cold air that streamed into the room. Finally, the sound of voices and running feet filled the corridor outside. Armed men in uniform poured into the room, members of the Kidotai, the well-known Tokyo police mobile strike force. An officer came up and saluted, then bowed. Nakajima returned only the bow and asked politely, "Are you prepared to assume control of the situation?"

The policeman quickly took in the scattered glass and

the looks of apprehension on the faces of those seated around the table. *"Hai!"*

Again, they exchanged bows. Nakajima slung his weapon and motioned for the others to follow his lead. He started for the door, but stopped when the policeman spoke again. "Warrior, may I know your name?"

"No. I am sorry, but you may not." He smiled. "Be careful with the documents. They may be of value." With that, he rounded the table and was gone.

Monday, 21 November, 8:15 A.M.
ICHIGAYA, JAPAN

Hiroshi Uno sat in his plush office at the Japanese Self Defense Headquarters complex and stared at the television. He fumbled for the remote control and again sat through the video clip of the raid at the Sasasone Building. During the lengthy wait after the initial attack, before the Tokyo police had arrived, he had had an opportunity to observe the assault leader. The man was obviously competent, but it was more than that. There was a controlled, mechanical viciousness to him. He was coiled and ready to strike at the slightest provocation.

"Incredible," Uno said aloud, "simply incredible."

The group that had captured Gotoda and his *yakuza* lieutenants was an element of a highly secret unit known as the Naginata Counter Force. Unlike their American special-operations counterparts, this unit was occasionally brought in to subdue elements of organized crime. The unit had been in existence more than seven years, well before Uno had taken office. During that time they had undertaken several very difficult and delicate assignments. Not once had they failed. By Western military standards, they were a most efficient unit with a superb operational record.

Still, Uno had to remind himself, they represented a potential liability. What if they were to fail in a mission or to somehow kill innocent civilians? The Japanese government had had more than its share of scandal and embarrassment lately, and a skillful politician was always mindful of calling the wrong kind of attention to himself or his department.

Uno was a guarded, taciturn man with a melon-like head and bland features. His shrewd, dark eyes were well recessed in puffy slits. He was wealthy, having made several fortunes in real-estate ventures and on the Tokyo stock exchange during the 1980s and had the foresight to go to cash before the markets had collapsed. Initially, Uno had sought a position in the new Mitsuzuka government in trade or finance, the real centers of power in Japan. Instead, he had been offered the position of director general of the Defense Agency. While it carried the rank of minister of state, it held considerably less influence than that of a senior bureaucrat in the Ministry of Finance or in the Ministry of International Trade and Industry.

The Defense Agency was an extraministerial body that reported directly to the prime minister, who was in turn responsible to the Diet. The Japanese Self Defense Force, the sole responsibility of the Defense Agency, was unique in its organization. To ensure civilian control of the military, all members of the armed forces in uniform were classified as special civil servants, subordinate to ordinary civil servants. This was just one of the measures adopted by the Self Defense Forces Law of 1954 to reduce the influence of the military on the government. Another check on the power of the defense establishment was the legal requirement that senior bureaucrats or "counselors" be assigned to the Defense Agency from other ministries on a rotating basis.

Hiroshi Uno had reluctantly accepted the appointment as director general, for the position afforded him some access to the centers of power. And it was not without some visibility. The United States had been pressing for a larger commitment from the Japanese Self Defense Force in United Nations peacekeeping forces. Some three thousand

Japanese soldiers had gone to Cambodia as a peacekeeping contingent during that nation's elections. Many in Japan viewed the deployment of these troops abroad as a measure of the nation's expanding role in international affairs, while others saw it as a violation of the constitution that forbade the practice. And there was the matter of the plutonium.

Japan had begun taking deliveries of weapons-grade plutonium from France in late 1992. Ostensibly, the plutonium was being stockpiled for use in proposed fast-breeder reactors, a technology abandoned by the United States and most other Western nations. The use of plutonium fuel in its reactors would also provide Japan the material to create nuclear weapons. No one felt that the technology required to produce a nuclear weapon would pose a serious problem for Japan. Uno turned to the man seated across the desk from him. "Sato-san, how was it that this matter was recorded?"

"It was Gotoda's practice to videotape these meetings," the man said evenly. "Apparently, he felt it gave him better control of his organization."

"Is there enough evidence in the documents and on this tape for a conviction?"

"That is hard to say. As you know, he has powerful connections. In any case, it is now a police matter. We were asked only to perform the assault."

Yasaka Sato was one of the assigned special counselors, on loan from the Ministry of Foreign Affairs. Uno studied him. Sato was intelligent and highly capable, and he had a good grasp of Tokyo politics as well as foreign relations. He had been detailed to the Defense Agency just over a year ago, and assigned as liaison officer to the Naginata Counter Force. His work was good and Uno trusted him— up to a point.

The video clip had sharply affected both men, but neither gave any indication. Sato was a bureaucrat and Uno a successful businessman, and neither had ever seen a man die, even on videotape. Until this moment, the operations of the Counter Force had been statements and numbers—statistics and completed mission reports. This was much different. And while they were very taken with this human drama, they were more impressed with the unpredictable nature of the raid. The results of these operations were far from certain; anything could happen.

"Sato, I am curious to know your opinion of the reliability of the Counter Force. Is this a military unit we can trust to back away from a situation that would compromise the interests of the state? More specifically, will they act strictly within the exact guidelines of a given mission tasking? Or do you feel they may be prone to, ah, shall we say, improvise or to exceed the constraints imposed on them from higher authority?"

Sato considered his reply carefully. "The Naginata Force is a very competent unit, and their deeds speak for themselves. It is my impression that they are a professional and well-disciplined group. Their senior officer, Colonel Matsumoto, is an experienced, conventional officer and not unaware of the sensitive political ramifications of his unit's mission. I also believe he understands that a single incident that brought disgrace to the nation or the government would bring an end to this venture."

Uno pursed his lips. "And the young men, the ones we have trained to give us this special capability. Do they consider themselves as modern-day ninja warriors, like we see in the movies?"

"They are in fact quite remarkable—very proficient and very disciplined. But in my opinion, they are soldiers." Again Sato measured his words. "Their qualifications and the aggressive nature of their training have developed a fighting man quite unlike the rank and file of the Self Defense Forces. And there is a spirit and elan among these men, as well as a passion for the art of combat, that we have not known since the war years."

"What you are saying, Sato, is that these men are samurai."

"Yes, Director General, they are samurai."

Uno leaned across the desk on his elbows. "But more importantly, Sato-san, can they be trusted, even in the face of death, to obey their orders and not exceed them?"

"As I said, Minister, they are samurai."

Sunday, 20 November, 1:35 A.M.
THE SOUTH COAST OF OAHU

While it was early Monday morning in Japan, it was still early Sunday afternoon in Hawaii. John Moody patrolled five feet above the white sand in sixty feet of clear water off Oneula Beach, stopping now and then to inspect a coral head or to look for shells. He was just beginning to hurt from lack of oxygen when he spotted the dark hump of a leopard cowrie, one he needed for his collection. The shell was nestled under a particularly large coral dome. He started for it but quickly drew back as twelve inches of moray eel emerged from a crevice in the coral just above the shell. Round wary eyes bracketed the green, dappled forehead. The mouth opened and closed menacingly. Now Moody really needed a breath, but the shell beckoned. He was considering how to deal with the eel in the short time remaining when a figure knifed in from above. With one gloved hand, the diver pinned the moray against the side of the crevice and palmed the shell with the other. As they drifted back to the surface, Don Walker grinned at Moody and slipped the cowrie into his collecting bag. It was their private law of the sea: you snooze, you lose. The find goes to the guy who gets it.

They paddled lazily on the surface, scanning the bottom. Moody inhaled deeply, filling his lungs to capacity and emptying them as fully as possible. The deep breathing cycle was important. For close to a minute, they huffed and blew like a pair of broached whales. Then Walker pulled himself forward and down in a single motion as he slanted for the bottom. Moody took another deep breath and bent to a pike position to follow him down.

Lieutenant John Moody and Petty Officer First Class Don Walker had served together for most of their military careers. At SEAL Team Two in Little Creek, Virginia, they had been assigned to the same operational platoon. Last summer both of them had been transferred to Hawaii. They were due for rotation within the teams, and Moody had been able to get both of them orders to SEAL Delivery Vehicle Team One. SDV Team One was located on Ford Island in Pearl Harbor, so they had landed in paradise together.

Oahu and the warm Pacific Ocean were a dramatic change from Little Creek and the mid-Atlantic. This was a diver's Shangri-la. They preferred free diving to scuba. The two of them usually worked in fifty to seventy feet of water, forty-five seconds on the surface and a minute ten seconds on the bottom. The idea was to breathe deeply while snorkeling to take on oxygen and, more important, to eliminate the carbon dioxide from your blood. It was not lack of oxygen that made you "want" to breathe, but the CO_2 buildup. By purging your system of CO_2, you could go without oxygen for longer periods. The trick was to stay down as long as possible, but not so long that you passed out from anoxia. There was a delicate balance. Blow and go, but get back to the surface before things start to become gray. Free diving was hard work and it could be dangerous, but this only added to its appeal.

Don Walker was an Arkansas dirt farmer who had joined the Navy with a dream of becoming a deep-sea diver. Instead, he had become a Navy SEAL. Men like Walker were not unusual in the SEAL teams; they and the SDV teams were well stocked with young men from the Midwest and the Great Plains. Many who grow up on the coast get used to seeing blue water, and the sea has no magic for them. For some adventurous souls who grow up landlocked, though, the sea beckons as if they were lemmings.

"One of these days, ol' Mr. No-shoulders is gonna get

you when you try that," Moody said as he leisurely treaded water, his snorkel dangling by his chin. He was from eastern Montana and still had a soft prairie drawl. He too had heard the call of the sea.

Walker fondled the cowrie. "One of these days. You 'bout had it, boss? I'm gettin' tired an' thirsty."

"I was hoping you'd say that."

Two hours of free diving was just about the limit of their endurance. It was like playing two hours of full-court basketball. But they had covered more bottom and seen more sea life than a scuba diver would have in twice the time. They had been working away from the boat, against the wind and current. Now they relaxed and let it carry them back to the launch. The Boston Whaler bobbed restlessly in the seaway on its tether.

Together they kicked up and over the side of the boat. Moody started the twin Merc 60s while Walker pulled the anchor aboard. Moody handed him a beer. The afternoon was a sparkler, and the horizon to the southeast off Honolulu was littered with sailboats. Moody hit the throttles and the Whaler leapt across the choppy water. Twenty minutes later they rounded Keahi Point and entered the mouth of Pearl Harbor. He throttled back to an idle, and they poked along up the channel toward the East Loch and Ford Island, enjoying the sun and the heat of the day.

"You see that hammerhead?" Walker asked, grinning knowingly.

Moody eyed him carefully and took a long pull on his beer. It was well known at SDV One that Moody hated sharks. "Don't screw with me, Don."

Walker laughed. "Jus' like a fighter pilot, sir, you got to keep your head moving. An' be especially careful on the way up." A fish swimming to the surface was a fish in trouble. Sharks knew this and so did free divers. More than once, they had been followed to the surface by a curious shark.

"No shit, a hammerhead?"

"Small one, 'bout five feet. He circled once and moved

on.'' Pearl Harbor was a breeding ground for hammer-heads. They were seldom a problem, but sharks were unpredictable, especially hammerheads.

"I don't care what you say, Don, they scare the shit out of me." Walker just smiled. "Another beer?" Moody asked, tossing his empty back into the cooler.

"Maybe one more. I should probably check out that harness assembly on the Number Seven boat. Chief wants to do a full-systems check tomorrow before we button her up."

"Problem?" Moody popped a can for himself.

"Not really. I got an intermittent signal on one of the communications pigtails. Just a matter of finding the bad connector and replacing it. Routine stuff." Walker's Navy rating was an ET or electronics technician, and the SDVs required a lot of attention. "We still scheduled for sea trials Sunday after next?"

"That's right, and I'll bet you just can't wait." They both smiled. Life at SDV One was an easy eight-hour workday with weekends off. Going to sea would put an end to that.

A half hour later, Moody eased the Whaler up to the pier on Ford Island. Along the way, they'd exchanged waves with girls in pleasure boats wearing bright bikinis. They'd also waved to sailors manning the rail of a destroyer standing out of Pearl—sailors who noted the gray hull of the launch and wondered what kind of Navy those two were in. Moody guided the boat smoothly into the slip, and Walker leapt up to the pier to secure the bow line.

Fifty-some years ago, massive battleships, the pride of the U.S. Pacific Fleet, had been tied up at Ford Island. But one quiet Sunday morning, the Japanese had changed all that. Now Ford Island was home for an assortment of tugs, utility craft, and SEAL Delivery Team One.

John Moody and Don Walker looked as if they could be brothers. Both were six feet tall, about 175 pounds. They were deeply tanned, with short, thick brown hair. And like clowns from the same circus troupe, their noses and lower lips were painted white with zinc oxide. Both wore sun-glasses with flat rubber head straps, canvas UDT trunks, and flip-flops. They were hard, muscular men, but neither had the bulk of a body builder. They gave the impression of good health rather than good looks. Moody was the lea-ner of the two, more angular, and he had more scars. One particularly large gash made an indentation in his calf; the wound was mottled with scar tissue and skin grafts, and made his legs slightly asymmetrical. They left the Whaler and headed for the SDV Team One building, casually lug-ging their fins, masks, and snorkels over their shoulders.

The SDV building was a large corrugated-metal structure built forty years ago as a seaprane hangar. Since then it had seen duty as a warehouse, maintenance depot, and small-boat storage facility. Now it belonged to SEAL Delivery Team One. The team had recently moved to Hawaii from Coronado, California, to be closer to the Pacific submarine fleet. Inside, semi-trailer container boxes, equipment pal-lets, and SEAL delivery vehicles littered the hangar bay.

The SDVs, resting on their trailers, lined the workbays along the rear wall of the hangar. Some had Plexiglas can-opies pulled back while others stood fully encapsulated, resembling dead whales on hospital gurneys. Still others were in various states of disassembly, connected to test equipment and monitors as if they were very sick and in need of life support. The Mk 9, Mod 1 SDV was a stumpy craft some fourteen feet long, smooth and round, like a giant black fiberglass larva. Stubby, horizontal bow fins grew from either side of the nose while a sonar transducer protruded from the front canopy windshield like a wart. At the stern, a single six-bladed propeller was bisected by hor-izontal stabilizers and a large rudder. In the way that an airline jet was sleek and beautiful, these were very ugly little craft. Moody had never before operated from an SDV. When he'd first seen one up close, he'd wondered if he'd made a mistake in requesting SDVs over an operational SEAL Team. But he and Walker had seen enough action with SEAL Two to satisfy both of them for a while. Besides, he was stationed in paradise.

Walker headed for one of the boats that was in intensive care. While he climbed into the SDV and went to work, Moody made for a line of office bays along the side of the building, offices reserved for platoon commanders. He slid behind an untidy desk and began to sift through his in-basket, initialing routing slips and leafing through a stack of correspondence. Occasionally he made a note at the bottom in neat, block print. Moody would have preferred to be out in the shop space helping Walker with the Number Seven boat, but that was not his job. He was Delta Platoon commander.

Delta Platoon had a complement of two officers and twelve enlisted men. All were SEALs and most, like Walker, were talented mechanics and technicians as well. The platoon maintained their two SEAL delivery vehicles and trained constantly to operate them in a number of diverse mission profiles. The platoon enlisted men kept up the boats and the officers handled the paperwork. Moody didn't particularly like this arrangement, but that's the way it was at SDV Team One. Even so, the platoon chief·had to shoo him away from the boats once or twice a week.

The office was small and very cluttered, as much a locker room as an office. A cabinet locker along the back wall held a single freshly pressed summer khaki uniform and an extensive collection of swim trunks, nylon running shorts, T-shirts, and sneakers. A thin, delicate Nishiki road bike leaned against a rusty coat tree. Rubber baseball cleats and a fielder's glove rested on the seat of a metal folding chair. A two-tier Navy-issue bookshelf crouched in the corner was crowded with administrative and technical manuals, but a portion of the lower shelf housed a number of ancient-history texts and Greek classics. Several years ago someone had given Moody a copy of Thucydides's *Peloponnesian Wars*. He had been a mathematics major in college, and when he'd discovered classical literature he'd felt like a celibate stumbling onto a whorehouse.

On top of the filing cabinet, next to a picture of his father sitting on a split-rail fence, was a tarnished belt buckle. The inscription on it read First Place, All-Around Cowboy, Calgary Stampede. As Moody paused from his paperwork to stretch, there was a symphony of popping and cracking from his joints. So far, his choices in life had not been particularly kind to his body. In the summers he had worked the rodeo circuit for spending money, then attended the University of Montana on a football scholarship. He had always been a good athlete, but football was his sport. After three years as all-Big Sky at wide receiver, the pro scouts had looked at him closely. But they'd all agreed: great hands, great moves, too slow.

So he'd left school and become a Navy SEAL. Grizzly fans still remembered the sticky-fingered receiver who would dive full-out for a low pass and scoop it off the top of the grass.

His eyes fell on the photograph of his dad and without thinking, he pulled open the desk drawer and took out a sack of duce. Then in a practiced, one-handed motion, he rolled himself a querlie and lit up, cinching the drawstring on the bag with his teeth. He smoked very little and, if he were honest with himself, would admit that he disliked the taste. But his uncle had taught him to roll his own when he was only twelve. Moody considered it a hard-won skill and too valuable to lose for lack of practice.

"My gawd, Daddy," he said to the man on the fence, blowing a cloud of acrid smoke across the desk, "how'd I ever get clear out here?"

His great-great-grandfather and great-grandfather had homesteaded in North Dakota along the Cannonball River before his dad's father had moved on into Montana and started their place on the Yellowstone. His dad and brother still worked the ranch. Moody had felt guilty about leaving for the Navy after college, but his dad understood and told him so. "We Moodys have always been ones to look for a better piece of pasture. We're plum outa land here, son, so you may have to go a ways to find yours. Maybe it's out there in th' ocean somewheres.''

Moody couldn't remember the day at home when he hadn't worked on the ranch—before school, after football practice, and until he'd left for college, all summer long. And his dad didn't take to dallying. He and his brother had a joke about their hard-driving pa; if it don't hurt, you ain't workin' hard enough. Moody had grown up with a healthy contempt for comfort, good training for a SEAL.

He finished with his in-box and turned to the PC on the credenza. He quickly brought up a file and began tapping out the platoon training schedule for the coming week. This was a familiar sight in the teams—a well-tanned, athletic-looking young officer in swim trunks and flip-flops hunched over a computer.

John Moody had been in the Navy for six years. For most of that time he had been with the East Coast SEAL teams in Virginia. This was his first West Coast assignment, SDV One being considered a West Coast team. Now he was making final preparations for Delta Platoon's deployment aboard the USS *La Jolla*, a 688-class nuclear attack submarine. It wasn't but a few years ago that the Submarine Service wanted little to do with the SEALs and their little wet submersibles, but the collapse of the Soviet Union had changed all that. As the American Congress looked for ways to reduce the defense budget, the American submariners desperately looked for work, even if it meant assigning one of their large, expensive hunter-killer boats to chaperone the SDVs.

Moody completed the platoon training schedule, shut down the PC, and headed for the showers. Fifteen minutes later he emerged in faded jeans and a flowered aloha shirt. He knew shorts would be more comfortable, but they'd look funny with the cowboy boots. After posting the training schedule on the platoon board, he met Walker, who had changed into similar attire. They hurried over to the foot ferry that would take them to Pearl mainside. Other passengers, dressed more in keeping with the Islands, gave them curious glances but the two SEALs ignored them. The short crossing was spectacular.

Moody had seen it many times before, but he never ceased to marvel at the late-afternoon, sultry beauty of Pearl Harbor. It was almost a religious thing. The sun was low and angry, made a burnt red by the burning sugarcane fields out near Makakilo. In contrast, the rugged Koolau Range to the east and north rose above the cane smoke to form a lush, jagged emerald wall. They were majestic, primitive mountains that dwarfed the high-rise condominiums sprouting around Aiea and Pearl City. Sunfish and Hobie Cats from the Naval Base Marina jousted with tour boats shuttling tourists to the sunken USS *Arizona*. Visitor traffic to the memorial always picked up prior to the anniversary of the attack on Pearl Harbor. In passing, Moody thought it curious that a large number of the visitors seemed to be Japanese. He shrugged and again gazed at the mountains against the crimson sky. At times like this he thought of the cold, damp winters in Little Creek and counted his blessings.

"So what's on the program this evenin', boss?"

"Same as every Sunday night. Go over to Trader Vic's for a burger, an' take a look at the latest crop of sex-starved secretaries just in for a week's vacation."

Walker smiled. "War's hell, ain't it."

"Hey, it's not just a job—it's an adventure."

Once they reached Pearl mainside, the two SEALs found their motorcycles. Walker had a big Suzuki and Moody a vintage Norton Atlas. They kicked them to life and roared off the base to the Nimitz Highway, then onto H-1 toward Honolulu.

Tuesday, 22 November, 6:32 A.M.
THE HENNA PENINSULA, OKINAWA

Shintaro Nakajima knelt quietly on the sand in front of the small sun-goddess shrine. The eastern sky was just beginning to turn a soft, mother-of-pearl pink. Soon the sun would again burst onto the land and change the ocean from its predawn gray to a deep cobalt blue. Unless his duties intervened, Nakajima rose early each morning to meditate and pray. For several days, a series of pre-winter storms had battered the home islands to the north. The last of them had passed just south of Kyushu, leaving a sharp winter chill in its wake. Usually Okinawa took the full force of the winter storms. Nakajima was dressed only from the waist down in loose-fitting cotton trousers called *hakama*, but he took no notice of the morning chill. He quietly said his Shinto prayers and humbly thanked *Amaterasu-o-mi-Kami*, the sun-goddess, for their success in the assault on the Sasasone Building. Nakajima did not consider himself a religious man but more of a student of religion, which is to say he was a student of Japan. He did, however, strongly believe in the value of prayer. His prayers were not demonstrations of supplication, nor did he ask for forgiveness. No true Japanese would ever kneel to petition one of his gods for absolution, let alone salvation. The closest thing Nakajima could envision to sin was the shame he would know if he failed in his duty. So he prayed for spiritual strength and to purify the rust that comes of life, tarnishing one's soul. In this way he sought to polish his spirit, like the ancient mirrors of the sun-goddess ritual. For Nakajima was not accountable in the way Christians were to their God. He was responsible to his family, his ancestors, and his nation, but certainly not to any god.

But if Westerners would have had difficulty with Naka-jima's devotion to multiple gods, they would never have understood his faithful practice of several religions. Some mornings he recited Buddhist sutras, for he derived a great deal of spiritual comfort and inner peace from the teachings of Buddha. As a Buddhist, he understood life in terms of cycles of suffering. There was comfort in knowing that a small measure of the strength and wisdom he achieved in this life would serve him well in future lives. On rarer occasions, he found himself in need of the moral precepts and structure of Confucius, from whom he learned that a good society and a good life were built on harmonious relationships. A man and a nation needed order and harmony.

Above all, though, Nakajima was a traditionalist. Shinto was the oldest of religions in Japan, primitive and loosely ordered. In the complex matrix of ancient beliefs and observances, he found a communion with nature and the religious underpinning to deal with his modern, changing world. The Shinto gods continually reminded him of his worthy ancestors, and that only through valor and spiritual purity could he, in turn, earn the respect and veneration of future generations after he crossed to the other side. Nakajima had a role to play. He was a living part of the sacred and timeless land called Japan. The Shinto gods taught him of the divine origin of the Japanese nation. He was determined to play his role well.

Completing his prayers, he rose and clapped twice, allowing the first rays of sunlight to play across his body. Nakajima's features were rounded and altogether rather plain, but with high cheekbones that suggested some far-distant Mongol ancestry. A portion of his neck, below his left ear, was scarred and pink from a scalding as a child. He was a compact man with good shoulders. When he relaxed, his hands hung well away from his slim hips. He had well-muscled pectorals and a flat, washboard stomach. His forearms were as large and veined as those of a body builder. It was a powerful, well-used body, with calloused feet and hands, and marked by old cuts and abrasions. Nakajima had devoted a significant part of his life to physical training and conditioning. But he knew physical strength was of little value without careful mental preparation.

Take-miki-zudhi, Valiant-August-Thunder, give me the strength and tenacity to overcome the obstacles before me. *Futsa-nushi*, Sharp-Cutting-Lord, grant me wisdom to act wisely and prudently. And Lord Jocho, by whose *Hagakure* all true samurai are guided, grant me courage. If duty requires my death, may I be privileged to die with honor. And if the choice between life and death is equal, may I unhesitatingly choose death. It is the way of the samurai and the path I have chosen.

Following thirty minutes of *kata* exercises, Nakajima toweled himself and carefully shaved. Then he donned a clean, starched shirt and a freshly pressed uniform with the epaulets of an *Itto Rikui*, a captain in the Japanese Self Defense Forces. Nakajima carefully inspected himself in the mirror. Then he left his quarters, walking at a brisk pace across the compound. The headquarters building was a whitewashed, cinder-block structure. Over the entryway were two crossed *naginatas*, staffs with broad, curved blades and a vicious hook at each tip. They had been carried by foot soldiers in the twelfth century as defensive weapons, highly effective in unhorsing mounted samurai.

"Officer entering the building," called the sentry at the door as he jumped to attention from behind the desk. The facility was protected by electronic security measures, but Colonel Matsumoto insisted on the traditional presence of a guard. Many JSDF installations presented more of a corporate image than a military presence. But then the JSDF was, by charter and practice, an impotent military organization. This was not a normal base, and the Naginata Counter Force was anything but a normal Japanese military unit.

Captain Nakajima returned the guard's salute and put him at ease. "Is the colonel here, Corporal?"

"Yes, Captain. He arrived about five minutes ago and went straight to his office." The sentry was a tall, rugged-looking man who had no difficulty meeting Nakajima's eye. "And begging the captain's pardon, it was my impression that the colonel appeared to be irritated that you were not here to meet him.''

"Thank you for your observation, Corporal. Resume your duties.''

They formally exchanged salutes and Nakajima continued down the hall, stopping at the door marked Commanding Officer. He stepped inside and carefully closed the door behind him; then he came to a rigid position of attention.

Colonel Matsumoto was a short, round man with a broad, wrinkled brow. His face was coarse and weathered, but his uniform was impeccable. He sat behind a large, well-ordered desk. The walls were bare and there was no standard military organization chart showing each unit's place in the JSDF command structure. But then the Naginata Counter Force was not found on any organizational chart anywhere. Matsumoto inclined his head curtly and inhaled through his lower teeth to register his displeasure, but there was a slight twinkle in his eye. A secretary slipped in bringing tea and quietly left.

"You are late, Captain.'' Their eyes met but Nakajima remained impassive. Both men knew he was on time. Nakajima bowed formally from the waist.

"My sincere apologies, Colonel.''

"Accepted, Captain. And may I commend you on your successful raid in Tokyo the day before last. Not only was it a success, but your unannounced entrance into the *yakuza* conference was captured on videotape.''

"Sir?'' Nakajima's eyes narrowed. The existence of the Counter Force was a closely guarded secret, as were the identities of the individual members.

"Do not worry, Captain.'' Matsumoto smiled. "The tape is in safe hands at the Defense Agency headquarters. But we must be mindful of this in future urban operations. Many of these modern buildings are being equipped with video surveillance, often for other than security reasons. Now, are your men ready?''

"Yes, sir. They are standing by in the inspection area.''

"Very well. Let us not keep *them* waiting, *hai!*" This time the twinkle was unmistakable.

Nakajima followed his colonel past the sentry and across the compound to a small parade ground. The base itself was a small installation, and Okinawa was a large island with a large military presence. The 3d Marine Division and the U.S. 17th Air Force, as well as the First Composite Brigade of the JSDF, were stationed here. Nominally, the base served as a test and evaluation facility to examine new small arms for the Ground Self Defense Force and the National Police, a task they did indeed perform. So far the small facility had remained obscure, and its real mission a secret.

"First Platoon, attention!" A senior first sergeant stood in front of twelve men arranged in two ranks behind him. Most were wiry, angular men, but a few were muscular and square-shouldered like their captain. All had a hard look to them. They wore the standard uniform of the Ground Self Defense Force, but with a red beret. Nakajima joined Matsumoto in returning the sergeant's salute.

"Gentlemen," the colonel began, "you have served your nation well and brought honor upon yourselves and the Naginata Counter Force. I salute your courage and your professionalism. It is a privilege to serve as your commander." Then Matsumoto bowed deeply from the waist. The first sergeant bowed slightly, acknowledging the respect he and the men were being shown. "And now, Sergeant, I will inspect your men."

The sergeant saluted and led the colonel along the first rank. Matsumoto moved slowly from one man to the next. He did not want to inspect these men; this was a chance for him to acknowledge each one individually. Had this been a real inspection, though, he would have found no discrepancies.

Nakajima stood to one side at attention. His impassive features masked the fierce pride he felt for these men. The Counter Force had but three operational platoons and a small headquarters element. He commanded First Platoon, trained specifically as a paramilitary and urban strike force, capable of conventional direct-action missions similar to the activities of the British Special Air Service or in covert, metropolitan counter-terrorist roles. These capabilities made them feared by the Japanese Red Army and *Chukaku-Ha* terrorist organizations. Their tactics and weapons were similar to those of the British and American special-operations forces or the American municipal SWAT teams. Years of training, punctuated by an occasional mission like the raid two nights ago, had made them more than brothers. Colonel Matsumoto completed his inspection and received the sergeant's final salute.

Nakajima stood with the colonel and watched as his first sergeant led the men from the parade area. They would be given leave for the rest of the day but would resume full training duties the following morning. The platoon was scheduled for an equipment parachute jump followed by an underwater compass swim with scuba.

"If I may ask," Nakajima said, "what was the reaction at the Defense Agency after seeing our work?"

Matsumoto smiled. "I sense it was a different experience for them, much different from reading one of your carefully worded after-action reports." The two began to walk slowly back to the headquarters building. "I believe it frightened them. They were able to see from the video how dangerous our work is and just how unpredictable the outcome can be. Our esteemed politicians know they need a military unit with our skills, but they are always worried that something will go wrong."

"Then we are a necessary evil?"

"Perhaps." They walked in silence for a moment. Then Matsumoto stopped and turned to the younger man. "You see, *Kohai*, our nation's leaders have guided us to unparalleled economic achievement. The basis of that success is long-range strategic planning—the result of a continuous and carefully constructed compromise between government and business. It is leadership by consensus. No one can doubt the merit of this approach, but it is slow and methodical. In this system, success and blame are shared. But our work is very difficult for men like Minister Uno to understand. It requires quick decisions and bold action. Sometimes there is no safe option, and often a high probability of failure. It also requires a leader who must act decisively—instinctively with little or no time for consultation. And if there is failure, blame cannot be shared.''

''So they need us, but perhaps they do not understand us.''

''That is a rational assumption. And so long as they need us, perhaps they will continue to allow us to function in our own way.'' Matsumoto again fell silent as they continued to walk, thinking carefully before speaking. ''I believe they understand we are a responsible and capable force, one that will act prudently. But Minister Uno and his superiors would quickly abandon us if the failure of a mission were to cause them embarrassment.''

Nakajima considered this. ''That is reasonable. We can attend to our duties, and they will not be blamed if we should fail.''

''And you feel this is a fair bargain, *Kohai?*'' *Kohai* was a term for a subordinate, but suggested a relationship more typical of that of an upperclassman and a freshman at the same prep school.

''Of course, Colonel.'' Nakajima framed his words with care. ''The *Hagakure* tells us that a warrior's first duty is loyalty to his liege. For us, that is to our nation and our nation's leaders. I also understand that for Japan to survive and prosper, it must change and must adopt new ways. Men like Minister Uno have their role to play. I am fortunate that in these modern times, I have been granted a way to both serve my country and to obey the *Hagakure*.''

Matsumoto smiled. The *Hagakure* was the teachings of the warrior-priest Jocho Yamamoto, considered the most complete work of samurai behavior. These teachings, so popular before the war, were now attracting an increasing number of young warriors, like Nakajima.

"And to follow the way of the samurai?" the older man said.

"Yes, Colonel, to follow the way of the samurai."

Matsumoto chuckled indulgently as he led Nakajima back into the headquarters building. "My young friend, I applaud your perspective and your optimism. Japan needs men like you, whether it realizes it or not. But I'm afraid the years have eroded my faith in our leadership. Perhaps it's a legacy from the postwar years when the shame of defeat so completely dominated us." A shadow passed across his face, causing his shoulders to sag and make him look older. Then he glanced at his watch and brightened. "Ah, we have time before lunch. Will you join me in the dojo for kendo?"

Nakajima bowed deeply. "I would be honored, Colonel."

Thirty minutes later, Nakajima and his colonel stood facing one another on a vinyl-covered rice mat. They wore light armor, helmets, and face shields, like two well-armed lacrosse players. Both men wielded *shinai*, a training weapon fashioned from a number of light bamboo blades tied and bound in cloth. They served as surrogates for the deadly two-handed swords. Nakajima carried his armor well, like a second skin, and the *shinai* seemed an extension of himself. Matsumoto was a stout man and the additional equipment made him appear something of a clown. His fat arms seemed too short for his bulk, and the helmet only seemed to enhance the size of his head. The *shinai* looked like a baton in his meaty hand.

Word quickly swept throughout the base that Colonel Matsumoto and Captain Nakajima were about to engage in kendo. This art, the "way of the samurai sword," had originated more than seven hundred years ago as a non-lethal form of combat—a way to test the skill of swordsmen without inflicting serious damage. By the time the two combatants had taken the first of their ritual bows, every member of the Counter Force not on duty had crowded into the dojo to watch.

The two men began to circle and feint. Nakajima was by far the quicker of the two, strong and with the reflexes of a cat. But the colonel was an aging master, or *sensei*, with a seasoned competence and sense of anticipation that allowed him to match the younger man. Nakajima was not unskilled at the sport, but all of his youth and speed were required to match the deftness of the older man. For almost a half hour they stalked each other. Periodically there was a flurry of stickwork as one or the other attacked. Their defensive skills were such that a blow was seldom landed, but when struck, was delivered with authority. Neither man held back. The armor prevented serious injury, but a clean strike would be remembered with a welt or a bruise. The crowd of men watched with pride and admiration. They cheered a successful attack or parry by either man.

Finally, Colonel Matsumoto stepped back, indicating he would proceed only if his opponent wanted to continue fighting. Nakajima removed his helmet, signaling he was agreeable to a rest. They smiled warmly at each other and bowed deeply.

Thursday, 24 November, 4:00 P.M.
SEA OF FERTILITY; LATITUDE 10°56'28" S
LONGITUDE 90°42'15" W

Almost exactly halfway around the world, two other men faced each other on a rice mat and bowed. Instead of a dojo, the unlikely location of their contest was the foredeck of a tramp steamer nearly a thousand miles off the west coast of South America. They were stripped to the waist and wore heavy cotton *hakama*. Both were barefoot. Once again, one of the contestants was young and the other older by a generation. The young man was lean and tightly muscled, his shaved head glistening in the midday sun. The older man's baldness was the price of his years. He was the heavier of the two, with a sinewy toughness that suggested tenacity and durability. Instead of *shinai*, they held two-handed *no-dachi* swords, long fighting weapons over five feet in length from tip to pommel. Their eyes met and, as if by some silent command, both swords flashed as they carved broad circles above and to either side of them. The polished steel moved in unison, with one streaking blade mirroring the movements of the other. It seemed as if the two swords knew the routine and the men were attached for the sake of form. Suddenly the swords halted in a vertical position in front of the men, then drew their handlers forward until the gap between the blades was less than six inches. Again, they flashed in tandem. The sword etiquette was as before, only this time they whirled about the men.

With their eyes locked, the combatants guided their metal surrogates though the precise, choreographed protocol. Razor-sharp steel flicked within inches of skin and scalp. Those who ringed the mat watched in fascination. It stopped as quickly as it had begun, with both swords snapping to the vertical between their handlers. The combatants stepped back and bowed.

Two men who were serving as seconds started forward with the sword scabbards when suddenly, the younger man cut a rapid figure-eight with his blade, the tip of the weapon carving graceful arcs off either hip. There was a hint of a smile on his lips. A murmur of excitement and approval rippled though the ring of onlookers. After a moment, the older man replied with a like gesture and the two men bowed low. The crowd became silent. Again, the two swords whirled and stopped. Then men and swords advanced and the dangerous ritual was repeated, only this time the tempo accelerated noticeably. When the action stopped and they had exchanged their bows, the younger participant was sweating profusely, but his eyes glowed in triumph and achievement. A sigh of relief passed among those who watched.

The older man's face was impassive. Then his eyes narrowed and he regarded his opponent with a calm, deadly stare. The younger man noted this and his eyes widened slightly. An uneasy quiet settled around the mat. Suddenly, the senior blade became a blur as its handler issued his challenge. His opponent swallowed slowly and took a deep breath before swinging his own blade in acceptance.

The two swordsmen began the ritual anew, but this time at a blinding speed. The younger man clearly struggled with the pace, while his opponent calmly looked out through hooded eyes, his own *no-dachi* seeming to spin as if driven by some unseen, unnatural force. The swords came vertical almost in unison. The combatants stared at each other a long moment, the eyes of the younger those of a snared rabbit. The corner of his mouth quivered slightly, but he steeled himself to the task. They stepped forward, and a moment later the men were encased in a silver glow as polished steel whirled about them. Suddenly, a nick appeared on the shoulder of the older man and a rivulet of blood began to cascade onto his biceps. There was absolute silence but for the occasional cry of a sea gull and the hiss of the blades; then it was over. Finally, swords and men stood facing each other, though the young man was shaking with emotion and exhaustion. It was with noticeable effort that he managed to step back and properly return his opponent's bow.

Then he noticed the blood that now covered the arm of the older man. "Tadao-sama, I have . . ."

"See to your sword."

He took a half step forward. "But you are . . ."

"*See to your sword!*"

Without another word, the younger man took a cloth offered by his second and carefully cleaned his blade. Then each man was handed a long, curved scabbard. Together they sheathed their weapons and bowed. Only the younger one remained bent at the waist.

"I ask your forgiveness, Tadao-sama. I have dishonored myself and drawn your blood. My life is in your hands."

Those who watched were silent, for the contest, which was to have been a demonstration of skill and swordsmanship, had become one of life and death. In this rare form of duel *suburi*, tradition allowed that the participant who drew the blood of his opponent could preserve his honor by offering the offended party an unchallenged stroke with his own sword. This tradition was seldom respected in modern times, but then *suburi* with sharpened *no-dachi* had largely been abandoned in the sixteenth century for this very reason. The practice itself was dangerous, and the price of honor often dismemberment or death. The older man twisted a cloth about his hand to keep his blood from soiling the haft of his sword, and once more unsheathed his blade. He stood looking at his opponent for a long while.

Insolent pup, he thought. His arrogance and pride far exceed his ability with a sword. For that alone I should feed his head to the fishes.

For several moments, Tadao pondered the worth of the man prostrated before him. The urge to strike was overpowering. He had already selected the exact location between two vertebrae where the best stroke could be laid. With a conscious effort, he restrained the sword from a fatal blow. Reluctantly, Tadao concluded that the young man was more valuable to him alive than as an example to the other impulsive young men who watched. And who knows, he thought, perhaps he will profit from this experience when the next test comes. Tadao stepped forward and gently stroked the man's shoulder with his blade, opening the flesh of his upper arm.

"You have not dishonored yourself, Taiyo. All things considered, you handled your sword well. But you should understand a *suburi* challenge may be answered with yet another challenge, and you would do well to carefully gauge your own skill as well as that of your opponent. Now we shall both have scars to remember this day."

"Thank you, Tadao-sama." The young man stood erect, recovering quickly, but still unsteady on his feet. Both men accepted compression bandages for their wounds.

"And now that Taiyo and I have entertained you for a

while, perhaps it is time to get back to your training duties.''

Those gathered on the foredeck parted as he casually walked back to the deckhouse of the vessel. Then they scattered to their duties. A short time later, Tadao stood on the port wing of the bridge and watched as his ship relentlessly pushed its way through the calm mid-Pacific.

They had been at sea for two days, having sailed from Lima, Peru. Like many emerging Third World cities, Lima was a polluted, bleeding sore. Tadao had endured the previous two weeks in the confines of the city and was happy to be at sea. As soon as they traded the sweet-ripe tidal stench of their berth on the Rimac River for the clean air of the open ocean, his spirits had soared.

Lima had not been his first choice for a staging area, but the port offered advantages too compelling to be overlooked. He had found it easy to buy weapons and ammunition, especially since he was prepared to deal in dollars. With heavy American pressure on the Colombian cartels, Peru now played an increasingly important role in the drug trade. Equipping a small army was just another cost of doing business. Nor did the expensive additions and unique modifications to the ship raise any eyebrows.

Besides, there was the large expatriate Japanese community. He and his men had been able to move about the city attracting very little attention. After it was over, their journey would surely be traced back to Lima. Tadao felt no remorse for the Japanese-Peruvians, nor for their Japanese-born president, Alberto Fujimori. No true Japanese could really live anywhere but in Japan. They journeyed to foreign lands to conquer them and to bring Japanese cultural and spiritual superiority to the subjugated, but not to live there.

The *Sea of Fertility* was a well-used coastal freighter just under 280 feet at the waterline. The keel had been laid in Singapore right after the war. Scars and gouges along the sides documented years of service and uncounted backwater ports of call. The battered hull had numerous coats of paint, the most recent heavily streaked with running rust. The shipyard in Lima had just rebuilt the small but adequate Daimler-Benz engine. Additional fuel tanks had been added to the internal spaces to dramatically extend the ship's range, and a portion of its cargo hold was now sectioned into living quarters for up to eighty men. Belowdecks, additional galley space had been installed to serve them.

There was a certain weary nobility to the old ship. It had a gentle grace and sense of proportion that hinted of an era before mass-production—a time before zone outfitting and computer-assisted assembly yards. The majestic prow quickly gave way to a clean deck line that rose quietly to a rounded, yacht-like stern. The superstructure rested just abaft midships, surrendering foredeck space for balance and harmony. The plating of the deckhousing was rounded and pleasing, not square-cut as with newer ships. A single king post and two pole derricks in the center of the foredeck served a pair of beam-and-board cargo hatches, one forward and one aft. This traditional design was functional as well as aesthetic and gave the ship a sea-keeping ability far better than modern ships twice its size.

In some ways, Takashi Tadao was like the *Sea of Fertility*. He had the look of a middle-aged Japanese laborer or rice farmer. His hands were calloused, and he wore a serene, almost bovine look. His features were bland by Western standards, except for the nose, which was sharp and dipped rakishly toward his upper lip. The dark eyes were impassive but missed nothing. When they settled on something or someone, they became penetrating, even predatory. Tadao was not a tall man, perhaps five feet six, but he had a compact, efficient build. When he moved from one wing of the pilothouse to the other, it was with the grace of a natural athlete. Though he stood quietly off to one side and said little, his presence dominated the bridge. He was a *daimyo*.

Tadao had grown up in a small village near Nagoya. The poverty of postwar Japan and occupation by the Americans was the legacy of his youth. A brilliant student with near-perfect test scores, he had qualified for a scholarship to study in America. He had been reluctant to leave Japan for any reason, but his father would not hear of it: "They have conquered us and there is much to learn from them. You must go. Just remember that your soul is Japanese, and that your ancestors composed poetry with brush and rice cloth long before there was such a thing as America." Tadao had attended Cal Tech and, like many bright young Japanese sent to school in America, had taken a degree in engineering, with honors. But at night, he had studied history and philosophy.

On his return to Japan, he had immediately entered the priesthood, later taking his vows with a militant faction of the *Yamabushi* order. While others of his generation had led Japan from the postwar depression to the status of an economic superpower, Tadao had turned to the old ways. From time to time one of his former classmates, now a senior corporate or government official, would seek him out, asking him to serve in one capacity or another. He invariably dismissed them, often upbraiding them for having replaced traditional Japanese virtues with their new commercial gods and Western values.

Tadao often felt that he had been born too late—a seventeenth-century man confronting the twenty-first-century world. He fully understood the miracle that was the technological resurgence of Japan; he simply refused to participate. While he never again entered secular life, he became something of a spiritual adviser and counselor to several rich businessmen. Tadao himself renounced personal wealth, but he was not above using the influence and means of the wealthy toward his own ends.

Following his return from school in America, he had been drawn to the teachings of Yukio Mishima. At one time, he had been the youngest member of Mishima's Shield Society—a secret army one hundred strong, pledged to guard the ancestral values of Imperial Japan. Most thought the society had died with Mishima's heroic suicide in 1970. It had not. Tadao had long nurtured a vision of a different Japan, purified of its Western influences and returned to the traditionalism of the past. Several years ago, he had begun to preach the substance of that vision and had found eager followers. Now many of those same followers were here with him on the main deck attending to their training.

The young men began group calisthenics or paired off for martial-arts training. Tadao watched quietly from the bridge like an indulgent parent. Finally, he allowed himself a slight smile. In a short while, he reflected, these warriors will swarm to the attack. Japan and all the world will know again of the samurai spirit. But we are more than samurai; we are *ronin—shishi* dedicated to the overthrow of the corrupt, commercial *shoguns* that now rule our nation. For a brief moment, Tadao's nostrils flared and his face took on a terrible ferocity. Then he composed himself and retired to his quarters to pray.

Tuesday, 29 November, 7:35 A.M.
JOHNSTON ISLAND

The sign on the office door said The Mayor of Johnston Island. Inside, Jim Bruso scowled as he sat at his desk plowing through a stack of paperwork. Occasionally, the grumbling became audible. "What a waste of time.... They gotta be shitting me.... Now who the hell thought up this one?"

It was a morning ritual. First he neatly sorted the material into three piles: one, do today; two, do later; three, trash it. Then he took the second pile and forced himself to allocate each piece of paper to pile one or three. The surviving documents he dealt with, reluctantly.

Jim Bruso worked for a government contractor, which meant that indirectly he worked for the U.S. government. Only as a government contractor, he couldn't allow himself to fall into the do-it-tomorrow, civil-servant mind-set, nor could he permit himself the luxury of normal government working hours. The terms of the contract had to be met, no matter how long it took. Over the years he had developed a deep-seated hatred of paperwork and of those who made their living by its skillful manipulation. As a result he was not always terribly fond of his employer, the Emerson Management Corporation, or of the U.S. government.

However, Emerson liked Jim Bruso. He was a people person, very good at getting them to work together under difficult conditions. Most of the twelve hundred civilian and government employees who lived and worked on Johnston Island said Jim Bruso made Johnston Atoll tick.

Emerson was in the business of managing the day-to-day housekeeping activities at remote government- and defense-related facilities like Johnston Atoll. Their duties included public works, vehicle upkeep, food service, power generation, fresh-water management, building maintenance, trash removal, waste treatment, and port services. They called Bruso the mayor, but the job description was more that of the chief cook and bottle washer. He was responsible for the mundane but essential tasks—routine, thankless jobs that were taken for granted unless they didn't get done. It was a lot like being a housewife, Bruso often thought.

He jabbed the intercom on the desk, ''Rosie, you seen the colonel yet?''

''Not yet, boss.''

''Let me know when he gets here, okay?''

Bruso turned back to his paperwork and a casualty report on the emergency power generator at the waste-treatment facility. The important business on the island was done by the real civil servants, mostly civilians working for the Department of the Army, and by the prime contractor, Thermal Technology. They were in the business of the storage and destruction of chemical weapons. Emerson, and Jim Bruso, did everything else.

Bruso stood up and stretched. He was dressed in what he had come to regard as his uniform: tan cotton slacks, a short-sleeved white shirt, and a tie. Johnston Island was an informal work place, but he always wore a tie and insisted that his supervisors also wear them. Jim Bruso was on the wrong side of fifty, but he looked younger. His red-brown hair was quickly turning gray but enjoyed a thick, thatched texture. A cowlick that refused the attentions of a comb rode like a flag on the stern of a yacht. Most of those on the island were a shade darker from the sun, but Bruso was one of those fair-skinned people who turned red and sprouted freckles. There was a large, emerald dragon tattooed on his left forearm, a reminder of a less responsible time in his life. He had dark, serious eyes that could be overruled by an infectious, crooked smile.

Bruso was solidly built and he had a quiet, matter-of-fact presence that compelled people to listen when he spoke. That was important. The men and women who worked the camps, whether it was an oil platform in Malaysia, a research facility in Greenland, or here on Johnston Island, were a rugged lot—many of them unsuited to a nine-to-five job on the mainland. They were a diverse and sometimes dysfunctional group, yet few practicing psychologists or MBAs knew as much about people and how to get them to work together as Jim Bruso.

The intercom chirped. "Sir, Colonel Trafton just walked into his office."

"Thanks, I'll be right out." Bruso collected his note pad and sunglasses and made for the door. As an afterthought, he pulled two large Cuban-made coronas from his desk drawer.

"Rosie," he said as he passed her desk, "I left a few things on my desk that need typing, and I still need the figures from the department heads for the monthly report."

"No problem—I'll see to it."

"You're a sweetheart. Hopefully, I'll be back in by mid-morning." She gave him a skeptical look as he went out.

He walked a short distance down the hall to an open doorway labeled Commander, Johnston Atoll. The outer office held a metal desk manned by a sad-faced Army staff sergeant.

"Y'all go right in, Mr. Bruso," said the sergeant. "Th' colonel's expectin' you."

"Thanks, Buford. Your daughter have that baby yet?"

"Not yet, but she gettin' right close. Don't know 'bout this grandfatherin' business, though."

"Trust me, Buford, you're a natural."

Bruso knocked politely and walked in. The corner location and commanding view of the wharf area said it was an important office. A scattering of plaques and diplomas on the walls complemented the clutter on the desk. The arms of a green metal government-issue swivel chair, like a large pair of forceps, had a large Army colonel clamped firmly by the hips. The colonel's feet were crossed on the desk, and he had a telephone wedged between his jowl and shoulder. He clenched a hand over the mouthpiece.

"Jimbo, come on in; grab a chair. Coffee?"

"No thanks, Colonel, I've already had my limit."

Colonel L. William Trafton, U.S. Army Corps of Engineers, was the atoll commander. He was responsible for everything within a three-mile radius. He was also Bruso's boss, or at least one of them, and if there was a problem that didn't involve chemical weapons storage or disposal, Trafton turned to Bruso. Since those two operations ran pretty much without incident, the colonel spent a good share of his day on the telephone with Bruso. And he didn't hesitate to call Bruso at night, no matter how trivial the problem.

"I'll just be a sec. It's just after lunch back there, and I want to get the general before he goes into another meeting."

Bruso waved his hand in a gesture of patience. Trafton teethed on a pencil and hummed, while Bruso began a visual tour of the memorabilia on the walls.

The Johnston Atoll Command was a responsible and career-enhancing post, and atoll commanders were usually rewarded with a cushy stateside tour when they were finished. Trafton, like Bruso, was one of the few on the island authorized to have their families with them. This was a special concession, since their duties seldom allowed them time off the island. Trafton and his wife had elected not to take their kids out of school, so his family waited for him back in Arlington. Bruso had been married for a short time, but his wife had quickly grown tired of the separations and life in remote places.

"Thank you, Lieutenant." Trafton took his feet from the desk and sat, more or less, at attention. "Well, good afternoon to you too, General. How're things at the Pentagon . . . oh, sorry to hear that." Trafton covered the receiver and whispered, "Cold as a witch's tit." Then he listened for a minute. "You say next week for sure? Yessir . . . yessir . . . understood sir. We'll be ready, and we can just about guarantee you some sunshine here. . . . Very good, sir . . . understood, sir. Goodbye."

"Company?" said Bruso. They both dreaded VIP visits.

"Afraid so. General Taggart and a member of the Senate Armed Services Committee will arrive on the Circuit Rider next week. I'll let you know how many will be in the official party as soon as we receive the visit-request message. Knowing the general, he'll want us to play the perfect hosts here at Club Fed."

"Understood." Bruso flipped open his note pad and scribbled a few lines.

"Ready?" Trafton asked.

"Ready."

Each Tuesday Bruso and Colonel Trafton made a tour of the island together. Neither man intended this to be a formal inspection, but everyone knew when the atoll commander and the facilities manager were out and about.

Five minutes later they were in Bruso's International carry-all and pulling away from the administration building. In deference to Trafton, Bruso rolled up the window and turned on the air conditioning. Trafton started to light a cigarette, but relented when he saw Bruso fingering one of his cigars.

"I understand we had a little trouble at the Tiki late last night?" Trafton began. The Tiki Lounge was a bar and grill, and provided what social life there was on the island. It was a cinder-block affair with a palm-frond false ceiling and big-screen TV.

"That's right, Colonel. Nothing more than a little shoving and a few words. I've already handled it."

They completed a loop around the administration building and made a slow pass down Main Street, a single blacktop strip laid across a crushed white coral base. Main Street separated the administration complex from the runway. Cinder-block buildings, sometimes several deep, crowded the street on either side. They housed living quarters, general-storage areas, and maintenance facilities.

"Did Dallas kick the shit out of Atlanta or what?"

Bruso didn't care much for football, but no one on Johnston Island could be totally unaware of the Monday night NFL game. "Atlanta's got no defense," he replied, repeating a comment he'd heard at breakfast.

"And Dallas's got the horses," Trafton added knowingly. "No doubt about that."

Bruso stopped for a few minutes to talk with the duty NCO in front of the military police barracks. He had a small contract security force, but a company of MPs stationed on the island handled most of the security chores.

They drove back past the wharf area located across the street from the administration building. When the construction of the chemical-disposal facility had begun back in 1988, the harbor had been dredged to allow deep-draft cargo vessels to unload at the quay wall. A lot of things had changed on Johnston Island since the decision had been made to build the plant. Next they set out on the perimeter road that would take them around the island. It was Bruso's second patrol that day. He always inspected his facilities at sunup.

All twelve hundred people at Johnston Atoll lived on Johnston Island, by far the largest of the four islands in the atoll, yet only a little over one square mile in size. It was an oblong piece of coral eight hundred statute miles southwest of Hawaii, with palm trees, submerged coral reefs, and

white, sandy beaches. The north equatorial current warmed
the atoll, and it was cooled by the northeast trade winds.
Instead of a high-rise luxury hotel and golf course, Johnston
Island was dominated by a large concrete runway capable
of handling military transports and the huge chemical-
disposal plant complex. It was a factory town in the middle
of the Pacific. Most of the inhabitants called it the Rock;
the name Club Fed had come from a congressional staffer
whose senator had objected to the cost of running the island.

The carry-all took just a few minutes to round the eastern
end of the runway and reach the turnoff to the main
chemical-storage facility on the southeastern tip of the island. A pair of MPs at the gate looked smart and made a
show of stopping them for identification before waving
them through. Bruso smiled, knowing the duty NCO at the
barracks had alerted them.

The chemical-storage complex was a great deal more ex-
pansive than it looked. Rows of long, low, concrete-slab
buildings housed racks of chemical-agent containers. Below
these were additional underground storage facilities, designated areas reserved for the agents whose containers were
reaching the end of their service life. Then there were the
special-storage facilities—small, detached metal buildings
that held the special nerve agents. All of the chemical
weapons on Johnston Island were deadly, but there was one
class of nerve gas—a variant of the deadly agent VX—that
due to its concentration, lethality, and persistence, was designated for special handling and storage. They occupied
segregated, negative-pressure containment vaults that
looked like reinforced corn cribs.

Bruso and Trafton spent a few minutes with the officer
in charge of the complex and then were again back on the
perimeter road. They made a brief call at the small air terminal on the south side of the runway and continued around
the western tip of the island to the disposal facility. The
primary work of the island, and the reason for the large
number of people there, was the business of destroying

chemical weapons. The Johnston Atoll Chemical Agent Disposal System, or JACADS, occupied a strip of land along the north side of the runway, further west and downwind from the main housing and office facilities. For the most part, the trade winds came squarely out of the east. The main building resembled a large coal-fired power generation plant.

Bruso was responsible for everything on the north side of the runway, but his responsibility stopped at the JACADS fence. An alert contract security guard waved them through, and they parked in the visitors' spot near the plant offices.

"Doctor Demming will be with you in a moment," the receptionist told them. Bruso smiled his thanks and took a seat while Trafton began to fidget. He started to pace, tapping his well-chewed pencil on his thumbnail. This was as much a part of the weekly drill as the island tour. Several minutes passed. Bruso relaxed and thumbed through a magazine while Trafton roamed about the comfortable reception area.

"Good morning, gentlemen—Colonel; Jim. Always good to see you."

Dr. Gary Demming was the JACADS director and quite young to hold such an important and sensitive position. But he had been a key player in developing the system technology and had headed the design team that had built the facility. He was trim and a bit of a dandy for an academician, with fashionably cut long hair and a single gold chain around his neck. On the occasion of Trafton's visits, he pulled his hair back to a small sprig of a ponytail. There was a single gold Cross pen in the breast pocket of his immaculate white lab coat. Demming knew they were coming, yet he always made them wait.

"Sorry, gentlemen, I was held up. Can I get you a cup of tea, or would you just like to wander around the shop a bit?"

Trafton was a coffee drinker, as Demming also knew.

"Why don't we just take a quick walk about the facility, Doctor?" the colonel replied.

Demming led them from the reception area down a spotless, brightly painted corridor. After a short elevator ride, they were deposited on a wide catwalk that ringed the main incineration plant. The facility had the enormity of a hydroelectric power plant and the cleanliness of an operating room. Inter-connected piping, valves, gauges, and huge compressed-gas flasks surrounded the large bulk of the central combustion chamber. Immense, complex, vent stacking rose from the chamber. It was like a set from a Steven Spielberg movie.

They made a counterclockwise circuit of the plant, Demming and Trafton walking together with Bruso trailing behind. The JACADS director ambled along like a squire touring his estate. He carried a clipboard cradled to his breast, but didn't refer to it.

"On-site chemical storage remains at approximately 63 percent of capacity. Deadly agent storage space is at 91 percent. We've been averaging just over five thousand pounds of material destroyed each day. Of that, five hundred pounds are the special nerve agents. The two defective air-sampling monitors have been replaced, and all 106 of them are on line and functioning properly. All emissions for the past week have been well within contractual limits." Demming removed a single, neatly typed sheet from the clipboard and handed it to Trafton. "The figures are all there."

Trafton folded the paper without looking at it and began to question Demming on specific aspects of plant operation. They quickly fell into a technical discussion of thermal co-efficients and absorption factors. Bruso allowed them to move ahead of him a few paces, and their conversation was lost in the murmur of the ventilation system. Trafton and Demming were the senior military and civilian representatives on the island, and while Trafton had the final word, it was a continuous struggle.

They also represented the two kinds of people who came

to remote places like Johnston Island. Some, like Trafton, did·their job well enough and little else. There was every form of recreation possible on the island and an excellent library, but Trafton spent most of his time watching TV and seldom missed the evening barbecue at the Tiki Lounge. Demming, on the other hand, ran five miles each morning before work and was active in the skin-diving club. Since Johnston Atoll was a registered bird sanctuary with several unique species, he had become an amateur ornithologist. Demming was the type who spent his evenings with Berlitz language tapes or *Scientific American*. He would leave the Rock mentally and physically better than when he arrived.

Bruso knew both types well. He tried not to place too much emphasis on what people did on their own, so long as they were on time for their shift and ready for work. Nonetheless, experience had taught him that those who spent their spare time in active pursuits tended to be better employees and co-workers.

Trafton stopped abruptly. "I guess that about does it. You ready to head back, Jim?"

"Ready when you are, Colonel."

"Then we're on our way. Oh, one thing I almost forgot, Doctor—you too Jim; have your people review the hurricane emergency procedures. I understand there's a low-pressure system building up just south of the Marshall Islands."

Bruso pulled out his note pad and added a few scribbles. Dr. Demming just smiled and nodded. The chemical-disposal plant was the only hurricane-proof building on the island.

Wednesday, 30 November, 1:10 P.M.
SEA OF FERTILITY; LATITUDE 04°45'15" S
LONGITUDE 132°12'36" W

The ship had been at sea long enough for its complement to have settled into a routine. Southeast trade winds
had gently followed them from the coast of South America,
and for the most part the seas had been calm. The eastern
mid-Pacific was unpredictable this time of year, even this
close to the equator, but each day had been much like the
last, sunshine and a gentle swell. Four days out of Lima
they had steamed through a series of squalls, but a fresh-
water cleansing of the decks had been well worth the modest seaway caused by the storm.

Takashi Tadao mounted the bridge, as was his custom
after the noon meal. Today, as during the two previous
days, he was dressed in a light kimono and *hakama*. He
now seldom wore Western clothes. Tadao usually occupied
the port wing of the bridge, which usually meant that the
master and his mate kept to the starboard side. He stood
with his arms folded, lost in meditation. For almost a half
hour, he did not move. Then for several minutes, he carefully put himself through a series of stretching exercises,
methodically working each part of his body. Refreshed, he
walked back through the pilothouse, pausing at the chart
table. The master was immediately at his elbow, pointing
out the ship's location.

"We are in this area, Tadao-sama, about four hundred
and fifty miles northeast of the Marquesas Islands. On your
instructions, we are scheduled to come right fifteen degrees
to a new course of three-zero-four in about two hours."
They had been on a base course of two-nine-zero since
leaving Lima ten days ago.

Tadao studied the chart. This was as close as he wanted
to come to a populated area, although Hiva Oa, the principal island of the Marquesas, was barely fifteen miles long

and Ua Huka even smaller. They had spotted several contrails from airliners that morning, probably headed for Faaa Airport on Tahiti in the Society Islands, another eight hundred miles further southwest from the Marquesas. On a small-scale map, numerous islands seemed to blanket the South and mid-Pacific, but in reality they were tiny specks with vast stretches of water between them. How did the ancient mariners do it, Tadao wondered. They navigated these tremendous distances between islands in their open canoes.

This reminded Tadao of Yamamoto's attack on Pearl Harbor, which had been as much a feat of navigation as a military victory. The Imperial Fleet had been at sea for almost two weeks in the North Pacific, most of that time in storms with no stars to mark their position. Yamamoto's strike force had sailed undetected over four thousand miles by pure dead reckoning—quite an accomplishment, even a half century ago.

"Where is our position, exactly?" Tadao asked.

"One moment, please," the master answered, stepping over to the satellite navigation receiver mounted on the bulkhead. He tapped a code into a small instrument that was no bigger than a cigar box. The receiver issued a high-pitched chirp and a small slip of paper. The master brought the slip back to the chart table and carefully marked off the longitude and latitude.

"We are here, Tadao-sama."

"Thank you, Captain," Tadao replied politely, dismissing him. They exchanged bows, and the master retreated to the starboard bridge wing. Tadao was not trying to be rude, but the master did not as yet know the destination of his vessel. What Admiral Yamamoto wouldn't have given for the navigation equipment aboard this little ship, Tadao mused.

But he knew that while some satellites were orbited as aids for navigation, others were put in space to closely monitor the movements of warships and fleets. Hopefully, they will overlook a small freighter steaming independently, he thought, knowing it was quite likely they would. There were as many as fifteen thousand merchantmen under way around the world at any one time.

Tadao took a pair of dividers and began to examine their track. Since leaving Lima, they had covered nearly four thousand miles of ocean. He laid a ruler along the track of their new course. They would keep to that heading for another five days, passing within a hundred miles of Palmyra Atoll, the last point of land before they reached their destination. Then they would turn north toward Hawaii. Shortly after that, the ship's master would learn the destination of his vessel.

Tadao walked out on the port bridge wing to be alone. They were well past the halfway point of their seven-thousand-mile journey. He faced west toward Japan and bowed his head, clapping twice, then opening his palms. "Honorable Yamamoto, Admiral of the Imperial Fleet," he called quietly, reverently. "Hide us from the eyes of our enemies and guide us to our destination, for we too will attack at dawn."

Tadao was silent for a while, then clapped once more to end his devotion. He stepped to the front of the bridge wing to watch a group of men gathering on the main deck just aft of the forecastle. It was time for weapons practice. The armorer had laid out several automatic weapons and the men were loading magazines. Empty paint cans would be thrown from the bow to serve as targets. Tadao sighed. He yearned for the time before firearms, when issues had been settled with two-handed swords and by the courage and skill of the men wielding them. But these are modern times, he thought, and a warrior must avail himself of the modern tools of warfare.

Tadao shook his head and began to pace slowly along the metal grating of the bridge wing. The invention of the arquebus, a predecessor of the rifle, had marked the end of samurai armies and fighting with swords. But perhaps even a modern superpower is vulnerable to a timely, well-aimed blow from a swordsman, Tadao thought, a swift stroke delivered with ferocity and precision. He lingered just a moment before taking the stairs down to the main deck. One of the men handed him a loaded Uzi. Tadao chambered a round and nodded to the man on the forecastle, who flung a gallon can out away from the ship. As the can kissed the water some sixty feet off the port bow, it was lost in a tight group of mini-geysers from the 9mm rounds.

Later that evening, after Tadao had finished his evening meal and prayers, there was a soft knock on the door. He glanced briefly from the single porthole in his stateroom. The sun, which had just slipped beneath the horizon, now painted the high cirrus clouds in vivid shades of pink, gold, and purple.

"In a moment," he called, turning back to the sea and sky. The closer a man approaches his destiny or the likelihood of his own death, Tadao realized, the more he savors nature and the splendor about him. It was a phenomenon of which he had read a great deal, but had never fully understood until now. Tadao had never felt himself unappreciative or cavalier about beauty, especially the beauty of nature.

But it's true, he thought. Each passing day my senses grow sharper and the grandeur of this world becomes more crystalline, more pure. How fortunate that I am allowed to undertake such a quest, and be able to die at a time of my own choosing. Can it be that I am now permitted to more fully grasp this beauty in order to purify my spirit for the journey ahead?

When the brilliance had faded to dark purple and gray, he turned from the porthole. Tadao opened the door and returned the bows of his visitors. "Welcome. Please, enter."

Two men slipped off their sandals and stepped inside. Their manner showed respect for the honor of being invited to the *daimyo*'s cabin. Both men were dressed for the occasion in loose jackets called a *haori* and matching *hakama*. The room was spacious for such a small ship, with an area for a desk and a low, square, lacquered table. The bunk had been removed, but there was a tatami mat and a coarse blanket neatly folded by the far bulkhead. A standing shoji screen partly hid the entrance to an adjoining shower. Japanese classics and martial-arts manuals lined the corner bookshelf.

"Please, may I offer you tea?" Tadao wore a *yukata*, a light cotton robe, wrapped about his broad chest and tied securely about his waist with a cloth sash. The two men bowed at the waist and murmured their thanks, then knelt on the rice mats by the table. They were in their late twenties with a serious, competent look to them. Tadao knelt to join them. He dipped a bamboo ladle into an iron hibachi and poured boiling water into three cups containing a measure of powdered green tea.

"I have asked you here to tell you of our exact destination and of the task before us." Tadao had not yet told his followers of their mission. "But first, I must ask two questions. They are not meant to question your loyalty, but to reaffirm your commitment to our cause. Many years ago when you secretly joined the New Shield Society, you pledged your lives to the preservation of the traditional ways of Japan and to the emperor. Have you now any reservation concerning that pledge?"

"No, Tadao-sama," they said in unison and with a certain indignation.

"And are you prepared to die willingly for the emperor and Imperial Japan?"

"*Hai!*"

"Very well. I will now show you why we have traveled so far from the Chrysanthemum Throne and why such careful planning has gone into this undertaking." Tadao paused to unroll a chart of the mid-Pacific. "In a week's time we will attack an American military installation. The facility is not well guarded, at least not in proportion to its strategic importance. But it is a very critical installation." He took a pencil to the map. "We are here. In another four days we will be at this position, about a thousand miles south of

Hawaii. From there, we will swing north on a course for the island of Oahu.''

"We are to attack Oahu?" said one of the men.

"No, Araki, not Oahu or any of the Hawaiian Islands. When we are approximately seven hundred miles south of Hawaii, we will turn left and proceed at full speed for our destination, this tiny island right here."

Both leaned forward, squinting at the black fleck on the empty stretch of Pacific Ocean. "Johnston Atoll?"

"Exactly. Specifically, the island called Johnston Island. Here, this may make things clearer." Tadao unfurled NOAA Chart 83637, detailing Johnston Island and the seaborne approaches to the atoll. "Our mission is the capture of Johnston Island. It is a small island, perhaps only three kilometers in length, but very critical to the Americans. Each of you will lead an element of the attack. If my plan is carried out precisely, we will achieve total surprise and sweep across the island like a plague of locusts."

"I am honored, Tadao-sama, but may I ask why this particular island?" Beneath his *haori* he wore a bandage on his arm.

"Of course, Taiyo," Tadao said as he studied them intently. Outwardly, he was very calm, but there was fire in his eyes. "Johnston Island is a storage site for a large portion of America's chemical-weapons arsenal. When we seize the island and control this cache of chemical destruction, America and its Japanese commercial allies will have to pay attention to us. The whole world will pay attention!"

Araki and Taiyo carefully studied the features of Johnston Island, often referring to the scale at the bottom of the chart.

"And what of the island defenses, Tadao-sama?"

"We will be outnumbered ten to one, but most of them are civilians and scientists. And of the few soldiers among them, not one is *samurai*. Now, here is my plan."

Tadao spoke for fifteen minutes, outlining his strategy to storm and hold the island. He talked at length and in detail of the island's garrison and the large chemical-storage facility. The two younger men listened, showing no emotion, but their hearts were pounding. One of them checked the date on his watch.

"Then we will attack on the morning of December seventh—December eighth in Japan?"

"Precisely. We will storm ashore at the same time Admiral's Yamamoto's air group swooped down on the American ships in Pearl Harbor. And we will see if the Americans are any better prepared than they were in 1941. Are you with me?"

Taiyo leaned forward bowing, his forehead a few centimeters from the mat. "I am honored to serve Tadao-sama. It will be victory or death."

"Victory or death," echoed Araki, also bowing to the floor, trembling with emotion.

"So be it," said Tadao. He placed a hand squarely on each man's knee, then bowed deeply before rising again to meet their eyes. "Victory or death."

Thursday, 1 December, 6:49 A.M.
THE WHITE HOUSE

Robert William Garrison, president of the United States, was religious about being at his desk no later than 6:45 each morning. Per his instructions, a pot of freshly brewed Starbucks coffee, a bran muffin, and a bowl of fresh fruit were laid out on the desk along with his morning reading. The material was in two stacks, one for public sources and one for classified documents. He poured his first cup of coffee and began with the national newspapers. Five to seven minutes were allotted to each, and less time was needed with the *White House News Summary* since many of the articles were reprints from the other papers. Occasionally, he scanned the Pentagon's *Early Bird*. The president was not so much interested in military news as much as he wanted to know what his military leaders were reading. Garrison could read at an incredible rate and had a near-photographic memory.

He tackled the classified material along with the muffin, which had the consistency of compressed sawdust, and began his second cup of coffee. The classified documents contained summaries from CIA, DIA, State, and his national security adviser. It was a little game with Garrison to see just how much of the so-called classified information was in the newspapers. Then there were selected narratives that focused on actual or potential crisis spots around the world. Most of his predecessors had relied on oral briefings, but Garrison preferred to read. At 7:50, the coffee and the muffin conspired to force Garrison from his desk into what he referred to as the Oval Office water closet and his staff called the presidential shitter. There he read the daily summary from his chief economic adviser.

Garrison had stormed into the White House behind a populist coalition and critical miscalculations by his political opponents. Even the veteran pols had underestimated just how effective a handsome, unmarried senator could be when he campaigned with a vigorous vision of the future and proposed very few specific programs. The voters knew what they didn't want and Garrison had been careful to avoid that. He was tall, charismatic, sincere, naive, and a great deal more intelligent than most Washington insiders realized. The new president talked like a liberal but didn't always act that way. He had an incredible work ethic, and no president since Dwight Eisenhower made more effective use of his staff. His first two years in office had not been without controversy, but even his critics conceded he was learning. After a rocky start, a second term was beginning to look promising.

The voice of Garrison's secretary greeted him as he returned to his desk. "Mr. President, Mr. Sizemore and Ms. Breamer are here for their eight o'clock meeting."

Garrison acknowledged without taking his eyes from a report on projected money supply figures. He finished it and quickly scanned two more rather troubling pieces on domestic industrial production, making a few notes on a legal pad. He was the first president in recorded memory who knew shorthand. A staffer came to collect the material and his notes, which would be typed and given to his chief of staff for action. Garrison polished off an orange slice and stepped from behind the desk. Brushing crumbs from his lap, he walked to a door leading to one of the reception areas.

"Rita, Martin, come on in. Sorry to have kept you waiting." It was exactly 8:00.

Cabinet members and staff often met their boss in the Oval Office like this. The president wanted to be known as a shirt-sleeves kind of a guy, but the crisp blue oxford cloth was well starched and accompanied by dark slacks, polished wingtips, and smart silk tie. He held a cup and saucer with one hand and had a ready handshake with the other. Robert Garrison had the smoothness of an advertising executive.

Martin Sizemore was his secretary of the interior and Rita Breamer his senior congressional liaison. Garrison escorted them to the leather-padded, cane-backed chairs in front of the desk and returned to his seat.

"I understand we have some problems with our domestic chemical-storage facilities?" Garrison often began meetings with an ambiguous, open-ended question. White House advisers had learned that this did not necessarily mean the president was unknowledgeable on the subject.

"Not so much problems with the chemicals or storage facilities as with Congress," Breamer began. Both she and Sizemore had notebooks opened on their laps. "There are eight storage facilities in eight different states that serve as depots for about 81 percent of our chemical-weapons stockpiles. The congressional delegations of those eight states are unanimous in their opposition to on-site destruction of the chemicals. Money for the destruction facilities has been partially appropriated, but like all projects of this size, the cost has escalated well past original estimates. The delegations of the eight host states have marshaled enough support in both the House and the Senate to pass a moratorium on any form of chemical-weapons destruction.''

"I understand these chemical weapons were to be destroyed by incineration, is that correct?''

Breamer and Sizemore nodded.

"Good Christ, who in the hell was so gullible to think that the citizens and their representatives would allow the federal government to burn deadly chemical weapons in their backyard? It's ludicrous when you think about it.''

"Well, sir, it's a problem that's been brewing for over a decade.'' Sizemore flipped through his notes. He would have been far more comfortable with a DOD weapons expert making this part of the presentation, but Garrison liked his top advisers to have a reasonable command of the technical details. In truth, the president didn't entirely trust his military advisers, and since Interior had a peripheral interest in chemical-weapons destruction, Sizemore had been called in. "The Army is the service component responsible for chemical arms. In 1984 they developed a technology for burning the weapons in special incinerators that operate at close to three thousand degrees Fahrenheit. This method was blessed by the National Academy of Sciences and the Chemical Material Destruction Agency. Of course, this was several years ago when emissions from burning, any kind of burning, were far less of an issue. Now everyone from local community groups to members of Congress are calling for a ban on the incineration of chemical weapons in their states.''

"I assume we've looked at alternate methods?'' prompted Garrison.

"Yes, sir.'' Sizemore now read from his notes. "We've experimented with chemical neutralization, supercritical water oxidation, steam gasification, and plasma arc pyrolysis. Each offers the advantage of lower emissions, but at tremendous cost—well above the fifteen billion now estimated for the incineration plants. Cryofracture, that's where the weapons are dipped into liquid nitrogen and then broken apart before burning, has some advantages, but not much.

To their credit, the Army has designed a pretty good incineration plant, and there's a prototype in operation. It's an automated and explosive proof operation, with an elaborate scrubbing system for the emissions. And less polluting than a coal-fired power plant. It's just that we're not burning coal."

"You're referring to that incinerator out in the Pacific—the Johnston Atoll plant?"

"Yes, sir. The plant's been operating for several years now without incident. It's my understanding that the efficiencies aren't what they expected, but it is destroying chemical weapons and doing it safely. Remember the hundred thousand NATO chemical artillery shells Reagan promised to remove from Germany by the end of '92?" Garrison nodded. "Well, Bush honored that commitment, and the shells were shipped to Johnston Atoll. They just finished burning those projectiles a few months ago. That's the good news. The bad news is, those hundred thousand shells represented only about 1 percent of our chemical weapons."

Garrison stared at him a long minute. "Martin, just how much of this stuff do we have laying around?"

"Laying around may not be quite the best term for it, Mr. President, but to answer your question, close to sixty million pounds."

"Sixty million pounds!" Good Christ! Garrison thought. The things you learn after you get into the White House.

"Yes, sir," Sizemore replied weakly.

There was a long pause, then Garrison turned to Breamer. "Rita, what's your slant on this?"

"It's politics, sir. That, and there's a trust and credibility issue. The technology works. What the Army didn't count on was public reaction. Local communities and the environmental groups are against burning, period, and they're digging in to fight it. We can make a good case that it's a responsible course of action, but the state and local governments will still oppose it. Most of the approvals for plant construction and the operation of these sites are with federal agencies, and that part could probably be pushed through. But there's nothing in it for these congressmen and senators to support this undertaking over the objections of their constituents.''

"Can we reason with them on this?''

"I doubt it, sir, and if we could, they'd probably want more than we could give in the way of compensation with federally sponsored programs.'' Breamer would have used the word *pork* but she knew Garrison disliked the term. "And there are a few side issues. Some of them are afraid the government will use the incinerators for low-level toxic-waste disposal after the weapons destruction is finished. And of course there's the question of jobs. Many of those facilities and depots are there only to provide storage for the weapons. Remove the weapons and you remove the bases and the jobs.''

"Can we safely move the weapons to Johnston Atoll and have them destroyed there?''

"That's an option,'' said Sizemore, "and it's been well studied. Our domestic stockpiles could be moved just like the artillery shells from Germany, but in most cases we'll have to ship chemical agents across state lines to a port of embarkation. That's sure to create a storm of protests. Greenpeace would be all over us for taking them to sea. The same reactions you would expect from the movement of nuclear waste.''

"Yes, but we don't have the technology to deal with nuclear waste. It appears we do have the means to safely destroy chemical weapons.''

"I understand, sir, but it's the not-in-my-back-yard syndrome. You can also expect a strong reaction from the governor of Hawaii and the Micronesian Federation if Johnston Island is to be the destruction facility for all our chemical weapons. They've already complained about the operations currently in progress.''

"Rita?''

"Politically, and I mean congressionally, it seems like we'd encounter less opposition by moving the weapons. I just don't see Congress allowing the construction and operation of incineration plants at the eight domestic storage sites."

Garrison smiled ruefully. "And I guess I can't just sit on my ass and pass it on to the next guy like my predecessors did."

"No, sir. The Global Chemical Weapons Treaty, which we lobbied for and are signatories, says we have to destroy all chemical weapons by 2004."

Garrison considered this over steepled fingers. He knew the 2004 date was soft. The Russians have a helluva lot more chemical weapons than we do, he thought, and they won't meet the deadline, not unless we pay for it.

During his first year in office, Garrison had been roundly criticized for indecisiveness. Since then he had moved quickly and firmly on several issues and had been lauded for his courage—a man who could make the tough choices. Decisiveness was popular unless you stomped on too many toes or in too many rice bowls. Twice Congress had opposed him, and twice he had taken his case to the people with positive results. His ratings in the polls had soared. He called it the Gipper gambit, for Ronald Reagan who'd used it so successfully with a Democratic Congress. Perhaps, Garrison thought, this could be another one of those hard issues.

"Martin, get with DOD and work out a detailed study for the transportation of chemical weapons to Johnston Atoll. Rita, I want you to prepare an assessment as to where on the Hill we can find support for this, and where to expect opposition." He studied his calendar a moment. "Let's meet here on Monday the twelfth, same time. Okay? Questions? Good—let's get to work."

Sunday, 4 December, 8:30 A.M.
PEARL HARBOR

John Moody stood on the rounded hull of the USS *La Jolla*, well aft, some twenty feet from where the black skin of the tapered steel cylinder slipped into the warm waters of Pearl Harbor. He watched intently but said nothing while a man on the pier barked orders. "Easy . . . down easy . . . easy. Pay attention, goddamn it! Give me some boom extension . . . that's it . . . that's it . . . hold what you've got! Now, down easy."

This was perhaps the most critical part of his platoon's deployment aboard the *La Jolla*—the loading of the SDVs aboard the submarine. Senior Chief Will Stockton supervised the loading. A five-ton mobile crane had just eased the Number Seven boat off its trailer and was now inching it toward the deck of the sub. Walker and several of the other SEALs handled tag lines—applying tension here, slacking off there, at Stockton's direction. Four SEALs stood by the dolly on the deck of the sub just aft of the dry deck shelter. Stockton made a pinching motion with his thumb and index finger, directing the crane operator to lower the SDV slowly. When the little boat was hovering over the dolly, the men on deck aligned it carefully before Stockton allowed it to come to rest.

The SDVs were of a frame and fiberglass construction and couldn't bear their own weight out of the water unless properly supported. The dolly on the deck of the *La Jolla* had only one function: get the fragile submersible to the dry deck shelter and onto its cradle inside. They were similar to the folding gurneys used in ambulances.

Stockton boarded the submarine and directed the final movement of the boat into the shelter. It was like muzzle-loading a large jelly bean. When the Seven boat was secure, he headed back out to the pier to prepare the Number Two boat for loading.

A pleasant chaos surged along the pier. There was something festive and expectant about a ship preparing to get under way, even a submarine making ready for a short, pre-deployment cruise. Sailors and civilian shipyard workers bustled about. Everyone seemed to be in a hurry, but they smiled and exchanged greetings. There was a sense of purpose. Those who were going to sea were leaving their families and could only look forward to endless twelve-hour workdays in confined spaces. Still, there was a feeling of anticipation and excitement. Once at sea, those same men would begin to look forward to returning home. A sailor's life was often one of looking forward to things being different. As tradition demanded, the speaker on the sail of the sub loudly sounded four bells and announced the arrival of its captain: "*La Jolla* arriving!"

Commander Robbie Kemp pedaled up the pier and parked his bicycle in the space reserved for the commanding officer's car. He was a slim six-footer with a forceful presence. Kemp had the distinction of being the third black officer in the history of the United States Navy to command a nuclear submarine. It had been a long pull from South Central L.A. to the top of his class at Annapolis. From there he had gone on to achieve high marks at the Navy's Nuclear Power School. Ten of his last sixteen years in the Navy had been at sea, mostly in attack boats. The job had cost him his marriage, a handsome five-figured income in the private sector, and what most men would call a normal life. Kemp had paid his dues.

During his plebe year at the Academy, he had gone aboard the USS *Richard B. Russell*, a newer 637-class boat. From that moment on he had known that someday he would command a nuclear attack submarine. Twenty years later he achieved his goal. The USS *La Jolla* (SSN-701) was a Los Angeles–class boat, sixty-nine hundred tons of technology with a single purpose: seek out enemy submarines and kill them. Kemp had dreamed of hunting Russian fast-attack subs in the Sea of Japan, or waiting off the Kuril Islands to pick up one of their boomers to shadow on patrol. But now there were no enemy ballistic-missile submarines on patrol. Even the Russian fast-attacks seldom left port. *La Jolla* didn't have the twelve vertical-launch Tomahawk missile tubes that were fitted to the more modern 688-class boats. It was purely a hunter-killer.

Or in this case, a mother hen to the SEALs and their toy submersibles. Kemp eyed the SDV sitting on the pier. Damn SEALs! If his boat had had a bank of Tomahawk tubes, he'd have been in the Gulf or the Adriatic with a chance for some real action instead of playing nursemaid to Jacques Cousteau and his junior frogmen. Kemp paused at the gangway to allow Chief Stockton to come ashore. The chief tossed Kemp a hurried salute and immediately fell to the task of rigging the Number Two SDV for lifting. Instead of boarding, Kemp watched while the second minisubmersible was hoisted aboard his boat and eased into the shelter.

The dry deck shelter, or DDS, was a large cylinder with a pressure access hatch in the bottom that mated to the forward escape trunk of the *La Jolla*, right behind the sail. It was a pressurized housing that served as a watertight garage for the two SDVs. The escape trunk provided access from the submarine to the shelter. From there the small submersibles and their SEALs could sortie, through the large circular, bank-vault type door on the rear of the DDS, to the open ocean. The shelter was designed to be flooded to allow the SDVs to leave the parent sub for a mission. After the SDVs were recovered, the shelter was drained and the little craft could be serviced in a dry environment.

Any 688-class attack boat could carry the DDS, allowing the SEALs a number of host submarines from which to choose. But for Commander Robbie Kemp, the dry deck shelter was like a chancre on the nose of a starlet. Why, he asked himself again, did the fucking Navy allow this wart to be clamped to the back of my beautiful submarine!

"Morning, skipper." Kemp's executive officer was waiting for him on board at the foot of the bow.

"Morning, XO. How we doing?"

"Making all preparations to get under way, sir. We'll shift to ship's power at 1300 and the tugs will be alongside at 1430. High tide is 1515. As soon as the SDVs are secure, the SEALs and their equipment will be fully loaded."

"Very well. COMSUBPAC will probably be down to see us off. Have the quarterdeck prepared to render honors."

"Aye aye, sir."

Kemp walked aft to the dry deck shelter. The huge, hydraulically operated door stood open. Inside several SEALs squirmed over and around their little craft, clamping them to their cradles and re-stowing equipment within the cramped shelter. Senior Chief Stockton stood at the opening with his hands on his hips, giving orders while Moody watched. The SEALs were dressed in pressed camouflaged fatigues, starched caps, and spit-shined boots. Kemp had to admit they were a sharp-looking bunch.

"Good morning, Mr. Moody."

"Morning, sir." Moody snapped to attention and saluted. Like Kemp, he was dressed in summer khaki. This was the first time Kemp had seen the officer in charge of his SEAL detachment in anything but fatigues or swim trunks.

"How was your load-out, Mr. Moody?"

"Just fine, Captain. Our personal gear is all stowed below or in the shelter. Your people have gone out of their way to make us feel at home. We really appreciate it, sir." The complement of the *La Jolla* had been scaled back to ninety-eight men to make room for Delta Platoon, but with fourteen SEALs and their gear, it was still crowded, very crowded.

"How're your boats?" Even though Kemp was less than excited about his assignment to carry SEALs, he was still a professional.

"Both fully operational, sir. We just installed the new obstacle-avoidance sonar and all on-board equipment has been freshly calibrated. We were also able to take aboard an additional set of batteries for each boat.''

"So you're fully ready to commence operations tomorrow?''

"Yes, sir.''

The *La Jolla* was scheduled for two weeks of refresher training in Hawaiian waters. Both the SEALs and the crew of the submarine had to practice the delicate underwater ballet of launching and recovering the SDVs while under way. The SEALs needed to practice their skills at docking the mini-subs and in underwater navigation, and the *La Jolla*'s maneuvering team needed to practice trimming the boat. It was quite a trick to keep the sub at a constant depth at slow speed while the dry deck shelter was flooded and drained. One disadvantage of the modern nuclear submarines was that they were not designed to sit on the bottom, so all operations had to be conducted under way at low speed.

Kemp glanced down at the single row of ribbons Moody wore above his pocket just under his SEAL pin. The Navy Cross and a Navy Commendation Medal bracketed a Purple Heart.

"Very impressive, Lieutenant. The Gulf War?''

"No, sir.''

"Bosnia? Mogadishu?''

"No, sir.''

"Then I assume you probably can't talk about it, right?''

"That's right, sir.''

Kemp chuckled to himself. So Moody was the one who did it! A highly classified penetration into Russian waters had reportedly been made by the Navy's only operational conventional, non-nuclear submarine. Kemp had heard that the mission was to recover a team of Navy SEALs parachuted in to gather evidence that the Russians were selling nukes to the wrong people. Word was that it had been a very dicey extraction and that the SEALs had encountered stiff resistance on the way out. The Navy Cross was second only to the Congressional Medal of Honor. They weren't passed out for routine missions, nor were Purple Hearts awarded for training operations.

"Very well, Mr. Moody. Carry on. And by all means, please let us know if you need anything."

"Aye aye, sir."

Kemp returned Moody's salute and started forward. He was intercepted by a petty officer with a message board. He frowned at the gaping cylinder perched on the back of the *La Jolla* and the two squat craft nestled inside. He shook his head and frowned. It's fucking discrimination! Why couldn't they have given me a boat with Tomahawks?

Monday, 5 December, 8:15 A.M.
CAMP H. M. SMITH, HAWAII

"Attention on deck!"

Everyone in the small, crowded amphitheater came to their feet, including a half dozen admirals and generals seated around a curved table in front of the risered theater seating. Arranged directly behind them in the first elevated row were key senior officers and civilian experts who could be called on if the CINC had questions about the briefing.

"Good morning, ladies and gentlemen. Take your seats and let's get started." Admiral Joseph Harrington found the high-backed swivel chair reserved for him at the center of the front table.

An Air Force major stepped to a podium offset from a huge rear-projection screen that dominated the front of the amphitheater. The lights dimmed and a map of the Pacific and Indian Oceans appeared. The reading light at the podium glowed under the major's chin, giving him a Lon Chaney look.

"Good morning, Admiral. Welcome to the weekly theater briefing. My remarks this morning will be classified at the secret level. We'll begin with the naval components in the eastern Pacific.''

The Pacific Theater stretched from the West Coast to Mombasa and from Australia to the Aleutians. Harrington listened patiently as the major dutifully presented not only the Navy's order of battle in his area of responsibility but also those of the Army and Air Force, reviewing regimental strengths and squadron availabilities.

All he really wanted to know was the status of those resources he would most likely need in a fast-moving crisis: the Army Ranger battalions and the Air Force F-15Es. His strategic assets consisted of an aging wing of B-52s based in Guam. Trident ballistic-missile submarines roamed the North and mid-Pacific, but they were not under the control of CINCPAC or Commander-in-Chief, Pacific Theater.

"That concludes my portion of the briefing, Admiral. Are there any questions, sir?"

"Not at this time, Major, but thank you. Excellent briefing."

"Thank you, sir."

The major breathed a quiet sigh of relief and surrendered the podium to an Army lieutenant colonel who took up the disposition of "enemy" forces. He began with North Korea and moved on to the Middle East. In closing, he spent a few minutes on the People's Republic of China and touched on terrorist organizations known to be operating throughout the theater. He was replaced by a briefing officer who expanded on the political instability in East and Southeast Asia, and on the few leftist movements still active. Most guerrilla forces now opposing established governments no longer called themselves communists.

"Is there any current joint military exercise play?" Harrington asked.

"No, sir," replied the Air Force brigadier general who served as his Deputy Chief of Staff for Plans, or DCOS N5. "There's nothing until Exercise Team Spirit in February, and once again, that will depend on tensions between North and South Korea. For now, we're planning on it."

"I see. Anything more on that helo we lost late yesterday? It was a Marine chopper I believe."

"Affirmative, sir. It was an H-46 from the *Saipan*." The speaker was a Marine colonel sitting almost directly behind the admiral. Harrington spun around to face the man. The Marine wore naval aviator's wings. "As of 0600 Kilo time, the search for survivors was abandoned. They found the oil slick and some debris, but the four crewmen are still missing and presumed lost."

"Thank you, Colonel." Harrington turned to his N3, or DCOS for Operations, who was a rear admiral. "I want a full report on that crash. That's the third Marine 46 we've lost this year, correct?"

"That's correct, sir."

Harrington pursed his lips and was silent for a good thirty seconds. The room was quiet except for the hum of the air conditioning.

"Bob," he said to his N3, "I want all the 46s grounded until we get to the bottom of this. Those birds are old, but we shouldn't be losing them like this. That chopper could have crashed with a platoon of young Marines. Stand 'em down."

"Aye aye, sir."

"Anything else?" Harrington asked looking up and down the lead table. "N1? N2? N4? Very well, thank you for your time." He pushed himself to his feet.

"Attention on deck!"

"Please, carry on," Harrington replied, but everyone remained standing until the CINC left the room.

Back in his office, the admiral grimaced as he scanned his calendar. His senior legal counsel had asked for a closed-door meeting with him at 9:30, which could only mean an incident of sexual harassment at Camp Smith or that one of his staff officers had come out of the closet. Neither prospect thrilled him. He swung around and looked down the valley across Pearl Harbor. The rain clouds boiled over portions of the Koolau Range, promising some magnificent afternoon rainbows.

Camp Smith sat well back on Halawa Heights overlooking the Naval Station piers, Ford Island, and Hickam Field. The base was named for General H. M. "Howling Mad" Smith, USMC. It was an old concrete and stucco construction with the look of a two-star hotel in a Third World country. The building had a shabby dignity that spoke of better times in a different era. A circular drive and several splendid banyan trees, whose roots were rumpling the pavement, graced the main entrance. Abundant hibiscus and bougainvillaea made the old structure almost cheerful. Camp Smith was the headquarters of CINCPAC.

Admiral Joseph P. Harrington, Jr., was an unlikely man to wear four stars, let alone achieve command of the Pacific Theater. He was a solid officer, highly proficient but quiet, and a surface warfare officer—a cruiser-destroyer man. Harrington himself was the first to admit that the competition for senior flag rank had been culled of some pretty good men by dramatic reductions in the submarine force and by the Navy Tailhook scandal. Many of the fast-track golden boys were now civilians. But Joe Harrington's timing had been good. When the Pacific CINC billet had come open, the Chairman of the Joint Chiefs had said, "We don't need any problems out there. Find me a solid professional who's long on integrity and short on ego." Harrington had been selected in favor of more senior admirals who muttered about the unfairness of the system but could truthfully say nothing against the new CINC.

"Admiral?" His executive assistant's voice broke into his thoughts.

Harrington touched the intercom. "Yes, Julie."

"Captain Neuchterlein from the Judge Advocate's office is here."

"Tell that ambulance chaser I'll be right with him."

"Yes, sir. And don't forget, we have a meeting with the leaders of the Japanese-American Friendship League at 1000. They want to finalize the agenda for the Arizona Memorial service. It's the day after tomorrow."

"Thanks, Julie. I hadn't forgotten."

Tuesday, 6 December, 6:00 P.M.
SEA OF FERTILITY; LATITUDE 17°04'56" N,
LONGITUDE 165°52'32" W

Takashi Tadao stood on the bridge of the old
tramper studying the sky. Fat clumps of cumulus clouds,
like distant heads of fresh cauliflower, dotted the horizon
in every direction, seemingly reluctant to approach the ship.
Tadao had not expected a cloud cover on their last daylight
transit, although he certainly had hoped for one. He wondered if even these scattered pockets would be of some
help. Turning from the open bridge, he walked back into
the pilothouse and stared at the chart.

Early on the fourth, they had come within 250 miles of
Christmas Island, then 200 miles north of Palmyra Atoll
just after midnight on the fifth. Just before sunrise, they had
swung to a northerly heading that would take them to Hawaii. At dusk they had come sharply left to three-two-zero
and brought the ship up to sixteen knots. Night steaming
was relatively secure, but in the daytime they were vulnerable to visual detection by satellite or reconnaissance aircraft. On this course, there could be no masking their
destination; they were headed straight for Johnston Atoll.
Tadao had known they would be vulnerable during the daylight hours of 6 December, but standing on the wing of the
bridge most of the day, he felt very exposed. In the radio
room, two men carefully listened on the maritime bands
and ship-to-shore frequencies, but they had been silent. Tadao looked up at the clock. 6:15 P.M.

"Captain!"

"Yes, Tadao-sama."

"At twenty knots, when will we arrive at Johnston
Atoll?"

The master fell to the chart with a set of dividers. He
took distance to a nautical slide rule with the new speed.
"We will arrive at the atoll at 0545."

"And what is our fuel state?"

The master consulted his fuel logs and made a few notes. "At twenty knots, we will use a third again as much fuel. It is well within our capacity, but we will arrive there with only a single day's reserve. We cannot leave without taking on more fuel."

"Very well. Take us up to twenty knots." So, thought Tadao, we are not unlike the young kamikaze pilots of the war who left their airfields with only enough gasoline to reach the American fleet.

Back out on the bridge wing, Tadao willed the sun to go down, but it remained suspended defiantly some thirty degrees above the horizon. He clapped twice and lowered his head in prayer. May the *kami* that protect our islands find us on this great ocean and make us invisible from the eyes of the *gai-jin* until it is time for us to strike!

The bridge and pilothouse vibrated slightly as the *Sea of Fertility* quivered at being asked to take on more speed. It bucked gently as it began to dig into the swells rather than ride over them.

Their luck held, apparently, or the Shinto gods heard Tadao and intervened. At the headquarters of the secret National Reconnaissance Office, there were more compelling priorities than a small freighter that had wandered out of the shipping lanes. Most of the hard surveillance requirements were still centered on Russia and the new republics of Central Asia. The intelligence establishment now labored, with marginal success, to monitor the nuclear weapons of the former Soviet Union. Nonetheless, Johnston Atoll was one of the U.S. defense facilities the NRO was charged with protecting. And due to its unique and remote location, Johnston Island relied heavily on the vessel-surveillance capability of the NRO.

It was not a visual watch with a photo-interpreter monitoring the sea and airspace around the island. An automatic surveillance system electronically sifted radar, infrared, and visual data from satellites that passed over or near the atoll. The system would alert the CINCPAC Crisis Action Desk at Camp Smith if any vessel approached within two hundred nautical miles, but the *Sea of Fertility* would not reach that point until 8:30 that evening, just after the sun slipped below the horizon.

That wouldn't help either, though, because the particular satellites passing overhead during the next eight hours had only optical sensors. There were no available IR satellites or Navy RORSats, the highly sensitive radar ocean-reconnaissance satellites specifically designed to detect surface traffic at night.

After the sun had set, Tadao turned to the ship's master. "I will be in my cabin. See that I am awakened at three o'clock or called immediately if there is any challenge to our progress."

"*Hai*, Tadao-sama."

After a quick meeting with his two lieutenants, Tadao retired to his cabin. Following a short period of meditation to calm his spirit, he carefully bathed, dousing and scrubbing himself in preparation for the important day ahead. Refreshed, he laid down on the tatami mat and fell fast asleep.

Wednesday, 7 December, 3:55 A.M.
HICKAM AIR FORCE BASE, HAWAII

Initially, it had seemed like glamorous duty. Plenty of air time, remote destinations with exotic names, and lots of time off between trips. The Air Force considered it good duty, even for a crew chief with as much time in as Senior Master Sergeant Andrew Pierce. The time off had not lost its appeal, but the flying was very repetitive. Week in and week out: Johnston Island, Eniwetok, Truk, Yap, Guam, Wake, and back to Hickam. Every once in a while they stopped at Saipan or Tinian. And there was a rare trip to Majuro, Ponepe, or Rota.

Soon they all looked the same—coral and concrete with

fierce tropical heat, overly air-conditioned crew lounges, and bad food. They called themselves the Circuit Riders, the C-141 Starlifter crew that serviced the former U.S. Trust Territories and possessions, like Johnston Island, in the Pacific. As crew chief, Pierce was responsible for everything but flying the aircraft. He was very busy on the ground and had plenty of time in the air with little to do.

Right now he was preparing the 141 for a scheduled 6:15 departure. Aside from a full load of cargo that had to be sorted, weighed, palletized, and loaded in the reverse order of their scheduled stops, they had VIPs aboard.

"Hey, Master Sergeant, how many we got?" An airman in dirty overalls towed a small cart with cleaning supplies behind him.

"Two. I want that head scrubbed from top to bottom, fresh towels, a full soap dispenser, a new box of toilet-seat covers—the works. An' break out the porcelain mugs. When the O Club opens, slip over there and get some cloth napkins. I want the coffee and tea ready, but don't make it till just before takeoff."

"Female, huh?"

Pierce looked up from his clipboard and removed the half-chewed cigar from his mouth. "Worse than that, a lady senator. We also drew an Army two-star."

"How far they goin'?"

"Just to Johnston Island."

"All this fuss for a two-hour trip." The airman whistled softly. "So who gets left behind this time?"

"Captain Rieling for sure. You up, DiGiorgio?"

"Shit, I wish. Naw, I think it's Eddie's turn."

Because some of the crew rest stops and layovers were short on adequate facilities, the Circuit Rider crew was all male, but it didn't necessarily have to be. Whenever a high-ranking governmental official or member of Congress was aboard, a female was shifted into the cockpit, either as a co-pilot or navigator, and one of the enlisted crew members was rotated. The airmen, male and female, understood it was a matter of convenience, but the Air Force wanted to avoid any perception of gender discrimination or favoritism. Only the command pilot and Pierce were exempt from substitution.

Ten minutes later a young airman stepped through the forward hatch of the Starlifter. She filled out a starched set of fatigues just a little too well.

"I'm looking for the crew chief?"

"Right here. And you are . . ."

"Airman First Class Gregory, checking in for the flight." She carried a small canvas overnight bag.

"Okay, Gregory, think you can handle manifesting the rest of this cargo?"

"In my sleep, Master Sergeant." She grabbed the clipboard from him and went to work.

Wednesday, 7 December, 6:01 A.M.
SEA OF FERTILITY; LATITUDE 17°53'21" N, LONGITUDE 168°72'15" W

"How far?"

"About thirty-five miles, Tadao-sama," the master replied. "I don't expect we'll pick it up on radar, or them us, for another forty minutes."

"Sunrise?"

"In about a half hour—at 6:27."

Tadao nodded. He was dressed as he had been when they'd sailed from Lima, in old seaman's clothes and a faded baseball cap. There was little to do but execute the plan. Preparations for the attack had been completed early the day before. The assault teams and section leaders had been extensively briefed, using a large table-size clay model of the island. Each man had his weapon, assignment, and an issue of ammunition. What they lacked in number would be well compensated for by shock and terror—*if* they could achieve complete surprise. And if we do not, thought Tadao, we will show the *gai-jin* how well we can die. Like their leader, the men had been up for several hours. Topside, the ship still looked like a tramper. An inspector who demanded to go belowdecks would soon learn there was something very different about this little freighter, and he would quickly die with that knowledge.

"Very well, let it begin." Tadao turned to a seedy-looking Caucasian who stood in the pilothouse by the radio on the rear bulkhead. "Proceed, Mr. Baxter."

The man had a sallow complexion and looked drawn. He wore cotton slacks, a white shirt that hung outside his trousers, and expensive street shoes. His nose was red, almost raw, and he often took a rumpled handkerchief to it. He picked up the handset. The radio was tuned to 2716 Hertz.

"This is the MV *Sea of Fertility* calling Johnston Control. *Sea of Fertility* calling Johnston Control, over."

His speech was very precise, with a hint of a British accent. There was no immediate response so he repeated the call. Finally the speaker in the pilothouse crackled.

"Ah, roger, this is Johnston Control. Go ahead, over." The voice sounded as if it had just been called from sleep.

"Johnston Control, this is the MV *Sea of Fertility* out of Panama bound for Hong Kong. We are presently thirty-five miles southeast of your location. I have a very sick crewman aboard and his condition is deteriorating rapidly. Request permission to make a port call for emergency medical attention."

"This is Johnston Control. Understand you have a medical emergency and are requesting a port call, is that correct, over?"

"That is correct, over."

"*Sea of Fertility*, are you aware that Johnston Island is designated a Naval Defense Security Area and closed to the public, over?"

The man smiled, then took on a serious expression. "Damn it man, I've got a lad here that's burning up with fever, and I judge his condition to be critical. Now can you help us or not?"

There was a pause before the reply came. "Okay, *Fer-*

tility, understand you have critically ill aboard. Stand by. Johnston Control, out."

He looked up.

"Very good," Tadao said. "The man has gone to wake his supervisor for further instructions. It will be a few minutes. Remain nearby."

Baxter nodded. He walked out onto the bridge wing and lit a cigarette. Suddenly he coughed loudly, a fluid-filled cough that came from his lungs. Ten minutes later, the speaker came to life.

"MV *Sea of Fertility*, this is Johnston Control, over." A new voice, one of authority, had replaced the drowsy radio operator.

"This is the *Sea of Fertility*. Go ahead, over."

"This is the harbor master speaking. The area you have entered is under military control, and ships approaching within one hundred miles are supposed to notify us of their intentions. Please state the nature of your emergency and why you haven't notified us sooner, over."

"This is the *Sea of Fertility*. I didn't intend to get this close, and now I'm not sure I have a choice. We have a crewman who is violently ill. A few hours ago he began vomiting and running a temperature of 104 degrees Fahrenheit. I repeat, one zero four degrees. He's gone into a coma and I'm afraid we might lose him. Do you have a doctor there, over?"

There was a pause. "*Fertility*, we have a doctor and complete medical facilities. Can you take a helo aboard, over?"

"We cannot. Our foredeck is obstructed by derricks and our afterdeck is too small. And I would be afraid to winch him up in his condition. Do you copy, Johnston Control?"

"Johnston Control, I copy. What is your length, displacement, and draft, over?"

"My vessel is 280 feet and we displace thirty-one hundred deadweight tons. We draw ten feet forward and fourteen feet aft."

"Ah, roger, I copy 280 feet with a maximum draft of fourteen feet—displacement, thirty-one hundred tons. *Fer-*

tility, do you have the American sailing directions for this port, over?''

Tadao nodded to the man on the radio. "Yes we do, over.''

"Very well, proceed to a position two miles south of the R-2 Lightbuoy as it says in the sailing directions. If permission is granted for you to enter port, a pilot will board you at that location. Guard this channel and check in on the half hour. We should have you on radar in a short while. Do you copy, over?''

"Understood, Johnston Control. MV *Sea of Fertility*, out.''

Ten minutes later the first man who had answered on the Johnston Control circuit called with a list of questions. Baxter told him the ship had a crew of nine, all Korean except for the owner's representative, who was English. The vessel had no cargo and was sailing in ballast for Hong Kong, where it was scheduled for scrapping in Macau. All this information was verifiable in the Lloyd's Shipping Directory. They were advised that the master was to collect all cameras and that they were not to dump trash within five miles of the atoll. If a port call was authorized, they were to remain under power while alongside the pier, and no one but the sick crewman could leave the vessel without permission of the commander of Johnston Atoll. All the while, the *Sea of Fertility* steadily closed on the atoll from the southeast.

"I have a definite radar contact, Captain,'' said one of the mates. "It should be the loran tower on Sand Island.''

"Range?''

"Twenty-seven miles.''

The sun had not broken the horizon, but there was a warning glow in the eastern sky. Tadao approached the captain. "How long before we make visual contact?''

"We should be able to pick up the tower and the mass of the chemical plant at about twelve miles. The outline of the island at eight to ten miles.''

Tadao was silent for a moment, pacing slowly around

the pilothouse before again turning to the captain and Baxter. "You know your duties. Are there any questions?" Both men shook their heads. "Very well. Send Horiuchi to the infirmary, and call me immediately me if there is any further contact."

A small cabin one level below the pilothouse served as a sick bay. It was little more than a first-aid station with a single cot, an old clinical blood-pressure station, and a resuscitator/aspirator unit. Tadao arrived there a moment ahead of Horiuchi, a lean man of indeterminable age with the look of a feral cat. Another man was with him, dressed in a tattered set of dungarees, but he had quick, athletic movements and a sense of purpose that said he was more than a merchant seaman. Tadao bowed from the waist, head low for a long moment.

"Are you ready, Horiuchi-san?"

"I am, Tadao-sama." He bowed slightly from the waist, acknowledging the respect extended him by his *daimyo*.

Tadao poured a chalky liquid from a metal flask into a porcelain cup and offered it to him with both hands. Horiuchi immediately drank it. Tadao met the eye of the other man.

"See to him." The younger man bowed and Tadao left.

Horiuchi laid down on the canvas cot. Ten minutes later his temperature soared and he began to vomit. After emptying the contents of his stomach, he continued to retch violently.

At sea near the equator, with very little dawn, the sun seemed to leap into the sky as if the gods had simply turned on the lights. Twenty-five minutes after sunrise, the structures on Johnston Atoll were visible on the horizon. Shortly after that, the islands beneath the structures appeared as if they were a single piece of land. At 7:40 they saw a speck of a small craft coming out to meet them.

"This is Johnston Control calling the *Sea of Fertility*, over."

"This is the *Sea of Fertility*."

"Johnston Control. Continue to a position two miles

south of the R-2 Lightbuoy. You will be met by a pilot vessel with a pilot and a medical officer aboard. You are cleared to enter the harbor under the direction of the pilot if the doctor judges that your medical situation requires a port call for humanitarian purposes. The pilot will provide you with a list of port regulations. Be advised that winds are from the east at fifteen knots. High tide is plus one at 1000. Do you have a bridge-to-bridge transceiver, over?''

"Yes we do, over.''

"Very good. Your pilot vessel is on channel thirteen. These are shoal waters, *Fertility*. Pay attention to your pilot and good luck. Johnston Control, standing by.''

"Understood, Johnston Control, and thank you. *Sea of Fertility*, out.''

Baxter wearily put down the handset and took up a hand-held Motorola transceiver. Tadao turned to his two lieutenants, Taiyo and Araki, who had just come onto the bridge. They were dressed in desert-pattern camouflage fatigues, the kind that had now replaced the Vietnam-era jungle cammies in the Army surplus stores. Automatic weapons were slung across their backs, barrels pointed down, much like the samurai of the fourteenth century had carried their *no-dachi* swords. Taiyo had a short dagger thrust in his web belt. Both men had nylon vests loaded with grenades and extra magazines strapped to their torsos. They wore black baseball caps and had radio transceivers clipped to their belts. They looked like members of a SWAT team.

"Get to your stations. When the attack is sounded, let no power on earth keep you from accomplishing your mission.''

They exchanged formal bows and the two soldiers hurried below. Tadao looked across the bow to their destination, a point just south of the atoll. He looked so harmless in his rumpled seaman's clothes and cap, but there was a savage, determined look on his face. By now they could clearly make out the pilot boat waiting for them, wallowing in the seaway.

Wednesday, 7 December, 8:15 A.M.
CIRCUIT RIDER STARLIFTER; AIRBORNE, 110
MILES NORTH OF JOHNSTON ATOLL

"More coffee, Senator?"

"Thank you, but I've had quite enough." Nancy Blackman, the freshman senator from Utah, was a relaxed, confident woman in her late forties. She had the quiet assurance of someone who had been successful in the private sector before entering politics. The largest stockpiles of America's chemical arsenal were located in her state.

At one time Blackman had headed the largest real-estate development firm in Utah. When California had passed Proposition Thirteen, she'd recognized that the California business community would have to shoulder a much larger portion of the tax burden. She'd also known that the massive social and educational infrastructure of the state could consume large quantities of tax dollars, and that the liberal Californian politicians would see that this infrastructure was well fed. This was bad news for business, but not for Blackman. Her firm had developed a solid reputation for helping tax-weary California businesses to relocate in Utah, which had made Nancy Blackman a multi-millionaire.

Two years ago on a local talk show, they'd asked her why she hadn't run for governor. "The governor's doing a good job," she'd replied. "What we need to do is to replace the nitwits in Washington." The discussion had led her to a challenge for the incumbent's Senate seat. Nine months later, she'd run away with the election.

Blackman had joined the Senate quite skeptical of the political process and with an absolute disdain for bureaucracy. But she listened carefully and asked very direct questions. Senator Blackman sat on the Senate Arms Control Subcommittee as well as the Armed Services Committee.

Utah's Tooele Army Depot held 42 percent of the nation's chemical weapons. A destruction plant similar to the one on Johnston Atoll had been built at Tooele, but the incineration of chemicals there was on hold. There were powerful lobbies in her state, both for and against the operation of the disposal plant. In Utah, they were as concerned with jobs as with the environment. The Army, which favored on-site disposal at all eight regional storage facilities, saw Senator Blackman as a potential key backer of their plan for on-site disposal. She had been invited for a visit to Johnston Island to see just how non-invasive and environmentally safe the disposal operation really was.

"Tell me, General," she began, "the Johnston Island plant has been operating at only 60 percent of its capacity. Is there some problem with design of the plant?"

General Paul Taggart was in charge of the Army's chemical-disposal program. Whether or not Blackman came around to the Army's way of thinking could depend heavily on the success of her visit to Johnston Island.

"We don't think so. But the technology's new and the operation hasn't been without a few glitches. Efficiencies are improving, though. Given the controversy surrounding the disposal project, we've decided to move forward very carefully."

"How about the storage of these weapons? I know in Utah, we're worried about the emissions from the incinerator there, but we're also concerned about leaks in the storage containers."

Taggart removed his glasses and sucked thoughtfully on one of the bows. He was a tall man, direct and intense. "For now, we believe the chemical agents are safe and well contained. But there's a finite life to some of the storage containers, and there's always a risk, however small, in handling these containers. In some cases, they could be difficult to repackage. In the long run, we think it'll be safer to destroy them on site." He shrugged. "We feel we have a safe and workable technology to accomplish that, but I guess you folks in Congress are going to be the final judge of that."

Blackman understood where Taggart was coming from,

but she found his, and the Army's, political naïveté frustrating. She was also a little tired of being patronized by men like Taggart. "That's correct, General. And ultimately, we're responsible to the voters if there's a problem or an accident. How do you feel about moving all the chemical weapons to a single facility for destruction?"

"Like Tooele?"

"Or Johnston Island."

Taggart thought for a moment. "Well, Senator, it would seem we trade one ticklish situation for another. From my perspective, the problems with moving the weapons are the same as with on-site destruction; they're political. So, it seems we're trading one controversy for another. Sure, we can move them. If they'd been needed in time of war, we'd have moved them and little would have been said about it."

Perhaps, Blackman thought, nodding.

A uniformed crewman stepped down from the flight deck and approached. "Excuse me, Senator, General," she said. "The aircraft commander sends his compliments. We're about forty miles from the atoll and should be on the ground in fifteen minutes. It's been our pleasure to serve you, and we hope you have a pleasant stay on Johnston Island."

"Thank you, Lieutenant," replied Taggart.

They watched the pilot return to the flight deck. "I'm curious about something, General. I know the restrictions have been lifted, but do most female pilots in the Air Force still only fly non-combat aircraft?"

"Sorry, Senator, I'm just a foot soldier and an engineer. But it's my understanding that women in the Air Force now fly everything from word processors to F-16s."

"And you don't have a problem with that, do you, General?"

"Are you crazy, Senator? Of course I don't." They both laughed.

Wednesday, 7 December, 8:20 A.M.
JOHNSTON ISLAND

Jim Bruso had been up for several hours and had already made his normal inspection of the various community support facilities for which he was responsible. He looked up from his paperwork as Colonel L. William Trafton burst through the door.

"Christ, when it rains, it pours!"

"Good morning, Colonel. Something wrong?"

Trafton wore a newly pressed, class-B uniform. He had a fresh shave and the odor of Noxema followed him into the room.

"Jim, I need some help. I got General Taggart and a U.S. senator due here in about ten minutes, and we may have a medical emergency on our hands."

Bruso had already heard. "You mean that merchantman with a sick crewman?"

"Yeah. I sent Doc Frankel out with the pilot. If that guy's really as bad as they say he is, I told the harbor master to let them come in. They can stay at the quay wall long enough to take the man off and get him to the hospital to see what's wrong. If they do come in, could you be on the wharf to meet them?"

"No problem, Colonel, I'll handle it. You take care of General Taggart and the senator."

"And it's not just a regular senator; it's a lady senator."

Bruso chuckled at Trafton's distinction. "Even better. Maybe that will keep the general distracted."

Trafton walked over to the window and looked out. "I guess we have no choice here if this is a genuine medical emergency, but I want that ship out of here as soon as possible." Trafton had the habit of using Bruso for a sounding board, especially when he was agitated. "And Demming better have that plant looking good, or Taggart will have his pompous little ass for lunch—mine too. I just wish that damn ship could have waited a day or two.''

"Relax, Colonel, it'll all work out. This a big ship?''

"Apparently not. The harbor master says it's a coastal freighter in transit to Hong Kong to be scrapped.''

Trafton glanced at his watch and quickly made for the door. "Thanks again, Jim.''

Bruso smiled and shook his head. He watched from the window as Trafton jumped into a carry-all and peeled out of the parking lot, throwing coral dust on all of the other vehicles. Then he picked up the phone to call the harbor master.

The *Sea of Fertility* came to a northerly heading and slowed to bare steerage way. The pilot boat came alongside to port in the lee of the ship. A Jacob's ladder was lowered to it. A man in uniform came over the rail first, followed by an older man who moved like a seaman. As soon as they were aboard, the pilot boat bore off and took a lazy station on the ship's starboard quarter.

"Welcome aboard,'' the master said in broken English. "I am Captain Chou, master of *Sea of Fertility*. This is Mr. Baxter, the owner's representative.''

"Hullo there, and thank you for coming.'' Baxter greeted them warmly, shaking each one's hand.

The pilot spoke first. "I'm Clancy Ellison, the Johnston Harbor pilot.'' He had watery blue eyes bisected by a broad, veined nose. He also had the weathered look of a man who had spent a lot of time at sea. He wasn't that old, perhaps close to sixty, but his creased, worn features suggested he was a man who hadn't always taken care of himself. "This here's Doc Frankel.''

"Hello. I'm Major Jonathan Frankel, Army Medical Corps. Perhaps you should take me right to your sick crewman.'' Frankel carried a tan canvas medical kit on a sling over his shoulder. It contrasted with his green utility uniform. A gold leaf marked one collar point, complemented by a caduceus on the other.

"Excellent. Kim, would you take the doctor to sick bay. Mr. Ellison, I'll accompany you and the captain to the bridge." A man in dungarees nodded and led Frankel aft. "After you, Mr. Ellison."

Ellison thought it strange that someone other than the master would be giving orders, but he shrugged and followed Chou up the stairs. You see everything on these merchantmen, he thought.

Once on the bridge, he surveyed the inside of the pilothouse. Aside from the master, Baxter, and himself, there was a mate at the helm and a bland-looking man dressed in seaman's clothes and a baseball cap who kept to the port wing of the bridge. Ellison noticed the ship was very well equipped for a tramper. Probably updated to make the trans-Pacific crossing, he concluded.

"You like-a tea, sir?"

"Yes, Captain. That would be most kind of you." Ellison disliked tea, but he had spent time in the Orient and knew it would be impolite to refuse.

"Tell me, Mr. Baxter," he said after the master left them, "I'm surprised to find an owner's rep aboard. It seems a bit unusual."

Baxter lit a cigarette, offering one to Ellison, who refused. "I'm an accountant, and I've been at the home office for going on fourteen years now. In all that time I've never been to sea. I've had some health problems lately, so it was suggested that an ocean voyage might do me some good."

Doesn't seem to be helping, Ellison thought. The guy looks like death warmed over. "So, have you enjoyed the trip?"

"It's been, well, different. I've had some time to myself—a chance to tie up some loose ends, if you know what I mean."

Ellison didn't, but he smiled anyway. His years in the merchant marine had been a steady diet of watch-standing and ship's work. Again he looked around the pilothouse.

He had a vague feeling something was out of place, but he couldn't put his finger on it. Ellison and Baxter worked at small talk while the master stood nearby, speaking only if spoken to. A crewman brought him a mug of strong tea. Finally, Major Frankel entered the pilothouse from an internal passageway.

"Major?"

"We have a real sick man down there. I don't know what's wrong with him, but if I don't get him stabilized and get some fluids in him, we could lose him."

"Can we take him ashore in the pilot boat?"

"Not a chance. I brought along a portable IV and he's on it now. The only way he can be moved is by litter. If we're going to save him, you need to get this ship to the quay wall where we can put him directly into an ambulance. And the sooner the better."

"Okay, Doc. We'll get right to it." Ellison turned to Chou. "Captain, are you ready to enter port?" The master nodded.

The doctor excused himself and went back to his patient. Ellison stepped onto the starboard wing of the bridge and took out his Motorola transceiver.

"On the pilot boat. You there?"

There was a burst of static from the handset. "Yeah, Clancy."

"Okay, Ned, we're gonna take her in. Thanks."

A bearded man leaned from the window of the launch and waved. The craft issued a blue-black belch of diesel smoke and began to wallow back toward Johnston Island.

"Break, Johnston Control, this is the pilot, over."

"Johnston Control. Go ahead, Clancy."

"The crewman here is in pretty bad shape and the medical officer wants to be in port to take him off. I estimate we'll be alongside the quay in about forty-five minutes unless we run into a problem. Can you have some line handlers and an ambulance standing by, over?"

"Understood, Clancy. ETA forty-five minutes and you want the meat wagon on the pier, over."

Ellison grinned. "That's correct, and pass the word on over to Jim Bruso. Pilot, clear."

Ellison stepped back into the pilothouse. He took a Johnston Island Harbor chart from his map case and unfolded it on the chart table. He put one hand on the master's shoulder and pointed through the pilothouse window toward the land.

"Okay, Captain, see that nun buoy right there . . . that's it, just to the left of the big smokestack." The master nodded. Ellison directed him to the chart. "That's the approach buoy to the channel. I want you to make for that buoy at ten knots and take it abeam to starboard, about fifty meters, okay?" Chou nodded. "As soon as you pass the approach buoy, come to a heading of three-five-zero magnetic." Again the master nodded. "We'll get a visual bearing on the two range towers on the north side of the harbor. From there it's standard channel markings, red to starboard, green to port. But you have to mind your helm. The channel's only about 140 meters wide."

Chou audibly sucked air across his lower teeth. "So. What speed you recommend in channel?"

"Slow to six knots once you pass the approach buoy. And you may have to carry a little right rudder to compensate for the westerly wind."

Chou said a few words quietly to the helmsman and then joined Ellison out on the starboard wing of the bridge. The pilot launch was halfway to the harbor, clearly marking the center of the channel. The bow of the *Sea of Fertility* began to swing as it picked up speed and steadied down on the approach buoy. They were on their way to Johnston Island.

Ellison still had the feeling something was wrong. The captain's mannerisms seemed strange, unlike those of other Koreans he'd met. He didn't recall Koreans saying "so" as this man did, and inhaling forcefully through clenched teeth. It had been a while, but Ellison could have sworn he remembered Korean as a more guttural and abrupt language. Suddenly, his attention was claimed by a thundering noise from above.

Everyone looked up as a huge C-141 transport shrieked overhead. It dropped its gear and continued in a westerly route as if it had some other destination. Then it dipped a wing and turned back into the wind for its approach to the Johnston Island runway.

The Starlifter taxied back down the concrete strip and turned onto the large parking apron on the north side of the runway. A ground crewman with wands lured the transport up to the west end of the apron. With a final howl, the big bird neatly pirouetted in front of the passenger terminal and came to rest.

Two passengers waited outside the terminal to fly west. They had a well-fed, professorial look to them and carried vinyl lap-top computer cases, which ID'ed them as tech reps. No sooner had the engines shut down than a pair of forklifts converged near the tail of the aircraft. Electric motors screamed painfully as the rear ramp and upper door yawned open. Colonel Trafton stood at attention on the left side of the aircraft, just forward of the wing by the passenger access. A crewman jumped down first and set a step-stool under the door. A woman appeared next, followed by General Taggart. Trafton and Taggart exchanged salutes.

"Good morning, Senator, and welcome to Johnston Island. Nice to see you again, General. Pleasant flight?"

"Perfect. Senator Blackman, this is Colonel Trafton, the commander of Johnston Atoll." They smiled and shook hands.

"Real happy to have you here, ma'am. Welcome to the Rock."

Blackman thanked him as she took in the clear skies and warm, clean air. She wore a cotton chino skirt, tailored denim blouse, and sensible shoes. The senator was a tall, handsome woman. Her dark hair was cut in a loose pageboy that rippled in the morning breeze.

"So what do you have on for us this morning, Colonel?" said Taggart.

"I thought we'd go straight to the JACADS plant. Doc-

tor Demming is waiting for us there. He's scheduled a facility briefing that will take about an hour. Then we'll begin
a tour of the plant. I assume you still plan to leave this
afternoon.''

"That's right. The Air Force was kind enough to make
a C-9 available to come and get us. It's supposed to be here
in time for a 1600 departure.'' Taggart chuckled. "Sixteen
hundred—that's four o'clock, Senator.''

"Thank you, General.'' She knew 1600 was 4:00 P.M.,
and her look told him so. "Shall we get started?''

"Our transportation is right over here,'' said Trafton
hastily. "This way, please.''

As they walked through the terminal, General Taggart
motioned Trafton aside. "One of the pilots said something
about a maritime emergency or something—heard it on the
radio. What's this all about?''

"A small freighter passing nearby had a crewman fall
ill. It happens every so often, and they know we can provide hospital care or fly them out. From what I understand,
the man's in pretty bad shape. The facility manager's handling it.''

"Bruso, right?''

"Yes, sir.''

"Is something wrong, General?'' Blackman asked.

"Not at all, ma'am,'' said Taggart. "Some problem on
a passing merchant ship, but it's under control. Here, allow
me.'' He opened the rear passenger door of the carry-all
and helped her in. As they drove along the perimeter road
around the west end of the island, Trafton maintained a
running monologue on the history of Johnston Atoll.

The *Sea of Fertility* crept into the harbor turning basin and
gently came around to a westerly heading. The northeastern
tip of Johnston Island passed slowly down the port side.

"Rudder amidships . . . all stop.'' The master relayed the
commands to the helmsman.

Ellison spoke into the Motorola. "Okay, Boats, come up
under my starboard bow and make up alongside.''

"Roger, Clancy."

The small Navy tug all but disappeared under the flare of the ship's bow. Nylon hawsers were passed down and the tug was made fast. Ellison noted there were two crewmen standing along the port rail with mooring lines at the ready.

"Okay, Captain, let's take her in. Rudder, left fifteen degrees; engine, ahead standard." Ellison calmly gave rudder and engine orders to the master, who relayed them to the pilothouse. At intervals, Ellison passed instructions to the tug over the Motorola. The wind was behind them, slightly off the port quarter, and the *Sea of Fertility* was rather nimble for a freighter. Standing on the port wing of the bridge, Ellison brought it smartly alongside the quay.

The quay wall was constructed of concrete-backed sheet piling with rubber-bumpered wood pilings and creosoted cross members to cushion vessels alongside. After the lines were over, Ellison thanked the master of the tug and watched as a mobile crane hoisted a brow into place. Jim Bruso was the first one up the gangway, followed by the customs inspector. A square, military-type ambulance had already backed up to the brow. The rear doors stood open while the two paramedics lounged nearby and smoked. Two canvas-covered flat-bed stake trucks sat idling at the far side of the wharf area by the access road. Bruso soon arrived on the bridge wing. The customs officer disappeared with the master to inspect his papers.

"Difficult trip?" Bruso asked Ellison.

"Not really. She's a pretty steady old gal."

"How about the crewman?"

"Not so good. Doc's still afraid he might lose him."

From where Bruso and Ellison stood on the wing of the bridge, they had a commanding view of the forward part of the ship as well as the entire wharf area. To either side along the shore, there were single-story warehouses and open storage areas bounded by chain-link fencing. Unlike a commercial facility, the waterfront was uncluttered and very clean. In front of them over the bow, some three-quarters of a mile west down the northern shore of the island, sat the huge bulk of the JACADS facility. From their vantage point, they could see the extensive piping and conveyor systems that served the plant, and the three tall red-and-white-banded smoke stacks.

Abeam from the ship and directly across the road that paralleled the waterfront were the administration building and exchange complex. It was 9:15 and the island was well settled into the daily routine. A few workers had paused to watch the ship tie up, but most had gone about their business.

"Where's Doc, anyway?" Bruso asked.

"I don't know. As worried as he was, you'd think he'd have the guy out on deck and ready to go. Hang on . . . there he is."

Down on the main deck, two men carried a litter from the deckhouse forward to where the brow connected the ship to the quay. A blanket covered the man in the litter, and his head lolled from side to side with the motion of the stretcher. Dr. Frankel followed them up the deck and onto the brow.

"Y'know, Jim. There's something kinda weird about this ship. I can't really put my finger on it, but I—"

"Hold on, Clancy. Who's that down there behind the stretcher, anyway?"

"Doc Frankel, who did you . . . wait a minute . . . that's not Frankel!"

Then it began.

The two litter bearers set their patient down by the ambulance and instantly pulled automatic weapons from under the blanket. The patient himself leaped to his feet, also armed. From within the ship, police whistles sounded. A hatch on the foredeck was lifted clear by one of the derricks, and armed men began pouring from the hold, running single-file for the brow. They wore light-brown desert camouflage uniforms, but with black sneakers instead of boots. Most of them had nylon or mesh vests with grenades and ammunition pouches attached. And all wore white headbands with hand-painted Japanese characters. They moved with discipline and precision. A man with a black baseball cap headed the file.

The first men ashore fanned out in a skirmish line and began advancing on the headquarters building. An occasional muffled staccato of suppressed automatic fire broke the morning quiet. Bruso and Ellison watched, rooted in horror.

"Oh God, *no!*" gasped Bruso.

Finally he and Ellison pulled away from the scene below them and started for the pilothouse. Blocking their entrance was the old seaman with the ball cap, the man Ellison had seen on the port bridge wing when he'd first come aboard. But the seaman had disappeared.

In his place stood a figure dressed in a tan pima-cotton uniform with a choker-type collar. The jacket was a tunic with a flap that buttoned down the right side of his breast and a line of false brass buttons down the left side to give balance. The collar, sleeve piping, and the strip along the outside of the trousers were dark red. His shoulder epaulets had no marking, but there were two small stars, one on either side of the collar fastening. He too had a white headband tied about his forehead inscribed with Japanese characters. Two swords were belted to his side, a *daisho* pair— one short and one long. He held a submachine gun with a thick, silenced barrel. The weapon suddenly barked, pinning Ellison against the bridge-wing railing. When the 9mm burst released him, he slumped to the deck in a sitting position and fell forward across Bruso's feet.

"Do nothing foolish or make any attempt to escape, or you will die like the pilot," the man said. Bruso, reeling in disbelief, obeyed. "Good. Now, I assume you are in charge?"

Bruso nodded dumbly. It was like a dream—a nightmare! Above the pilothouse, a large flag rose to the yardarm and boldly unfurled in the stiff breeze. It was a Japanese flag, but not the Hi-No-Maru, the sun-disk flag of modern Japan with a red circle on a white field. It was the battle flag of the Imperial Japanese Army—menacing and colorful, with the rays of the rising sun radiating from the center. Bruso numbly turned to the activity below. The last of the attackers had cleared the gangway. First one truck, then the other, roared away from the wharf loaded with armed men. After that a half dozen or so climbed into the ambulance and screeched after the trucks. Another dozen fanned out along the waterfront. Several mounted machine guns appeared along the main deck.

Bruso turned back to the pilothouse, half expecting the uniformed apparition with the headband to be gone. He was not. Nor was the shouting along the waterfront or the occasional burst of gunfire. Reality began to sink in. His feet were warm and wet, causing him to step to the side. His shoes were filled with Ellison's blood.

"What is your name?" the man asked.

Bruso stared at him, unable to speak. The weapon didn't make that much noise, but the clang and whine of the bullets as they skipped into the deck plating beside him did.

"What is your name?"

"Bruso," he heard himself say over the ringing in his ears. "Jim Bruso."

"Ah! So you are Bruso . . . good. Very good." The man in the tan uniform smiled cruelly. "Now listen closely, Mr. Bruso, and I will tell you what you must do if you wish to be alive when the sun sets on this historic day."

The man continued to speak, but Bruso only half heard him, his mind racing to catch up with events. *This day . . . this historic day. My God, it's December 7—again!*

Yoshiro Taiyo sat in the cab on the passenger's side giving instructions to the driver. He again tested his arm against the elastic bandage that bound his upper arm. It was wrapped tightly to keep the wound from opening, yet still allow him an adequate range of motion. He had a map board on his knees with the route to his objective clearly highlighted. Behind him on the canvas-covered bed were fifteen heavily armed men. They drove quickly, but not so fast as to call attention to themselves. Their target was the military police company headquarters and barracks complex located between the administration building and the runway. Taiyo had to assume the MPs had been alerted, but if their luck held and they hadn't, a speeding truck would surely get their attention.

As they turned onto Main Street and approached the MP headquarters, Taiyo smiled. During their extensive briefings on the ship, he had learned that many Americans, especially those in the military, smoked cigarettes, but they were prohibited from smoking inside their buildings. The two soldiers casually smoking on the wooden steps told him what he needed to know. He gripped the driver by the shoulder.

"Banzai! Drive right to the door!"

The building was no different than a dozen others that lined the street—whitewashed, cinder-block construction with a rust-streaked air conditioner hanging from every other window. A flag with the colors of 28th Company, Schofield Barracks MPs, fluttered from a wooden staff planted in a circle of coral rocks near the walkway. The two MPs lounging on the porch watched as the truck jumped the curb and took out the flagpole, coming to a stop just ten feet from them. For a moment Taiyo didn't move, marveling at how closely the building resembled the clay table model they'd studied during their preparations. And it was all exactly the same as the color photos! He fumbled for the door handle and leapt from the cab.

Men poured out of the back. Most were armed with Uzi submachine guns and a few with shotguns. Each knew exactly where he was going. The canvas behind the cab was thrown aside, revealing two men with Uzis fitted with thick sound suppressors. One of the MPs started for the door while the other just stared, dumbfounded. Rounds slammed into them as they danced and tumbled like the marionettes of a palsied puppeteer.

The first men from the trucks raced for the barracks behind the headquarters building. Concussion grenades were tossed into the buildings, blowing out the windows and stunning those inside. Then the attackers rushed inside and the killing began in earnest. Back on the truck, two more men with Heckler & Koch 91 heavy assault rifles began clearing the street in either direction. They knocked down a soldier a half block up the street and raked a pickup truck, causing it to career into a telephone pole. With short, surgical bursts, they picked away at anything that moved.

Taiyo appeared on the porch of the MP headquarters building and took out his radio. "This is Strike One. The military police headquarters and barracks are secure. We are also in control of their armory. Now proceeding with phase two."

The truck, canvas stripped back from the top and sides, rolled slowly up the street. An Imperial battle flag now fluttered from a staff tied to the front bumper. Taiyo stood in the bed behind the cab, flanked by the two men with heavy assault rifles. On either side, members of his attack force moved quickly from building to building in two-and three-man teams, searching for weapons and any sign of resistance. Anyone in uniform was shot outright and civilians warned to stay inside until instructed to come out. It was a street scene from the fall of Nanking in 1937.

Riding in the other truck, Araki and his men sped around the perimeter road on the eastern end of the island. Their objective was the chemical-storage complex, just over a mile by road from the ship. They were still several hundred yards from the entrance when the gunfire and explosions from the grenades began to rumble across the runway.

During security drills conducted periodically on the island, the ten-foot-high section of chain-link fence that protected the storage complex entrance was rolled into place. At that time, the two MPs on gate duty would don flak jackets and helmets and shove loaded magazines into their M-16s. One guard would check the credentials of those wanting to enter against the access list while the other provided security from the safety of the sandbagged guard post. Today, they had been told there were VIPs on the base, and both of them had reported for their shift in freshly starched camouflage fatigues. They were on the alert for staff cars, but not for trucks moving at high speed.

The storage complex was just over a half mile from the MP barracks and slightly upwind. The two MPs on duty heard the explosions and stood by the guard shack trying to figure out what was going on. "Where's it comin' from, Frank?"

"I dunno. I thought they closed the range whenever there were VIPs on the island."

"Yeah, me too. Some asshole probably just didn't get the word. Get on the horn to the barracks and see what the fuck's goin' on."

Both soldiers looked up in time to see a stake truck rumble off the perimeter road and come charging toward the complex. They watched the truck bear down on them until it was too late. One was run down and crushed under the wheels while the other was cut down as he tried to get back to the guard shack. The truck didn't stop until it reached the center of the complex at the storage control office, another single-story, cinder-block building. Men dropped from the back of the truck. Some fanned out through the complex while a half dozen, led by Araki, burst through the door of the office. After two quick bursts of fire, all was quiet. Several terrified civilians were locked in a conference room. Araki ordered the two men and one woman in uniform outside and shot them.

No more than five minutes after the truck had entered the storage facility, it was again on the perimeter road. This time there were only a dozen men in the back. The vehicle raced westward along the south side of the island toward the disposal facility.

Minutes before Araki's truck and his twelve men passed the access road to the airport terminal, the ambulance with seven men turned off the perimeter road and braked to a halt at the base of the control tower. Fully armed combatants crouching behind assault rifles and submachine guns ran to their assigned places. Two of them rushed up the stairs and took command of the tower, while the rest secured the terminal area and the flight crew. The two controllers in the tower died quickly.

One of the Japanese in the tower smiled as he surveyed the deserted hardstand below. The big C-141 rested docilely on the hot tarmac fifty yards from the terminal. His instructions were not only to take the control tower, but to capture the transport and the air crew intact. He took out his radio and reported the success of his assignment. Then he and another attacker slung their weapons and began to drag the corpses from the tower. After that they settled down and began to familiarize themselves with the tower radios.

Surprisingly, the only real resistance came from the civilian guard at the disposal facility, one of Bruso's men. Like many in the contract security force, he was a former Army enlisted man. He was also a handgun enthusiast. As the truck with Araki and his men bore down on him, one of the men behind the cab sprayed the gate area with automatic-weapons fire. The guard drew his Ruger 357 and dropped to a shooting crouch. He managed to get off four rounds before a soldier in the truck found him with his Uzi. One of the Ruger's big rounds tore through the radiator, causing steam to blanket the windshield. The driver slowed until he remembered his training and stuck his head out the side window to find his way. The other three bullets left spiderwebs in the front windshield. Two of them passed through, one grazing the thigh of a man standing behind the cab. The third took Araki in the middle of the forehead, killing him instantly.

The truck braked to a halt exactly where Bruso and Colonel Trafton had parked two days earlier, about the same time of day. Camouflaged figures in white headbands streamed from the truck into the building. One of them stopped to open Araki's door, shoving a hand in the middle of his chest to keep him from falling. He quickly checked the dead man's eyes and saw they were beginning to dilate. He tore the radio from Araki's vest and hurried after the others, allowing his dead leader to tumble from the seat into an awkward heap on the blacktop.

The attackers raced through the building unopposed. Several of them ran straight for the disposal control room, a large sterile, airtight space with thick windows overlooking the main incinerator assembly. The room was packed with instrumentation and several white-coated civilian plant operators. They seized control of the room and ordered the terrified technicians to continue with their work. One of the Japanese told them in slow, precise English to complete the burning of chemical agents in the current destruction sequence, but to terminate the conveyor system that added new munitions to the system.

Another group broke into a plush conference facility. One of the attackers raised his weapon to fire on the two men in uniform, but another stopped him. The captives were roughly searched, handcuffed, and pushed back into their chairs. The man with the radio reported that the disposal facility was secure, adding that Araki had been killed in the attack. Then he reported that he had captured the atoll commander and what appeared to be another high-ranking military officer.

Jim Bruso now stood against the pilothouse, facing an armed man dressed as a merchant seaman. Bruso's Marine Corps training was close to three decades old, but he could tell the man with the Uzi was a soldier, not a sailor. The bald man in the strange tan uniform stood on the bridge wing with a portable transceiver in each hand. Every few minutes he spoke a few brief words into one of the sets. Incoming transmissions were also brief and disciplined. When the firing broke out at the MP compound, there was no mistaking the bark of the non-suppressed automatic weapons or the muffled crump of grenades exploding inside buildings. Bruso had been with the 26th Marines at Khe Sanh. That was a long time ago, but he knew the sound of a firefight. He also knew the sound of a one-way firefight. A bitter rage began to build inside as he thought of the slaughter that must be taking place. The island was totally unprepared for this kind of armed assault, and Bruso quietly prayed that none of his people would be foolish enough to resist. These people are Japanese, he reasoned, and part of some sort of a paramilitary force. Why would we be attacked by the Japanese? The shock was wearing off and he began to think more clearly. Not *the* Japanese, but a group of dedicated, well-armed Japanese terrorists!

The man in the tan uniform turned to him. "So, Bruso, our attack is going according to plan. Within minutes we will be in complete control of the island. As I assume command I will expect you to cooperate and obey my instructions, quickly and without hesitation." His measured English was precise, with only a hint of an accent.

"What do you want? Why are you doing this?"

"In good time. As soon as the administration building is secure, I will shift my command post there." A burst of static came over one of the handsets. Tadao put it to his ear. *"Hai . . . hai . . . hai . . . domo arigato!"* He turned away from Bruso and spoke into the other radio.

Bruso's attention was then captured by activity near the entrance to the administration building. He watched in disbelief as the American flag was taken down and replaced by the Imperial Japanese battle flag.

"Bruso, do you recall the last time a Japanese invasion force raised our flag on conquered American soil?" He just stared at Tadao. "Few people do. It was when we occupied Attu and Kiska in your Aleutian Islands." Tadao continued, with a touch of reverence in his voice, "That was well over fifty years ago. We abandoned Kiska, but our soldiers died to a man in the defense of Attu." Again, the radio crackled. "It is time for us to go ashore, Bruso. Please, follow me."

As they started to leave, Baxter strolled out from the pilothouse onto the bridge wing.

"Ah, Mr. Baxter. Will you be joining us ashore?"

"I don't think so. I think . . ." A cough shook him to

the core, but he quickly recovered. "I think you can agree that I've held up my end of the bargain."

"And you now want us to honor our side of the agreement."

"I suppose," he said, lighting a cigarette. "I really have no wish to further be a part of this."

"Fucking traitor," Bruso mumbled.

Baxter gave him a twisted smile and stepped to the railing with his back to them. The man with the Uzi moved back toward the pilothouse and motioned for Bruso to do the same. Tadao carefully set the radios by the door to the pilothouse and in one swift motion unsheathed the long sword, the *katana*. He discarded the scabbard and wielded the sword with both hands.

"Good God, you can't *do* this," Bruso said softly.

The blade made a singing sound as it completed a full arc above Tadao, then snapped forward and cleanly severed Baxter's head from his body. His head reached the deck plating just ahead of the torso and rolled a few feet into the scupper. The rest of Baxter quivered for a few seconds and began to pulse blood from the truncated neck. Bruso stared in horror as Tadao drew a white cloth from his tunic and began to carefully wipe the few red beads from his blade. He tossed the cloth aside and returned the sword quickly to its scabbard. Then he bowed ceremoniously to the form on the deck.

"Shall we go now?"

Bruso couldn't move. He was not unfamiliar with bloodshed and death, but that was in war—in another place and time.

Tadao smiled condescendingly at him. "He was not a traitor, you know, at least not from his point of view. He had the AIDS virus and the disease was in its final stages. We knew this when we contacted him and sought his assistance in this undertaking. For his cooperation, a sum of money has been placed on deposit to care for his family. He died bravely with honor and dignity at a time of his own choosing, Bruso. Can a man ask for more?"

Bruso finally tore away from the corpse and stared at Tadao. "You're out of your fucking mind," he heard himself say.

A flash of anger passed across the other's features, but he quickly regained his composure. "Perhaps, Bruso, but that is *your* point of view. And I place little credence in the perspective of *gai-jin*. Come, we must go!"

He descended the stairs to the main deck. Bruso followed, prompted by the muzzle of an Uzi in his spine.

Wednesday, 7 December, 11:36 A.M.
CAMP H. M. SMITH, HAWAII

Admiral Joe Harrington sat at his desk reviewing yet another budget revision. On the desk beside the money figures was the operations schedule. Like all theater commanders, he was being asked to do more with less. He was wearing a white T-shirt, white trousers, white socks, and white shoes. On a coat tree by the door hung his service dress-white blouse, complete with high starched collar and gold shoulder boards, each carrying four silver stars. The hanger and blouse had a severe port list caused by the mass of medals that smothered the left pocket. He would have changed to a working uniform, but he was scheduled to speak at a retirement luncheon for the PACFLT Command Master Chief.

Harrington had just come from the Arizona Memorial. He had attended other Pearl Harbor Day ceremonies at the memorial, but this was his first as Commander-in-Chief, Pacific. The force chaplain and a Shinto priest had offered prayers for all the souls lost that day and in the war years that followed. Harrington and a senior member of the Japanese consulate in Honolulu had made brief remarks, consoling words about past misunderstandings and a future built on trust and friendship. The American admiral and the Japanese consular officer had laid wreaths on the water, and the photographers from the wire services had had a field day.

He pushed the papers aside and took a sip from his mug. But how do the Japanese *really* feel about Pearl Harbor, he wondered. How would I feel attending a similar ceremony at Hiroshima? For some reason, the Arizona Memorial was the number-one attraction for Japanese tourists in Hawaii, more popular than Sea World Park and Hanauma Bay combined. Harrington had watched them line up at the memorial, laughing and taking pictures, like junior-high kids on an outing. Many American tourists thought their conduct was rude and insensitive, even sacrilegious. Harrington didn't think so. They're just very different from us, he thought. We don't understand them any better now than we did in 1941.

He had not been totally comfortable during the ceremony that morning, and he was very glad it was over. Harrington was too young to remember the attack on Pearl Harbor, but he distinctly remembered the end of the war in the Pacific, V-J Day. He and his mother had walked from their house on 8th Avenue up to Orange Avenue, the main street in Coronado. Horns were blowing, and people were hanging out of car windows and shouting. His mother told him this meant his father would soon be home. Later that evening, he was playing on the front porch when the two somber-faced officers came up the walk. He knew at that very instant his father would never come home again.

Harrington truly couldn't remember his father, but his mother had talked about him a lot. Sometimes that was all she talked about. Periodically, an old shipmate would stop by and the stories would begin. The senior Harrington had commanded a five-gun Fletcher, screening battleships as they pounded the coast of the Japanese home islands. On news of the surrender, the task force had pulled back out to sea to await further orders.

That evening a single kamikaze came in on the deck with the sun behind him. They never saw him until it was too late. His father was severely wounded but wouldn't leave the bridge, directing the fire-fighting teams and counter-flooding that were to save his ship. But he'd lost too much blood and died before he could be transferred to the cruiser hovering alongside.

"And the war was over," Joe must have heard a hundred times. "What a terrible waste." As the son of a Congressional Medal of Honor winner, an appointment to Annapolis was waiting when he finished high school. Joe Harrington's career in the Navy had been highly successful, if not meteoric, but even with four stars, he still lived in the shadow of a father he'd never known.

Harrington pushed himself away from the desk and went into the small bath that adjoined his office. After he relieved himself, he paused at the wash basin and splashed water on his face. The man in the mirror had generous, regular features, bushy eyebrows, and thick white hair. On a good day he could pass for distinguished, but today he looked like he could use some more sleep. He was of average height, with a deep chest and narrow hips. The linen trousers had a difficult time gripping his waist and had to be assisted by suspenders.

"Excuse me, Admiral, but we may have a problem here."

Harrington came out of the head wiping his face and forearms with a hand towel. "What is it, Bob? You look a little flushed." Rear Admiral Bob Kiner was his N3.

"The comm station just received a strange transmission from a ham radio operator on Johnston Island. You're not going to believe this, sir, but the ham says they're under attack. Claims there are men with automatic weapons running around and bodies lying in the streets. The radio operator talked with him for about five minutes before he went off the air. Our people here at the comm center think there's something to it." Harrington crossed the room and lowered himself to his chair. "And that's not all," Kiner continued. "He says they're Japanese."

"Japanese!"

"Yes, sir."

Harrington felt an uneasy prickle on the back of his neck. But he was not a man given to emotion or haste. "Have we tried to raise them through normal comm channels?"

"Yes, sir. No response."

"UHF?"

"And SATCOM, Maritime Mobile, short wave, telephone—everything. All dead. We've been calling since it came in," he checked his watch, "about ten minutes ago, and we can't raise anyone. At first I thought it was someone's idea of a sick joke. Now I don't know what to think."

"Atmospherics?"

"I don't think so. We're talking to Midway, Eniwetok, and Truk just fine."

Harrington was silent for a moment. "Bob, you were a comm officer way back when. What're the chances all these systems could go down at once?"

"Very unlikely, Admiral. I'd say next to impossible."

Harrington was silent. Could it be happening again? There were chinks in the concrete of several buildings down at Hickam Air Force Base—damage caused by strafing by Japanese planes in the attack on Pearl Harbor. They had been left deliberately, to remind future generations of airmen and sailors of the terrible price paid by the unprepared.

"How quickly can we get something down there?"

"We have an A-6 at Barbers Point on half-hour standby. Probably the best reconnaissance bird we have available right now."

"Launch him. How about a CAP?"

"We could scramble a section of F-15s from Hickam for a combat air patrol."

"Do it. Surface assets in the area?"

"The *Vinson* battle group is seventy miles southeast of the Big Island. They're inbound from the mainland and have been cleared for the ranges on Kahoolawe this afternoon and tonight. They were due in Pearl tomorrow afternoon."

"Have them turn southwest for Johnston Atoll at best

speed. I want them on alert with an E-2 airborne. Get cracking, Bob."

"Aye aye, sir."

As Kiner hurried out, Harrington punched a button on one of the desk sets. A second later a youthful voice came across the speaker. "Communications Center, RM1 Teeters speaking, sir."

"Teeters, this is Admiral Harrington. Get me the communications watch officer."

"Aye, sir. Wait one."

Harrington thought of telling him to hurry, but it wasn't necessary. Everyone hurried when the CINC called.

"This is Lieutenant Commander McAlexander, sir."

"Commander, listen up. I want the following going FLASH precedence to the Chairman of the Joint Chiefs, info PACFLT, COMSEVENTHFLT, and the commander of the Army 25th Division here on Oahu. Classification, top secret. Are you ready to copy?"

"Yes sir."

"From: CINCPAC. Subject: Possible incident or armed attack on U.S. installation. One: Have received unconfirmed reports of an armed attack on Johnston Atoll/Johnston Island. Presently unable to establish communication of any kind with Johnston Island. Two: Reconnaissance aircraft and combat air patrol launched from Oahu, ETA eighty minutes. *Vinson* battle group steaming for the area, ETA," Harrington quickly estimated speed and distance, "twenty-four hours. Three: Details to follow as they are received." Harrington thought of including the part about the attackers being Japanese, but decided against it. "End of message."

The watch officer read it back to him and rang off. Harrington sat staring at the two picture frames on the corner of his desk. One was a color photo of Sarah and the two girls—women actually, both in college. The other was an old black-and-white of his mother and a naval officer. He had lieutenant's stripes and an easy, confident grin. His combination cap cover was dark, like the ones they wore fifty years ago. "Do you think they could still do it, Dad?"

he asked the lieutenant quietly. "Could they still come in on the deck with the sun behind them?"

Harrington stood up, turning to the window and the peaceful harbor below him. He watched for several minutes as a frigate stood out from the Naval Station past Ford Island. Then he turned back to his desk and punched the intercom.

"Yes, sir."

"Ask General Sheppard to come up here."

"Aye aye, sir."

Harrington retreated into the head to change into a working uniform.

PART TWO

THE DAY
OF THE
DAIMYO

Wednesday, 7 December, 1:32 P.M.
BARBERS POINT, HAWAII

Navy Two-six Bravo lifted off from NAS Barbers Point and banked south, straining for altitude. The A-6E Intruder was an electronically sophisticated aircraft with a tired airframe. It was like an alert old lady with a frail, stooped body. The A-6 was an ugly aircraft, unlike the sleek new F/A-18s, with a big nose and a skinny tail. But it had tremendous range and could carry a lot of bombs. Intruders had served the Navy as heavy attack bombers for more than three decades, airframes that had been flying well before many of their pilots had been born.

The Intruder carried a two-man crew, or in the case of Two-six Bravo, a two-person crew. Today's mission was not bombing, but visual reconnaissance. Lieutenant Anita Greyling was the command pilot, and the naval flight officer, or NFO, strapped into the seat on her right was there to navigate, help with the radios, and direct the FLIR—forward-looking infrared sensor. Two-six Bravo was one of the USS *Vinson*'s aircraft that had flown to Barbers Point ahead of the battle group. It hadn't been a full scramble, but they'd wasted no time getting airborne once the call had come in.

"What the hell's goin' on, Nita?"

"You got me, Rick. They said get airborne and fly southwest. Something about a visual confirmation. Your comm gear all on line?"

Lieutenant Rick Leonard surveyed his communications

panel and the maze of dials and switches crowded around the cockpit. "You want it; I got it. We can talk to the president or I can call you a cab. Maybe somethin' local." A slack-key Hawaiian ballad sifted through the earpieces in Greyling's helmet.

"Not bad, Rickie, but maybe we better check in." Greyling thumbed the comm key on the control stick, extinguishing the ukeleles and guitars. "Barber Control, this is Navy Two-six Bravo climbing through nine thousand on a vector of two-three-zero. You have traffic for us, over?"

"Roger, Two-six Bravo, stand by." Greyling and Leonard exchanged a bored look. Probably a radar tracking exercise, thought Greyling as she scanned her instruments. She noted that she still had over fourteen thousand pounds of internal fuel plus a total of six thousand pounds in the two wing tanks and the single centerline tank. Whatever it is, she thought, we're not going to run out of gas anytime soon. The Hawaiian music again surged through her helmet, nothing but vowels and harmony. Leonard had begun to sway, as much as his seat harness would allow, and strum an imaginary uke.

"Two-six Bravo, Two-six Bravo; this is Barber Control. Request you shift to channel fourteen secure, that is one-four secure. Your control is Barndance, I say again, Barndance. How copy, over?"

"Ah, this is Two-six Bravo, Roger. Shifting to Barndance on channel one-four secure—" Greyling glanced to Leonard, who nodded—"Two-six Bravo, clear."

Leonard made the frequency shift and gave a thumbs-up to his pilot, and Greyling again pressed the comm key. "Barndance, this is Navy Two-six Bravo outbound from Barbers Point on two-three-zero. Understand you have some work for us, over?"

There was a delay and a burst of static as the secure-voice transmission came through. "Affirmative, Two-six. I have a recon mission for you and will be controlling you for Tango Echo Yankee. This is not a drill, Two-six Bravo. I repeat, this is not a drill. We have a problem out there and we want you to take a look at it. A combat air patrol should be joining you any time.'' Leonard pulled off his gloves to thumb through his call-sign book. Greyling began to search the sky and found a section of F-15s floating off her starboard wing, two thousand feet above.

''Roger, I have my CAP at two o'clock high.'' The lead F-15 rocked his wings as a signal that he was on the circuit. ''What is our mission, Barndance?''

As Barndance gave her the details of the reconnaissance mission to Johnston Atoll, Greyling made notes on her thigh pad. Partway through the mission brief, Leonard reached over and wrote ''Tango Echo Yankee = CINC-PAC actual.'' So, Greyling thought, this little drive-by-look-see was for the big admiral up on the hill. She glanced again at the two F-15s riding shotgun, and they now didn't seem all that reassuring.

''Two-six Bravo, be advised that we have reason to believe Johnston Island may not be in friendly hands. Recommend you consider the atoll hostile and take appropriate evasive maneuvers. Good luck, Barndance standing by.''

Greyling acknowledged and looked at Leonard, who again shrugged, but his eyes were a little bigger as they peered over the rubber edge of his oxygen mask. Without thinking she scanned the cockpit, quickly and professionally, trying to imagine what could be going on at Johnston Island. Greyling knew they stored chemicals there. Maybe that had something to do with it; maybe there was a chemical spill and everyone was dead.

She again interrogated the Johnston Island TACAN, as she had a few minutes earlier, but it remained silent. The TACAN was an automatic, omni-directional radio beacon that should have been emitting a continuous signal. Chemicals wouldn't affect a TACAN beacon, so someone must have turned it off. That's really strange, she thought, but it doesn't really matter.

They were outbound on the Barbers Point TACAN, and she was told that an E-2 Hawkeye from the USS *Vinson* would soon be in the area to serve as an air controller.

"Hey Rick, how much time we gonna have?"

Leonard was busy punching in target coordinates and remaining onboard fuel data into the computer. "We'll have about thirty-five minutes on station depending on how hard you push it over the target." The A-6E had long legs, but seven hundred nautical miles each way over open ocean was stretching it. Greyling nodded and carefully adjusted the throttles for maximum efficiency.

Greyling took Barndance at his word and carefully circled the atoll at one thousand feet from ten miles out, just within visual range. She could make out two rising wisps of dark smoke but little else. Leonard worked the radios and listened along known commercial, military, and maritime frequencies. Nothing. Johnston Island was electronically dead. After the second circuit, Greyling called Barndance and reported they were preparing for a visual pass.

"You ready, Rick?"

"Let it happen, Cap'n."

"Tiger Lead, this is Two-six Bravo. I'm going in hot and low for a visual pass, over."

"Roger, Two-six. We'll bring our orbit down to angles four decimal five and keep an eye on you. Good luck; Tiger Lead, out."

Greyling gently pushed the nose over and put the hazy speck of land in the center of her windscreen. She pulled the Intruder back level at fifty feet. The airspeed indicator wound up to five hundred and fifty knots. It's probably a joke to the F-15 jocks, thought Greyling, but this is balls to the wall for an A-6. But those guys'd be real sweaty-palmed flying this low—routine stuff for us. She glanced up quickly and saw the two Air Force jets streaking above her in a loose combat spread. Then she concentrated on the island ahead.

The Intruder was flying north to south and crossed the island between the harbor and the JACADS plant. A half mile out, she popped up to five hundred feet. They could see more from that altitude, and Greyling could take time from flying the aircraft to look around. Leonard locked the FLIR on the ship in the harbor. The FLIR was a hemispherical wart on the chin of the bomber. It could sense and record an image based on surface temperature differentials and would then create a picture almost as detailed as a photograph. The device also had a stable element that allowed it to hold a lock on a designated target while the aircraft maneuvered. They were only over the island a few seconds, but the A-6 had excellent cockpit visibility. They could clearly see vehicles smoldering and forms lying in the street. From her seat on the left side of the aircraft, Greyling glimpsed the rising sun flag flying from the administration flagpole. After clearing the south end of the island, she pulled the Intruder back into a gentle climb.

"What you got, Rick?"

"A pickup turned on its side and burning, and two bodies laying nearby that I could see for sure. They got cars and trucks parked on the west end of the runway to block it. And there's a 141 parked on the tarmac. Christ, it's like something from the *Twilight Zone*. What the hell's going on down there?"

"I don't know, but I want another pass to confirm it. You get a FLIR paint?"

"That's a charlie—good copy." Leonard held on as Greyling pulled the Intruder through a tight turn and they started back down.

"Nita, hold on a sec!" He cocked his head and carefully worked the vernier on one of the radios. Greyling eased the Intruder up into a shallow orbit at just over seven thousand feet, still well south of the island. Leonard's head snapped up. "Listen to this on the air-sea rescue channel!" he said on the intercom.

"Mayday, Mayday, Mayday." The voice was clear but the signal very weak. "This is X-ray Tango Three-One-Seven down on Johnston Island. Repeat, X-ray Tango Three-One-Seven down on Johnston Island, over."

Leonard signaled that she could transmit. "X-ray Tango, this is Navy Two-six Bravo. We copy you weak but readable; what is your situation, over?'' Greyling wasn't flying the plane anymore. The autopilot held them at altitude in a lazy, fuel-conserving orbit. She pressed the sides of her helmet to hold the earpieces more snugly.

"Thank God. Navy, this is X-ray Tango. I'm a C-141 on the Johnston Island strip. That you who just buzzed the field, over?"

"That's affirmative, X-ray Tango. What's the problem, over?"

"I'm not sure. Some armed men have taken over the control tower and there's been a lot of gunfire. There's two dead soldiers, American soldiers, at the base of the tower. From what I can see from the cockpit, they've blocked the runway and taken over the island. Uh, over."

Greyling gave Leonard a puzzled look and fingered her transmit button. "Okay, X-ray Tango. What's your name and exactly where are you right now, over?"

"This is Master Sergeant Andrew Pierce. I'm the crew chief of the 141 Circuit Rider. Right now I'm hiding in the aircraft. They haven't come out to look at the plane yet, over."

He's inside the plane, thought Greyling, and using one of those small survival radios. That's why his signal's so weak. "Understood, Master Sergeant. I want you to sit tight and I'll get right back to you; how copy, over?"

"Roger, Navy, but hurry. They could come here any time, over."

"Hang in there, Sarge. I'll be right back to you; Two-six Bravo, out."

While Lieutenant Leonard shifted radios, Sergeant Andrew Pierce huddled in the corner of the sweltering cockpit of the Starlifter. There was something unusual about the transmission from Two-six Bravo and Pierce needed a minute to put his finger on it. The voice of Two-six Bravo was that of a woman, that was it. And, now that he thought about it, a fairly young one.

Greyling checked in with Barndance and told them about her contact on the ground. She also asked more questions than they could answer. Five minutes later she was back to Pierce.

"This is Navy Two-six Bravo. You there, Sergeant?"

"Right here; go ahead, Navy."

"Okay, Sergeant, here's how it is. You're the only one on Johnston Island we can talk to right now. Everyone else is silent. From what we know and what you've told us, it looks like the island has been taken over by some sort of military force. Did you get a look at any of those guys, over?"

"Not really, except that they were soldiers and they had white headbands on, like the sweatbands tennis players wear only there was writing on them. That's about all, over."

"Understood, Sarge. Now I need you to do something for me. Can you disable the aircraft from where you are, over?"

"Disable my bird?" Even under the circumstances, this bothered Pierce.

"That's affirmative, Sarge. Can you fix it so it can't take off, over?"

"Well, I suppose so. Yeah, I can do it, over."

"Then do it. After you've disabled the aircraft, I want you to find somewhere to hide inside the cabin so if the bad guys board the plane, they won't find you. And if you have time and can do it without being seen, get a section of the antenna wire to your radio outside the aircraft. You got that, over."

"Okay, Navy. You want me to sabotage my bird and then hide out with the radio. Wilco, but what's going on, over?"

"I wish I knew, Sergeant. But the Commander-in-Chief, Pacific, wants you to down your aircraft and then hide out. Those are your orders. Listen up on your radio again at 1600 this afternoon local time for further instructions and after that, on the hour. Whoever relieves me on station will have further instructions. You handle that Sergeant, over?"

"Do I have a choice, Navy? I can handle it; just have someone back to me at 1600, over."

"You got it. Good luck Sergeant; Navy Two-six Bravo, out." Greyling and Leonard gave each other a look that said "poor bastard," and Greyling took the Intruder off autopilot.

"I want another look at that place, Rick. You ready for a pass?"

Leonard scanned his radios and the FLIR, then reached over and tapped the fuel gauges. Just under eleven thousand pounds left. "Okay, but make it quick. We're near critical on fuel, and I hear there's sharks in these waters."

Greyling already had the bomber into a shallow dive. "Tiger Lead, this is Two-six Bravo. I'm going back in on the deck, south to north this time, over."

"Roger, Two-six Bravo. We'll follow you across."

The Intruder cut the southern coast of the island west of the chemical-storage facility, this time crossing the runway at three hundred feet, and exited directly over the harbor. Leonard locked up the administration building with his FLIR. On this pass they confirmed their initial visual sightings. Only this time, they felt several sharp thumps as they passed over the vessel tied up in the harbor. Neither aviator had experienced ground fire, and it took a moment for Greyling to realize just what had happened.

"Hey, Rickie, I think we took a few hits on that pass."

"No shit! I can see a hole in the starboard aileron!"

"How big?" From Greyling's position in the left seat she was unable to see it.

"Just a small hole with a little tear in the skin, but it wasn't there a minute ago. How's it feel?"

Greyling scanned her instruments and saw nothing wrong. She had the Intruder in a gentle climb, seeking altitude and safety. Then she put the aircraft in a gradual turn toward Oahu. Gingerly, she tested the flight controls; all responses seemed normal.

"Tiger Lead, Two-six Bravo. We took ground fire on

that last pass. Can you come down here and give me a look-see, over?''

''Ah, say again, Two-six.''

Greyling frowned under her mask and toggled the comm button. ''You heard me, Lead. We took fire and I have a damaged aircraft. Request a visual pass ASAP, over.''

As the Intruder continued up through ten thousand feet, Greyling and Leonard exchanged an occasional ''holy shit'' glance. The F-15 that drifted down and slid underneath them found three more bullet holes but no fluid or vapor trails. As Navy pilots in Vietnam and the Gulf War had learned, the A-6 was a pretty tough old bird.

''Navy Two-six Bravo, this is Barndance. Do you have anything to report, over?'' In her concern with the ground-fire damage, Greyling had all but forgotten her controller.

''Roger, Barndance, this is Two-six Bravo. We just completed our second visual low-level over Johnston Island with IR confirmation. We also just completed our first combat action over occupied territory, over.''

''Barndance, Two-six Bravo. Did you say combat action, over?''

''That's affirmative, Barndance. I'm heading back to Barbers Point with light ground-fire damage.'' Greyling gave a summary of what they had seen during their second pass as her eyes continued to scan the instruments for any sign of trouble. Already she was reviewing emergency procedures in case the damage was more extensive than it appeared.

Hey, she thought suddenly, I'll bet I'm the first female naval aviator to sustain battle damage. She shook off the thought and concentrated on her instruments and the problems that might be ahead in getting her aircraft back to Hawaii. What if I lose an engine, or the flaps or gear won't come down, she thought. And what if I have a slow fuel leak from the groundfire damage. Jesus, am I glad I don't have to go back aboard the boat!

Wednesday, 7 December, 2:10 P.M.
THIRTY MILES SOUTH OF HAWAII

While Lieutenant Anita Greyling nursed her wounded A-6E back to Barbers Point, Petty Officer Don Walker flew his Seven boat through the cobalt-blue Pacific. Periodically he scanned the instruments on the lighted console. Main batteries, 43 percent; boat, air, 1,200 psi; breathing air, 1,500 psi. Today, as on most training runs, they were breathing from open-circuit scuba. For their battle problems and on actual missions, they would use recirculating, closed-circuit diving rigs that gave off no telltale bubbles. The ammeter showed power consumption at 40 percent, which meant they were loafing along at four knots. There were other gauges that gave him depth, heading, trim, and told him of the health of his navigation and communication equipment. Walker took them all in with a glance and concentrated on his compass. His ears did the rest. The SEAL SDV pilots flew their craft with their ears, as they were much more sensitive to depth than were the gauges. The various navigation systems presented their data to the pilot through tones in his earphones. Walker and the Seven boat were nearing the end of a five-hour navigation exercise, a drill that called for them to run a prescribed route with five course and speed changes. Now they were on the final leg to a rendezvous with the *La Jolla*. He checked the chronometer on the console and the notes on his navigation slate. Right about *now*, he thought, and turned on the Doppler sonar.

Walker swung the boat fifteen degrees left and right of his base course listening for a return. As he came back to port, it was there. He estimated the signal strength and made a final course adjustment to intercept the mother sub, then cut off the sonar. Excess sound in the water was as dangerous for the SDVs as for the big submarines. "Five bucks says we get a visual in exactly three minutes.''

Moody sat next to Walker, in the navigator's position. He too had heard the pinging, but he studied the visual presentation on the sonar scope as well. Moody thought for a moment. "This course and speed?" The Seven boat was a wet submersible, which meant there was water inside the boat as well. Moody and Walker both wore a second-stage scuba mouthpiece with a waterproof seal that formed a small, dry oral cavity. This gas pocket in the mouthpiece made speech garbled but possible.

"This course and speed," Walker replied.

"You're on—mark." Moody scribbled the time on the Plexiglas windshield with a grease pencil and they began to search the blue-green void ahead and below them for the ponderous bulk of *La Jolla*.

To reduce the risk of collision, which would destroy the Seven boat and do absolutely nothing to the big sub, the SDV flew at thirty feet and the mother sub at fifty-five. At two minutes fifty seconds from the mark, Moody started to smirk behind his mouthpiece. Then a blue-black shape began to emerge from the green curtain at nine o'clock low. Walker had hit the rendezvous point dead on—again.

No matter how many times he had seen it or how hard he tried to visualize the meeting in advance, Moody could never quite prepare himself for the awesome experience that was an underwater submarine rendezvous. It was so *big*. He felt like he was riding in a shuttle craft on its way to an encounter with an intergalactic space cruiser. And in a way, he was. The mother sub crawled out of the emerald shadows, part beast and part machine, representing a kind of alien sanctuary. At night the meeting was even more dramatic. In the dark, with just colored strobes to determine the sub's attitude and speed, the immense underwater bulk could still be felt, and that was more eerie still.

Walker pushed the stick over and down to bring the SDV on a parallel course with the *La Jolla*, and kicked the speed up to six knots to overtake it. The little boat maneuvered like a baby hippo. He gave a wide berth to the mother sub's big multi-bladed screw and crept up toward the sail on the starboard quarter. On deck two SEALs, tethered to the hull some twenty feet behind the yawning opening of the dry deck shelter, watched their approach. One of them held a winch cable that would be shackled to the nose of the Seven boat to guide it into the shelter.

Carefully, Walker eased the little craft to a hover over the deck and gently brought it down between the two underwater deckhands. It was like landing a helicopter on the deck of an underway destroyer. He had to judge his speed and altitude carefully, compensating for the swirling currents caused by the *La Jolla*'s sail and the dry deck shelter.

But Walker was good, one of the best SDV pilots in the platoon, and he gently brought the Seven boat to the deck of the submarine. Once the little sub had a line through its nose, he carefully jockeyed the rudder and buoyancy controls to help it as it was drawn into the shelter. When the SDV was inside and locked into the cradle, he secured the power and began his post-flight checklist.

The two SEALs in the rear compartment climbed out and drifted up to congratulate Walker on another precision rendezvous, made that much sweeter since he had lifted a five-spot off the boss. In Delta Platoon, as it was throughout the teams, everything was competitive, and money often changed hands as the SEALs wagered on their skills.

The Mk 9, Mod 1 SDV had a forward compartment for the pilot and copilot-navigator and a rear compartment that would hold four very cramped SEALs along with their equipment. Normally they trained with a crew of four—two forward at the controls and two aft, observing. For battle problems that called for them to simulate a mission, the boats carried a full complement of six with equipment. On the navigation training runs, like the one they had just completed, it was very boring for the two SEALs in back, so they often took along paperback novels to pass the time. It was like reading in the swimming pool, and the course of these training missions could be traced by the pages torn off and discarded along the route through a cracked hatch of the SDV.

Walker's Seven boat was finished for the day, but the Number Two boat had yet to make its training run. As he unstrapped himself and looked around, Moody was surprised to find the crew of the other SDV nowhere in sight. Senior Chief Stockton, also in open-circuit scuba, hovered effortlessly near the top of the shelter as he supervised the recovery operation. Moody gave him a questioning gesture, and Stockton drew his hand across his throat to indicate he had canceled the other training mission.

As soon as the two deck handlers were back into the shelter, Stockton signaled for the shelter to be depressurized and drained. A deep base warning buzzer filled the chamber as the massive door of the dry deck shelter swung shut. An extensive underwater lighting system served them, but it somehow never seemed as clear as the blue-green world outside. Steel locking bars dogged the door to the shelter and high-pressure air started to bleed into the top of the steel cylinder. The water level began to drop.

Moody knew his head was above the water line when the visibility went to zero. He was in a dense cloud, like a steam bath, only it was cold, and the hiss of expanding air was deafening. Returning to his natural element was not a pleasant experience. Once the water drained out, the shelter was decompressed and brought to the "surface" or a normal pressure of one atmosphere, the same as inside the mother submarine.

Walker and Moody sat in the SDV and waited for Chief Stockton to signal that they were on the surface. As standard training doctrine dictated, they "rode" their scuba regulators to the surface. The mist cleared away as the chamber was vented.

"On the surface!" yelled Stockton. "Okay men, let's get this gear secured and a post-dive inspection on the Seven boat."

Moody pulled off his face mask and took a gulp of the moist air. Delicious. There was a red circle around his eyes and nose from the mask and another around his mouth and chin from the scuba communications mouthpiece. Next he pulled off the neoprene diving hood. The waters off Hawaii were warm, but a man couldn't sit motionlessly in a wet submersible for more than a few hours without some protection.

Stockton stood near the front of the shelter, wearing only canvas UDT trunks. He had a single aluminum scuba bottle on his back and his mask was pushed up on his forehead. The chief was a twenty-five-year SEAL veteran as well as a Navy master diver. Stockton had thick legs and a barrel chest with a matching pair of doves, one tattooed above each nipple. He was in his early forties and looked older. Many of the land-warfare requirements of a SEAL were beyond him, but underwater he still moved with the ease and grace of a large mammal. He had sharp features and a 1960s-vintage flattop, cut very close on the sides. Senior Chief Will Stockton seldom smiled, and Moody had yet to hear him really laugh, but he had a wry, sophisticated sense of humor that suggested keen intelligence. Stockton stood at the side of the SDV and helped Moody clear away his straps and regulator pigtail. Then he took Moody's slate, which contained the courses, speeds, and navigational data from the training run.

"How's it going there, Senior Chief?"

"Fine, sir. I hear you owe Walker some money."

"Some more money," called one of the SEALs.

"He was lucky."

"Again, sir?"

"Yeah, again. Say, I thought the Two boat was scheduled for a run. Something wrong?"

"Maybe," Stockton replied, "but not with my boats. I was told to secure the shelter as soon as we got you aboard. The skipper wants to see you as soon as you can get below."

Moody eased himself over the side of the SDV and worked his way forward to the access trunk. He was a little rubber-legged from five hours in the water. "Any idea what's up?"

"No, sir."

He unzipped the wetsuit jacket and pulled it off. "Well, I guess I'll grab a quick shower and go find out."

"Sir, I got the impression Commander Kemp wanted to see you as soon as you got aboard. I mean like right now."

"Okay, Senior, I'll get right on it." Moody pulled off the neoprene pants and booties and dropped into the escape trunk.

Once inside the sub, he took a moment to towel off and pull on a pair of sweats before making his way forward to Commander Robbie Kemp's stateroom, collecting a cup of hot coffee enroute. He was still chilled from the training run.

"You wanted to see me, skipper?"

"I sure do, Mr. Moody. Come in and have a seat." There was only room for two chairs in the small room. Even on a big attack boat like the *La Jolla*, the commanding officer's quarters were little more than a broom closet. Moody grabbed the vacant chair. "This came in from CINCPAC via COMSUBPAC about forty minutes ago." He handed Moody a yellow teletype message draft. It was classified Top Secret/SPECAT.

"Sir, I'm not cleared for special category TS."

"You are now, Lieutenant. Read it."

The message was brief and to the point, with very few details. Moody read it twice and handed it gingerly back to Kemp.

"Terrorists on Johnston Atoll—Japanese terrorists."

"Looks like it. You guys are supposed to have antiterrorist training. You know anything about Japanese terrorists?"

Moody took a sip of coffee. SEALs were trained in counter-terrorist operations, but more from a tactical, urban-warfare perspective. They were not antiterrorist specialists like the Army's Delta Force, at least it was not their primary mission. Moody had attended a two-week Air

Force school that focused on the terrorist personality and various active groups around the world. They had studied Japanese terrorists, but only briefly.

"Sir, I'm no expert, but most of the terrorists we've been concerned about are the Arab variety because they've targeted American citizens and installations. The others, like those in South America, Europe, and Japan, have mostly been nationalists and pretty much stayed within their own borders, except maybe those in exile."

"So you know nothing about Japanese terrorists?"

Moody thought for a moment. "The only thing I really remember from my training is they're likely to be fanatical and they don't make idle threats."

"Well, we've been ordered to make for Johnston Atoll at best speed and stand by along with the *Vinson* battle group. We'll be there in about twenty hours. Tell me, Mr. Moody, if they asked you to sneak in there with one of your SDVs, could you do it?"

"If there's a deep-water access or any kind of harbor, we can get in. Under certain conditions we have the ability to do shallow-water reconnaissance work, maybe even get a team across the beach and ashore to set up an OP."

"An observation post?"

"Yes, sir. Usually two men with a radio and a pair of binoculars—strictly a sneak-and-peak operation."

"Okay. What if they ask you to go ashore and do something more than just observe, like storm a bunker or take over the airport?"

"Then we better get our hands on some weapons. All we have now are side arms and a few submachine guns for training purposes—defensive weapons for the SDV crews. And we don't carry ammunition aboard for pre-deployment training."

Kemp studied Moody over steepled fingers. "Very well, Mr. Moody. Why don't you get together a list of whatever equipment and weapons you'll need if the order comes down for you to go ashore and do some real SEAL work."

"Aye aye, sir, but this is an SDV platoon, not a direct-action platoon. My men are trained primarily for harbor penetration, ship attacks, and shoreline reconnaissance. Beyond that, our job is to deliver other SEALs to the objective area. We're bus drivers.''

"Yeah, well, I'm an attack-boat skipper, and I'm trained to hunt and kill enemy submarines. So here I am chauffeuring you kids and your toy subs around. Sometimes, Lieutenant, we can't do just what we want.''

"Yes, sir, I'll get right on it.'' Moody rose to leave.

"And Mr. Moody.''

"Sir?''

"Take that equipment list straight to the comm shack. We'll slow down and come to periscope depth long enough to send it out. Then come back here. I'm having a chart of Johnston Atoll sent up and I want to go over it with you.''

"Aye aye, sir.'' Moody set out to find Senior Chief Stockton; he'd need his help with this. He thought about a quick shower, but went for some more coffee instead.

Wednesday, 7 December, 3:27 P.M.
CAMP H. M. SMITH, HAWAII

"Reporting as directed, Admiral.''

"Come on in, Jack, have a seat. I assume you've heard about our problem on Johnston Island?''

General John Wesley Sheppard strode across the office and took a seat at the small conference table in the CINC's office. He nodded politely to Rear Admiral Bob Kiner, who sat at Admiral Harrington's elbow shuffling message traffic.

Sheppard was a striking man, with reliable shoulders and something of a young Errol Flynn look to him, very much at home in uniform. He gave the impression of someone who knew what he was talking about. "Yes, sir,'' Sheppard answered, "but only that some kind of small military force has taken Johnston Island. Just what happened down there?''

Sheppard's official title was COMSOCPAC or Commander, Special Operations Command, Pacific. The job was a high-visibility position with a lofty title, but he was really just another senior member of Harrington's staff with specific responsibilities. Sheppard was one of the new breed of Army general officers who had not been a combat arms officer in Vietnam, which meant his left breast hadn't the multiple rows of combat decorations of his predecessors. And while he had been a "snake eater"—Special Forces soldier—for his entire career, he also had an advanced degree in computer science and a PhD in psychology. Sheppard had graduated near the top of his class at West Point, and leadership came easily for him. In Pentagon circles he was known as a clear thinker—a Green Beanie, but a heads-up guy.

Admiral Harrington looked to his N3. "Bob, you want to give him the short version?"

"This is what we *think* happened." Kiner moved quickly, concluding with the A-6 mission and the contact with the crewman hiding in the C-141 Starlifter. The junior admiral laid down the sheaf of messages and rubbed his chin thoughtfully. "Taking that island is a pretty tall order. There're over twelve hundred people stationed there and a company of MPs as well as a contract security force." A messenger slipped in and handed Kiner a piece of paper. He scowled and handed it to Harrington. "You better take a look at this, sir." It was a copy of the C-141 Circuit Rider's manifest. A single name was highlighted. Harrington read it in a glance and passed it to the Army man.

"So we have to assume," Sheppard said, "this terrorist force has twelve hundred hostages, and one of them is a United States senator."

"We have no other choice," Harrington replied. "You have any suggestions, Jack?"

"Not at the moment, sir. We have contingency plans that generally cover this kind of thing, but nothing specific for Johnston Island. And nothing for this many terrorists or this many hostages. Right now we desperately need information. Sir, I've recalled my staff and started a data dump on Johnston Atoll. Along with the *Vinson* battle group headed for the area, I recommend we take steps to preposition special-operations reaction teams and have the *Tarawa*'s Marine Expeditionary Unit begin making plans for an amphibious assault on Johnston Island. I've already requested that a battalion of Rangers at Fort Lewis be placed on thirty-minute standby and ordered a pair of AC-130 Specter gunships from the 16th Special Operations Squadron at Hurlbert Field in Florida. There's a platoon of Navy SEALs aboard the *La Jolla*; COMSUBPAC has ordered them to rendezvous with the *Vinson* battle group. We should also have one or two direct-action SEAL platoons flown here from Coronado. In addition, I recommend that you go out to JCS and request support from the Delta Force." Sheppard paused, scanning his notes. "Who'll be handling the communication with this guy in the 141 on Johnston Island?"

"We have an E-2 Hawkeye from the *Vinson* orbiting the atoll," Kiner said. "They'll be guarding his frequency."

"If they can patch him through to my operations staff, I'd like to control him from there. I'll have one of my planners ready with a list of questions for him. I assume there's been no word from the terrorists or whatever they are?"

"Nothing yet, but the comm center is calling them every fifteen minutes. I'm sure we'll hear from them when they're ready to talk. Bob," Harrington said, turning to his N3, "let's get a request up the line to JCS for the Delta Force. Jack, you're my action officer on this. For now it's a planning exercise, but we may have to move quickly. Work the problem and keep me informed of any developments. If it comes to a head, I'll want alternatives—lots of them. Bob will get you whatever you need." Harrington paused and passed a hand thoughtfully across his mouth. He lifted his eyebrows and turned back to Sheppard. "Questions?"

"Just one, sir. I understand we're dealing with the Japanese here?"

"It appears this may be true," Harrington said guard-edly, not sure exactly why he was being so cautious. "At least they seem to be Oriental. And the aircraft reported a Japanese battle flag flying from the administration complex on Johnston Island. Anything else?"

"Not at this time, Admiral."

"Good, let's get to work. I've got a call to make to a very anxious Chairman of the Joint Chiefs."

Wednesday, 7 December, 2:45 P.M.
JOHNSTON ISLAND

Takashi Tadao stood at a window in the adminis-tration building and surveyed the wharf area. The island was firmly under his control and tan–camouflaged figures with headbands, their weapons now slung, patrolled the wa-terfront. It had taken them less than forty minutes to seize Johnston Island, and that much time again to neutralize the few isolated pockets of resistance, not that the Americans had put up much of a fight. His forces had suffered one dead and two wounded, and the U.S. military presence on the island had been wiped out, literally. It would have been no different had they attacked a Japanese installation, Ta-dao thought, for Japan was now a nation of shopkeepers and bankers. But that is why we have come here, he thought, to change all that.

Then his eyes fell on the Imperial battle flag, snapping at the pole in the afternoon trade winds. He stood a bit more rigid, if that was possible. At this moment, he felt he knew the same sense of pride and conquest as General Ya-mashita had at Singapore and General Homma in the Phil-ippines. But that was a time when Japan had abounded with able leaders and warriors to follow them. Perhaps it will be that way again, he thought.

Following the subjugation of the island, Tadao toured his conquest in one of the stake trucks, standing in the open bed behind the cab, acknowledging his men. When they saw him, they raised their hands over their heads and shouted "Banzai!"

He knew it was important for them to see him and to allow them this small celebration as conquering warriors—this was their birthright. Tadao recalled the news clips of American soldiers parading in the streets after their adventure in the Gulf War. Heroes All, the banners had proclaimed. The Americans had their victory, thought Tadao; now I'll have mine!

On his tour of the island, he also inspected the placement of explosives at the chemical-storage facility. He had carefully chosen those agents stored in the special-containment vaults for the explosives. The big chemical-destruction facility was now shut down, and all had gone according to plan. He sensed the presence of one of his men and turned from the window.

Tadao had commandeered the operations center for his headquarters. The large office was lined with phones and desks and littered with paperwork. The windows enjoyed a commanding view of the waterfront. There was a complete communications facility in the next room, now manned by his people, as well as the surface-surveillance radars that warned of approaching ships. "Tadao-sama, they are here."

"Very well. Send them in."

Colonel Trafton, General Taggart, and Nancy Blackman formed a solemn procession as they marched into a corner of the room that served as an informal reception area. Jim Bruso rose to meet them. Two men in camouflage with automatic weapons stood off to one side.

"Welcome to my command center," said Tadao. "Please, have a seat."

Colonel Trafton stepped forward. "I demand to know what is going on." He was sweating and his features were pinched and red, but there was a fierce look to him. One cheek was puffed and dark and one eye nearly swollen shut. The others followed Bruso in finding a chair.

Tadao regarded him coldly. "If you will be so kind as to sit, Colonel, I will tell you why we are here and the nature of our mission on Johnston Island."

Trafton slumped heavily in a chair by the wall with his eyes malevolently fixed on Tadao. The rigid figure began to pace the reception area before his prisoners. He still wore the tan uniform with the high red collar, but he had removed his headband. The two swords remained belted to his side. He stopped to address them with his hands clasped behind his back, occasionally rocking forward on the balls of his feet.

"Johnston Atoll is now under the control of samurai from the New Shield Society. I am Commandant Takashi Tadao. We are a small, highly disciplined force and represent the warrior spirit of our ancestors, a force once prevalent in Japan. Our actions here are the vanguard of a movement that will sweep our sacred land and return our nation to the traditional values of the true Japan. We hold hostage not only the lives of everyone on this island, but the stores of chemical munitions located here as well. Our demands are simple and nonnegotiable." Tadao took a single, carefully folded sheet of rice paper from his tunic. "I am told this female is a United States senator." He smiled indulgently at the idea of a woman in this position. "My study of your government would suggest that she is the most senior American representative on the island. Very well—she will be allowed to convey our demands to your government."

Tadao stepped toward Blackman and held out the sheet of paper. She reached tentatively for it, but Trafton rose and snatched it away.

"I am still in command here, and if there is to be any negotiations on my island then it will begin with me."

Tadao seemed not to react to this outburst, but his eyelids lowered slightly and his nostrils flared. Bruso noted this and a chill passed through him. Colonel Trafton read the text of Tadao's demands.

"This . . . this is ridiculous! You can't be serious; this is crazy . . . you're crazy!"

The smaller Japanese dropped to a quarter crouch and set his rear foot at ninety degrees to his lead foot, which pointed at Trafton. Tadao extended his left hand gracefully toward the colonel while the right one drew behind him, elbow high. Then in a movement that was almost too quick to follow with the eye, his right hand, palm extended, shot forward and buried itself in the center of Trafton's chest. The movement was reversed so quickly it was difficult to be sure that it had really happened.

But it had. Trafton grunted from his bowels and fell back into his chair, then slid awkwardly to the floor. His eyes bulged as if straining to understand what had happened, while his jaw fell slack. Following a long, tortured exhalation, the eyes went blank and began to dilate. The American colonel's sternum had been pushed back into his chest cavity with sufficient force to crush his heart like a ripe tomato.

"Your island commander was a fool," Tadao said casually, and then, as an afterthought, "but he died painlessly. He was dead before he reached the floor." Tadao shrugged imperceptibly and then bowed to the form sprawled on the floor.

The other three stared in horror as he took the paper from the dead man and offered it to Senator Blackman. She took it numbly, but could not take her eyes from Trafton. When she finally did look up at his killer, there was a cold rage stamped on her features. Tadao noticed this and smiled.

"You are angry—good. It will give you strength. But do not underestimate my resolve or my belief in our cause. You will either read my demands to your countrymen or I will kill you and hand the paper to the next senior person, and the next, until my demands are made known."

"You have no choice, Senator," said Bruso gently, "and those listening will at least know you're safe."

"He's right, ma'am," added General Taggart, his voice a whisper.

"Very well, Mr. Tadao," Blackman said, rising. "I will do as you ask."

"Excellent." Tadao beamed. "If you will follow me to the communications room, we have the transmission frequencies prepared for your announcement." As Blackman moved to follow him, Tadao turned to Bruso and Taggart. "You may as well come with us. Since all the world will soon know of our glorious enterprise, perhaps you should, too."

Wednesday, 7 December, 8:50 P.M.
THE WHITE HOUSE

Robert Garrison, normally a very controlled man, was unable to sit behind the desk any longer. While Gates Carlton, General McKenzie, and Dr. Epstein sat patiently, the president roamed the Oval Office with his hands thrust deeply into his trouser pockets. It was well past the dinner hour, and none of them had even thought about food. To further display his frustration, Garrison had slipped his collar button and loosened his tie, ever so slightly. He liked small meetings, at least in the beginning, to sort out his position on matters. The larger gatherings would follow. Garrison knew the ever-vigilant White House press corps judged the size of the crisis by the size of the meeting. He also knew this crisis would remain under wraps for no more than an hour; too many people already knew about it. The president stopped by the side of the big cherry-wood desk and leaned stiff-armed on the polished surface. "I still don't see how in the hell our security at this facility could have been so lax. How could they have just sailed right in there and taken over?"

General McKenzie simply stared across the desk. He'd suggested more than once that cuts in the defense budget were excessive—that these cuts left many defense facilities undermanned, but this was not the time to again point that out.

"And now," Garrison continued, "they want me to say I'm sorry—that we're sorry!"

"Sir," Carlton began, "this isn't getting us anywhere. We don't have much time, and for now we have to accept the fact that a group of Japanese nationals, whatever their motives may be, have occupied a sovereign and very important piece of American property." Gates Carlton was an old college chum of the president and headed the White House inner circle. Garrison trusted Carlton and had made him his secretary of state. Carlton was a lanky, angular man with a narrow face and bushy, brooding eyebrows. White House staffers said he looked like a basset-hound owner. He had unruly brown hair that seemed to resist any attempt at orderly barbering. Carlton was approaching fifty like a man who had been grooming himself for the task for decades. He was affable and disarming, known as someone who could get things done. Gates Carlton was also one of the few in the administration who could maneuver the president, and he knew this meeting had to move forward. "I've sent the Japanese a complete and unedited text of the communiqué from this Commandant Tadao. It went directly from my office to their foreign minister. I followed it up personally with a phone call."

"What did he say?"

Carlton shrugged. "Typical Japanese response. 'We are most concerned; we are shocked by this turn of events; we will give this careful consideration.' I was also able to get a facsimile of the Japanese battle flag flying on Johnston Island sent to them from Hawaii. That ought to get their attention."

"Well, it sure as hell got mine." Garrison returned to his chair and the two documents in front of him. One was a simple two-paragraph message. The other was a grainy, black-and-white photo developed from the FLIR imagery of the A-6 Intruder. One would have thought it an old photo except for the modern buildings and the date-time strip in the lower right-hand corner that said it had been taken barely two hours ago. He tossed the picture back onto the desk.

"What have you got on this, General?"

John McKenzie, Chairman of the Joint Chiefs and the nation's senior military officer, sat ramrod-straight in an ill-fitting suit bought off the rack. At the president's request, senior military advisers wore civilian attire to White House meetings. Carlton often joked that you could take the general out of the uniform but not the uniform out of the general. "Sir, for now we're doing everything we can to collect information on the situation. As you know, the aircraft that obtained this picture was damaged by ground fire. It appears their defense of the island is confined to small arms. We now have some Navy reconnaissance aircraft working the area at medium altitude, so we'll have detailed photo coverage within the hour. From the information we do have, and right now it's pretty sketchy, they seem to have a sizable armed presence—perhaps a hundred men or more. If we have to use force, it won't be a police action or a raid by the FBI Hostage Rescue Team. It'll have to be a full-scale military operation."

"Can you do this?"

"Yes, sir," McKenzie said immediately, but then paused to phrase his words carefully. "We have the *Vinson* battle group in the area with its amphibious ready group standing by. I'm sure the eight hundred Marines aboard, with their supporting arms, are more than a match for these people. But a standard amphibious operation, with an over-the-beach attack or a vertical assault with helicopters, may not be the best alternative. If our landing force is opposed, the casualties among the local population could be high. And there's the matter of the chemicals. The embarked Marine Expeditionary Unit has only limited capability to operate in a chemical environment."

"Are the Marines the only option?"

"For now. My special-operations planners are working the problem right now. I've asked them to come up with a feasible plan within twenty-four hours. Elements of the Delta Force and a battalion of Army Rangers are being moved to Hawaii for contingency purposes. I'm sorry, sir, but we have very few military options at this time.''

Garrison studied the two pieces of paper on his desk for a long moment while he pinched the bridge of his nose with his thumb and index finger. ''So what about these chemicals and the explosives they say they've placed on them, General?'' he said, tapping the documents. ''Just how much danger is there?''

''Sir, that's why I asked Dr. Epstein to sit in on this meeting. He's one of our leading experts on chemical and biological warfare and on the storage of our existing chemical stockpiles.''

Epstein had the look of a bureaucrat, with thinning hair and mild eyes heavily framed by glasses, but a keen, intelligent expression said there was more to this man. Garrison couldn't help but notice his hands, which were long and thin, more like a woman's. Epstein wore light wool slacks and a corduroy jacket, unbuttoned, that revealed several pens in the breast pocket of his shirt. He moved every few minutes, trying to find a comfortable position.

''All right, Doctor, how bad is it?''

Epstein crossed, then uncrossed, his legs and dabbed nervously at his upper lip with a handkerchief. ''To be perfectly frank, Mr. President, it couldn't be much worse. To begin with, there's a great deal of nasty stuff on Johnston Island, but most of the chemicals are first- and second-generation agents. Some of the binary compounds are benign unless someone there is clever enough to know how to combine them. But even these binary weapons are not appreciably more dangerous than the rest; they were engineered for stability, not enhanced lethality. That's the good news. Among the special weapons stored on Johnston Island are two enhanced variants of the nerve agent VX. These are the ultimate chemical weapons, perfected at the height of the Cold War in response to Soviet tactical chemical doctrine. They were developed to let the Russians know that if they ever used battlefield chemical weapons, we would retaliate with a massive chemical depopulation of the Soviet Union. These are some very, very dangerous chemicals. You see, we—''

''I can't believe this,'' Garrison said, raising his hand to interrupt. ''You're saying we're capable of national annihilation by chemicals; that's absurd! Hell, don't we have nukes for that?''

''Of course we do, Mr. President, but strategic chemical weapons are not absurd when you apply Cold War logic.'' Epstein tugged at his earlobe and took on a forced Socratic tone. ''During the Cold War, NATO's strategy was to defend Western Europe against a Soviet or Eastern Bloc conventional attack. We knew we couldn't stand up against a massing of their armor. This was no secret, and our battle plans included the use of tactical nuclear weapons to defend Western Europe. There was no choice; we couldn't hope to stop them with our conventional forces. The Soviets always maintained that if we used tactical nukes, they'd respond with strategic nukes. So for the duration of the Cold War, it was a stand-off; we threatened tactical nuclear response and they threatened strategic nuclear Armageddon. It was a form of MAD—mutual assured destruction. Fortunately, the Soviet Union folded before somebody's bluff was called.''

''So what does this have to do with chemicals?'' Garrison asked impatiently.

Epstein inclined his head in a show of indulgence. ''Everything, sir,'' he replied. ''The Soviets were far more advanced than we were in the use of battlefield chemical weapons and their armored units were trained to operate in a chemical environment. We had no tactical chemical doctrine that remotely matched their capability. Furthermore, the Pentagon and the administration feared public reaction if we pushed for better battlefield chemical weapons and tactics. And there was the morale of the troops to think about; it scares the hell out of them, not to mention the discomfort of running around in those bulky chemical-exposure suits." Epstein paused to again pat his lips with a handkerchief. "None of this was acceptable, so we developed two new VX agents—the ultimate chemical weapons. If the Soviets used tactical chemical weapons, we'd respond with strategic chemical weapons."

"And just how deadly are these new VX things?" Garrison's attention was now riveted on Epstein.

The scientist's intelligent features became strained to the point of looking painful as he framed his words. "Both agents are deadly, but the Soviet Union is a very big country. To achieve a widespread and comprehensive morbidity with light concentrations, the kind of concentrations that favor airborne dispersion over an extensive area, we developed a nerve agent with a rather peculiar pathology. The inhalation of just a few molecules will cause an immediate deterioration of the central nervous system and total disability within an hour. While death is certain, it is slow and very painful. Shall I describe the symptoms?"

"That won't be necessary," Garrison replied, turning to McKenzie. "Did the Soviets know we had these chemical super-weapons, General?"

"Yes, sir, and that was the whole point of it. And a case can be made that our chemical weapons, like our nuclear arsenal, has served us very well. Each side knew an attack on the other, even with theater-based nuclear *or* chemical tactical weapons, was an invitation to national suicide— again, mutual assured destruction. But few in the public sector knew that MAD extended to the chemical arena. Even in the Gulf War, Saddam Hussein refrained from the use of chemicals for fear we would respond in kind. Even a thug like Saddam fears chemical retaliation."

Garrison slowly shook his head in disbelief. "I had no idea," he said quietly. The president's healthy, outgoing manner usually made him seem larger than life. But over the past few minutes, he seemed to grow smaller and become almost frail, as if he were being compressed by the weight of this new information. Robert Garrison was a veteran politician, and that was all he was. He had never been in the private sector and he was one of the few command-ers-in-chief in this century who had never served in the armed forces. For him war, even the threat of war, was irrational and a failure of statesmanship.

"It's understandable, Mr. President," Carlton said gently after a long pause. "Chemical weapons are a form of madness no one wants to think about."

"Perhaps," Garrison replied, regaining some of his composure, "but now we have to think about it. This madman Tadao says he's placed explosives on the chemical weapons and will blow up the entire stockpile. I assume this will be fatal to everyone on Johnston Island who has no protection. Is that correct?" There was a long pause. "Doctor Epstein, I said is that correct?"

"Yes, sir, that much is correct," he said as the pained expression returned to his face, "but I'm afraid it just may be a great deal more serious than that."

"Good God, man!" Garrison blurted, "just how much more serious could it be than the lives of twelve hundred people?"

Epstein took a deep breath. "Sir, the lives of everyone on the Hawaiian Islands are at risk, and the potential danger extends to the Northwest Coast of the United States and the West Coast of Canada."

"You'd better explain that, Doctor," the president said coldly.

"The enhanced VX agents are airborne contaminants, designed to remain aloft for days and dispersed by air currents. The agent known as VX-3 has an active life of twenty-four hours; then it combines with nitrogen atoms to form an inert gas. But VX-5 is a very persistent agent. It will remain active and deadly for up to a week, perhaps ten days. Normally the northeast trades blow from east to west, and any airborne contaminants would be carried west, devastating Micronesia and perhaps Melanesia. But unfortunately, or fortunately if you're a Micronesian, there's a good-size tropical storm brewing just south of the Marshall Islands, and it appears to be heading east and north. From what the people over at NOAA tell me, this is a pretty serious storm. It appears to be strong enough to buck the trade winds and carry past Johnston Island to Hawaii. Sir, do you remember Hurricane Iniki that hit the islands a few years back?'' Garrison nodded. ''This storm is not nearly that size so it won't be packing the destructive winds of Iniki, but all it has to do is just get there.''

''And you're telling me there's enough of this VX chemical to kill people in Hawaii?''

''Mr. President,'' Epstein said evenly, ''there's enough VX-5 on Johnston Island to kill half the people in Russia across an area the size of Siberia. If these agents get aloft and if that storm takes them directly to Hawaii, there will be nothing but plant life remaining after the storm passes.''

''But you said something about the West Coast and Canada,'' Garrison said, speaking rapidly. There was a hint of panic in his voice. He ran his tongue quickly over his lips and swallowed hard. The president was clearly struggling to retain his composure, glancing from Epstein to Carlton or McKenzie, like a trapped animal looking for a way out.

''Yes, sir, I did. A tropical storm usually gives birth to a number of thunderstorms which generate a great deal of unstable air, causing surface air to be taken up to great altitudes. If some of these toxins reach the jet stream and upper air currents, they can easily reach the West Coast. By jet stream, the West Coast is only seventy-two hours away. I doubt the loss of life will be as complete as in Hawaii, but a catastrophe by any reckoning.'' Epstein hesitated before continuing. ''I'm sorry I can't be more encouraging, sir. This is my field of expertise. The study of atmospherics and wind currents is very much a part of what I do.''

This time there was a long silence before the president managed to speak. ''Doctor Epstein, I'm going to want a second opinion on this, but I sense you're giving me the true picture.'' He again paused. ''Tell me, what's a man like you doing in this kind of business?''

He didn't have to spell it out for Epstein; the scientist

knew exactly what Garrison was asking. He straightened in his seat and looked directly at the president.

"Since I was a child, I've had a fascination with the Holocaust. While I was studying chemistry at Columbia, I became drawn to the mechanics of just how so many of my people could be exterminated with the use of chemicals and poison gas. I knew it was morbid, but somehow I was drawn to it. Finally, I decided that if I could do something—if I could prevent it—no one would ever use chemicals on Jews again. The decision was not an easy one," he said, smiling ruefully, "and to this day my own mother will not allow me to speak of it in her presence. However, I concluded that if America was to protect the free world from nuclear weapons in the hands of totalitarians, we must also protect them from chemical weapons. So I became an expert in the field and helped to develop some of our most deadly agents, including VX-3 and VX-5." He bowed his head a moment to compose himself and continued. "And the sad thing is, we almost made it. It almost worked—until now."

"I see, Doctor. Do you have any recommendations on what we should do if this terrible genie gets out of the bottle?"

"Yes, sir," Epstein replied in a barely audible voice, and this time he couldn't meet the president's eye. "If the enhanced VX agents are set free by an explosion, you must do immediately what the destruction facility at Johnston Island has been doing for the past two years."

"And that is?"

"You must burn them, sir."

"I'm not sure I understand," Garrison replied with a puzzled expression.

"Mr. President, you'll have to drop a nuclear weapon on Johnston Atoll."

The shock on Garrison's face was mirrored by his secretary of state. It was if someone had slapped them. Only General McKenzie seemed immune from the shock of Epstein's proposal, but then he was more familiar with decisions of life and death—or at least better at shielding his emotions while they were made.

"There must be another way," Garrison finally managed. "There has to be."

"Sir, I helped develop those agents; I'm responsible for this! In God's name, if there were any other solution I would tell you, believe me I would!"

Garrison studied Epstein for a long moment, then pursed his lips, seeming to come to some sort of decision.

"Very well, Doctor, I think I understand what you're saying. But so far, no chemicals have been released. And if they are, unless that storm materializes and the danger to Hawaii is confirmed, there's no way I'm going to consider dropping an atomic bomb on twelve hundred American citizens."

"No, Mr. President, you *don't* understand! Even if there's no storm, airborne VX molecules can find their way a great distance from their release point. And even in the very unlikely event of a ten-day dead calm, you still have to use the bomb if the chemicals are set free. Nothing will be able to save those people on Johnston Island. Unless you take action, they'll all die horrible, horrible deaths!"

"Of course," Garrison replied softly. "Of course." Epstein was flushed and beginning to sweat, and the president could see that he was emotionally at the end of his tether. Somehow, this seemed to give him strength. The president rose briskly, signaling an end to the meeting. "Very well, gentlemen. You've given me a great deal to think about. General, I want to know what, if anything, can be done to assault that island and keep this lunatic from detonating the explosives on those chemicals." He walked around the desk and offered his hand to Epstein, some of his old charm returning. "Doctor, I know it was as hard for you to tell me these things as it was for me to hear them. Thank you for your candor. Any further suggestions you may have will be most welcome."

As McKenzie led Epstein to the door, Garrison motioned for Carlton to remain. Epstein stopped at the door and turned. "Don't let them die like that, sir," he pleaded. He was now crying openly. "You can't imagine the suffering they'll go through."

After they had left, Garrison returned to his chair. He rubbed his face, trying to purge the weariness that had suddenly overtaken him. It was all so overwhelming. Then he turned to face Carlton across the desk.

"How much longer until the press comes out with the capture of the atoll?"

Carlton looked at his watch. "I'd say no more than half an hour. We've prepared a bulletin for a release to the wire services. It'll hit the late-night news, but most of the country won't learn about this until tomorrow morning. Except Hawaii; it's quarter to six there.

"But these demands Tadao has come up with are another matter," he continued. "CNN received a copy of them right after we got ours. We had to promise them an exclusive televised interview with the secretary of the Army about Johnston Island in exchange for a twenty-four-hour hold on the story. This could be pure dynamite. If there's not a quick settlement of this thing, then I recommend you go on TV and tell the people what's happening *before* the demands are made public by the media."

Garrison leaned back in the leather swivel and closed his eyes, trying to purge the image of Epstein's pleading face. "I don't know what the Japanese are going to do, but there's no way I can go along with this, Gates. No way—I just can't."

"But what if Epstein's right, Bob," Carlton said softly. "What if it's not just the lives on Johnston Island, but all of Hawaii." Garrison stared quietly at the desk for several moments, then looked up. "I still can't," he said, but with less conviction.

Thursday, 8 December, 11:03 A.M.
TOKYO, JAPAN

Late evening in Washington, D.C., was late morning in Tokyo, the following day. The room was more crowded than the prime minister would have liked, but that was how it had to be. There were many present at the meeting he would need to call on for support as well as those traditional opponents who would require special attention. At times like this, he envied the power of a dictator or even the executive privilege of the American president. But that was not how decisions were made in Japan, or at least not how they were made in Japan today.

Prime Minister Narihiko Mitsuzuka and the other key members of the government had learned of the capture of Johnston Island at eight o'clock that morning. He had immediately called for a high-level meeting of his cabinet and political faction leaders in the Diet. Since it was 8 December in Tokyo, it was just now dawning on many of those present that this attack on Johnston Island had taken place on the anniversary of Pearl Harbor. The subtle murmuring around the room had reached an audible buzz, displaying the anxiety of those assembled. Finally, Mitsuzuka rose and cleared his throat. There was immediate silence. The expression on the prime minister's face showed the gravity of the situation. He bowed low to show his deepest regret.

"Honorable colleagues," he began. "You are all aware of the events that took place on the American island in the Pacific. I take full responsibility for this unfortunate incident. I should have insisted on a closer scrutiny of the rightist elements in our nation. Therefore, I ask your forgiveness." Again, he bowed deeply. "Now it seems we must come to some sort of position on this matter. The Americans will have to deal with this situation, and I am led to believe there may be considerable loss of life. They know it was not Japan who did this, but the source of their problem is Japanese. I fear public opinion in the United States may force their government into a hasty reaction that will be detrimental to Japan. You have before you the information transmitted to us by their government. The American newspapers have this information, so our own media will soon learn of it. I humbly ask for any counsel that may help us to avoid further humiliation and to contain this embarrassing problem." He bowed one more time, but less dramatically, which indicated he was prepared to assume his role as national leader.

"Mitsuzuka-san. You don't suggest that we in any way support the demands of this terrorist?" said an older, distinguished man at the end of the table. His tone was respectful, but detached.

"Of course not," Mitsuzuka replied, seeking to understand the agenda of the older man. He took up a single sheet of paper and adjusted his glasses. "The terrorist leader has made two demands. First of all, he has asked that the emperor assume his, quote, 'ancient and traditional duties as the cultural and military leader of the nation.' The second," Mitsuzuka said, removing his glasses and looking around the room, "is that the American president personally and publicly apologize to the emperor for America's aggression and crimes against the Japanese people during the war." He paused to measure his words. "Regarding the emperor as a military leader, this is a direct violation of our constitution. As for an apology from President Garrison . . ." he opened his hands in a helpless gesture. "In any case, acquiescing to the demands of terrorists is something both we and the Americans have agreed not to do; this is by a resolution sponsored by the United States at the United Nations."

"So what have we done about this?" asked the elderly man politely. His voice was neutral and betrayed none of his feelings on the issue. Masayoshi Oka was a powerful member of the Diet, with his own constituency. He had often been a political ally of the prime minister, but not always.

"I have sent a carefully worded message of regret to President Garrison and a pledge to assist him in any way to help resolve this crisis. I also plainly stated that these demands in no way reflect the thinking of the Japanese government or the Japanese people. So far, they have asked only for the information we have on the terrorist leader, Takashi Tadao, and we have complied with that request."

"And just who is this Tadao? I know only that he is a rightist of some intellectual ability and that he has the ear of some old-line industrialists. What more do we know of him? Is he in some way connected with that Nomura idiot who committed sepuku a few years ago?"

"Apparently," Mitsuzuka replied, carefully measuring the proper amount of respect and patience in his tone, "he has secretly revived the Shield Society, the neonationalist group founded by Yukio Mishima that was active in the late sixties prior to Mishima's death. We have nothing that would connect Tadao with Shusuke Nomura, other than that he too was a rightist. Before his death, Nomura was an unsuccessful political candidate who advocated change within the system. Tadao, it seems, favors stronger action. With your permission, I have asked Inspector Hayashi from the Ministry of Justice to provide us with a short biography of Takashi Tadao. Inspector?"

Hayashi was a stocky man with a shaved head. He stepped to the table and withdrew a small spiral notebook, the universal badge of police detectives. His bow was low and respectful, but curt. It said that while his ministry may have to share some responsibility for what took place on Johnston Island, he personally did not.

"Takashi Tadao, or Commandant Tadao of the New Shield Society as he now calls himself, is a very dangerous and formidable man." Hayashi detailed a short history of Tadao's personal and political life. He described a man of ability and influence, one who merited respect, and he cautioned against underestimating him. Then he snapped the notebook closed and bowed his head to show he was finished.

"Does anyone have questions for Inspector Hayashi?" Mitsuzuka intervened.

"Perhaps one or two," came the voice from the end of the table. "Since this Johnston Island deals with chemical weapons, does this Tadao have any connection with Shoko Asahara and the Aum Shinri Kyo sect, the ones who put sarin gas in the subways?"

"There is no evidence to support that Tadao would have anything to do with those people. Tadao is a traditionalist and the Aum sect is more of a futuristic, religious cult. A man like Tadao would consider them trivial and unimportant."

"I see," Oka replied, "and what, in your opinion, will Commandant Tadao do if his demands are not met, or the Americans attempt to recapture their island by force?"

"He will carry out his threat," Hayashi said immediately. "He would prefer that the Americans attack, for then he can release the poison chemicals and die with a sword in his hand. But if the Americans do nothing and try to wait him out, I believe he will release the chemicals and then take his own life. A man like Tadao would not undertake this venture without carefully preparing himself for death. In all probability, he will view himself a failure if he is alive when it is over."

"And in your experience, short of meeting his demands, is there anything you know that will convince him to turn away from this course of action?"

Hayashi paused a moment before answering. "Tadao, like Mishima before him, is a samurai in that he reveres the emperor. The emperor and the imperial nature of Japan's history hold a sacred meaning for these men. Perhaps some intervention by the emperor may serve to defuse the situation. But then Tadao may also feel the emperor is now no more than a hostage of the Imperial Palace, which is perhaps why he has asked for a restoration of imperial authority."

"Like the emperors of the Tokugawa Era, who were dominated by the shoguns of that period."

Hayashi inclined his head in respect for Minister Oka's observation. "Precisely," he replied.

"Any further questions?" said Mitsuzuka, suggesting he wanted to move forward. There were none. "Thank you for your help, Inspector," he said politely. Hayashi bowed and left the room. "Now, I must soon speak directly with the American president. Does anyone have anything more that we may offer to the Americans, other than my apologies and further information on 'Commandant' Tadao as it becomes available?"

Mitsuzuka was about to adjourn the meeting when a man in the back of the room rose to be recognized.

"Yes, Minister Uno."

Uno bowed to the men at the table. "My humble observation is that the Americans will attack the island and try to recapture it. They do not seem to be patient in these matters, and it is in keeping with their nature to take strong action." Uno glanced around the room. Sensing a general agreement, he proceeded. "In all probability, they will begin the attack with a probe by one of their antiterrorist units, perhaps their highly publicized Delta Force. As many of you know, we have within our defense organization a well-trained, paramilitary force with an impeccable record in counter-terrorist operations. They are a superb fighting unit, and they could prove most effective against this renegade force that is essentially a small samurai army."

"You are referring to the Naginata Counter Force?" There were many carefully masked expressions around the room. Many did not know of the Naginata Counter Force, but no one asked for clarification.

"Yes, Prime Minister."

"But," interrupted a young minister seated near Oka, "from what the inspector has told us, certain death awaits any attempt to stop Tadao."

"That is correct, Minister," Uno replied, bowing his head slightly, "but would we not save much face if Japanese soldiers were a part of the mission to recapture Johnston Atoll, no matter how impossible that mission may be?''

Again, Uno sensed agreement around the room.

Wednesday, 7 December, 6:15 P.M.
JOHNSTON ISLAND

The day had been long and very hot. Master Sergeant Andrew Pierce estimated the temperature inside the aircraft at well over 115 degrees. Fortunately, the aircraft had an ample supply of drinking water. He had taken the blankets from the emergency provisions and used them to make a nest for himself under the metal deckplates of the Starlifter. The air was a little cooler there, but not much. This wasn't the most comfortable accommodation, nestled among the cable runs and hydraulic tubing, but it was the best hiding place he could find. Twice that day they had come aboard the aircraft. The first time, Pierce guessed them to be men who had taken over the control tower and passenger terminal. He didn't speak Japanese, but their conversation was light and punctuated with laughter—a universal banter common to soldiers of all armies, a language familiar to Master Sergeant Pierce. They'd left after a brief inspection of the aircraft.

Much later that afternoon, another group had come aboard. This was a more orderly and disciplined boarding, and some of the talk was in English. Pierce recognized the voice of the aircraft commander, Captain Reiling. His captain was questioned extensively about the aircraft, its range, and serviceability.

"And you will be able to take off from here and with enough fuel to reach the Japanese home islands?'' The voice was accented, but with a cold authority.

"Sure,'' Reiling had replied defiantly, "unless someone has been tampering with the plane.'' He spoke more loudly than necessary for normal conversation. Pierce figured Reiling would know he was missing from the crew members captured in the terminal, and would guess that his crew chief was hiding in the aircraft.

"There had better be nothing wrong with this airplane, Captain, or you will answer to me, personally—with your life."

"So what will you do then, hotshot—get one of these monkeys to fly it for you?"

There were sounds of a scuffle and the thud of a body hitting the deck-plate above him. Then it was quiet except for Reiling's moaning. A terse exchange in Japanese faded along with the sound of Captain Reiling being dragged from the plane.

Pierce had remained frozen beneath the floor for a very long time, knowing he had in all probability signed his aircraft commander's death warrant. Earlier that day, he had destroyed the ignition switches, which were critical to engine start-up sequence. The Starlifter would need replacement parts and several hours of maintenance before anyone would be able to turn the four big J-79 turbofan engines. Pierce had carefully removed the access panel and smashed the solenoids under the flight engineer's console. There was no apparent damage to the console, but the switches were worthless. That the commander at Pearl Harbor, and now Captain Reiling, had ordered him to do this was of little solace. He shook himself from these reflections and flicked the penlight across his watch, noting that it was almost 1900.

Carefully, he cracked the deckplate above his head and listened, then eased it high enough to peer around inside the cargo bay. He could see only about half the length of the interior due to the cargo pallets that filled a portion of the aircraft. Finally he emerged and silently made his way up to the flight deck, sliding quietly into the pilot's seat. Dusk was now beginning to creep over Johnston Island, but he had an excellent vantage. There was little chance of his being seen from the terminal or the control tower, yet there was enough light for him to examine the island. From this position some twenty-two feet above the runway, he cautiously surveyed the tarmac for roving guards. Then he took out his survival radio and attached it to a thin wire antenna that now dangled from the cockpit window.

"This is Pierce," he spoke quietly into the transceiver. "Do you read me, over?"

"Roger, Master Sergeant, this is Barndance Control. I hear you loud and clear, how about me, over?" This time the voice came from an intelligence specialist sitting over a plotting table with a huge color mosaic enlargement of Johnston Island. The imagery had been gathered by Navy F/A-18D(RC) aircraft just a few hours earlier. A Navy E-2 Hawkeye was patiently orbiting Johnston Island at thirty thousand feet, serving as an airborne transponder. The Hawkeye received Pierce's signal, boosted it, and retransmitted it on a dedicated frequency to the crisis-management center at Camp Smith. "I copy you five-by, Barndance. What do you want, over?"

The man at the plotting table sensed something in Pierce's voice that was different. "You okay, Master Sergeant?"

"Yeah, just a little tired and more than a little scared. Let's get on with it, over."

"All right, here we go and we'll have to hurry; it'll be dark there soon. You have the binoculars, over?"

"That's affirmative."

"Good. Now on a relative bearing, using the nose of the aircraft as zero-zero-zero, tell me what you see?"

Pierce looked straight ahead over the rounded snout of the C-141 and described vehicles blocking the runway and the buildings on the north side of the runway. After several questions that pressed him for clarification, Pierce shifted his glasses thirty degrees to the right and repeated the process. Using Sergeant Pierce as his eyes, the photo-interpreter directed him in a full circle. Several other photo-interpreters and intelligence officers listening on the circuit began to plot the information on the enlargement.

Thursday, 8 December, 3:10 P.M.
JSDF MOUNTAIN TRAINING CAMP, OKINAWA

Captain Shintaro Nakajima carefully removed his foot from the crevice allowing his entire weight to hang from fingertips that dug into the inch-wide ledge above him. Then he carefully pulled himself up to an eye-level position and remained suspended while his feet sought yet another purchase. He tested the new foothold carefully before transferring his weight. His hands searched for a place to grasp and the cycle was repeated. Other members of his platoon were scattered across the rock face. The climb was difficult but well within their ability. Except in this climb, they also worked against the clock. All of them knew that rock climbing became exponentially more dangerous when one hurried, but Nakajima and his men were in a business where speed could save their lives. More important, speed could also allow them to complete their mission successfully. A team of good sport climbers would have safely made this summit in three hours. Nakajima expected his men to do it in less than an hour.

As the last man cleared the rock face, Nakajima tapped the button on his wrist chronometer. "Fifty-six minutes, thirty-six seconds," he announced. "Excellent." The men clustered around him broke into smiles. It was all the reward they required for their work on the face. His platoon had spent the morning hours on the lower portion of the face practicing mountain rescue techniques—skills that would help them descend with a wounded comrade or a rescued hostage. Their afternoon climb was the final training evolution. A cold wind had come up to add to the challenge, and yet, while Nakajima and his men had broken a sweat under their parkas, none were breathing hard. He was pleased with their performance and told them so.

"And now, men, as a reward for your fine effort on the

way up, you may descend at your own pace and in a manner of your own choosing. Dismissed.''

He watched as they dug into their packs for their descent lines, like a group of school children rifling their lunch pails. Long nylon ropes uncoiled down the four-hundred-foot cliff. They then lashed Swiss seats about their waists and attached snap links.

"On rappel!" yelled the first as he leapt over the edge. Another followed, then another. One man was on the ground almost immediately, covering the distance in three bounds. It was a controlled free-fall, yet he stepped onto the gravel below as if stepping off a bus. Another toyed with the face, scampering left, then right, in a pendulum motion as he zigzagged to the bottom. Most of the men ran down the face head-first, Australian fashion, controlling the rope with one hand while holding the other one free as if cradling a submachine gun. Nakajima, the last man off the summit, bounded to the bottom in an upright, conventional manner, quickly and professionally.

"Captain Nakajima! Captain Nakajima!" called a soldier who ran to meet them as the climbers were retrieving their equipment. He was a member of the training-support team.

"I'm right here, Corporal. Please state your business."

The man bowed respectfully. "Colonel Matsumoto just radioed. He wishes you to return to the base as quickly as possible."

"It will take us but a few minutes to get our gear aboard the trucks. Call and tell the colonel we will leave immediately for the drive back."

"Oh no, sir! There is a helicopter on its way. The colonel wishes you to fly back." As the man spoke, Nakajima heard the beat of a helo heading for them. His trained ear told him it was coming fast at low altitude.

"So," Nakajima replied turning to his platoon. "Sergeant Ozawa, take charge and see that the men get back to the base as quickly as possible. It seems there may be some work for us in the near future. I will be flying back to the base ahead of you. Report to me when you return."

Nakajima returned his sergeant's salute and handed him his climbing pack. A Kawasaki-built McDonnell-Douglas OH-6D popped over the ridge and tail-walked to the base of the cliff, shedding speed and altitude as it blanketed the platoon with dust. Nakajima leapt into the open door before the skids touched the ground, and the little helo sped away.

He assumed it was a matter of some urgency so he resisted the temptation to change into a fresh uniform, going straight to Colonel Matsumoto's office. Reporting to a superior in less than his best uniform was a sign of disrespect, but Nakajima knew his colonel would understand.

"Ah, *Kohai*, thank goodness you are here. We may have some very serious business to attend to. Come, sit." Matsumoto attached a great deal of importance to protocol and normal courtesies. That he would dispense with them suggested the matter was quite urgent. Nakajima took a seat without a word. "Tell me, do you know anything of a man called Takashi Tadao?"

Nakajima thought carefully before answering. "Only that he is a rightist of considerable reputation. He is an imperialist and a protégé of Yukio Mishima. At one time he was also a priest of the Yambushi order and a very capable martial artist. As I recall, he was a kendo master and some years ago won the national . . ." Nakajima flushed and lowered his eyes.

"Yes, *Kohai*, please continue."

"He narrowly defeated a superb swordsman by the name of Major Hideki Matsumoto for the national kendo title."

The older man chuckled without smiling. "Well said, Captain, but he beat me soundly. What else do you know of him?"

"I remember an article written about him and his fascination with death—almost an erotic fascination. As I recall, Tadao maintained that freely choosing to die is the ultimate manifestation of free will. I have heard nothing about him for some time, perhaps several years. Is he still alive?"

"Very much so. Read this." Colonel Matsumoto handed

him a yellow message facsimile. It was a secret cable from Director General Uno that summarized the situation on Johnston Island. While Nakajima tried to comprehend the terrible dilemma this would cause for the Americans, he had to admire the boldness of the action.

"And what has he asked for?"

"He has demanded that the emperor be restored to his pre-war status and influence, and that the American president apologize for the war—publicly apologize."

"That would suit a follower of Mishima. Did he set a time limit on these demands?" Without realizing it, Nakajima had immediately begun to think in terms of a counterstrike.

"Not yet," Matsumoto replied, "but he has threatened to kill everyone on the island if he is opposed."

"How many men has he with him?"

"That remains unclear, but there seems to be close to eighty, perhaps more, and there are over a thousand American hostages on the island, mostly civilians."

Nakajima inhaled audibly. "Then he has made a suicide pact between himself and anyone who would attack and try to rescue the hostages. The Americans have an impossible situation on their hands."

"Not just the Americans," Matsumoto said evenly. "The director general has offered our services to assist with the recapture of Johnston Island."

Thursday, 8 December, 4:30 A.M.
450 MILES SOUTH OF HAWAII

The *La Jolla* had covered well over four hundred nautical miles in less than twelve hours. Normally this would have been a relatively easy high-speed transit, but dragging along the dry deck shelter had required a flank bell for the whole trip. Sprinting at high speeds, even a sleek boat like the *La Jolla* put a great deal of sound into the water, and the DDS had made it even noisier. Although the Russian subs no longer came out to challenge them, American attack-boat skippers still felt there was something immoral about making noise underwater. The *La Jolla* had now reduced speed to "ahead slow" as it approached the battle group.

Commander Robbie Kemp rode the eyepiece of the Type 18 main periscope from the pedestal flooring to a standing position. From there he hung on the shears while making a 360-degree rotation. He wore his combination cap backward in Gunther Prien fashion, but Kemp was the wrong generation, nationality, and color for an old U-boat skipper.

"I have two starboard running lights on the horizon, zero-four-zero. Bring up the radar mast."

A few seconds later a quartermaster called out, "Radar holds a number of surface contacts. Closest contact identified as the *Carl Vinson* fifteen hundred yards on the port bow. The *Tarawa* is astern of it—range, nineteen hundred yards."

The plotting team on the *La Jolla* knew exactly where the *Vinson* and the members of its battle group were, but bringing a submarine to the surface, even in open water, was a very carefully formatted maneuver. Essentially an armored vessel, the sub had been designed to withstand the pressures of deeper water. More than one surface vessel had been gutted and sunk by a blind submarine on its way to the surface. Kemp shifted the periscope to the infrared mode and took one more turn. Satisfied, he turned to the diving officer. "Okay, Ted, take it up."

The young officer reached for the 1-MC mic dangling on its cord from the overhead. "Now, surface! Surface! Topside watchstanders, stand by your stations." The control room burst into a flurry of hushed activity, with orders quietly called out and acknowledged. There was the appearance of a great deal of confusion. Kemp watched critically as his crew professionally went about their business.

"On the surface, Cap'n," the diving officer reported. "Surface steaming watch has been set."

"Very well, Lieutenant—nice job." Then he turned to Moody, who was standing in the rear of the control room trying to stay out from underfoot. "Are you ready to get under way, Mr. Moody?"

"Yes, sir. It'll take us about five minutes to rig the CRRC on deck. Then we'll be away."

"We'll maneuver on the surface to get you a little bit closer. Be sure to get a radio check with us and the *Tarawa* before you launch and just before you get under way. You have a transponder with you?"

"Yes sir, and the *Tarawa* has our squawk."

"Good. It's a big ship, but the sun won't be up for another hour or so, and it's pretty dark out there. We'll stay on the surface long enough to make sure you're headed in the right direction." The *La Jolla*, a modern submarine, was ill suited for surface operations and, with the weight of the SDV shelter perched on the afterdeck, was rolling badly.

"Will you be able to stay in contact with us while submerged, skipper?"

"The *Vinson* has a GERTRUDE channel for short-range underwater communications. We'll be in the area and they'll keep us informed."

"Cap'n," the OOD interrupted, "the SEALs request permission to open the dry deck shelter door and launch small craft."

"Permission granted. I guess you better make your way aft. By the way, who are you taking with you?"

"Senior Chief Stockton and my lead SDV pilot—Petty Officer Walker. Sir, if we have to bring equipment aboard, how do you want to do it?"

"Helo it onto the stern, and we'll take it aboard through the DDS. And pray for a calm sea or it can get exciting."

"Same for personnel?"

"Same for personnel."

"Request permission to leave the boat, sir."

"Granted," Kemp replied, returning his salute.

Moody headed aft, pulling on a light Goretex foulweather jacket as he hurried from the control room.

Ten minutes later Moody sat on the port spray tube of the CRRC, or combat rubber raiding craft, a small Zodiac-like boat. Barely four feet from him on the starboard tube was Chief Stockton, but Moody had to strain to see even his outline. The little craft pitched and wove through the swells like a motorized cork. Walker manned the tiller of the outboard and could see no better than Moody. Occasionally they blindly plowed into a breaking wave that washed over the spray tubes and soaked everyone aboard. They had a lighted small-boat compass, but it swung wildly as the waves pushed them about.

Moody clutched the safety rope with one hand and the radio with his other, relaying "come a little bit left—come a little bit right" directions from the radar operator on the *Tarawa*. Walker and Chief Stockton bailed. Even on a warm, tropical ocean surrounded by friendly ships, it was a dark and forbidding transit. Finally they picked up the stern light of the big LHA—helicopter assault ship—and the warm glow of its well deck.

Moody didn't so much see the big ship as he felt its presence, like driving into the shadow of a mountain. The well deck of the *Tarawa* was a terribly convenient feature of this class of LHA: a huge gate in the stern of the ship opened and allowed sea water to flood a section in the after part. It was designed so the *Tarawa* could give birth to landing craft and amphibious tanks that carried Marines to the beach. Moody's small craft entered the stern gate like a Volkswagen Beetle driving into a barn. Once inside, they beached the CRRC on the metal ramp at the forward end of the well deck. Soon after they had landed, the stern gate rumbled closed and the dewatering process began.

Several sailors helped them carry the boat up the ramp and secure it. Even with their waterproof parkas, the three SEALs were soaked. Fortunately, Senior Chief Stockton had insisted they pack extra uniforms in a waterproof bag. Moody looked like a drowned rat as he made his way up the ramp. He squished when he walked.

"Lieutenant Moody, welcome aboard the *Tarawa*." A tall, thin Marine, in starched fatigues and spit-shined boots, held out his hand.

"Thank you, Colonel. Glad to be aboard."

Thursday, 8 December, 8:50 A.M.
HICKAM AIR FORCE BASE, HAWAII

General Jack Sheppard paced along the tarmac and searched the southern horizon for the *Vinson*'s COD, or carrier onboard delivery, aircraft. He paused to draw on his cigarette and continued his vigil. A quick glance at the Camel straight brought a frown from him. He had started smoking at Ranger school and had never quite been able to kick the habit. Nearby, the members of his battle staff milled about. A small pile of overnight bags, attaché cases, and map cases rested by the door to the operations building. Sheppard absent-mindedly field-stripped the cigarette, briefly reflecting that most of his military career had been spent waiting—usually in the wrong place. He had just missed Vietnam, and it seemed that somehow he was always where the action wasn't. Panama, Grenada, the Gulf War; he'd missed them all. Jack Sheppard had an impeccable military record, with extensive command and staff experience, but he had not once led, planned, or commanded an actual combat operation.

By Army standards, and most certainly by Special Forces criteria, Sheppard's career was very successful. But in this man's Army, lack of combat experience made one an associate club member—ineligible for regular membership. In his heart, he knew he was a good soldier and combat experience was more of a macho thing, a rite of passage. He also knew that a senior commander was more of a manager and logistician than a warrior. But when the war stories began at the officer's mess, he could only listen along with the other noncombatants. He was simply a cop, a very good one, who had never drawn his gun. Most of his classmates from the Point had had their chance to act in a time of crisis. Until now, he had been denied his.

When word had come down from the CINC that a small military force had captured Johnston Island, Sheppard had instinctively known this would be his last chance to take an active role in a combat operation—not to lead an assault, but to direct the operation. He knew it would be a special-operations tasking; it was too big for law-enforcement action and too small for conventional Army forces, especially with civilian hostages involved. *Go easy*, he told himself.

Careful planning, careful staff work, and solid logistical support were the key to operational success. It was a tough problem, no question about that, and they still lacked solid intelligence. But he had a damn good staff and a number of well-trained special-operations units from which to choose. He pictured the terrorists fleeing before the assault of one of his Ranger battalions, but he quickly pushed the thought from his mind. For now it was a planning drill and ultimately, the odds favored a resolution by negotiation rather than direct combat action. Still, he'd be ready; this could be his chance.

"General, the duty officer says the COD flight is about fifteen minutes out. Seems they had some sort of a fuel problem and were late in leaving the carrier."

"Thanks, Richie," Sheppard replied to his aide. Even Captain Richie Fagan, who had seen action in the Gulf, wore a subdued combat infantry badge on his starched camouflage blouse. "Damn squids are never around when you need them."

"Airborne, sir." Captain Fagan exchanged a chuckle with his general. A squid was a none-to-flattering name for a sailor.

The tardy flight reminded Sheppard of another pimple on the smooth complexion of his military career—the United States Navy. The creation of the U.S. Special Operations Command several years ago meant those in Special Forces were really no longer a part of the Army. In essence, Spe-

cial Operations Command was a fifth service. This new
organization was a tri-service command that, while numeri-
cally dominated by the Army, was a composite force from
the other services. Sheppard had served two staff tours at
SOCOM in Tampa, Florida, and both times his reporting
senior had been a naval officer. He had worked hard during
those tours of duty and had been commended for both. As
a reward, or perhaps as punishment, he had been assigned
to the Pacific Command, the only theater commanded by
an admiral. It was the largest, and next to Central Command
in the Middle East, the most active theater command, but
it was a Navy area of operations. His boss, the CINC, was
an admiral.

A dot on the horizon finally sprouted wings and soon
turned into a C-2 Greyhound, the Navy's current COD aircraft. The big twin turboprop touched down and hurried
over to where they waited. USS *Carl Vinson* was blocked
across its tail in black letters. An enlisted crewman directed
Sheppard and his staff aboard and gave them a quick safety
briefing while the two pilots remained at the controls. They
began rolling as the crewman retrieved the access hatch and
secured it.

The flight was routine, but rough and noisy compared
with a commercial jet. They loitered around the ship while
the *Vinson* took a section of F-14s aboard, then settled into
the pattern. It was steaming into the wind with close to
forty-five knots blowing across deck. The COD landed at
about eighty-five knots, so the aircraft had to struggle to
catch the moving airfield. It was a very soft trap.

Sheppard led his staff out of the COD and directly onto
a waiting SH-60F Seahawk helicopter that would take them
to the *Tarawa*. He had thought of running the operation
from Camp Smith, where the communications and intelligence coverage would be superior. But the operational support would come from the *Vinson*'s battle group, and any
direct-action mission would be staged from the *Tarawa*.

A few minutes later they settled onto the deck of the
boxy LHA. The ship's operations officer took the staff to

the flag plot, where they immediately began to set up a battle watch. Sheppard was led to the flag officer's quarters.

The suite was spacious and well appointed, with a sitting room complete with a small conference table. A curtained door led to the sleeping quarters and private toilet. The bedroom had a porthole that framed an escort vessel steaming on the *Tarawa*'s starboard beam. Along one wall of the sitting room was internal communications equipment that connected the room with the ship's bridge and combat information center. On the other wall, over a Naugahyde couch, was a large framed print of an armed Marine contingent marching through the streets of Tripoli. A green felt cloth covered the table. Cups and saucers attended a china carafe of hot coffee flanked by a crystal cream-and-sugar service. Soft music played over the ship's entertainment system. Directly above him was the flag plot that would serve as his command center for the planning and execution of any action taken against Johnston Island.

Fucking Navy, Sheppard thought, as he tossed his gear bag on the couch. As a second lieutenant he'd slept rolled in a poncho liner in the field with his platoon. When he'd been a company commander, it had been a sleeping bag in the corner of a command bunker. Once promoted to field grade, he'd been allowed a canvas cot in the command tent; as a battalion commander, he'd had his own cot and tent. And now I'm about to fight the Japanese from a condo with an ocean view, he thought.

When he turned and opened the door, a Marine lance corporal snapped to attention and saluted. "What're you doing here, son?" Sheppard asked, as he returned the Marine's salute.

"Sir, I'm assigned as the general's orderly, sir."

"What's your name, son?"

"Lance Corporal Peppard, sir."

"Okay, Corporal; I want you to find my operations officer, Colonel Simms, and have him report to me ASAP. Then tell the comm center to get me copies of all the traffic on Johnston Island for the last three hours. And when you've finished that, tell the landing force commander I'd like to see him in forty-five minutes—say 1300. Got all that?''

"Yes, sir.'' Peppard remained at attention, mentally reciting his instructions.

"Well?''

"Sir?''

"Get moving, son!''

"Aye aye, sir,'' and he disappeared down the passageway.

Sheppard walked back into the sitting room. He took a battered tin cup from his vinyl bag, one he had taken from a field mess years ago, and filled it with coffee from the china carafe.

When General Sheppard and his staff set down on the *Tarawa*, it was just after 11:00 A.M. on 8 December. At Kadina Air Force Base on Okinawa, the time was 6:00 A.M. the next day. Captain Nakajima and six of his men waited quietly in the corner of an empty hangar. Their gear bags and weapons boxes were paraded neatly along the wall of the hangar. The weather was chilly and wet, and their breath issued brief clouds in the cold building. There was no banter or joking as would be the case with a group of U.S. servicemen, nor was there any complaining about waiting in the cold. They simply stood there, speaking softly among themselves.

Then a figure entered through a small door at the other end of the hangar. He walked briskly toward them. With no command given, the small group transformed itself into a rank behind Nakajima. He saluted, knowing that the men were at attention behind him.

"Place your men at ease, Captain,'' Colonel Matsumoto said, returning the salute. Nakajima spoke a single word to his men without taking his eyes from Matsumoto. The colonel turned away, motioning Nakajima to follow. They walked slowly and Matsumoto said nothing until they were out of earshot from the others. He was clearly troubled.

"I will not attempt to deceive you or to make this matter seem what it is not, Captain. I am afraid that you and your men are being offered to the Americans as a way to ease our political conscience."

"But with respect, Colonel, is this not our duty?"

"It is, but our leaders have made more than just an offer of assistance. They have strongly suggested that any action to repatriate Johnston Island should consist of both American and Japanese attackers." Nakajima looked at his colonel but said nothing. "You understand, *Kohai*," Matsumoto continued in a gentle voice, "that those in Tokyo see this as a hopeless mission. I fear they may be correct. They feel that if American lives are lost in such an attack, then we will save face if Japanese lives are also lost."

Nakajima considered this a moment, but his thoughts immediately ran to the tactical implications. "I understand, Colonel, but surely the American commander would not tolerate a foreign element in his attacking force." Nakajima tried to imagine having American soldiers suddenly thrust into his platoon on the eve of a mission. It was not a pleasant thought.

"The American commander may have no more choice than you or I. My orders are to make the best squad of the Naginata Counter Force available to the Americans. But I feel your fate is in the hands of the politicians as much as the American commander who, like us, must do as he is ordered."

Nakajima stopped and bowed. "I am honored that you selected me, whatever the mission. My men and I will do our best to justify your trust. And perhaps, in some small way, we may be able to assist the Americans with their problem."

"Perhaps," Matsumoto replied, trying to keep the bitterness from his voice. He framed his words carefully, "but if a samurai is sent into an impossible situation, it should not be under the command of a *gai-jin*."

"I accept this mission, freely and without reservation,

under *your* orders, Colonel. And we are prepared to die if that is how it must be.''

"You honor me, *Kohai*,'' the older man replied, bowing low. "I will pray to the *kami* for your safety.''

"With all respect, Colonel,'' Nakajima said as he too bowed, "pray for our success.''

"There is another matter,'' Matsumoto said as they continued walking. He chose his words. "This Tadao, whom you may have to face, is a most worthy and dangerous adversary. When we fought for the kendo championship, I was a better swordsman than he—the better technician, if you will. But he was a better fighter. I could not match his ferocity and determination. If you meet him, you must use your tenacity and cunning as well as your skill.'' The older man stopped and was silent a moment before he continued. "It may be that you find him an honorable man, even virtuous. Even I cannot, in some ways, but admire the boldness of his action. You may respect this man, but you must also fear him and, if possible, stop him.'' Matsumoto was about to continue when Nakajima bowed his head to interrupt.

"Please, if I may, Colonel, I believe I understand. We are both samurai. My lord is the way of Japan today. Tadao's is the way of Japan of a previous era—a time before I was born. He must serve his lord and I mine. I admire and respect this bold warrior. Nonetheless, I will fight this man with all my skill and heart. To do less would dishonor myself, you, and all that I hold sacred. It would also dishonor Tadao-sama. I am samurai. To do otherwise is unthinkable.''

The colonel again bowed. "You are wise for a man of so few years, *Kohai*. May the *kami* that protect our divine land guide you on your mission.'' Outside the hangar, a piercing wail announced the approach of a jet aircraft. Matsumoto cleared his throat as he composed himself, jerking the bottom of his uniform blouse straight. "I see the transport that will take you on your journey has arrived,'' he said in a strained voice. "I will accompany you to your plane."

The two men walked back to where the others waited without speaking. The six soldiers came to attention as the colonel and their captain approached.

Thursday, 8 December, 4:10 P.M.
THE WHITE HOUSE

Most Americans were now aware that a terrorist group had captured Johnston Island. It had taken almost a full day, but the tragedy had finally shouldered aside the college-football bowl pairings as the lead story. The wire services had been quick to point out that the attackers were Japanese. There was nothing yet public on the demands of the terrorists, but there was speculation—everything from reparations for Hiroshima to the cessation of all trade between Japan and the United States, an idea not unpopular in many sections of America.

But few people really knew where Johnston Island was, and fewer still knew that it was in the business of chemical-weapons storage and destruction. Only a chance interview with a Greenpeace advocate or a former Cold War protestor spoke of the huge stores of chemical weapons on Johnston Island. The media was out scouring the nation for former military officers or retired Department of Defense employees who knew anything about chemical weapons. In the scramble, some reporters failed to make the distinction between chemical and biological weapons. Official sources had remained silent, but that was about to change.

President Garrison sat back in his chair with a large terry-cloth towel draped around his chest and shoulders. Television cameras and lighting tripods ringed the large cherry-wood desk. Black rubber cables snaked across the floor, all but obliterating the presidential seal woven into the carpet. Technicians with picture IDs and secret servicemen filtered through the equipment. A makeup man, who thought the president was some kind of hunk, professionally went about his work with powder and brush. Garrison, who disliked TelePrompTers, read through the double-spaced, typed statement his speech writers had prepared. He would deliver this address from the Oval Office. The spin doctors knew there was nothing more sincere than a sober-faced president sitting at his place of work. The desk was neat, but there was a stack of papers near his elbow and a well-stocked pencil cup. Two gold pens stood at attention, peeking from his shirt pocket.

"As you can see, we've consistently referred to them as a band of terrorists." Gates Carlton sat on a corner of the desk and paged through a copy of the text. "We first mention their nationality on the second page, where we say they have connections to the Japanese militant right; then on page four we refer to them as a 'militant Japanese faction.' All other mentions of Japan allude to them as a co-victim of this terrorist act."

"We have to refer to these guys as Japanese?"

"No way around it," Carlton replied. "It's been in the morning editions and on radio and TV nonstop. Our initial indications are that this attack has touched a raw nerve across the country, primarily because the attackers are Japanese. We may have a ground swell on our hands."

"Really that bad?"

"Jesus, Bob," Carlton said, lowering his voice, "they attacked an American base on the anniversary of Pearl Harbor. They hold a thousand American hostages. Half the people out of work in this country think it's the fault of the Japanese and half of those employed in manufacturing think the Japanese threaten their jobs. They're looking for a reason to bash Japan. Can you imagine the talk around the bar down at the American Legion? We have a serious problem on Johnston Island and another with public opinion right here at home."

"Okay," Garrison replied dubiously, "what else?"

"I've touched briefly on chemicals. We have to mention

it, but I think it's best if we speak only about Johnston Island as a destruction facility. We talk of a 'potential hazard to those Americans being held there,' on page three. The official press release on Johnston Island will describe it as a pioneering effort in the eradication of these dangerous agents of mass destruction. The rest is filler with the usual words of consolation for the families of the hostages; we're working the problem—inappropriate to comment on the status of ongoing negotiations—doing everything we can, and so on.''

Garrison glanced in the mirror and pulled the towel from his neck. ''That'll do, Robert; could you excuse us, please?''

''Of course. Break a leg, sir,'' the makeup man said as he retreated.

''Huh, oh yeah, thanks Robert.'' He turned his attention fully to Carlton.

''Christ, Gates,'' he said in a nervous, quiet voice, ''just what in the hell *are* we going to do about this mess?''

''I honestly don't know. The first thing is to find out just who we're dealing with and see if we can reason with him. The FBI has the corporate knowledge on terrorists. Faxes have been flying between the Bureau's Special Operations and Research Unit in Quantico and the Japanese Ministry of Justice. The attorney general tells me the Japanese are being very cooperative. FBI is working this problem, and the data's been sent out to Langley for CIA's input. They're trying to assemble a personality profile on the guy, but I understand it's moving slowly. This Tadao's not a known terrorist or on anybody's watch list so there's not much on him. Who knows—maybe he just wants some media coverage, or wants to talk with somebody important.''

''Speaking of the media, how're *we* doing?''

''The press secretary says it's still a little early for that. That's why we have to go ahead and assume a proactive stance. But from what our PR guys say, there's a lot of voters out there who just plain don't like the Japanese.''

''So what you're saying is that if somebody in government has to wear a black hat, let's make sure it's Prime Minister Mitsuzuka and not me.''

''Something like that, but we have to be careful. The Japanese banks are not in the greatest shape right now and they're still the major foreign holder of our national debt. By the way, I saw the Japanese ambassador just after lunch. I could hardly carry on a conversation; he was bowing every other word. Between apologies, he offered the services of their secret counter-terrorist unit. Our embassy staff in Tokyo knows very little about them, but our people at Langley say they're supposed to be very good—maybe the best.''

''So what do you recommend?''

''I see no reason not to go along with them on this. We've already made arrangements to have these men join our naval task force near Johnston Island. Allowing a few of their people to be involved could prove very important with the media, in both countries. Besides that, no matter how this thing gets resolved, we'll still need the Japanese when it's over, probably more than they'll need us.''

Garrison nodded his approval, but he was having trouble looking that far ahead. ''So what if this Tadao fellow won't budge; what if he sets a deadline and continues to ask what we can't give him? What then?''

''Well, then we may have to call his bluff and let him make the next move. Or perhaps General McKenzie will have a workable military option before that deadline arrives. Meanwhile, we have to consider what to do if he blows up the chemical weapons stored there.''

''You mean dropping the bomb,'' Carlton added grimly. ''But how will we know if he does set off the explosives and releases the chemicals?''

''That's been worked out by NSA. They've parked a high-resolution satellite in a synchronous orbit over Johnston Island. They'll know on a real-time basis if there's an explosion on the island.''

''But just because there's an explosion doesn't mean the

chemicals will be set free, or that those released are the super chemicals Epstein talked about.''

''They know exactly where these agents are stored, down to within a few feet, and they'll be able to tell from the damage to the holding vaults if there's a chemical release. I understand the resolution on these spy satellites is quite incredible, especially in an area like Johnston Island where there's so little pollution. I found it hard to believe, but they say they'll be able to see people dying in the streets. Then we'll have to make the decision to incinerate the island with a nuclear weapon.''

Garrison's weariness was beginning to show through the makeup. ''So what should we do, Gates?''

''I recommend we tell the Air Force to get a bomber airborne and in position to deliver the weapon if that's what ultimately has to be done. For now it's just a contingency, but the alternative, however unlikely, could be disastrous.''

''That storm in the Pacific still brewing?''

''I'm afraid so. It's moving slowly, but it's headed straight for Johnston Island.''

Garrison pursed his lips and was silent for a moment. Then he gave his secretary of state a bewildered look. ''Good Christ, Gates. I wanted to be president—the chief executive. We wanted the White House so we could help the nation move ahead to a new prosperity in the twenty-first century. The job of commander-in-chief just came with the office.''

Carlton had known Garrison a long time, and he was beginning to see the signs of panic. He leaned closer and put a hand on his arm. ''Look, Bob, neither one of us may like to admit it, but our military advisers are probably some of the best people we have. McKenzie and his service chiefs may be a little hidebound, but they've been in uniform for three decades. They have no agenda but sound military options. And the FBI terrorist specialists are the best in the world.

''Until we're given a reason to do otherwise, we have to do this by the numbers. Study the problem, hope for the best, prepare for the worst. We've got to look as good as we can and play for time. The hard decisions will come later, and we'll cross those bridges when we get to them—you'll see. Right now the American people need to hear from their president. They need to know he's got a problem but he's on the job.''

Garrison drew a deep breath. "You're right, Gates, thanks. Tell McKenzie to make the preparations he needs to drop the bomb, but preparations only.'' Garrison grimaced at the thought, but he sat a little taller in his chair and straightened his tie. "I didn't ask for this goddamn thing to be laid at my door step, did I?''

"No, Mr. President,'' Carlton replied, "you certainly didn't.''

"Two minutes, Mr. President, two minutes.'' Technicians melted back among the equipment and a ring of cameras raised their snouts to look at Robert Garrison.

Carlton stepped away from the desk. The president rolled his shoulders in a circular motion, tilting his head left, then right, as he settled in behind the big desk. He was like a fighter getting ready to answer the bell. Thirty seconds before air time, Garrison quickly scanned his speech. Then he took another deep breath and faced the cameras. Carlton covered his mouth to hide the smile. When the cameras were on him, President Robert Garrison reverted to candidate Bob Garrison—poised, confident, very sure of himself.

In a pressroom in the basement, an announcer behind a formal podium faced a single camera. "Ladies and gentlemen, the President of the United States.'' The network feed then cut back to the Oval Office.

"Three, two, one, and now!'' A man with headphones dropped his hand and pointed to Garrison.

Then the president told his fellow Americans of the heinous act visited upon one of their islands in the Pacific, and just how hard he was working to do something about it. He talked about the demands made by the terrorists, both of Japan and of the United States, and how the Japanese were cooperating fully. Garrison smoothly explained that while Japan and the United States had once been enemies, the friendship the two nations had built over the last fifty years would help them to resolve this emergency. Then he asked for the nation's patience and prayers while he and his administration worked to resolve the crisis. And when he expressed sympathy for those who had friends and relatives on Johnston Island, there was no question of his sincerity. He scarcely looked at the printed text and he was magnificent.

Thursday, 8 December, 10:15 A.M.
JOHNSTON ISLAND

Jim Bruso sat to one side of the raised dais between Senator Blackman and General Taggart. Like the general, he had his hands cuffed in front of him. All three watched as the other islanders were directed into the small auditorium. Scientists, warehousemen, secretaries, truck drivers, electricians, supervisors, cooks—they all looked the same: defeated. Confusion, intimidation, and weariness were written on their faces as they walked quietly in single-file, taking their seats starting from the front of the room. Tadao stood center stage, just behind the lip of the raised floor, and glowered at his captives. Few could meet his brooding eyes.

The auditorium had a capacity for just over three hundred with comfortable, spacious seating. As the captives took their seats, no one spoke a word. There was an occasional muffled cough, but well stifled as if the perpetrator wanted to avoid calling attention to himself. The room was heavy with fear, and there was a smell of sweat and soiled clothing. For what seemed a long time, Tadao stared into the silent crowd. A good number of these people were a part of Bruso's contract force, and he watched them with a measure of sadness and rage. He also watched their captors.

They were arrogant and condescending, occasionally

prodding one of the Americans with the butts of their rifles. Bruso noted that they didn't handle their weapons with the care and ease of professional soldiers, not like the men he had served with in the Marine Corps. They could probably shoot well enough, but they were not full-time soldiers. Most of them now had two swords belted to their sides, as did their leader, and he was sure this was something new. Those in the auditorium who were there as guards stood on both sides of the room with their weapons at the ready. Perhaps it was for show, but if there was any shooting, they would have to fire at each other as well as at their captives. Even so, Bruso conceded that they were well disciplined, if not soldierly. Last night he'd noticed the two men guarding them had been rotated several times, which meant they were sleeping while many of their captives were not. Could that mean they were preparing for a lengthy occupation?

The night had been a long one and Bruso had begun to reflect on the speed and precision with which this force had overwhelmed the island. The attack was too swift and devastating to have been carried out without a tremendous amount of planning and preparation. Tadao and the members of his force were well informed. They knew precisely where to go and exactly who were the key people on Johnston Island. How had they been able to have trucks available and waiting on the pier to support the attack? How did they know so much about our communications equipment and security measures? If I find out who helped these animals do this to us, Bruso swore, I'll kill him or die trying.

"Citizens of Johnston Island, listen to me." Tadao's voice was soft and icy as it carried across the sea of sullen faces. "We are the warriors of the New Shield Society. Our cause is the spiritual salvation of Japan, and you are now our prisoners. You have no rights or privileges other than those I choose to grant you. Do as you are told, and only as you are told, and we will treat you humanely. Disobey my orders or the orders of my men, and you will be punished—severely. When you leave here, we will allow you a meal before you return to your holding area. Soon we will begin discussion with your government concerning the terms of your release. Should any of you have thoughts of resistance or escape, consider where you are. We are in total control of this island, and on my orders, explosive charges have been placed on the chemical weapons. Any attempt at escape or rescue and I will order the charges detonated.''

There was a collective gasp as a fresh wave of terror swept across the large room. Several began to weep softly. Each knew the quality of death that awaited them if there were a major chemical release.

''But you must remember,'' Tadao continued as the room fell quiet, ''that your fate rests with your own behavior, just as it does with the actions of your government.'' He paused, smiling cruelly at them. ''We Japanese know the value you Americans assign to life, even if we do not completely understand it. I am sure your government will bargain in good faith for your release. And now, since your island commander is no longer with us, perhaps you would like to hear a few words from your Mr. Bruso.''

Tadao had said nothing to Bruso about this, but he was not totally unprepared. The Japanese leader was a shrewd man, and Bruso knew that he and the others were on the podium for a reason. The mere act of his walking to the center of the stage and facing those seated with his hands bound had its effect. Bruso looked across the crowd of familiar faces.

''Frank, Rose, Donnie, Kathy, Tom,'' he began as his eyes swept across them. ''I can't tell you how embarrassed and sad I am to be standing before you like this. None of you deserves what has happened, but that doesn't change the fact that it has happened. I'm not going to tell you not to resist or to not try to escape, but as we've all seen, these men can kill without any reservation and often without purpose. So I believe that resistance is very dangerous and serves no purpose other than getting more of us killed.

''However, I will ask you to care for each other and keep faith with each other. We've always worked as a team here on the Rock, and we need to continue it. It will help us to get through this.'' Bruso paused, searching for something else to say, and Senator Blackman stood up. A guard started toward her, but Tadao froze him with a glance.

''My name is Senator Nancy Blackman from the State of Utah.'' Her voice was soft, but clear and steady. ''Until yesterday, I was a stranger to Johnston Island. Now I'm one of you. I cannot tell you what our government will or can do, but I can assure you they will not forget us and will do everything possible to gain our release. Now I'm going to ask each of you to take the hand of the person on either side of you—that's it, hold hands.'' The armed Japanese along each wall came alert and looked about, frowning furiously while Tadao remained impassive. A few of those on the end of the rows reached forward to touch those seated in front of them. ''That's it—good. Now let's pray quietly for each other and for a speedy end to this tragedy.'' Blackman took Bruso's hand and bowed her head. There was absolute silence. Bruso finally tore his eyes from the senator and lowered his head.

Bruso had not heard Tadao move, but suddenly he was standing at his elbow. ''Thank you, Senator,'' Bruso said. Heads raised and the spell was broken. ''That's all we can do, people, pray and look out for each other. God bless all of you.'' He turned and followed Blackman back to his chair. Alone, Tadao surveyed the crowd, arms folded across his chest.

''Very well. We have no objection to your prayers, but it is your actions that will dictate your treatment. And now you will be escorted to the dining facility for a meal. Other meals will follow unless your conduct is inappropriate. If you do not follow instructions, you will not be allowed to eat. Dismissed!''

The guards directed them from the auditorium in single file. On their way to the cafeteria, they were made to walk past the rows of corpses from the previous day's massacre. Inside, Bruso sat staring at the empty auditorium. Tadao told them that after the first group returned to the holding area, another group would be brought in for the briefing. Bruso reflected on what had just taken place. It somehow all seemed so unreal. It was as if he were being made to live through a bad dream. He found himself beginning to wonder if this wasn't just that, a horrible, painful dream— hoping he'd wake up to another routine day on Johnston Island. But it wasn't a dream. Like the others, he was becoming weary and his mind looked for an easy explanation, a safe way out. There just wasn't one. He also wondered if he could face yet another assembly of his fellow hostages, but he knew he had no choice.

While the next group of hostages filed into the auditorium on Johnston Island, it was 7:40 the next morning in the Mariana Islands. Colonel Anthony Fortino had just left his home in Oceanview and was on his way to Anderson Air Force Base. He drove the old Ford Fairlane faster than he should, but the road that snaked around the northern tip of Guam was deserted this time of morning. As he roared through Agafo Gumas, his pager went off. Without taking his eyes from the road, he fumbled for the microphone hooked to the radio under the dash. The mike eluded him, but he found a portion of the coiled black cord and finally wrestled it to his chin.

"Anderson Field, this is Fortino. My beeper just went off; what's the problem, over?"

There was no response so he repeated the call. What th' fuck, over, he thought. They know I'll be there in a few minutes. He stabbed the Ford with his right foot and it accelerated through eighty. Then the speaker under the dash crackled.

"Skipper, this is the squadron duty officer; you there, over."

Fortino recognized the voice. "I'm here, Frank. Christ, I'm only about five miles from the main gate. What's the problem, over?"

"You have code seven, Colonel, over."

"What the hell's goin' on, Frank? We haven't done one of those in over a year."

"Well, sir, we're going to do one today, over." The duty officer's voice was even. To say more would be a security violation, but Fortino could detect the stress in his voice.

"Understood, Frank. See you at the admin building. Fortino, out."

He eased off on the gas pedal, wanting a few minutes to think before he arrived at the base. A code seven was the clear transmission term for a launch with nuclear weapons. It wasn't a full-blown scramble, but the next thing to it. Code sevens were normally reserved for heightened conditions of readiness, like Defense Condition 2, when the United States wanted a portion of its bombers airborne in case of an enemy attack. There hadn't been a *real* DEFCON 2 since the Cuban Missile Crisis. It had been a frequent drill back in the Cold War days, when there had been a Strategic Air Command to counter the Soviet nuclear threat. But SAC had been closed down following the partition of the Soviet Union.

Colonel Anthony Fortino was the commanding officer of the 512th Heavy Bombardment Squadron, one of the last active B-52 squadrons. Their current model, the B-52H, had an updated electronic suite, but it was the same forty-year-old airframe. In the hands of an experienced crew using low-level tactics, it was still a very good strategic, deep-penetration platform. And they still trained for the strategic nuclear mission, but most of their training was devoted to medium-altitude strikes with conventional weapons to support the next major regional conflict. The 52s were old and slow, but they could still carry a lot of ordnance a long way, as they had on the ARCLIGHT strikes during the Vietnam War.

But what could possibly have happened, thought Fortino, to cause a nuclear launch? The sentry at the main gate knew the Fairlane. He stepped out to wave it through and almost got run over for his trouble.

The next gate, one that admitted personnel and vehicles to the squadron buildings and the hardstand where the B-52s were parked, was normally unmanned. This morning there was a helmeted air policeman with a flak-jacket and an M-16. He too knew the car and the colonel by sight, but he carefully inspected Fortino's ID before raising the metal pole gate to allow him through. Fortino raced over to the squadron administration building and screeched into his reserved parking slot. His squadron duty officer, Major Frank Leach, stood inside the door waiting for him.

"Okay Frank, what's the deal?" Fortino was intense and very animated. He looked like a big Danny DeVito with shorter, thicker hair.

"I don't know, skipper." He handed Fortino a red folder with Top Secret/CO's Eyes Only stamped across the front. "This came in about fifteen minutes ago." It was a FLASH message from their parent command, the 410th Heavy Bombardment Wing.

"And you didn't read it?" Fortino had left standing orders that the duty officer read *all* incoming correspondence. Fortino trusted his staff. They were to take action as required, then notify him.

"No, sir. Just as it was coming in, I got a call on the secure line from the wing operations officer. He said I was to proceed as if it were an actual code seven launch and under no circumstances was I to read the message."

"But you did take just a teensy-weensy peek at it, didn't you, Frank?" Fortino asked, ramming an unlit cigar into his mouth. He gave his command duty officer a coy look.

Leach blushed and swallowed. "Yes, sir, I did."

"And?"

"I read about half of it, sir. Then I got scared and quit."

Fortino eyed him closely; he was really scared.

"Squadron recalled?"

"Yes, sir. I notified everyone on the rotation and they're on their way in."

"Good. Sergeant!"

"Yes, sir."

"Get me and the major a cuppa coffee." Fortino turned abruptly and walked away, reading the message in the red folder as he did. Major Leach followed him into his office.

Thursday, 8 December, 1:30 A.M.
VINSON BATTLE GROUP, 150 MILES NORTHEAST OF JOHNSTON ATOLL

General Sheppard did not receive a copy of CINC-PAC's message to the 410th Heavy Bombardment Wing ordering one of their squadrons to prepare a bomb that would incinerate a thousand American citizens and a United States senator on Johnston Island. Instead, he received a message that Admiral Harrington would be flying to the *Tarawa* to brief him personally on the crisis. This had sent up red flags along the chain of command. Admiral Coyle, Commander of the Pacific Fleet; Vice Admiral Quinlan, Surface Force, Pacific; Vice Admiral Guibert, Commander Seventh Fleet; and Rear Admiral Lawler, Commander of the *Vinson* battle group all wanted to know why the CINC was flying to one of their ships to speak personally with an embarked staff. All had been notified as a matter of courtesy. Each admiral knew it had something to do with the Johnston Island affair, but they were in the chain of command and wanted to know what was happening. General Sheppard, who reported directly to Admiral Harrington, could give a rat's ass about what every other admiral in the U.S. fucking Navy thought.

Late that morning, he had met with Colonel Lister, the landing force commander and commander of the Marine Expeditionary Unit aboard *Tarawa*. Sheppard liked Marines and, more important, he respected them. He knew that Marines were truly a breed apart. Every man and woman in the Marine Corps was a rifleman, not a rifle-person, and all other duties were secondary. A typical Marine platoon was composed of a dedicated-but-green second lieutenant, a dedicated-and-competent noncommissioned officer, and a group of underachievers who had been thoroughly brainwashed to perform a particular set of tasks, precisely and without question. The result was a superb conventional fighting unit. Earlier in his career, Sheppard had often heard about the Marine brotherhood and dismissed it. By the time he'd put on his general's star, he'd been around long enough to know there was something to it. A significant number of congressmen and senators felt the same way, and the Marines had not had to endure the budget cuts and force reductions of the Army, Navy, and Air Force.

Lister was lean and taciturn, short on sophistication and long on common sense. On balance, Sheppard felt he could trust him to do what he said he could do and not overstate the capabilities of his Marine Expeditionary Unit. That was important.

Sheppard did not yet know the role Lister's Marines would play. He needed a troop commander who could accurately assess the prospects for success in various scenarios. Lister himself was clearly not happy about the idea of sending his Marines into a chemical environment, but he candidly presented the MEUs limited ability to deal with chemicals. On the positive side, many of his NCOs were Gulf War veterans. Sheppard was relieved to learn that a good portion of the eight-hundred-man MEU had been extensively trained in peace-keeping operations, which meant they were drilled in urban fighting and small unit tactics with civilians present. This could be important if they found themselves having to fight from building to building to flush the defenders from Johnston Island. But it had been a long time since United States Marines had had to dig out Japanese defenders from a Pacific island.

Lister had brought a Navy lieutenant to the meeting, the officer in charge of the SEAL detachment aboard the *La Jolla*. The lieutenant surprised Sheppard by pulling out a chart of Johnston Island and outlining a plan for his minisubmarines to sortie from the *La Jolla* and penetrate Johnston Island harbor or approach the shoreline undetected. He thought it would be feasible to get a few men across the beach and into a position to observe parts of the island. The three of them had then studied the reconnaissance-photo mosaics.

The SEAL officer felt it would be possible to get a small squad close to the chemical-storage area and destruction facility undetected. He was casual and a bit too cocky for Sheppard's taste, but he was sharp enough to request a night photographic mission to establish the night-lighting pattern on the island. When word came down that Admiral Harrington was on his way, he handed Lister and the lieutenant off to his staff.

Sheppard was waiting by the *Tarawa*'s island when the SH-3G touched down on the carrier's flight deck. A loudspeaker bellowed over the helo's turbine whine to sound eight gongs followed by "Commander-in-Chief, Pacific, arriving." Sheppard greeted him, along with the commanding officer of the *Tarawa*, and led them inside. The CO invited the CINC to the wardroom for coffee, but he declined.

"Thank you, Captain, but I need to speak with General Sheppard immediately."

Sheppard led them up four flights of steep metal stairs to his quarters. Admiral Harrington was accompanied by his staff N3 and Rear Admiral John Lawler, the battle-group commander. Since Sheppard was junior to the three Navy admirals, he poured the coffee.

"Thanks, Jack. I'm sorry to bust in on you like this. Normally my place is back at Camp Smith, and I don't like to interfere with my operational components. But we have some new information on Johnston Island and it's not pretty. Therefore, I wanted to brief you personally. I've asked Admiral Lawler here to join us since he'll also be involved." Harrington paused, looking from Sheppard to Lawler and back. "General, if we're forced to mount an operation against Johnston Island, you'll be my on-scene commander. Admiral Lawler and the *Vinson* battle group are now assigned to you as a supporting element. You'll have the entire resources of the Pacific Command at your disposal, and anything else you may need.''

Sheppard exchanged a quick glance with Lawler, which told him the battle-group commander did not like the arrangement. It was unusual for a task-group commander to be subordinated to the embarked element commander, but that was what Harrington had just done. He didn't really expect Lawler to like it; Lawler had two stars and he had only one. But the CINC made the rules in his theater, and Lawler was unlikely to question the arrangement, at least not openly. Admiral Kiner sat poker-faced at Harrington's elbow and said nothing.

''Now let's talk about Johnston Island. I'm afraid the fate of the American hostages there may become a secondary consideration. I'm going to ask the N3 to give you the details. Bob?''

''Okay, gentlemen,'' Kiner began, taking a red folder from his briefcase, ''this is how it stands.''

For fifteen minutes, he reviewed the recent developments on Johnston Island, the demands of the terrorists, and the deadly realities of the enhanced VX chemical munitions that were wired with explosives. He handed Sheppard a profile of Tadao. The document had been assembled by the FBI's Behavioral Science Unit and was not three hours old. Kiner also had recent weather maps that showed a tropical depression just east of the Marshall Islands and moving steadily for Johnston Island. Finally, he told them of the risk to Hawaii if the VX agents were set loose in the path of the storm.

Both Sheppard and Lawler sat stunned. ''You mean the entire population of Hawaii is at risk?'' Sheppard managed.

''That's correct,'' Kiner replied, ''and possibly portions of the West Coast as well.''

''So as you can now see,'' Harrington intervened, ''your number-one priority is to prevent those charges from being exploded. If there's some way to render the explosives safe or to overwhelm the terrorists before they can set them off, I need to know that and soon.'' The senior admiral rubbed his hands together slowly and looked at Sheppard. "Jack, you'll also have to level with me about what our chances are. If there's no feasible way to do this, I'll need to know that too."

"So if I send a team to Johnston Island to disarm the explosives near those chemicals and they fail," Sheppard said quietly, "there's a good chance they'll not come out alive."

"Better than a good chance, Jack. If those agents are released, I believe the president will immediately authorize dropping an atomic bomb on the atoll. That's what his senior science advisers are telling him to do."

Sheppard and Lawler exchanged an apprehensive look. Harrington continued. "A B-52 squadron on Guam has been placed on alert. Within a few hours they'll have an aircraft on station with a nuclear weapon on board, a pretty fair-sized one from what I'm told. I'm sorry to have to bring you this news, gentlemen, but that's what's on the table. Naturally there's going to be some pretty serious talking between our government, the Japanese, and this Tadao guy on Johnston Island. As you'll see when you study the man's profile, he's not one to compromise or back down. But for now, that doesn't concern us. Jack, I want options ranging from special operations to a full-scale amphibious assault. I'll want your best recommendation as well. And God help us if we're directed to exercise one of those options. I understand it takes time to pull this together, but I'll need something from you by 0800 tomorrow morning, Honolulu time."

Harrington reached over and decanted himself more coffee. "I'm afraid that's all I have for now. Any questions?"

"Yes, sir," replied Lawler. "You said it was a big bomb. I'd like to get a burst radius on that weapon. I have eight thousand men and women embarked in my task force, and I'd like to keep them out of range if possible."

"Good question." Harrington looked to his N3, and Kiner referred to his notes. "If you stay fifty miles away from the atoll," Kiner replied, "preferably to the south, you'll be safe. You could probably close to within thirty miles before running into a problem. You'll have some base surge to deal with, but very little radioactivity. It's supposed to be a big bomb, but a clean one. We're having an expert flown out from Lawrence Livermore plus some radiological contamination teams. They'll be aboard *Vinson* by tomorrow morning. Not that it's relevant now, but we dropped two nuclear weapons on Johnston Atoll in the early fifties.''

"Very well," Lawler nodded. "Can I brief my ship and air-group commanding officers? Personally, I think they need to know."

"Permission granted," said Harrington, "but keep the ships in your task group under strict electronic and communications security. All of this information, particularly the nuclear option, is absolutely top secret."

"Aye aye, sir." Lawler looked at Sheppard. "General, we'll do everything we can to support this mission. I only ask that you don't endanger my sailors any more than necessary."

Sheppard studied Lawler, trying to decide if the battle-group commander was honestly pledging his support or just covering his butt in front of the CINC in case things got nasty. He concluded it was the latter and turned back to Harrington. "By 0800 tomorrow, Admiral?"

"Zero eight hundred, Jack. And there's one other thing." Harrington pursed his lips, seeking the right words. "It seems there's this crack Japanese counter-terrorist outfit called the Naginata Counter Force. The intel types say these boys are the best there are. A small group of them is being sent here and placed under your command. I've been asked by the Chairman of the Joint Chiefs—actually, directed is a better word—to include them in any direct action taken against Johnston Atoll."

"A small group, sir?"

"Seven of them," Kiner offered quietly.

Sheppard could not hide his disbelief. "Begging the admiral's pardon, sir, but you're not telling me that if I have to assault that atoll, I have to include some Japanese outfit?'' He knew he was out of line, but the enormity of the task before him was starting to overwhelm him. He was about to continue, but the CINC raised his hand.

"Jack, this team of Japanese specialists is already on their way. They'll be here sometime around midnight, maybe earlier. My orders are very specific; you are to include them in any action taken against Johnston Island. Now, I'm sure you can appreciate that bringing them into this was not a military decision.'' This was as far as he wanted to go in saying that the politicians were interfering where they shouldn't. "These Japanese may or may not be of any practical use to you, but there are *my* instructions. I want you to include this Japanese team in your operational planning. But, if you feel they will in any way compromise your ability to get the job done, you have my authorization to exclude them from an actual mission. Is that satisfactory, General?''

Sheppard glanced quickly away from Harrington's determined features and caught the surprised look on Kiner's face. He knew Harrington was disobeying a direct order, and he loved him for it. The admiral was placing the final decision with his operational commander and his military career alongside it.

"Sir, it's ah, well, more than satisfactory. I appreciate your . . .''

Harrington again raised his hand. "These are dangerous waters, Jack. We have those poor souls on Johnston Island to consider as well as the lives of the men we may have to send in there. I have to do my job so you can do yours; it's what we're paid for. It's your show, Jack. Get those options and probabilities to my staff by tomorrow morning. I'm told the *Tarawa* has a direct secure voice link to Camp Smith, so I'll want to hear from you personally as well. Admiral Kiner will see you get anything else you need.''

Sheppard took a deep breath. "Understood, sir.''

Harrington rose. "I have to get back to Hawaii. General McKenzie wasn't too keen on me coming out here, but I told him it was necessary. Good luck, Jack. I'm counting on you."

Sheppard stood and took the admiral's hand. "Thank you, sir. I'll do my best."

"Don't bother showing us to the flight deck. I'm sure you have work to do." Kiner and Lawler rose to follow the CINC out.

"Admiral Lawler, I'd like you to stay behind for a short while, if you could," Sheppard said. "I'll have one of the *Tarawa*'s birds run you back to the *Vinson*."

Lawler made the mistake of looking to Harrington, just for an instant. The CINC gave him a cold look as he paused at the door, then led Kiner from the room. Lawler started to speak but Sheppard silenced him, motioning the Navy man back to his chair. Then he poured the admiral another cup of coffee and waited. A few minutes later the 1-MC announced, "Commander-in-Chief, Pacific, departing."

"Now Admiral, you and I are going to quickly come to an understanding, because neither of us has time for any bullshit. First of all, I'll do everything in my power to keep your ships out of harm's way. That's a promise. But I'll not be second-guessed on how to carry out my mission. You are my principal supporting element. You'll be consulted; your opinion will be solicited. As the afloat group commander, you're invited to call matters to my attention that will contribute to the success of the mission. If ships and personnel are needlessly being put at risk, tell me about it. But on all matters concerning this operation, including the support from your battle group, my judgment is final. You report directly to me and no one else. I don't give a shit if you go over my head later on, but you come to me first, is that clear?"

"That's very clear, General."

"Excellent. Now if you don't think you can live with this arrangement, and I mean right from this moment until we're done with this mess, then now's the time to speak up. I'll call the CINC back and he can decide whether you get a new operational commander or I get a new battle-group commander. What'll it be?"

Lawler was silent for a long moment. This arrangement was clearly *not* to his liking; it effectively put this snake-eater in command of his battle group. But, Sheppard was also clearly the CINC's boy and Lawler knew Harrington would back him all the way.

"Okay, General; you're the boss."

"Fair enough." Sheppard held out his hand. Lawler hesitated for a second, then took it.

Fifteen minutes after Harrington's departure, Colonel Lister and Lieutenant Moody joined General Sheppard and Admiral Lawler around the table. They surrounded an enlarged and annotated photographic overlay of Johnston Island. Lister and Moody briefed the two senior officers on their plan. It called for special-operation probes on the chemical-storage area and at the chemical-destruction facility, quickly followed by an assault by the Marines. The *Vinson*'s air group would provide tactical air support with AC-130 gunships held in reserve. The general concept appeared workable, but the countless details vital to a coordinated attack had yet to be worked out.

"Gentlemen," Sheppard began, "that looks like a fine plan based on the available information. There's been some new developments." He told them of the new VX agents and the threat to Hawaii. When he had finished with the part about the B-52s and the nuclear weapon, the room became silent. General Sheppard allowed the Marine colonel and the SEAL a moment to digest the news, and continued. "So, it's imperative that we defeat the explosives on the chemical weapons, and based on recent intelligence, we can concentrate on the storage facility. It appears the chemical-destruction operation has been shut down. Now, unless someone can convince me otherwise, I see no advantage in committing the Marines, or any other large force, until the chemicals are neutralized. That means your sole objective is the chemical-storage area, specifically those bunkers where this VX is stored."

After a long silence, Colonel Lister spoke. "I agree with you, sir. We'll be prepared for an amphibious assault or a vertical assault, but really it all comes down to keeping those chemicals in their containers." Suddenly they were all looking at Moody.

"You still think you can get in close to shore and get some people across the beach, Lieutenant?" Moody's eyes were riveted on Johnston Island. He heard the question and he desperately tried to concentrate on it, but his mind was racing ahead. For the last twenty-four hours he'd tried not to think about possible exposure to chemicals. He'd fought off the terror of it, thinking that they'd carry gas masks or find an observation post that was upwind from the storage area. He'd convinced himself that they could plan around the chemicals, maybe even use their diving rigs to avoid having to breathe the air. Now he found himself wondering what it would feel like to be vaporized in a split second. Or was there any feeling to it?

"Lieutenant Moody?"

He tried to sound normal, but his mouth was dry. "Yes, sir, I believe we can get a team across the beach. Getting into that storage facility and defeating the explosives is another matter. I guess it could be done, if we're lucky and the firing devices aren't too sophisticated. We'll need some technical help. Let me get together with my petty officers and see what we can come up with." Moody shook his head and forced a smile. "Whoever goes in after those charges is going to be one motivated dude." It was an awkward attempt at humor and it came off badly.

"Is that going to be you, Lieutenant?"

Moody shrugged. "Yes, sir, I guess so, unless I can think of a better way. God knows I'm open to suggestions. Is there any hope for negotiations with these guys?" He spoke slowly, as if he had cotton in his mouth.

"Very little, I'm afraid," Sheppard replied. He handed Moody the FBI report on Tadao. "Unless they can somehow be tricked into believing their demands will be met, the experts believe they'll carry through with their threat.

And speaking of Japanese, there's one other piece of news. There's a hotshot Japanese counter-terrorist squad being flown in late this evening. I want you to meet them and see if they can be of assistance. You're welcome to accept or reject any help they may be able to give you.''

Moody just nodded. He was already on overload and this was just another bizarre piece of the puzzle. You want me to talk to some friendly Japs about the terrorist Japs? he thought. Sure, why not? ''What's my time line on a mission concept?'' he managed. The mission concept was an outline of the attack plan.

''I'll want to see something by 0700 tomorrow.''

''Aye aye, sir. If there's nothing else, I'd like to find my chief and get busy on this.'' Moody's color was none too good and he seemed anxious to leave.

''Very well, Lieutenant. I want you to work closely with my staff operations people. If there's anything you need, it'll be airlifted by priority aircraft. Keep me posted.''

''Sir, you can count on that.'' Moody again shrugged and got to his feet. ''Excuse me, gentlemen,'' and he was out the door.

The remaining three officers looked at each other. Colonel Lister spoke first. ''General, it's obvious that getting to those explosives is the whole ball game. Then we can deal with the terrorists and hostages. Moody seems like a good man, but are you sure he's the right man for this job? With respect, sir, I understand these SDV platoons are trained for harbor penetration and to deliver other SEALs to go ashore to carry out the mission. Isn't this a job for a special antiterrorist team like the Delta Force—or at least a SEAL direct-action platoon? And,'' he added quietly, ''if you don't mind my saying, the lieutenant looked a little shaky.''

Sheppard tugged at his ear thoughtfully. ''No, I don't mind, and furthermore, I agree with you; he looked damn scared. Normally, I'd be inclined to call in the JSOC people and go with a group like Delta Force, but they're not fully trained in submarine operations and we don't have time to bring them up to speed. And our Mr. Moody's not all he seems. Here, read this.'' Sheppard pushed a folder between Lister and Lawler. The Marine opened it for both men to read. It was a personal message from General Thon, Commander of the U.S. Special Operations Command in Tampa, addressed to Sheppard.

The text outlined a super-secret mission into northern Russia more than a year ago led by a Lieutenant John Moody. They were compromised and had to fight their way out against heavy odds. Moody was wounded in the process, but managed to get out with all his men and accomplish an important and dangerous mission in the process. The message closed with a comment by Thon: ''My recommendation for the Medal of Honor was downgraded to a Navy Cross for security reasons since hostilities do not officially exist between the U.S. and Russia, but the man rated it!''

''That's incredible,'' said Admiral Lawler. ''What the hell were we doing with a special-operations team in Russia?''

''Seems it had something to do with a serious incident of nuclear proliferation. The administration, at least the last one, was determined to oppose the spread of nuclear weapons, even if it meant sending people into Russia.''

''Incredible,'' Lawler said again, ''but the colonel has a point. He did look a little shaky.''

Sheppard saw a hint of a smile on Lister's stern features. ''Colonel?''

''I withdraw my reservations. The kid's scared because he's been there. In the Corps, we'd say he's gone eyeball-to-eyeball with the Big Bulldog in the sky. I'll keep watch on him, but I think he'll be okay. Given the capability of the surface search radars on Johnston Island, an underwater approach is probably the best way to do the job. It'll be a complex operation, but I'm not sure we have any other options. We have to go with Moody.''

The three men sat in silence until Sheppard rose, signaling an end to the meeting. "Gents, I think we all have work to do."

Moody moved quietly through the ship until he came to a hatch that led from the *Tarawa*'s island superstructure to the flight deck. Passageways that led to exterior hatches were bathed in red light to allow those preparing to leave the interior a chance for their eyes to become accustomed to the darkness.

Moody pushed past the blackout curtain and slipped through the metal door into the night. He walked along the island toward the bow, instinctively wanting to avoid the open expanse of the broad flight deck. The sun had dipped below the horizon less than an hour ago, and a strong quarter moon had taken charge of the sky, cutting a rumpled, silvery path from the horizon to the *Tarawa*. It reminded Moody of an episode from *Victory at Sea*.

The battle group was steaming south at a leisurely twelve knots. He crossed the flight deck and eased past a line of bulky CH-53D Sea Stallion transport helicopters squatting along the port side of the flight deck, nose to tail with rotors folded, looking like giant sleeping cicadas. Several smaller helicopters and two AV-8B Harriers were spotted aft of the island on the starboard side.

He moved forward cautiously, allowing his senses to merge with the sea and the salt air. The gentle motion of the ship was more noticeable on the bow, but the forward edge of the flight deck was quiet and peaceful. Machinery noise and the persistent hum of the ship's air conditioning were all well aft. Gliding seventy feet over the water on the bow of a helicopter carrier at night was a little like being the hood ornament of an old Chrysler on a moonlight drive in the desert.

Off to starboard, a small group of sailors smoked and talked quietly. Occasionally the *Tarawa* would bite deeply into the Pacific and there was a soft crushing sound as the ship's stem parted a swell. The trade winds were still blowing gently out of the east, so the wind over the deck came at him from eleven o'clock. Only a few stars challenged the moon in the east, but the western sky was magnificent. And for a few moments, Moody allowed the splendor of what was before and above him to overshadow his fears. Just a few minutes earlier, the terror of what he might have to do had caused him to all but run in panic from General Sheppard's cabin.

The fear had begun aboard the *La Jolla*, even before Commander Robbie Kemp had told him of the capture of Johnston Island. He'd sensed something was wrong when Chief Stockton had signaled the cancellation of the platoon's SDV training. After the chief said Kemp wanted to see him, he'd started to become apprehensive. Then when Kemp had given him the details of the capture of the island, he'd somehow *known* that the platoon would be committed; he'd just known it was going to be for real.

"It just doesn't make any fucking sense," he told the oncoming wind.

There were only about eleven hundred active, operational Navy SEALs. Their training was long and dangerous, and they were deployed with fleet units and advanced bases around the world. Nonetheless, the probability of a SEAL being involved in a direct-action mission was low. Even during the Gulf War, with seven platoons in the theater, very few SEALs had seen meaningful action. As one weary chief petty officer put it, "Never have so many trained so long and hard for so little." Moody was now looking at what could be another difficult mission. If the odds of a real, direct-action mission in a SEAL's career were small, Moody asked himself, what were they for two such missions? And why me?

He tried to think ahead. They were all professionals and the mission to Johnston Island would hold no illusions for any of them, least of all Moody. Their enemy was a suicidal fanatic who, in all probability, would be expecting them. If they failed to disarm the explosives, their reward would be an excruciating death from chemicals, or their bodies would be instantly fused with the sand and coral of Johnston Island to form glass, a hard silicone compound marred only by the carbon impurities of their flesh. Since Moody was a veteran, he knew all too well what it was like to be scared and to worry for the lives of his men. Combat experience is a valuable thing, but it also robs a young warrior of his fantasies about the romance of combat, and along with it, much of his enthusiasm. Moody found he had to remind himself that this was real, not just some elaborate dream.

He had come directly onto the flight deck from the general's quarters so he could be alone with his fear and, if possible, come to terms with it. Once they were into the planning phase and mission preparation, there would be no time for it. The men would watch him carefully, and they had to see confidence and purpose—not fear. Moody often wondered whether he would do things differently if the men weren't there watching him. He gave the orders and they followed them, but they also expected him to be courageous. He could hide the fear, but that didn't make it go away.

The heavens and the vastness of the ocean made him feel appropriately insignificant, but his fear of death felt no smaller. Christ, he thought, a week ago I was in paradise. The drinks had fruit in them and the women were abundant and easy. What happened?

"Hey, sir, that you?"

"Oh, hello, Senior Chief. Yeah, it's me."

"What're you gonna do, sir, make a leap for it?"

"I was thinking about it, Senior, but then you'd be stuck with all the paperwork. Just to show you the kind of guy I am, I'll wait till I'm on liberty back at Pearl and drink myself to death."

"That's thoughtful of you, sir. The mission's a go, isn't it?"

"Looks like it. There's a lot that could happen to keep us out of it, but I wouldn't bet on it."

Moody told Stockton about the chemicals and the bomb, and about what would happen if they didn't succeed.

The chief gave a low whistle. "Who's going in?"

"Walker and Berta will drive, and I'll lead the attack element. I'll want you on the boat to manage the launch and recovery operations." Stockton started to protest, but Moody silenced him. "No arguments on that one, Senior. We'll need a clean launch, and I want you running the shelter in case there's an abort and we have to get back aboard quickly."

They were both quiet for a moment, then Stockton spoke. "The platoon's still pretty green, sir."

"Yeah, I know, but Walker and Berta know what they're doing, and a few of the other guys have been around for a while. The backseaters don't count for much until we get there and cross the beach. And I got an idea or two how we might pull this off."

"When's the mission concept due?"

"The general wants it by 0700 tomorrow."

Stockton again whistled. "We better get hot, sir. That's not a lot of time."

They walked together back across the flight deck to the island. Two miles off the port quarter, the *Vinson* heeled to port, turning into the wind and coming up to thirty knots to launch aircraft.

While Moody patrolled the flight deck of the *Tarawa*, Captain Nakajima stood on the tarmac at the Wake Island airport, seventeen hundred miles almost due west of the *Vinson* battle group. The sun had just slipped below the horizon, and the hardstand still radiated the day's heat. Wake, once an important defense facility and refueling stop, was now little more than a weather station and wildlife refuge. The airport served as a military practice field and emergency strip. Nakajima looked out to the north across the lagoon of the horseshoe-shaped island.

He had a keen sense of history, and he knew that Wake Island had been pounded by Japanese carrier aircraft in 1941 in preparation for what the Imperial Navy felt would be an easy victory. The 450 Marines on Wake had felt differently. They'd fought valiantly against overwhelming odds, a harbinger of the fierce island fighting to come in the Pacific. Following Wake's capture, land-based aircraft from this very airfield had provided cover for the Imperial Fleet on its retreat from the disastrous battle at Midway. That great sea battle had cost Japan four of its large aircraft carriers and the core of her experienced carrier pilots. After Midway, Japan had never again mounted a serious offensive effort against the United States.

Nakajima, along with his six men and their equipment, had comprised the aircraft's sole cargo. The C-141 Starlifter could easily have taken them nonstop from Okinawa to Hawaii, but both Washington and Tokyo wanted the small Japanese contingent moved in strict secrecy. With the exception of a UN Japanese peacekeeping contingent that had been sent to Cambodia in 1992, this was the first time the Japanese government had deployed an armed force away from the home islands since World War II.

The crew of the Starlifter had been courteous and professional, but Nakajima had noticed something different in their manner. Conversation among the Americans stopped when he approached, and there were the semi-furtive, sidelong glances. During his limited contacts with American servicemen on Okinawa, he had found their manners curious, but they had generally been outgoing and good-natured. The crew of the C-141 were none of these things. After the plane landed, he sought out the aircraft commander to thank him. The American Air Force major barely acknowledged him and only reluctantly returned his salute. The ground facility personnel at Wake were equally cool. Now they stood waiting outside the small terminal, wondering what it would be like aboard a ship in the American fleet.

Shortly after the Starlifter left Wake for Hickam Field in Hawaii, a pair of small twin-engine jet aircraft appeared on the horizon. They buzzed the field once in formation before peeling from the landing pattern and settling neatly onto the runway. While the aircraft were taking on fuel, one of the pilots came over to meet them. Unlike the trim Air

Force crew in their well-fitted blue coveralls, the Navy pilot wore a sweat-stained gray flight suit, and his hair was matted from several hours in a flight helmet.

"Howdy, I'm Lieutenant Greg Johnson. You th' guys I'm s'posed to take back out to th' *Vinson*?"

Nakajima concentrated on his words. Those from the south of the United States were sometimes difficult to understand. "We are here to join the American forces near Johnston Atoll," he replied formally. "I am Captain Nakajima of the Japanese Self Defense Force."

"Uh-huh. You got orders, pal, and maybe some kinda identification? Seems there's been a rash of Japs in the area pretendin' they're somethin' they ain't."

Nakajima took a leather case from his jacket and produced a set of orders. He retrieved his ID from his shirt pocket and handed it to the pilot.

"Reckon that means you're one of th' good guys instead of one of th' bad ones on Johnston Island, huh?"

Americans continually amazed Nakajima. The man had repeatedly insulted him, yet he knew the smile on the pilot's face was genuine, and that the man clearly meant him no ill will. "We've come to help defeat those on Johnston Island if that is your meaning."

"Close enough, Captain," the pilot replied. "Do your men understand English?"

"Some more than others. Perhaps it will be better if you speak to me and I will speak to them."

"Okay. My instructions are to get you to th' *Vinson* as quickly as possible so we'll take off as soon as we've refueled. The S-3 Viking is an antisubmarine aircraft. She wasn't designed for passengers, but she's got the range and the speed to get us back to the battle group in a hurry. We'll split your gear an' your men between th' two aircraft. It won't be a comfortable trip, but we'll have you aboard the *Vinson* in about three hours."

Twenty minutes later, Nakajima was strapped into a makeshift canvas seat with his legs on top of an equipment bag. The interior of the Viking was small, noisy, and crammed with electronics equipment. He scanned the faces of the two men sitting across from him. They appeared impassive, but he knew these men well. Fear was difficult for them, but he could see they were apprehensive. So was he.

Dangerous assignments were nothing new to Nakajima and his men, but they had always operated in the Japanese home islands within a friendly environment and a familiar command structure. Support requirements had always been provided with respect and courtesy. More important, he had always been in control of the tactical situation; the men under him and assigned supporting elements had been under his command. In matters of operational planning and tactical execution, his judgment had been final. So, he told himself, I am no longer in control of events.

But it was more than that. The Viking climbed through ten thousand feet and the small cabin became cool. A chill passed through him, and he knew it wasn't entirely from the cold air. For all his martial training and self-discipline, Nakajima felt detached and isolated. Even the presence of his men could not keep him from feeling alone. The inner peace and tranquillity, so much a part of his being, had suddenly deserted him.

Why do I feel so lost? he asked himself. It certainly is not the prospect of death. Has not my whole life been a preparation for that very moment? He sensed the next few hours in this cold, crowded metal cocoon could be his last opportunity to resolve these feelings and regain the internal accord that nurtured his spirit. Oblivious to where he was and to those around him, he sat forward and bowed his head. He clapped his hands twice to begin to pray.

His gods did not desert him; they immediately united with his being, which momentarily became infinite. The spirits of the different godly functions reminded him that he was, above all things, Japanese, and that this did not change because he was far from Japan and among strangers. The *kami* that were a part of the sky and air and earth of his sacred land were never far away, no matter where he was. More than that, they were a part of him. And there were the voices of his ancestors, the warriors of ancient Japan. They too would help show him the way. He could trust in his training and physical strength, but he must also have faith in who he was. You are Japanese, said voices from antiquity.

The spirits of samurai who had fought and died centuries earlier closed ranks around his soul. If your thoughts and actions honor us, they told him, you may draw from our strength and we will not abandon you.

He ended his prayer, greatly relieved and now more in harmony with himself. Nakajima allowed no outward show of his feelings, but the two soldiers across from him sensed a change in their captain. He seemed more relaxed, yet determined and sure of himself. This aura of confidence had a soothing effect on them. Soon both were dozing in their cramped seats.

Nakajima quietly analyzed his feelings. Japan, and the formal structure of Japanese society, made it easy to be Japanese. This became more difficult away from the home islands, but not impossible. While Japan was changing, and not necessarily for the better, it was still very different from the rest of the world. Financial interests now controlled Japan, but even this modern, commercial society still honored a warrior. If a man was samurai in spirit, even a corporate samurai, there was respect.

After all, was it not this new breed of financial warrior who had returned Japan to world stature? America had required two centuries to emerge as a world economic power. Japan, a smaller, defeated nation with few natural resources, had done it in two decades. Certainly such achievement deserved respect.

Then, he mused, there were the Americans; they seemed to have no concept of respect. They often lacked dignity, even among themselves. Their manners were coarse and abrasive. Nakajima sometimes wondered how a nation so unsure of itself and so impure could remain a world power. Perhaps it was because they were an immigrant nation with a short history and few traditions, and this made them so adept at change. Or, Nakajima concluded, perhaps it was simply because their land was not the home of the Sun Goddess and their leaders not descendants of the gods. They were masters in the adaptation of technology for military use, and their actions were unpredictable—often irrational. But this giant, stumbling child, however crude and abrasive, had been rudely awakened just before mid-century and had defeated Japan, something no nation had ever done. Could this business at Johnston Island have the same effect—and the same result?

Nakajima had carefully studied America and its armed forces. Their military had taken the best from the European model and had been one of the first to develop an officer corps based on ability. But the Americans seemed to be leaderless in the wake of the Soviet collapse, and preoccupied with social issues. Their army, even the elite forces, seemed to have lost its focus. Now Nakajima and his men would have to serve with that army and take their instructions from the Americans.

Then he thought of Takashi Tadao and of the near-impossible mission before them. If the choice between life and death is fifty-fifty, he recited reverently, immediately choose death. Nakajima smiled. In the way of military technology, we can learn much from the Americans, but if our mission is one of certain death, then the Americans can learn a great deal from us.

Nakajima made himself as comfortable as he could and closed his eyes. How ironic, he thought, that my own death could come at the hands of a samurai while fighting on the side of the *gai-jin*. The notion brought another smile, a sad one, and he fell asleep.

Flag plot was short for flag officer's plotting room, a surviving convention from the days when admirals followed the movements of their fleets and ships in battle with models on large plotting tables. The modern version of the flag plot aboard *Tarawa* was a large space on the 0-3 level just below General Sheppard's quarters.

This facility was a scaled-down version of the crisis-management centers found at Camp Smith and other theater command headquarters. The room was crowded with communications consoles, status boards, and TV monitors—it had the look of a video arcade with bad lighting. From here, the general's special-operations staff would maintain a twenty-four-hour, three-section battle watch until the crisis was resolved. Political decisions and the fighting, if it came to that, would happen elsewhere, but Sheppard would manage the crisis from the flag plot on *Tarawa*. His staff had trained for this for years, but in support of a general war scenario rather than as a primary player. At one end of the room, a padded captain's chair perched on a raised platform to allow the operational commander a clear view of his command center. A bank of colored telephone handsets that hung vertically from a communications panel near the chair's armrest was patched to the *Tarawa*'s communication center. Two were dedicated to CINCPAC, one of them to the crisis-action team leader at Camp Smith and the other directly to Admiral Harrington. A third handset was a dedicated line to Admiral Lawler on the *Vinson*. Two others were available for duty as needed. Real-time, secure satellite communications could link the commander to a squad of men in the field or to the president.

Moody sat at a chart table in the corner of flag plot across from Senior Chief Will Stockton. Walker sat next to the chief. The watch section went about their normal duties, but they were careful not to disturb the SEALs. Many of the watchstanders were veteran special-operations officers and senior enlisted men, several of whom had combat experience.

None of that mattered, for they were now staff officers, and the staffies, by convention, deferred to the operators. Most SEAL officers tried to avoid staff tours that took them away from the operational teams. Right now, a cushy staff job didn't look all that bad to Moody.

"So what do you think about the approach, Don?"

"The first part's doable. These currents can be tricky, but I should be able to find the entrance to the channel. If we run at about twenty-five feet, there should be no problem coming in by the channel. The trick will be leaving the channel and making our way across the shallows to the rally point near the storage facility."

A large-scale chart of Johnston Atoll covered the table. The blue portions around the islands were sprinkled with fathom markings. "If that storm blows in as expected, it'll make things a little rough in shallow water."

"But you can do it?"

"Yessir, I can do it. And if you can get th' sub in close, it'll help a whole bunch. It'll be a tough navigation problem if we launch the SDVs way offshore. Then we may have to chance comin' to th' surface in rough water to get a visual fix and we could risk broaching."

Moody nodded and turned to Stockton. "What you got, Senior Chief?"

Stockton pulled a green wheel book from his blouse pocket. "All gear we requested by message from *La Jolla* has been assembled at North Island and will be airborne within the hour. By the time it gets to Hickam, remanifested to a COD flight for the *Vinson*, and brought here by helo, it'll probably be late tomorrow morning before we see it. The shooters are coming from the SEAL unit in Guam and the EOD guy from West Loch in Hawaii. Look for them sometime late morning also. We talked about a direct-action squad from one of the West Coast teams, but I'm not sure we have time to get them here and through the launch and lockout procedures in time. Same goes for the Delta guys. Besides, I think you're right: we have enough talent in the platoon to go ashore and do the job."

Moody nodded. "Anything more on our Japs?"

Stockton frowned. "The watch team leader says they'll be here sometime around 2400 tonight, maybe later. Hey, sir, it's your call, but don't let the brass force anybody on us. I don't care how good these guys are, they got no idea how we do business.''

"You're probably right, Senior." Moody tried to picture sneaking into the objective at night with some Japanese guys in the back of his SDV. He smiled and shook his head. "Let's not count them out just yet, and we still have to include them in the planning. Oh, and before I forget, get a message sent to the *La Jolla* that I want the platoon to begin sleeping days and awake at night in preparation for a night mission.''

Stockton nodded and made a notation in his book. "That shouldn't be a problem for us. Looks like we have an all-nighter ahead of us if we want that mission concept ready for the general.''

"You decided who's gonna suit up for this one, sir?" asked Walker. This question would also be gnawing at the SEALs on the *La Jolla.* Normally, to be excluded from an operation would be a bitter pill, but maybe not this time.

"Not yet, Don. When we figure out how we're going to get there and exactly what we're going to do when we arrive, then I'll make the assignments. For now I'll lead, and you and Berta will drive.''

Walker shrugged and rose. "Coffee, boss—Senior Chief?''

Both men pushed their cups across the table.

Friday, 9 December, 5:45 A.M.
THE WHITE HOUSE

Gates Carlton sat by the fireplace in the Green Room and studied his friend Robert Garrison. The room had been turned into a parlor by Dolly Madison and was elegantly adorned with emerald furnishings. The speed at which Garrison flipped through the pages was startling, and had Gates not known better, he would have thought he was only skimming them. Garrison finished without saying a word, laying the document on an ornate eighteenth-century side table by the wingback. He sipped carefully from his glass of juice and said nothing for two full minutes. His attire was typically crisp, but the eyes said that President Garrison was very tired.

"Gates, do you really think there's something to this?"

Carlton had known this question was coming and measured his response. "Yes, I do." He had asked to see the president alone with the reports so they could discuss them in private. The president had a standing order that all conversation in the Oval Office would be tape-recorded. A private, unrecorded conversation meant a conversation in the Green Room.

"The Asian Studies Group," Carlton continued, "was a think tank commissioned by the last administration to study Asian societies. We've used their product over at State and so has Langley. They were able to link the culture of a nation to their political decision-making processes. In terms of the Japanese, they tried to predict how they make decisions and just how they will react to internal and external pressures."

"So they developed a decision-making model," Garrison said, referring to the document. Carlton nodded. "And were they successful?"

"For the most part. They predicted, for example, the Japanese government's response to that religious cult who let sarin gas loose in the subways. They seemed paralyzed. It took them weeks to get warrants and make arrests. This is a pattern in Japan when confronted with something new or unexpected."

"So what about Johnston Island?" Garrison asked.

"Except for their Ministry of Justice, which is providing information on the terrorists and this counter-terrorist team, they've done nothing. Our sources close to their government say there's a lot of talk and sucking air through teeth, but nothing of substance. The reality is that Tokyo has no effective governmental machinery to deal with this kind of thing. As you know, the Japanese government is a fragile coalition, and any strong stand against this terrorist group, or even a mild show of sympathy for them, would probably cause the government to fall. There'll be a lot of bowing and apologies, and they'll publicly label it 'an unfortunate situation,' but that's about it.''

''What else did this Asian Studies Group come up with that you feel could be significant?''

''Actually, the group no longer exists; their funding was cut about a year ago. It was a small working group headed by a Japanese-American by the name of Sam Sunaga. He's well thought of in academic circles and considered a leading Japanologist. I spoke with him briefly late last evening and he thinks this may just be the tip of the iceberg—that there is a sizable minority in Japan who will be sympathetic to Tadao's demands, if not the actual capture of Johnston Island.''

''You can't be serious?''

Carlton leaned forward. ''Sunaga explained that the Japanese people feel as much victims of the Second World War as aggressors. They see Japan's ascendancy in the twenties and thirties as the nation taking its rightful place as the leader of Asia. Then a small group of militarists took them to war against the United States. Once at war, the Japanese people had no choice but to fight to protect their land. They also feel that Hiroshima and Nagasaki more than compensated for the attack on Pearl Harbor.'' Carlton hesitated. ''It seems the Japanese people are very familiar with the suffering caused by the bombs dropped on Hiroshima and Nagasaki, but less clear on the origins of the war.''

''Meaning?''

''Meaning,'' Carlton continued, ''that many in Japan feel an apology by the president of the United States would not be out of line.''

''Out of line! Hell, I'd be impeached! And there're a lot of Americans out there who think the Japanese should apologize a little better for the war.''

Carlton raised his hands in a calming motion. ''I asked Sunaga about that. It seems the Japanese reluctance to apologize is related to their not wishing to offend their war dead.''

Garrison shook his head in frustration and took up his personal notepad. ''How about this other thing Tadao wants? Just what does he mean by the emperor must 'assume his traditional cultural and military role?' Does that mean he again becomes head of state?''

''In a way. In January 1946 Hirohito, probably at MacArthur's urging, declared himself a man, not a god. Tadao has asked the emperor to again become a god. Sounds silly to us, but many Japanese still feel the emperor is a god. Tadao wants him to acknowledge this publicly. As for the military role, if the military serve the emperor and not the bureaucracy, they become a national army, not an armed police force as they are now. This is critical if Japan is to ever again become a military power.''

''And the Japanese want this?''

Carlton shrugged. ''The Japanese people are by and large pacifists, but collectively they are a proud and wealthy nation. And the right is gaining strength.''

''So this Sunaga feels Tadao has the sympathy of the Japanese people?''

Again Carlton shrugged. ''That's what he said. This has to do with the lone-warrior or lone-samurai concept, a very powerful theme in Japanese history. It's a little like our cowboy of the old West or a serious version of Don Quixote. Seems the most honorable thing a samurai can do is place himself in an impossible situation, one where honor and loyalty are at stake and death is all but certain. This splendid and tragic death for a lost cause is quite revered by the Japanese.''

He leaned forward with his forearms on his knees. ''To die honorably in a hopeless situation is heroic beyond our comprehension. It's Nathan Hale and Davy Crockett and Joan of Arc and . . . Jesus Christ all rolled into a single noble, tragic figure. Tadao is that kind of hero. The Japanese government will publicly deplore Tadao's actions, but the Japanese people will secretly admire him. They'll admire him not for what he's done, but for why he's doing it. Does that make sense?''

Garrison raised his eyebrows in a neutral gesture. "So the Japanese right will gain power and get behind this Tadao?''

"According to Sunaga they'll treat him like a messiah. No one knows just how large and influential the right is. This kind of thing could bring them out of the closet. The Japanese media, unlike our own, practices a good deal of self-restraint. The papers will report it, but they won't sensationalize it. Our embassy in Tokyo has reported several demonstrations in support of Tadao, mostly from students. And three right-wingers have committed suicide as a show of support. Officially the Japanese will keep a lid on things, but I can tell you Mitsuzuka and his advisers are very scared.''

"Surely the Japanese wouldn't consider doing what this Tadao wants!''

"No guarantees," Carlton replied, "but the consensus of my experts at State is that Mitsuzuka will step back and allow us to deal with the situation. Langley concurs. They'll not come right out and refuse the demands, but they'll do nothing to comply. Basically they'll do what the Japanese do best—they'll wait.''

"What about the emperor?''

"No one knows. Probably what the government tells him to do, but no one really knows.''

The president nodded and was silent for several moments. "Okay, I'll buy it. Tokyo will smile and bow and do nothing. There'll be some agitators in the street, but nothing the Japanese riot police can't handle. Now, how do we think Tadao will handle the hostages?''

"Our satellite coverage and aerial reconnaissance are pretty comprehensive now and, I'm sorry to report, the number of corpses has risen to well over a hundred, most of them military personnel. We're afraid he could start killing and brutalizing the hostages as well.''

The president gave Carlton a haunted look. "But this is

almost the twenty-first century, and these people are acting like barbarians. Why?''

"We're not talking about modern Japanese society, we're talking about a small, dangerous element within that society. We have them too; look at some of these militias around the country—look what a couple of them did to the federal building in Oklahoma. The Japanese don't have an exclusive on the extremists. It just seems that theirs are better organized and a whole lot more committed.''

"Look, Gates, if we know these guys are systematically killing our people, we're going to have to do something about it.''

"I understand, but there's still the matter of the chemical super-agents. A meteorological team over at NOAA has pretty much validated what Epstein told us about this airborne particulate reaching Hawaii.''

"And the storm?''

Carlton looked at his watch. "It should reach Johnston Atoll in a little more than two days. It's on a heading that will reach Hawaii three days later.''

"Do we have a military option?''

"General McKenzie says he hopes to have a proposal to us by noon today.''

Garrison shrugged. "So I guess we wait it out. Still nothing more from Tadao?'' Carlton shook his head. "And how's the mood around the country?''

"Your broadcast did a lot to settle things down and buy us some time, but there's been a few incidents. They burned a Toyota dealership in LA last night and there was a big protest at a Japanese auto-parts factory in Kentucky. These are isolated incidents, but I think we need to get this thing under control and fast.''

Friday, 9 December, 10:05 P.M.
ANDERSON AIR FORCE BASE, GUAM

Colonel Anthony Fortino sat in the left-hand seat of the B-52H, standing on the brakes while the eight Pratt & Whitney TF33-P-3 jet engines began to spool up. The rows of gauges, switches, and circuit breakers that surrounded him were bathed in red light. It was all very familiar. He studied the tachometers for a moment and pulled the throttles back to idle. Beside him, his copilot, Major Ed O'Connor, patiently flipped through his checklist. Ahead through the cockpit windscreen, two strings of lights marking the edges of the runway raced in front of him, almost coming together on the horizon where the strip ended with a five-hundred-foot drop to the ocean.

The big Stratofortress was old, but then so was Fortino. The airplanes had been in the air longer than he had, but not by much. He loved the big lumbering bombers like some men loved their Edsels. At the Air Force Academy, his classmates had all wanted to fly fighters, but the small, nimble planes had never appealed to him. He'd always said, "When I look to my left, I wanna see nothing but engines and when I look to my right, I wanna see nothing but copilots." Fortino and his five crewmen sat waiting for clearance to take off. They were the third aircraft in the three-aircraft rotation.

After Fortino had read the alert message and had it authenticated, he'd called his wing commander for a personal verification. There was no mistake. He had been ordered to place an aircraft with two nuclear weapons in a holding pattern at forty thousand feet, eight hundred miles southwest of Hawaii, and keep one there until further notice. This was not a drill. They were to prepare to drop a nuclear weapon on Johnston Atoll on command. The mission order specified a three-hundred-kiloton weapon fused to burst at fifteen hundred feet. His wing commander had also breached security and told Fortino why he might have to bomb Johnston Atoll. The commanding general knew, even if the politicians and the Pentagon types didn't, that Fortino and his aircrews would need to know why they were being asked to drop a nuclear bomb on American citizens. But the knowledge didn't change their orders. Now Fortino's 512th Squadron was sealed off and the crews would remain in isolation until the crisis was resolved.

The mission preparation and execution had been well-choreographed and rehearsed during the Cold War. Everything was procedural. His squadron weapons officer authenticated the message by separate channels to release the weapons from nearby storage magazines. The nuclear safety officer keyed the cipher locks that would allow the weapons to be armed. Technicians, under layers of supervision, programmed the weapons for yield and burst height. Aircraft commanders and bombardiers signed for the electronic keys that would allow them to complete the final arming sequence once airborne. All this had been done before, many times, but the knowledge that this was not a drill made it a brand-new experience. Well-rehearsed procedures suddenly became foreign.

Half of Fortino's squadron aircraft had been configured to carry missiles, a mix of AGM-86 cruise missiles and AGM-69 short-range attack missiles. Current doctrine called for them to deliver nuclear weapons with cruise missiles. Cruise missiles were accurate and reliable, but unnecessary for this job. Nor would they need the precision of TV-guided smart bombs. The three aircraft designated for the mission were older planes, configured to carry free-falling, dumb iron bombs. With a three-hundred-kiloton weapon, pinpoint accuracy was not needed.

The mission was a simple one, at least tactically. When the aircraft commander received the order to drop the weapon and had the order authenticated, a single bomb would be armed. Target coordinates, drop altitude, bombing course and speed, and meteorological data had already been programmed into the weapons delivery system. When told to do so, the plane would overfly the target, drop the bomb, and take them away from the blast at the optimum course and speed. It was that simple. Choosing the crews that would fly the mission had not been so simple.

All Air Force bomber pilots knew about the *Enola Gay*, and *Bock's Car*, the aircraft that dropped the bombs on Hiroshima and Nagasaki. The personal lives of those B-29 crew members changed dramatically following those historic missions. If a drop was ordered, the crew that made it would have to deal with being the third aircraft in history to drop an atomic bomb on civilians. Only this time, those civilians would be American citizens.

A B-52H had a range of ten thousand miles, and loitering time over the target of almost sixteen hours. Fortino chose four aircraft for the mission, three principal aircraft with one held in reserve. Three primary birds would fly eight-hour shifts over Johnston Island. The relief would take place on station at forty-thousand feet near the target, allowing the off-duty bomber to return to Guam for maintenance and crew rest. Any of his crews could fly the mission. Fortino considered choosing them by lottery, but rejected it. It was a command decision and he was in command.

His executive officer or second-in-command would not fly; he would remain on the ground to attend to squadron business. Fortino and the next two senior aircraft commanders would fly the mission, with the third senior AC in reserve with the standby aircraft, armed and ready to fly.

At the squadron briefing, the other crews had made a show of their disappointment, but they'd been none too convincing. Fortino could see their relief. He had, however, made the flying rotation a matter of chance. They'd cut the cards and he'd drawn the number-three position. So now, if one of them did have to make the drop, that crew could rightly claim that it had been in the cards.

Fortino's eyes swept the instrument panels quickly and professionally. The aircraft was ready to do its job, but was he? Damn it all! he thought. Squadrons have personalities, even old B-52 squadrons waiting for the boneyard. His 512th Squadron had been a tight group and morale had been high; he had made it that way. Now there was a sharp division between those who flew and those who waited on the ground. The grounded crews were supportive, but when the assignments had been made, the old bonhomie had evaporated. Now the two groups hardly spoke.

Fortino also thought of those innocent people on Johnston Island. Christ, how will I live with myself if I have to make this drop? How will I handle it if one of my pilots has to make the drop? What do I say to him when he lands and steps down from the plane? Oddly enough, he felt it might be easier to do the job himself and not have to watch one of his other crews suffer.

"Tradewind Three-seven, you are cleared for takeoff on runway four, over."

"Roger," Fortino replied casually. He reached forward and gently touched a white plastic statue of the Blessed Virgin on the dash console. "Three-seven rolling." He crossed himself, as he did before every takeoff, and then pushed the eight throttles forward. The B-52 began to accelerate down the runway with the speed of an underpowered runaway motor home.

PART THREE

The Day of the Samurai

Friday, 9 December, 2:15 A.M.
NINETY MILES NORTHEAST OF JOHNSTON ISLAND

A sailor with Mickey Mouse ear protectors and goggles coaxed the SH-60 Seahawk over the port quarter of the *Tarawa*. With lighted wands, he enticed the large, screaming metal bug to an amidships landing spot. Then, like an orchestra leader completing the adagio, he eased the craft gently to the deck. The helo was not one of the *Tarawa*'s birds and had seemed reluctant to set down in a strange place.

The pilot cut the power and the big main rotor began to wind down. A crewman leapt quickly from the door, still connected by his communications umbilical, and stood by his machine until the blades had come to a complete stop. Then he slid the door fully open and beckoned the passengers out.

There were seven of them, each man carrying a canvas bag and a pack slung over one shoulder. Two of them dumped their loads onto the deck and returned to the helo for a large metal box, which they slung between them. They were met by the *Tarawa*'s chief master-at-arms, who led them to a hatchway cut in the ship's island superstructure. There he halted them and asked to see their orders. The man leading the contingent handed him a sheaf of papers and looked around at the vast flight deck and towering superstructure that ran along the ship's starboard side.

Not as large as the last one, he thought, the one they called the *Vin-son*, but a huge ship nonetheless. Nakajima

211

had been aboard ships of the Japanese Maritime Self Defense Force, but they were smaller, destroyer-type ships. He had also been on supertankers, rapelling from helicopters in mock boarding attacks, but the big tankers were more like floating metal islands—small cities at sea with little sense of movement.

This was different; these were ships—big ships. He found the names strange. The *Vin-son* was named for a civilian legislator, a member of the American diet, and this smaller one for an island in the Gilbert chain. Nakajima knew it had been the site of a fierce battle between the Japanese defenders and the U.S. Marines, one of the bloodiest of the Pacific war for the Americans. Three thousand Imperial Japanese Army soldiers had fought to the death, but the U.S. 2d Marine Division had paid dearly for the tiny island called Tarawa. A third of the five thousand Marines had never made it a shore, and many more had died on the beaches. And now he stood on the deck of the ship that commemorated that battle.

Nakajima had encountered Americans on Okinawa, but seldom officially. Usually they were off-duty soldiers relaxing in the city of Naha, or on their way to or from one of their bases. They were typical young Americans—loud, friendly, carefree. Members of the Naginata Counter Force were encouraged to avoid them. But these Americans appeared different; they were serious and very businesslike. Everyone seemed to be moving about the enormous decks with such purpose.

Their helo had been delayed on the big carrier while the ship launched and recovered jet aircraft. He had been fascinated by the complex nocturnal, mechanical ballet. Large, dark shapes whistled across the stern and all but crashed onto the deck, while others were hurled off the bow spitting cones of fire from their sleek tails. Perhaps, Nakajima reasoned, when Americans focus on a task, they can be quite good at it. If they can build ships like these and operate them with such skill, it is little wonder they were able during the war to sweep the Imperial naval forces from the Pacific.

Two men stood off to one side and watched the new arrivals. As the master-at-arms finished inspecting their papers, they approached the group. "Which one of you is in charge?" the taller one asked quietly.

"I am Captain Nakajima." He stood at attention and bowed formally from the waist.

"Well howdy, Captain," said the American as he extended a hand, "I'm John Moody—Lieutenant John Moody."

Nakajima hesitated and took the offered hand, again bowing but only slightly. Like most Japanese, he did not like to touch strangers. He recognized the importance of the Western handshake, but he still found it offensive. Nonetheless, there was a warmth and firmness in this American's grip.

"This here's Senior Chief Stockton." Nakajima took the other man's hand and inclined his head. Moody continued, "Seems we may be working together on this operation. While the chief sees to your men, why don't you and I have a little chat."

"A little . . . chat?"

"Captain, I think we need to talk."

"Ah," the Japanese replied.

Moody and Nakajima watched as Stockton stepped over and quickly found the Japanese sergeant. After a few words he grabbed the sergeant's bag and led them through a door in the superstructure. Following their departure, Moody motioned to Nakajima and they began to walk. They made a strange pair, the tall, angular American and the blocky Japanese captain. They had walked halfway to the bow before Moody spoke.

"Have a good flight?"

"Yes. It was an interesting trip."

"You're stationed on Okinawa, right?"

"That is correct."

Finally Moody stopped and faced the shorter man.

"Look Naka . . . Nakahima . . . Nakahama . . . uh, how do you say your name again?"

"It is Nakajima, Cap-tain Na-ka-ji-ma."

"Na-ka-ji-ma. Okay, got it. Do you have a first name?"

Americans! Nakajima drew himself up to his full height, coming almost to Moody's chin. "Of course. But is there something wrong with my title or my last name?"

Moody stood with his hands clamped easily on his hips, pinching the camouflage utility blouse around his slim waist. The quarter moon was high and to the south, gently washing the two men in pale light. Moody tilted his head and looked down at Nakajima.

"Hey look, friend. It looks as if I may have to go ashore on Johnston Island and try to stop this Tadao fellow. I may even take you with me. If I do, then there's a better-than-even chance we'll *both* be dead before it's over. If I have to die with a man, I want to call him by his first name."

For the first time since he'd left Japan, Nakajima allowed himself a smile. Americans were a curious and peculiar people. He expected that. Yet there was something strangely familiar about this one. He appeared relaxed, but he had a hard edge to him.

"So, you think this mission may require our death?"

"What do you think?"

Nakajima again smiled. "My close friends call me Taro. It is a childhood name that somehow has followed me; it is short for Shintaro. I would be honored if you called me Taro."

"Fair enough. And you can call me John."

"Very well, John-san." Nakajima bowed from the waist, and Moody, feeling awkward, did the same. Both men bobbed a few times, Nakajima observing proper courtesy and Moody trying to do the right thing. They looked like two penguins observing pre-mating protocol. It was an odd ritual on the moonlit flight deck of a ship named the *Tarawa* in the mid-Pacific.

"We don't have much time, Taro," Moody said as they

continued to walk. "Tell me what you know of this business?"

Nakajima reviewed what he had been told of the capture of the island and of Tadao's demands.

"And do you know what will happen if the chemicals are blown up?"

"All there will perish," Nakajima said simply.

"They will," replied Moody, "but that's only part of it." He then told the Japanese captain about the VX agents, the oncoming storm, and the B-52 that now circled overhead. When he had finished, Nakajima halted, trying to comprehend what he had just heard.

"You mean that all of Hawaii and millions of people are at risk?" Moody nodded. The Japanese inhaled audibly through his teeth and continued. "And that if the explosives set these chemicals free, then an atom bomb will be dropped on the island?"

"Now you understand the problem."

Nakajima peeled off his fatigue cap and ran a hand across the stubble on his head. "So. We must stop this. It cannot be allowed to happen." Nakajima was neither an economist nor a politician, but he knew that modern Japan depended on trade and on Western markets. In particular, those with the United States were essential to its economy. If an atomic bomb obliterated Johnston Island, relations between the two nations would be irreparably damaged. Japan's current recession would become a depression, one from which the country would be decades in recovering. Any relationship with the West based on trust would be damaged far longer. He looked sharply at Moody. "You have a plan?"

"Perhaps. Tell me about this guy Tadao."

For the next fifteen minutes Nakajima talked about Tadao, but he also talked about the way of the samurai. In simple, graphic terms, he spoke of their opponent's resolve, and of patriotism and commitment. "Tadao is," he concluded, "a samurai, and as I have explained, that is no small thing. He is a warrior who has pledged his sacred honor to this undertaking. To fail, or to act in a conciliatory manner, would jeopardize his place among the great samurai who have gone before him.''

"So if his demands are rejected, he'll set off those charges?"

"Without hesitation."

Moody considered this as they continued slowly about the deck.

"It seems," Moody offered, "that this Tadao is a lot like you."

Nakajima bowed his head. "You honor me. I too believe in the way of the samurai."

"If it comes to it, could you kill him?"

"*Hai*, without hesitation," he said evenly. "To do otherwise would dishonor myself and Tadao-sama."

They walked for several more minutes along the edge of the flight deck. Finally Moody drew a sack of tobacco and hunched over with his back to the wind as he laid a line of black shredded leaf down along the curved white paper. Nakajima declined to join him but watched with interest. Moody quickly licked and rolled the smoke, then fired it between cupped hands. He flicked the match away and drew heavily on the rumpled querlie. As he exhaled, he seemed to come to a decision.

"Are you and your men scuba-qualified?"

"We are all qualified divers," Nakajima answered.

"Do you know how to use oxygen rigs, specifically the Draeger?"

"The German-made rebreather? Of course."

Moody smiled. "Excellent. My chief petty officer and I have an idea how to do this thing, but it may not work without your help."

"Then perhaps, John-san, you should show me your plan."

Moody finished his smoke as they walked back across the flight deck on their way to flag plot.

Friday, 9 December, 10:00 P.M.
TOKYO, JAPAN

Prime Minister Mitsuzuka sat at his desk, savoring
a rare moment of quiet. The day had been long and difficult,
but he'd had many of those in his thirty-plus years in public
life. He was tired, but it was more than that. He was afraid.

Mitsuzuka owed his current position to a fragile coalition
of political parties and special-interest groups within the
Japanese diet. Each had its own agenda and wanted to be
heard. In the normal course of government business,
whether a trade pact or a tax measure or an agriculture bill,
each faction presented him with its position, for or against
it. He listened carefully, gauging the strength of the position
and the depth of commitment to the issue. Then with his
key advisers, he cautiously orchestrated the give-and-take
required to pass or defeat the measure. Sometimes, one or
two rambunctious members of the coalition had to be
brought to heel, but for the most part it was a conciliatory,
highly civilized process. The Japanese governed themselves
by continually seeking consensus. It had been that way for
almost four decades, but today was different. The time-
honored conventions of negotiation and compromise that
were the heart of the Japanese political process no longer
seemed to apply.

The Johnston Atoll affair had changed everything. There
was little his government could or would do publicly about
the incident. The small special-operations team had been
lent to the Americans in strict secrecy. Nevertheless, he had
spent the day receiving delegations of the coalition parties
to get their views on the matter. Most of the meetings had
begun in the normal courteous fashion, with legislators ex-
pressing their regret at this unfortunate incident.

But as the discussion moved to the reasons behind the
action and how to deal with the rightists in general, Tadao

in particular, difficulties arose. Members of the diet, political colleagues who were skilled at working through differences politely and with respect, suddenly became vicious. Years of civility and protocol were stripped away in a heated exchange.

For many, the Johnston Island incident was a call for all *true* Japanese to step forward and be recognized. The implications of Tadao's action were all but lost in the nobility and daring of his exploit. He had acted in secrecy and purely on principle to place himself in an impossible situation; he was the essence of a Japanese hero. In keeping with samurai tradition, his feat was seen as an act of revenge: for the older generations, revenge for the humiliation of the war—to the younger, revenge for the recent years of Western condescension and jealousy in the face of Japanese commercial success.

And it challenged the moral foundation of every Japanese. To denounce Tadao was to deny the traditional and spiritual distillate of Japan and the virtues of its ancient culture. But to agree with him, or offer support, was to condemn the new Japan, the modern economic superpower and its democratic constitution. Men Mitsuzuka had known for years, old political hands, exchanged words that two generations ago would have called for a fight to the death.

If this is how it is among the nation's leaders, he thought, what is it like among our people? As he considered this, the fear that had stalked him most of the day began to burn in his stomach. There was a knock at the door, and his aide stepped in and bowed.

"Excuse me, Prime Minister, but Minister Oka is here to see you."

"Very well," he said loudly, so his voice would carry to the visitor in the outer office. "Show him in at once." The prompt admission of the visitor showed equal measures of respect for the man and concern for the current crisis. Oka was not only a senior and influential member of the diet, he headed the largest of the coalition parties. The old man was highly respected in business circles as well as in government. Occasionally he and Oka had had their differences, but Mitsuzuka knew that his position as prime minister enhanced Oka's position and afforded him political leverage. He also knew that without the elder statesman's support, he would not hold his office.

Mitsuzuka met him at the door and the two men meticulously exchanged formal greetings. Oka's manner in observing these formalities told Mitsuzuka that he too was concerned about recent events. Mitsuzuka escorted the older man to two identical chairs that bracketed a low, lacquered table. When Oka refused to sit until he was seated, Mitsuzuka rightly guessed that his guest not only shared his own fears, but was very agitated.

"Honored colleague," Mitsuzuka began, "these are difficult times. I have spent the day with members of our alliance and they are divided over this matter. Harsh words have been spoken among friends that may linger long after this has ended." He paused to give weight to his words. "This troubles me deeply. I humbly seek your advice."

Oka leaned forward in his chair and inclined his head to acknowledge this show of respect. On Mitsuzuka's prior instructions, a young woman dressed in a traditional kimono brought in tea. After she'd left, the prime minister carefully poured for his guest and then for himself.

"You know that I once pledged my life to the emperor and to the defense of our sacred land." It was not a question, for it was well known that Oka had served in the Imperial Army. He had enlisted in 1938 and risen to the rank of major, serving with distinction in China and Burma. In Japan, he was revered by the active right as Americans do their astronauts. "That was a very long time ago, and I was young and foolish. Now I am old and foolish, but I remember one thing very clearly—as clearly as if it were yesterday. It was the contempt of my generation and the generation that proceeded me for anything not Japanese and anyone not born in Japan.

"We had good reason to feel superior. Before the turn of the century, we were a feudal land. Yet within but a few decades years we emerged as a modern nation and in 1905 defeated Russia, then a leading world power. In the thirties we dominated the Asian Pacific. The Greater East Asia Co-Prosperity Sphere, under our leadership, would have succeeded had we not brutalized the nations we conquered. They would have welcomed us as saviors, for we were strong and drove the white man from the Asian mainland, ending centuries of exploitation. But we were arrogant and made enemies of potential allies.''

He was silent for a moment while he mentally returned to a Japan that was, before the war. It was a bittersweet journey. ''You almost had to have seen us in our pride and glory of those times to fully appreciate the physical destruction and psychological damage of our defeat by the Americans. It almost cost us our souls—almost. Our conquerors defined the rules of the new warfare, business and commerce. And here we are, again a world power. Now, I am afraid we may again allow our pride and our contempt for others to defeat us.'' He lowered his head, this time to hide his emotion, and the prime minister was very moved.

''May I know if you have a recommendation?'' Mitsuzuka said gently.

Oka looked up. ''You must go to the emperor and ask him to order Tadao to relinquish his conquest and return home.''

''But do you think he will do so, even at the request from the emperor?''

''It does not matter what he does,'' the older man said, careful to contain an outward show of his impatience. ''It is what our people think. This island Tadao has captured, even with the numerous American hostages he has taken, is not important.''

''It is not?'' Mitsuzuka said, puzzled.

''Do you not understand? Can you not see the real danger? He has captured the imagination of our people, especially the so-called intellectuals and the young people. There lies the danger! If they follow him, we will again be on the path to national ruin. Once in this century is enough.

Tadao is a samurai; we have no power over him. The emperor must order him to surrender. If he obeys the emperor, the immediate problem is solved. Then we or the Americans will have to imprison a great national hero. If he refuses, we can brand him a renegade and an outlaw; then we can deal with him—purge him from the minds of our youth. A samurai who disobeys an Imperial edict is an outcast, a *ronin*. He is on his own. We can turn our people away from this romantic fool and show the Americans that he is a criminal—not a national hero!''

Mitsuzuka was deeply embarrassed that he had not seen the full danger Tadao posed. He bowed low. ''Honored colleague, thank you for placing this matter in perspective and helping me to see this threat more clearly.'' Oka inclined his head to indicate he accepted the apology. ''I will seek an audience with the emperor at once. May I ask you to accompany me to this meeting?'' It was widely known that Oka had once been a personal confidant of Hirohito, the late father of the current emperor. Oka again inclined his head.

Friday, 9 December, 6:02 A.M.
JOHNSTON ISLAND

Jim Bruso had finally managed a few hours of sleep. It was more than he'd had the night before and was the heavy, dreamless sleep of total exhaustion. He needed more, much more, but his internal clock would not allow this. His eyes fluttered open just before dawn, and the terror of the last two days was immediately upon him. He glanced over at the two forms on the floor next to him. As had he, they were sleeping fully clothed on the carpeted floor of the small office—no blankets, no pillows.

General Taggart was having a difficult time. Few general officers, Bruso acknowledged, have had to sleep in their uniforms for two days, and he was looking decidedly less military than he had on Wednesday when he'd arrived. But then Bruso had been a Marine and Marines were not so inclined to lose their starch. Bruso also knew that Taggart was a staff officer, Army Corps of Engineers, and that made him something of a civilian in uniform, at least to a Marine.

The general carried himself well enough and didn't complain, but he seemed naked without his authority. When Bruso or Nancy Blackman tried to talk to him, he was often unresponsive. Earlier that morning she had pressed him on the exact amount and type of chemical weapons stored on the island, and he had simply covered his head with his hands.

Bruso understood. He had seen that same vacuous, hollow disbelief in the eyes of his fellow Marines in Vietnam during the siege of Khe Sanh. Even strong men, when denied sleep and after seeing too much death, can lose touch with reality. Often after a few hours' sleep they were all right—sometimes not. There were moments during those terrible days, while the North Vietnamese mortars pounded them around the clock, when he'd seen it in the mirror.

Bruso lay on his back, now fully awake. There was really nothing he could do and he knew it. He looked over at the sleeping Taggart with a measure of compassion, like a seaman would a shipmate who was seasick.

Nancy Blackman was different. There was a sense of presence and calm determination about her. Over the past thirty-six hours, Bruso had begun to turn to her when he wanted to talk. He knew she was terrified, but she refused to allow this terror to degenerate into panic, or even resignation. He sensed that Blackman knew her captors thought less of her because she was a woman, and less still that she was a Western woman in a position of power. She had remained poised, as if determined not to allow Tadao to degrade her. Somehow, Senator Blackman seemed able to turn her fear into resolve. Bruso had thought about this over the past few days and concluded that perhaps this was the true basis of courage—the conversion of fear into hatred and then, action. For Senator Nancy Blackman, that action was to maintain her composure and dignity at all costs. Even Tadao had begun to treat her with respect. Bruso thought she was nothing short of magnificent.

He silently raised himself from the floor and stepped into the lighted hallway. When he pointed to the bathroom across the hall, the guard nodded curtly. The door remained propped open as he made his way to the basin. He scarcely recognized the haggard man who stared back at him from the mirror. Bruso winced as he pushed the handcuffs higher on his wrists and splashed water on his face. Then he relieved himself and washed as carefully as the manacles would allow. Leaving the bathroom, he felt only marginally refreshed, but more human. Nancy Blackman met him in the hall.

"Hello, Jim."

"Morning, Senator. Were you able to manage some sleep?"

She gave him a tired grin and a shrug. "Good morning!" she said brightly as she turned to the guard, flashing him a broad smile. Then she walked into the bathroom, pulling the door closed behind her. The guard frowned and said something guttural in Japanese. He started to follow her but got no farther than the door, unsure of how to proceed. Suddenly, he went rigid. Bruso turned to see Tadao walking down the hall.

"Ah, Bruso. Up early, I see." Tadao was freshly shaved and in a clean uniform. The two swords were belted to one side while a holstered pistol rode on the other hip. "I see you too are an early riser. How about your two comrades?"

Tadao glanced in the office and saw only Taggart, who was snoring. Then his head snapped around to the closed bathroom door. There was a rapid exchange between Tadao and the guard. It was clearly a reprimand and the guard lowered his head. The look on Tadao's face was dangerous as he slammed open the door to the toilet.

"Oh, good morning, Mr. Tadao." She addressed him in the mirror without turning around. Her blouse hung from a hook on the wall and she was bare from the waist up except

for her brassiere. A short stack of towels rested on the edge
of the basin and she was doing her best at a sponge bath.
"Something I can do for you?" Her tone was conversa-
tional, as if her husband had just walked into her dressing
room.

Bruso felt she may have gone too far, but Tadao only
smiled and inclined his head. "Since you ask, Senator, yes.
Please address me by my title, which is Commandant. Then
put on your clothes and join us in the hall."

He again closed the door and turned to Bruso. "She is
spirited and I will allow that, up to a point. You may tell
her that if she continues to test me, I may be forced to turn
her over to my men for their pleasure, and we will see just
how much spirit she has. Now, I understand that it is your
practice to tour the island each morning, is that not correct?"

"That's right," Bruso replied.

"Excellent. This morning we will do it together. The
lady may join us, after she has finished her toilet, of course.
We will allow the general to rest."

A green Army nine-passenger van waited for them at the
administration building. A small rising-sun flag adorned the
front bumper on each side. Tadao climbed up front with
the driver. Bruso and Blackman were herded into the second seat while two guards rode in back. The sun was just
lifting over the horizon as they made their way around the
perimeter road.

The island had changed little except for the absence of
activity. Periodically they passed a sentry armed with a rifle
and a radio, patrolling near water's edge. Several raised
their arms and shouted, "Banzai!" Tadao smiled and
waved. They paused briefly at the chemical-storage facility
while Tadao conferred with one of his lieutenants. Bruso
noted the vehicles parked along the length of the runway,
making it useless. As they returned to the administration
complex, Tadao directed them to the gymnasium.

"Perhaps you would like to see just how your people
are adjusting to their captivity?" he said. On their way to

the door, Bruso noticed that the wind had backed around and was now coming from the south. Overhead, the normally clear sky was flecked with patches of high cirrus clouds.

"You know we have a tropical storm coming?" Bruso said. "This building may not be safe under high-wind conditions."

"What would you have me do Bruso, herd them all into the chemical-disposal facility?" A look of horror crossed Blackman's face, causing Tadao to chuckle. "No Senator, it is not what you think. The disposal unit is a storm-proof structure, the only one on the island, is that not so, Bruso?"

"That is correct, Commandant," Bruso said stonily. His features had suddenly taken on a troubled, faraway look.

Tadao smiled indulgently as he held the door for them. Inside, the gym floor was a patchwork of sleeping forms and men sitting up, half awake. Others were just lying on their backs, staring at the ceiling. It was a scene from a Red Cross shelter following an earthquake or a hurricane. At least they had been given blankets. Trash from emergency food-ration containers littered the area. Bruso watched two men return from the restroom and another two leave. The only other movement was from those forms on the hardwood floor as they searched for a more comfortable position. A stale, sour smell hung in the air and promised to become worse as the temperature rose. The gym floor was a large area encompassing two basketball courts. Four men with automatic weapons patrolled the perimeter. More than eight hundred men were being guarded by just these roving sentries.

"Very efficient, is it not?" Tadao said, as if reading Bruso's thoughts. "If the two men allowed to go to the toilet try to escape, the two waiting their turn will immediately be shot. We have had no problems."

"May I see the women, please?" Blackman asked.

"Of course, Senator."

Tadao barked a few words to one of the guards, and he led Blackman away in the direction of the handball courts that housed the women. Along the way, she smiled an encouragement to several men sitting on the floor and stopped to lean down and take one man's hand. After she was gone, Bruso turned to Tadao.

"Do you mind if I talk with some of my people?"

"Not at all, Bruso. Just remember that their fate, as well as your own, depends on your total cooperation. Any mass uprising will cause a slaughter; I give you my word on it." As if by some silent cue, three more armed men entered the building and took positions along the walls.

Bruso walked into the sea of men, occasionally pausing to talk quietly or shake someone's hand. "Nothing yet, Art . . . we're still waiting . . . there's nothing we can do, Fred; we just have to wait it out."

He appeared to be meandering through the crowd with no purpose, but that was not the case. Every shop or department that worked under him had at least one man who knew everything about that particular operation. Sometimes it was the department head or shop foreman and sometimes not. Bruso knew exactly who these men were, and he was looking for one of them.

"Hello, Wilbur."

"Hi, Mister Bruso. When we gettin' outta here?"

Wilbur Cummings was what they called a lifer—a retired military bachelor who'd been on Johnston Island for eight years. He was like some veteran petty criminal who had difficulty adapting to life outside prison walls. Wilbur worked in the motor pool.

"Wish I knew—hopefully soon. I have to keep moving, but tell me something quickly. Back on Wednesday when this thing started, there were two stake trucks checked out with drivers—remember that?"

"Sure do. Nothin' leaves the shop lessin' it goes through me."

"I know that, Wilbur. Tell me about it."

A few moments later, Bruso returned to where Tadao waited with Nancy Blackman and the two guards. She noticed there was something different about him; there was a grim, hard edge to him that had not been there earlier.

"Jim, are you all right?"

"I'm fine," he said stonily, "just had some bad news about a coworker. You'll know about it soon enough. How're the ladies doing?"

"They're tired and scared, and one or two are borderline hysterical, but they'll be all right. You have some very strong women there, and they'll see to the ones who need help."

Bruso nodded. He could probably name them, he thought, although perhaps not. Often, the people you thought were weak or too self-centered to be of much use in a crisis were the very ones who came through when things got tough.

"These people need food—real food. When are you going to allow them to have something to eat . . . Commandant?"

Tadao smiled slowly. "They have again given us no trouble through the night, and they will be allowed food. And now, I have need for the senator to speak with your government. When we've finished with that, you too will be allowed to eat."

He turned to leave and they followed him out the door with the two guards close behind.

Friday, 9 December, 6:41 A.M.
EIGHTY MILES EAST OF JOHNSTON ISLAND

The SEALs and a few of the staff planners had moved into a small compartment next to flag plot. A Marine sentry guarded the door to the flag plot and another stood by the entrance to the room where the planning group wrestled with the details of the upcoming assault. Several men bent over a small conference table covered with photographs, diagrams, and charts of the atoll. Standing in the corner was a full-size colored cardboard rendering of a ter-

rorist in desert-camouflage uniform, complete with headband and submachine gun. The features were definitely
Oriental. Some of the black-and-white photos on the table
were grainy enlargements of figures patrolling the beaches,
bisected by the rifles they carried. They'd been taken from
high altitude, but they looked much like the large color
composite. A four-foot-square sandbox rested on a card table where a surprisingly realistic representation of the
chemical-weapons storage facility had been fashioned. The
sculpted sand was a burnt yellow-brown, the color of
crushed coral under a quarter moon. Bubble-plastic packing
material, sprayed flat black, formed the surface of the
ocean. Buildings of dark gray construction paper were arranged within a scale-model chain-link fence.

The architect of all this was a baby-faced Army captain
who had taken a degree from the Rhode Island School of
Design and applied his talents in a manner his mentors back
in Providence would probably have considered sacrilegious.
Throughout the night, whenever a new batch of photos or
drawings of the storage facility arrived, he would sort
through them and tack some to the bulkhead above the
model. Then he would descend on the layout, leveling a
slope here, moving a building there, gradually rendering the
miniature ever closer to the real thing.

A few hours ago a civilian had arrived on the *Tarawa*;
his firm had been the design contractor for the construction
of the storage facility. He'd brought several sheaves of
blueprints and was able pinpoint the special-containment
vaults that would house the enhanced VX agents. His contract for this consulting job specified that he would not have
to go within fifty miles of Johnston Atoll. Senior Chief
Stockton estimated that his daily fee to the government
would probably cover all the military salaries in the room
for a week.

Walker sat at the table with a chief boatswain's mate
from one of the frigates in the battle group. The chief had
been stationed on Johnston Island several years ago and had
served as master on a Navy tugboat there. He knew well

the waters around the island and the approaches to the harbor. Walker grilled him, referring to sections of laminated charting clipped into a binder—the same charts he would take with him in the SDV on the run to the island. He made notations in various colors of grease pencil.

Late the previous evening, Moody had taken him aside. "Don," he'd told him, pointing to a location on the chart, "I don't have time to figure out how to get there *and* what to do when we arrive. I'm going to count on you to get the SDVs here. If we can choose our time to make the hit, I'll want the boats in place by 0345."

With that direction, Walker had gone to work. He could only estimate how close the *La Jolla* could get to the island, which would determine the exact time to launch the SDVs. The lanky petty officer laid a track from the objective back out to sea and worked his way in. Johnston Atoll was perched on a shelf and surrounded by shallow water. There were questions of tide, depth, current, unplotted submerged obstacles, shore lighting, aids to navigation, and bioluminescence, to name a few. The tugboat chief had answers to only some of them. Walker had brought his submerged-attack checklists with him and did the best he could. Portions of the mission were not covered by standard procedure, so he improvised.

Moody sat at the table behind a keyboard. A laptop computer loaded with a set of mission-planning software had been flown out from SDV Team One back on Ford Island. The program walked him through the mechanics of launching a direct-action, over-the-beach mission from SDVs. It was highly detailed, but Moody had been forced to type Unknown or TBD—to be determined—in far too many places. There were annexes for logistics, communications, command and control, emergency recall, alternate routes to target, action on target, alternate actions on target . . . the list went on.

The basic plan for the attack still worried him. He had devised a clever strategy for the assault, one that might just work if everything came off on schedule. However, it was a complex plan and that itself was a problem. They would have no time for rehearsal; he was placing his trust in the skill of the SEALs—and his Japanese. Moody paused for a moment. *His Japanese*, for they were now his men too. And those going on the mission would have to do the job based only on what they learned at the briefings.

"Oh-shit-oh-dear," Moody mumbled as he snatched a look at his watch and turned back to the keyboard. "It's like I'm getting ready to play in the Super Bowl, and I'm drawing up plays in the dirt with a stick."

"Hang in there, sir. You're doing just fine."

Senior Chief Stockton seemed to be everywhere, but right now he was at Moody's elbow. Part of the night he'd been with Walker, helping him to plan the SDVs' approach to the target. All of their attention was focused on the run in; there was no plan for coming out. Either they succeeded in disarming the explosives, or they failed and it wouldn't matter. Periodically Stockton left the room to send a message to SDV Team One in Hawaii, requesting information or an additional piece of equipment. He contacted the *La Jolla* hourly to check on the preparation of the SDVs. Each time Moody completed a section of the mission concept, he toggled the print key and the laser printer issued a hard copy. Stockton proofed it while Moody moved on to the next portion.

Captain Nakajima sat on the other side of the table from Moody and Stockton, marveling at the process. The idea of having a plan for an attack formatted on a computer had never occurred to him. He understood what they were doing; the basic steps were much the same as if he'd been planning a raid. But to plan a difficult, complex mission in such detail, and in just a few hours, was beyond him. Nakajima was aware that the Americans were far more computer-literate than Japanese, but he'd never expected to find it so in their military. And it wasn't just Lieutenant Moody. Both SEAL enlisted men took to the computer to complete portions of the operational plan. The only time Nakajima had felt comfortable was when Moody had consulted him on a detail of the attack using the scale model.

Moody again looked at his watch and sat back. "That's it, Senior Chief, the last plan annex. You got anything there?"

"Just two corrections, sir. You're probably going to need a backup frequency for the Marine assault element, and I'd recommend you get them airborne a little bit sooner. Those CH-46s have goods legs and when you want 'em, you're gonna *really* want 'em—maybe sooner than you think."

"Yeah, good idea." Moody took the sheets and scrolled back on the computer screen to make the adjustments. Stockton retrieved the final section from the printer. While he read it, Moody rose and walked stiffly over to the coffee pot. It was almost empty and he had to tip it to get a half cup of the lukewarm fluid. It looked like used motor oil. Like Walker and Stockton, Moody wore a T-shirt and fatigue trousers. Only Captain Nakajima had remained in full uniform. Moody reached for his blouse and pulled it on.

"What do you think, Senior?"

"Looks okay to me. Anything else you'd like me to check?"

"Probably, but I've got about ten minutes to get this up to the general." He reached over and tapped in a short command. The printer began to whine softly and dispense text. "When that's finished, make a copy for us and get a copy on the secure fax back to Ford Island. I'd like our operations people to review the plan and see if we missed anything."

"Aye aye, sir."

"And when do the shooters and the EOD guys get here?"

"Latest is sometime before noon," Stockton replied.

"Okay, I'll want to have a mission-overview briefing at 0900. Have the staff round up the supporting-element commanders. We'll get the new guys up to speed after they get here. How about the final support briefing?"

Stockton flipped out his notebook. "I'd recommend 1600. We'll have to leave for the *La Jolla* by 1800 or we'll miss our window and have to wait twenty-four hours. Even then, it's going to be tight. You and the rest of the assault team are scheduled to rest between 1100 and 1500.''

"Uh-huh, I could just about use some rest." He turned to the squat man sitting quietly across the table. "Taro, you ready to go and meet my general?"

"Yes, John-san," he said rising.

They bowed to each other, causing Walker and Stockton to exchange sidelong glances.

"Hey, John. You want to see what your target will look like?"

"Sure."

The sand modeler turned out the lights and held the mockup in a flashlight beam, one with a pale yellow diffuser. The effect was eerie. A highly detailed, miniature version of the chemical-storage facility lay before them in the simulated moonlight, complete with lilliputian buildings and tiny storage bins. There were even small floodlights along the scale fencing, the kind you see on the HO-gauge train layouts. The three SEALs, whose business it was to approach coastal targets from the sea at night, were amazed at how real it looked.

"If you go in between three and five in the morning, you'll have a strong half moon in the west about like so." He moved the light in a thirty-degree arc. "If you approach the storage facility from the southwest, it'll be over your left shoulder, or not at all, depending on cloud cover from the storm moving in."

"That's terrific, man, really," said Moody. "I wish we could take it with us aboard the submarine."

"Maybe you can. Let me work on that."

Stockton flipped on the lights as he entered the room and handed Moody a revised copy of the mission concept and operational plan.

"Good luck, sir."

After Moody and Nakajima left, Stockton turned off the lights. He and Walker began to study the sand model, pressing their faces down on the plastic to get a waterline view of the target.

Friday, 9 December, 2:30 P.M.
THE WHITE HOUSE

Robert Garrison was at his place behind the big cherry desk in the Oval Office. Intelligence reports and newspapers covered the desktop. For the moment, the president had ignored his fetish for tidiness. He stared at the television monitor resting in the antique armoire along the west wall. CNN was covering the Johnston Island Crisis, as it was now called, as they had the Gulf War—nonstop. Their front-line news team was now strategically deployed to cover the story. Three reporters in Washington worked the capital beat, one each at the Pentagon, the State Department, and the White House. A member of the news team was with the Japanese community in L.A., while another in Hawaii patrolled the gates of the Pearl Harbor Naval Base. But the CNN reporter who seemed to be getting the most air time was Christiane Amanpour in Tokyo.

Earlier, she had been on a downtown street corner as one of the now familiar trucks laden with loudspeakers cruised the financial district blaring nationalist and military music. Patriotic banners and screaming youths wearing sashes and headbands clung to the truck. For the most part, Japanese on the crowded streets observed these proceedings with their typical restrained indifference. Then a sharp cameraman found his target and zoomed in for a close-up. A well-dressed elderly couple waved small rising-sun flags. When the truck passed in front of them, they raised their hands and yelled, ''Banzai!'' The video clip had been replayed many times.

Ms. Amanpour was now across the street from the Ministry of Defense. The Tokyo riot police had deployed with their batons, helmets, and thick Plexiglas shields. The protestors, mostly young people, formed into chanting, snake-like chains as they wound through the crowd. They bumped along in a ragged file, like some bizarre version of the bunny-hop. Organizers with colored arm bands and battery-powered megaphones shouted directions and encouragement. This was a familiar exercise for both demonstrators and riot police, but there was an elevated level of passion and anger to these proceedings, one that could easily escape the Western eye.

Suddenly, a demonstrator stepped forward and unsheathed a long samurai sword. His blade arced over the top of the line of shields and all but severed an arm wielding a baton. As the wounded man reeled from the rank, the swordsman filled the gap, slashing at the two men to either side. One of them managed to use his shield to good advantage, but the other was not so lucky. The blood from a severed carotid artery sprayed protestor and policeman alike. There was a pause from the shock of this unprecedented breach of demonstration etiquette. Then the police captain issued a shrill blast on his whistle and shields converged on the sword bearer. He was buried under a flurry of batons, but the action had caused a breach in the police ranks. Demonstrators poured through and the well-organized protest became a riot, to the detriment of the rioters. The police batons took a fearful toll. Finally the riot police managed to clear the area, leaving a number of dazed protestors in their wake, many of them bleeding from their mouth and ears. The street and sidewalks looked like the aftermath of an American campus antiwar demonstration in the early seventies.

President Garrison watched this along with the rest of America. He clicked off the TV and counted his blessings. At least for the moment, the domestic picture was far less troubling. As yet, there had been no massive demonstrations. Perhaps, Garrison reasoned, it's because Americans have been conditioned by a steady diet of TV violence and overseas military adventure. Reaction seemed confined to isolated incidents of vandalism in the major cities, usually directed at the most visible signs of Japanese presence—car dealerships. Local police had been able to control it, but there had been a few spectacular fire-bombings.

The single positive aspect of the crisis had been public reaction regarding Japanese-Americans. It was as if the nation, conscious of mistakes made with its Japanese citizens after Pearl Harbor, now sought to protect them. The media was out in force and had caught only a few incidents of harassment and jeering. Such occurrences had been isolated and directed at Chinese and Koreans as well as Japanese. A group of skinheads had gathered at a shopping mall in the Japanese community of Gardenia near Los Angeles to stage a protest, but they'd been met by an even larger and more militant number of local non-Asians. The police had ended up removing the skinheads for their own protection. Japanese communities throughout the nation were acting with caution, but their reaction to the capture of Johnston Island was one of outrage, even more so than with non-Japanese Americans.

As the CNN anchor in New York began an inventory of the response in foreign capitals, Gates Carlton slipped into the office. "We just received a message from Nancy Blackman," he said without ceremony. Garrison noticed his friend was flushed, and Gates Carlton did not ruffle easily. Carlton had taken up residence in an office down the hall, much to the relief of the career professionals at the State Department and the chagrin of Garrison's National Security Adviser. "Tadao's given us a date of sorts to meet his demands." He handed Garrison two sheets of message text as he coiled himself into a chair in front of the desk and loosened his tie.

"How's Nancy sound?" Blackman, like the president, was unmarried. Garrison had escorted the senator to a concert at the Kennedy Center a few months back. The reasons were mostly political, but the event had set tongues wagging all over the capital. He had found the senator attractive, charming, and politically formidable. They'd agreed to see each other again, but both were very busy and discretion was almost out of the question.

"The communications types said she came over very reserved," Carlton replied. "Langley's doing a stress analysis on her voice print now."

"How'd this come in?" Garrison asked as he began to read.

"Oddly enough, over the secure communications link between Johnston Island and the Naval Communications Station in Hawaii."

"Then he's not gone public with this?"

"Not yet."

Garrison began to read aloud. "This is Senator Nancy Blackman reading a message prepared by Commandant Takashi Tadao of the New Shield Society. 'The governments of Japan and the United States will be given until noon Saturday, December 10th, Johnston Island time, to obey my demands. These demands remain unchanged. Unless these conditions are met, the bloodshed will begin.' "

He quickly scanned the remainder of the text, which outlined the format and venue for public announcements that would compel Japan and the United States to comply with the demands. Garrison again read aloud, from the second page: " 'A copy of this text will be released to the major wire services in one hour.' This concludes the message from Commandant Tadao."

Garrison laid the sheets on the desk, leaning back in the chair as he carefully massaged his forehead with his fingertips. Carlton noticed that the president's customary crispness was gone and it was only early afternoon. His eyes were red from lack of sleep, and there was a nick on his chin where he had cut himself shaving.

"That's how long from now?" Garrison said, shaking off his fatigue.

"About forty minutes."

"I assume there's no way of jamming their transmission."

"Not really," Carlton replied. "NSA says it's all but impossible to maintain a twenty-four-hour jamming effort across the transmission frequencies available to them. And Tadao claims he has agents in Japan and America equipped with radio transmitters, so there's no way we could beam a bogus transmission just to him on Johnston Atoll.''

Garrison nodded. "Tokyo have this?"

"Yes, sir. Per your instructions, it was sent to their embassy by secure fax within minutes of our receipt."

The president was silent for several moments. "And we've still found no way to negotiate with this guy?"

This was not the first time the president had asked this question. "Apparently not. We've tried several different tacks and nothing has worked. We even offered to send Dave Steckle as an official envoy, along with a leading Japanese Shinto priest. Tadao will have none of it." Steckle was the U.S. ambassador to Japan.

"Damn!" The president pushed himself up from the desk and began to roam the office with his hands in his pockets. "Why won't the son of a bitch at least talk with us—meet us halfway? He has something we want. There could be some concessions. He's being unreasonable!"

Carlton would have smiled had the stakes not been so high. Bob Garrison owed much of his political success to his personal magnetism and his ability to persuade people to see things his way. During his short tenure at the State Department, Carlton had learned that dealing with the Japanese, even under the best of circumstances, was like watching paint dry. They were slow, methodical, and usually very stubborn. If men are from Mars and women are from Venus, Carlton was found of saying in private company, then the Japanese are from Neptune. There was no way in hell Bob Garrison was going to be able to charm his way through this situation.

"I took the liberty to fax this response to Doctor Sunaga at his home in Palo Alto."

"Sunaga?"

"The fellow out at Stanford who headed the think tank that studied militant Japanese culture." Garrison nodded his recollection. "I spoke briefly with him this morning and he's agreed to act as a consultant on this. Along with the

fax, I told him we might want to talk with him before Tadao
releases this statement to the public.''

"Or before someone leaks it to the press. Hell, Gates, I
have no idea how to respond to this.'' He glanced at his
watch. "We still have thirty-two minutes; get him on the
phone.''

It took the NSA technicians in the White House communications center less than a minute to make the connection and patch the call through to the speaker phone on the
president's desk.

"Doctor Sunaga, this is Gates Carlton. We spoke earlier,
sir.''

"Hello once again, Mr. Secretary.'' The voice had just
a hint of an Asian accent, but served to make his words
measured and precise.

"Doctor, I have the president here with me, and we have
a few questions for you.''

"Thank you for speaking with us, Doctor Sunaga.''

"My pleasure, Mr. President. I am not sure how I can
help, but I will try.''

Garrison gave Carlton a questioning look. "Doctor Sunaga,'' Carlton began, "I will assume you've had a chance
to spend a few minutes with the most recent communication
from Johnston Island. We were hoping that you might give
us the benefit of your opinion as to what Tadao might be
thinking or what he may be about to do?'' Garrison nodded
his assent to the question.

"What you ask is most difficult. First of all, his thoughts
probably would make little sense to you, or to me for that
matter, for he considers himself a warrior-priest and a samurai as well as a true Japanese. He is undoubtedly concerned that future generations of Japanese will regard him
favorably. And I am sure he is thinking about the quality
and setting of his own death.'' Sunaga paused a moment.
"It is also difficult to predict exactly what he will do, but
I am rather sure it will be theatrical, and by our standards,
very barbaric.''

Garrison sighed in exasperation. "Why is he doing this,

Doctor, and why now—why not six months or six years ago?''

"Again a difficult question, Mr. President. It is my personal belief that the Japanese right is very frustrated at this time. Prior to 1945, their animosity was focused on the West, specifically America and the colonial powers, like Great Britain. After the war and until recently, there was the Soviet Union and communist China. Japan and her new American protector-ally had a common enemy, the communists. And there are the four Kurile Islands that the Soviet Union took from Japan during the war. This is an important issue to the Japanese and a rallying point for the right. Now, we are sending aid to Russia and we overlook militarism in North Korea and mainland China. Many Japanese feel isolated, and to the Japanese right, we have once again become the enemy.''

"Is that why he has asked me to apologize for the war?''

"Perhaps. You see, Mr. President, as hard as it is for us to understand, there are those in Japan who feel we are responsible for the war—that the atomic bombs were unnecessary and that the occupation following the war added insult to injury. Tadao's demand for your apology will not be unpopular with a large number of Japanese.''

"I see,'' Garrison replied. "And what about this business with the emperor?''

There was a long pause, and the president was about to repeat the question when Sunaga cleared his throat. "Sir, my natural parents were killed during the war, but I was too young to remember them. I was lucky and was adopted at the age of six. My adoptive parents were American Christian missionaries, but I attended Japanese schools and did not leave Japan until I was almost twelve years old. Mr. President, I consider myself a Christian, and I've raised my own sons to be Christians. But I still pray to my parents, not *for* them—to them. And there is still a part of me, perhaps a very small part, that at least *wants* to believe that the emperor is a god. It's a part of the complex lore and belief system that is Japan. It's a part of me.'' Again, he paused. "Does this help you to understand the issue, sir?"

For several seconds no one spoke. "Yes—yes, it does," the president finally said. "Now tell me, Doctor, do you have any advice for me?"

"Mr. President, there is really very little I can offer. You are dealing with a very determined and, by Western standards, a most ruthless man. I was, however, intrigued that he conveyed his demands to you privately before going to the media with them. It could be that as a matter of courtesy, he is offering you an opportunity to publicly speak first—that he wishes this to be an open exchange."

"Courtesy?" Garrison shook his head slowly. "The man's captured an American installation and killed dozens of our citizens. Now you say he's being courteous?"

"I know this is difficult, sir, but this is very Japanese, or I should say, very Japanese for a samurai and an Imperialist."

"So what do you recommend?"

"If there were some way to allow him to save face and offer him an honorable death, he may listen, but even that may not satisfy him. And you must understand the small value he places on the lives of the hostages. If there is some small concession you could offer him, something that would show respect, it may serve to delay whatever he has in mind. Perhaps the only thing in our favor is that I don't believe Tadao wants to die of chemical poisoning if he can help it. He is not afraid of dying, but this may not meet his criteria for an honorable death. I am sorry I cannot be more helpful or encouraging."

"Thank you, Doctor," Garrison said. "We appreciate your time and your advice." After the connection was broken, he turned to Carlton. "Well?" he said with a show of resignation.

"You've got twenty-three minutes, sir."

Robert Garrison's particular genius was his ability to speak clearly and with absolute conviction with little or no preparation. He lifted several sheets from the corner of his desk and began to scan them. The president had superb speech writers, but he also had a small team of political analysts who provided him with carefully scripted phrases— idea bytes, he liked to call them. The text, which consisted of several pages of these one-liners, was constantly being revised and updated. He now studied the sheets with intense concentration, pausing at intervals to flip a page.

"Okay," he said, looking up to Carlton, "let's go."

The reporters in the White House pressroom scrambled for their chairs while the president took a few moments to change into a fresh shirt and sit for makeup. Fifteen minutes later he was ready. All the while he had the papers before him, scanning them in succession. Finally, just before he stepped to the podium, he took a three-by-five card and scribbled a few cryptic notes. As he had done many times before, he placed the card in his shirt pocket and never looked at it again.

"Ladies and gentlemen of the press, fellow Americans, and citizens of Japan." There was a slight stir from the assembled media as the president included the Japanese people in his remarks. "I wanted to take a few minutes and update you on events as we understand them concerning the unfortunate incident on Johnston Atoll. As you know, a group of Japanese militants has captured Johnston Atoll and made hostages of the American citizens there. These renegades are motivated, in part, by their desire for change in Japan. The leader of the terrorist force, Commandant Tadao, has asked that the emperor of Japan assume the position he held in Japanese society prior to World War II. This would have the effect of returning the Japanese people to the closed, insular society that characterized Japan before the turn of the century.

"So the change Mr. Tadao seeks is not mere political change, but a return to a previous era in Japanese history— a more militant and isolated time. It would also jeopardize the half century of friendship and cooperation our two nations have enjoyed since the end of that terrible conflict. And while our two nations have had their share of misun- derstandings, I believe these five decades of peaceful accord have brought progress and prosperity to the citizens of both lands. Now Mr. Tadao, who has seized our atoll in the Pacific, has placed all of this at risk.

"Then there is the matter of my apology for the events that led to the attack on Pearl Harbor and the war. I can do this—I can say those words." There was a stir in the gallery, and not a few of the older reporters wore a look of astonishment. Several were on the verge of coming out of their seats. "Like you, Mr. Tadao, for I assume that you are listening, I was not born when the war and the events that led to the conflict took place. Yes, I can say I'm sorry for the war and that I'm sorry for any actions on the part of my nation that may have contributed to causing that war. And I can truly say that I'm sorry negotiations between Japan and the United States that were under way just before Pearl Harbor failed."

The president paused a moment and looked away, gripping the edges of the podium as if trying to compose himself. It was very effective. "But can I make an apology for the American people—for the veterans who fought in that war or for the families who waited for their loved ones to return home? Or for the families whose fathers, sons, or brothers did not come home?" Garrison shook his head slowly and continued in a subdued voice. "No, Mr. Tadao. I am the president of the United States of America, but there are limits to my authority. I can tell you that personally, I am sorry our nations fought before we were born, but no more than that."

The president drew himself up and smoothly shifted gears. "Furthermore, I view this invasion by a group of hard-line, Japanese Imperialists on the anniversary of the attack on Pearl Harbor as totally reprehensible. In spite of my personal anger and strong feelings about this provocative act, my immediate concern is for the safety of those Americans on Johnston Island. Tadao has just issued a statement requiring that we comply with his demands by five o'clock Washington time, or he will cause harm to the Americans he holds captive. The current situation on this remote Pacific island and the lives he holds in the balance severely restrict my options. Normally, in situations where hostages have been taken, it has been our firm policy not to negotiate. And in this particular situation, strict compliance with the demands of Mr. Tadao may in fact be impossible. Nonetheless we will, in consultation with our Japanese allies, seek a resolution to the crisis. And we will consider all options.

"To those who have friends and loved ones on Johnston Island, I join all Americans across this great land in sharing your anxiety and your anguish. I assure you that I will do everything in my power to help our people there, to alleviate their suffering, and to bring them home safely and unharmed."

Again, President Garrison paused. "Ladies and gentlemen of the press, I have a great deal of work to do so there will be no time for questions. For those of you watching, I ask that each of you find a quiet moment and offer a prayer for our fellow Americans out there in the Pacific being held against their will. And may God bless all of us as we work for their safe release. Thank you."

The president strode from the room while the assembled reporters came out of their chairs, waving their notebooks and shouting questions.

Saturday, 10 December, 5:50 A.M.
TOKYO, JAPAN

A cold, damp wind had blown down from the Sea of Okhotsk, bringing snow to Hokkaido and the northern portion of the main island and sending freezing rain and fog into the Tokyo area. Dawn was still an hour away. Had it not been a weekend morning, the business commute would have been unusually ferocious.

While most in Japan slept, Prime Minister Mitsuzuka and key members of his government had continued the debate on Johnston Atoll. A heated political discussion had continued with differences sharply drawn between moderates and traditionalists, a division that often slashed across party lines. The right-leaning Renewal Party had all but endorsed the spirit of Tadao's action, while the Socialists wanted a stronger censure from the government.

As the back-room meetings dragged into the early morning hours, no small amount of time was devoted to the financial crisis awaiting them on Monday, when the banks and the Japanese stock market opened. Indications suggested there would be a massive sell-off, and Mitsuzuka was forced to consider closing the exchanges and banks, at least for one day.

Now, at last back in his chambers, with a copy of Tadao's last communiqué in his hands, he listened to the conclusion of the American president's speech. While the commentator reviewed the events leading to the capture of Johnston Atoll, Mitsuzuka sat in silence for several minutes. He too would have to address the citizens of his nation, perhaps before the day was over. Finally he turned to his companion seated nearby, who had kept the vigil with him for most of the night.

"May I know your reaction, Oka-san."

The older man sat staring into space, unmoving as if he had not heard the question. Mitsuzuka waited patiently for him to speak.

"It is all that we feared. Unless this situation can be resolved within a very short time, much that we have worked for and achieved since the war will be lost!" Oka had raised his voice, something he had never before done in Mitsuzuka's presence. Taking a moment to compose himself, he continued. "Both we and the United States are flirting with economic chaos if we fail to manage this situation properly. Neither of us can afford to disengage. Even false statements made only to bring about an end to the crisis could be disastrous. And militarily, our position is difficult. As the Chinese move to extend their influence in Asia and Russia stumbles toward anarchy, we will be isolated. And the North Koreans continue to be restless. If the Americans pull out, we will have no choice but to rearm and become a nuclear power. Feelings in our land run deep when it comes to arms and nuclear weapons. I fear it will tear us apart.''

"And do you have a recommendation?"

Oka frowned and shook his head slowly. "We can do nothing but wait on the Americans. Have we heard from the emperor?"

"I understand that he has agreed to help. At the moment, he is in consultation with leaders of the *Jinja Honcho*." Legally, this was an association that administrated the many Shinto shrines across Japan. In reality, they were a powerful influence on religious thought and the unofficial guardian of Japanese spiritual values. Their counsel was actively sought even by liberal politicians. "We will have his response shortly."

The old man bowed slightly in acknowledgment. Then his eyes became distant, as if his thoughts had shifted elsewhere, perhaps to a time a long time ago, a time before the war that men of his age remembered all too well. A shiver ran through him that nearly forced an outward show of emotion.

Friday, 9 December, 6:35 P.M.
THE WHITE HOUSE

General John McKenzie found President Garrison in the Situation Room in the basement. The Marine sentry felt a bit foolish at asking the Chairman of the Joint Chiefs of Staff for identification, but he had standing orders to check everyone—no exceptions. He carefully scrutinized the photo-ID tag clipped to the pocket flap of McKenzie's uniform before allowing him into the room. Inside, civilian and NSA technicians were busily monitoring the communications systems that kept the president in touch with his military chiefs and senior civilian agencies, domestically and around the world. McKenzie was glad the president had activated the Situation Room and the White House Crisis Management Team. He knew it was a difficult step for Garrison, as it meant he might have to take military action.

Garrison huddled in the corner with Gates Carlton and his press secretary, trying to gauge the public response to the president's address. The broadcast of Tadao's ultimatum by the networks was almost two hours old, and the three of them were screening opinion polls from around the country.

"Excuse me, sir, may I see you a moment?"

"Of course. Thanks, Linda," Garrison said in dismissal. "Keep us posted." She rose and gave McKenzie a neutral look on her way out. Initial reaction to his speech was guardedly positive and Garrison's spirits were buoyed, almost eclipsing his fatigue.

"Please join us, General." They were seated at a Formica table in the corner, one used for coffee breaks by the off-duty watch personnel. The Situation Room was a scattering of communications consoles and TV monitors, much like a crisis-management center at Camp Smith or flag plot aboard the *Tarawa*. The carpets were plush, there was wood paneling instead of metal walls, and some of the chairs had real leather, but the equipment was the same. Garrison glanced at his watch.

"I expected you over an hour ago. Is something wrong?"

"No, Mr. President. I apologize for being late, but my people out in the Pacific needed some additional time for a staff review and probability analysis of our operational plan. I'm able to report that we have a reasonable plan for neutralizing the explosives on the chemical weapons on Johnston Island."

Garrison slid a cup and saucer across the table to McKenzie and poured from a metal thermos embossed with the presidential seal. "I'm listening, General."

For the next ten minutes, McKenzie outlined the plan for

the SEALs to slip ashore on Johnston Island and render the explosives safe. Then he covered the second phase of the operation, which would be an assault by the Marines. When McKenzie finished, the president turned to his secretary of state.

"Gates?"

Carlton lifted his bushy eyebrows and rolled down his lower lip. "Just might work. Does this plan include the Japanese group that was flown in from Okinawa?"

"Yes, sir. In fact, it seems their participation is pivotal to the mission."

"What are the chances?" Garrison asked.

"We estimate a 30 to 45 percent probability for success. That's if we go in tonight. If the operation can be delayed for twenty-four hours, the chance for success could be as much as 55 percent, perhaps higher. However, if you want them to make the attempt tonight, the team has to be given the order within the hour. It's 2:45 P.M. on Johnston Island, and preparations have to go forward now or wait another twenty-four hours."

The president was silent for several moments, then lifted an eyebrow to his secretary of state.

Carlton grimaced. "It's a chance either way. I recommend waiting at least another day. I understand the emperor may try to intervene, which could have some bearing on the issue or at least buy us some time. It would also allow us to brief key members of Congress before taking action." He paused. "This may sound cold and it probably is, but if this Tadao makes good on his threat and there's bloodshed, it will make a chancy rescue operation a little more palatable, especially if things go badly."

All three men knew "palatable" meant politically acceptable. Garrison leaned back in the chair and closed his eyes.

"General?"

"Speaking for the men who will have to go on this mission, sir, we can use the time. The delay will allow us another day of photo-intelligence work and preparation. It'll also allow them more time to get the assault element into position. It could make the difference.''

The decision to wait, and not provoke an incident that could require dropping an atomic bomb on American citizens, was not a difficult one.

''Very well—we wait. Gates, I'll want some recommendations on what to say to Tadao and how to say it. Maybe your people or the folks out at Langley have some ideas as to whether we should give him a flat no or ask for more time. Mitsuzuka may even have some ideas on how to talk to this guy.'' Carlton was busy scratching down notes in a leather-bound notebook. ''General?''

''Yes, sir.''

''If you go ahead with an attack tomorrow night, at what point is it too late to recall your men.''

''Right now, the plan calls for them to hit the storage area between 4:00 and 4:30 in the morning. Unless they're compromised on the way in, they can be recalled right up until the time they go through the fence and attack the facility.''

''Okay, tell your people to prepare to go in tomorrow night. I'll withhold the final authorization until they're ready to launch the mission. But I'll still want to approve the final attack after they're ashore.''

McKenzie wanted to tell Garrison about the dangers of presidential micro-management and of previous disasters, from the Bay of Pigs to the Iran hostage crisis, but he refrained. ''Yes, sir,'' he said as he rose, sensing he was being dismissed. ''Naturally, we'll keep you posted on any substantive issues that may affect this course of action. Per your instructions, the B-52 will continue its orbit on station pending a recall by your order or an authorization to arm the weapon in preparation for a drop.''

''I understand that, General. Thank you.''

After McKenzie left, Garrison turned to Carlton. ''Gates,'' he said in a low voice, ''I'm scared.''

''So am I, Bob—so am I.''

For a short while the two of them sat in silence. If the

communications techs, NSA staffers, and military personnel who manned the Situation Room thought it odd that the commander-in-chief and the secretary of state were sitting in their coffee mess in their shirt sleeves, they gave no indication. Garrison drew a deep breath and looked at Carlton.

"All right, I'm going to want a closed-door meeting with a bipartisan group from the Hill. Let's keep it under fifteen, and include McKenzie and the director of Central Intelligence. I want them to know exactly what we're up against, and the reasoning behind this course of action."

"Are we going to tell them about the possibility of dropping a nuclear weapon on Johnston Island?"

"Absolutely. The War Powers Act specifically states that the president will not resort to nuclear weapons without consulting Congress unless an enemy strike is imminent." He smiled ruefully. "I have no first-strike authority. Legally, I cannot drop that bomb without consulting them—even if we're bombing our own people."

Politically, you don't want to drop it without consulting them, Carlton thought. But he agreed with the president; some decisions were too big to be made alone. "I'll get together with the Speaker and the vice president and prepare a list for your approval." He made a few more notes and rose from the table. "Anything else?"

"You can pray, Gates. That's what I'm going to do."

Friday, 9 December, 4:30 P.M.
SIXTY MILES EAST OF JOHNSTON ISLAND

The *Vinson* battle group leisurely steamed through a rolling mid-Pacific seaway. Occasionally, the formation turned in unison and sprinted into the wind while the big carrier launched or recovered aircraft. Then they returned to base course and a comfortable twelve knots. The wind was freshening and now from the southwest, but the sky was flossed with strands of high cirrus clouds that said the upper atmospheric winds were still building.

Aboard the *Tarawa*, Senior Chief Will Stockton made his way through officers' country, checking staterooms. He found the right door and quietly slipped inside. Stockton paused a moment to allow his eyes to adjust to the darkness. Then he found the bulkhead-mounted desk light and clipped it on, throwing light and shadow across the blanketed forms lumped in each of the two single beds. He quietly took a chair near the foot of one of the beds.

"Mister Moody?" No response.

"Hey, Lieutenant, wake up."

Moody bolted upright in the bed. "Is it time? What time is it?"

"Easy, sir, easy. It's about 1630 and—"

"Sixteen thirty—we're late! What the fuck's going on, Senior!"

"Relax, sir. We've been scrubbed for tonight."

"Huh—what!" Moody was fully awake now, and there was a wild look in his eyes.

"It's off for tonight. Word just came down, and they've decided to wait for twenty-four hours. We got another day."

Moody, sitting upright, now slumped back against the bulkhead, closing his eyes. The flood of relief was almost nauseating, but the respite was fleeting. Another day's preparation would certainly improve their chances, but the delay was just a stay of execution. Now there would be another day of apprehension and the fear quickly returned.

Their frantic preparation the previous night would have placed them on Johnston Island just before dawn tomorrow—Saturday morning. The five hours of scheduled sleep between 1030 and 1530 today were a part of that plan. Timing and rest intervals for the assault team were a critical component of mission planning. While Moody and Walker slept, Senior Chief Stockton had worried over the details of the operation. He also made the decision to allow them the additional hour of sleep when the mission was postponed.

"Okay, Senior, anything changed on the atoll?" Moody said huskily, as the emotion drained out of him. Before he'd turned in, the staff duty officer had briefed them on Tadao's deadline and the president's statement. Given Tadao's promise of bloodshed, he'd felt sure they would go in as soon as possible. Stockton pulled the chair closer and fished his notebook from his blouse pocket. He began to brief Moody like a father reading a bedtime story to his son.

"Okay, here's how we stand. The guys on the *La Jolla* been bustin' their ass on the boats and they're both mission-capable. They've been notified of the delay and have re-scheduled the mission pre-dive and pre-launch procedures. The EOD guy finally got here, just before 1200, and I think you better have a talk with him." Stockton gave Moody a quick look of caution and continued. "We got the shooters in from Guam, the ones we wanted—Tom Slyfield and Darron Jackson. Since we got the delay, they wanted to test-fire their weapons. It'll also give us a chance for a test of the NODs. I scheduled it for 2000 this evening." He flipped a page in his notebook. "All the gear and weapons we requested from Ford Island and Coronado are here. The Jappos an' a couple of the jarheads gave me a hand, an' we got everything stowed in waterproof bags and ready for transport to the sub."

"How about the weather?"

"Just like this for the next twelve hours, then it's supposed to start to kick up—first the wind, then the seas. Last time I was topside, the sky was lookin' kinda weird. They're saying the storm will build gradually and the main winds will be here early Sunday morning—about the time you're going over the beach. The good news is, the winds are lighter than we expected, in the fifty-to-sixty-knot range."

Moody shrugged. "We can't do much right now about the weather. It'll cause us some problems, but any diversion will be a help."

"I've scheduled us to board the *La Jolla* at 2200 to-night," Stockton continued. "We wait much later than that and the seas may pick up and give us some problems. If they stay reasonably calm like now, I think we can still load everything in a Mike boat and go alongside for the transfer. Two helos'll be standing by just in case."

Again, Moody nodded his approval. Slinging the equipment and people down to the sub from a helo at night was tedious and dangerous. There was little chance that the terrorists on Johnston Island would have access to satellite photos, but several nations beside the United States and Russia had orbiting intelligence satellites. They were taking no chances; the transfer had to be done at night. A sighting of a submarine on the surface near the battle group would surely tip their hand.

"How about the briefings?"

"I've rescheduled you for the support element briefing at 1800—about an hour and a half from now. Our radio frequencies have been authenticated and the radios are being set up and tested. The warning order is scheduled aboard the sub for 0045. You guys will bed down again about noon tomorrow. Then we'll see how close we can get to the target to launch the SDVs. I'll set the mission briefing for five hours ahead of the launch with time for a half-hour brief back. Then it's showtime." Stockton snapped his notebook closed. "How do you feel?"

"Like I could use a drink," Moody replied wearily.

Stockton smiled and pulled a bottle of Crown Royal from the pleated pocket on the side of his camouflaged trousers. He spun the top off and handed it to Moody.

He raised an eyebrow at the bottle and then at his chief. "Nice stuff, Senior, but you're not supposed to have liquor on board a Navy ship."

"It's okay, sir; it's medicinal."

"I see. And how'd you know I like Crown Royal?" Moody knew Stockton hadn't brought this aboard with him, and he was not about to ask him how he came by it.

"It's my job to know these things, sir. That's why I'm

a chief in this man's Navy and you're just a lieutenant."
Stockton looked at him evenly with no hint of a smile.

"Is this a private party or can the swabbies join in?"
Walker sat on the edge of the other rack, yawning and
scratching. He was completely nude. Moody handed the
bottle back to Stockton, who passed it to Walker. He took
a long pull before returning it to the chief. "Smooth as a
baby's ass," he said, savoring the taste. "I assume the mission's a no-go for tonight," he said as he pulled on his
trousers, "or has this operation officially been classified as
a kamikaze mission, and this is a substitute for the sake."

"We got a twenty-four-hour reprieve," Moody told him.

Walker considered this as he raked his hand through his
hair. "Another day t' pretend we're not scared shitless.
Such a deal. How're the boats?"

"I just spoke with Berta on the *La Jolla*. They're both
up and ready," said Stockton. "We'll be back aboard the
sub late tonight so you can check 'em out for yourself."

"Anything else?" Moody asked.

Stockton hesitated, rubbing his jaw. "Just one thing,
sir." He stoppered the bottle and slid it back into his trouser
pocket. "I think a couple of th' Japanoozers are a little
light in the loafers."

"Queer?" said Moody. "You're shitting me."

"I don't think so, sir."

"You sayin' we got some rump wranglers on th' team?"
said Walker.

Stockton just gave him a cold look.

"Swell," Walker continued. "Who's the lucky SEAL
who gets to snuggle in the back of an SDV with one of
those guys?"

Moody ignored him. "Just what makes you think so,
Senior Chief?" He quickly began to dress, and suddenly
he was very serious. Anything that could affect the mission
concerned him.

"I saw two of 'em holding hands in the berthing compartment, just for a moment. Then I kinda kept an eye on
them and well, it's just the way they treated each other."

"Could you be mistaken?"

"Maybe, but I doubt it. They're fags, sir."

"Shit," Moody said softly. He knew Stockton wouldn't have brought it up if he wasn't sure. "I really don't need this right now."

"What're you gonna do, sir?" said Walker.

"Guess I'll have to have a talk with Captain Nakajima," Moody said as he quickly dressed. "Senior, how you getting on with the Japanese top kick?"

"Sergeant Ozawa? Okay, I guess. He doesn't say much and he acts like someone starched his skivvies, but he knows his stuff. We checked the weapons out together, and he handles a submachine gun like a professional armorer. They've made some modifications to their MP-5s I'd like to copy."

"He straight?"

Stockton shrugged. "I suppose so and he's one hard son of a bitch, I can tell you that. If those Jappos on the island are half as tough as him, we got trouble."

Moody was silent for a moment. "You say we have an hour or so until the support briefing?" The support briefing was a gathering of the air-group squadron commanders, Marine assault element leaders, and destroyer gunnery officers—all of whom could be called on for support as soon as the explosives on the chemicals were disarmed.

Stockton glanced at his watch. "About an hour and fifteen minutes."

"Fair enough," Moody replied. "Let me grab some chow and I'll meet you in flag plot. I want to see the latest intelligence and then we'll go over the brief together." Stockton nodded and rose. Moody turned to Walker. "You ready for some chow, Don?"

"This mean I get to eat in the wardroom, boss?"

"No, it means we're both headed for the mess decks—it's quicker."

"Can we hold hands?"

"Don't talk like that in front of the chief. He'll be on to us. And no skipping in the passageways."

Stockton scowled and followed them out, scratching an entry in his notebook as he went.

Saturday, 10 December, 1:43 P.M.
TOKYO

Emperor Akihito sat in his private study in the Imperial Palace and contemplated the events of the past twenty-four hours. He had just finished a simple lunch of rice and vegetables. An attendant brought in a fresh pot of tea and silently retired. His study was a blend of old and new—the low, ornate table where he took his meals was from the Taisho Era and contemporary by comparison, but many of the furnishings dated back to the Kamakura Era. There were a few pieces of pottery from the Heian Period, priceless artifacts thrown by Ainu craftsman over a thousand years ago. A massive desk in the corner of the room had been the gift of a Dutch trader to a ranking member of the Tokugawa family. An oak credenza behind the desk held the tools of a modern executive: personal computer, fax machine, telephone, and small television. Leather-bound volumes of old and contemporary literature lined the walls. While Akihito sat on a tatami mat for the occasional meal he took in his study, the room held several expensive European-style chairs and a comfortable, padded settee.

The world of Akihito was far different from that of his father, who'd held the Chrysanthemum Throne from 1926 until his death in 1989. The horror of the war was a highly filtered memory for the then-crown prince. Akihito, who'd been sheltered as well from much of the shame and struggle of the postwar years, had finished his graduate studies in England, thus completing a comprehensive liberal-arts education. The emperor was a symbol of the Japanese nation.

He was consulted and advised, but he had no real political power. It was a job for life, replete with ceremony but no real responsibility. From this vantage point, Akihito had become an astute political observer, and elected officials sought his advice more often than was publicly known. And, as expected of a direct descendant of the gods, he was the highest-ranking Shinto priest in the land.

The Johnston Island affair had caused Akihito a great deal of personal anguish. He understood, perhaps better than many politicians, the terrible forces that were in play. Takashi Tadao appealed to the Japanese people at the very root of their souls, perhaps touching some ancient core of awareness long smothered by their modern world. Discipline and self-sacrifice, the foundation of the Japanese character, had allowed the nation to rise from the ashes of the war. But this industrial renaissance and national prosperity had done little to improve the Japanese spirit and sense of self. As economic growth slowed and the Americans pressed for access to Japanese markets, many Japanese, especially the younger ones, had begun to question commercial achievement.

For a time in the eighties, corporate and financial leaders had assumed the role of the new samurai and been respected and admired. But now times were changing, and more Japanese were looking to the past to redefine their national identity. They saw only the beauty and order and nobility of their history—none of the brutality and suffering. Japan's commercial leaders were tarnished by the recent recession and the politicians weakened by corruption and scandal. Now this Tadao had burst on the scene as a bold, noble lone samurai.

There was a soft knock at the door and a senior member of the Imperial Household Agency slipped inside. He advanced a few short paces and bowed low. "One-Under-Heaven, I am here to remind you of your address to the nation in thirty minutes. All preparations have been made. You will speak from a podium in the Main Reception Hall in accordance with your instructions. May I be of service in any other way?''

''No, that will be all.'' The man retreated noiselessly, leaving Akihito alone with his thoughts.

All morning he had received various officials and advisers for consultations on the crisis. A delegation from the *Jinja Honcho* had again called to offer their perspective on the matter. In the 1930s they had been allied with the Shinto militarists who had taken the nation to war, but now their members were pacific and proponents of nonviolence. Tadao's capture of the American island in the Pacific had shaken them profoundly. Potential impact on Japanese-American relations was immense, but the *Jinja Honcho* clearly saw a greater danger in the possible disintegration of modern Japanese society. Akihito found their arguments compelling, and the bleak assessment had been reinforced by a palace visit from a very worried prime minister and his father's old adviser, Masayoshi Oka.

Demonstrations in Tokyo and the other urban areas were growing in frequency and force. The emperor had as deep an understanding of Shinto as anyone, not only spiritually but historically. Furthermore, he clearly knew the destructive forces that lay beneath the surface of his polite, hardworking subjects. He took a last, careful sip of tea and rose from the table. Then he walked briskly to the Imperial suite to change for his address.

The setting for Akihito's address was most unlike that of a U.S. presidential press conference, or even of an important public announcement by the Japanese prime minister. Every conceivable detail, except the content of the speech, had been micro-managed by the Imperial Household Agency staff. Akihito, dressed in a dark suit, white shirt, and conservative tie, faced a single camera flanked by banks of portable lighting. The video feed would be distributed to the media through the Ministry of Home Affairs. A dozen Japanese reporters formed a small gallery off to one side, polite and orderly—very different from their

Western counterparts. The hall's immense, ornate wood paneling added dignity to the proceedings.

Akihito himself looked like a college president. A televised speech by the emperor was not an infrequent occurrence, but such events were normally confined to religious or cultural topics. For this address the Japanese people had been given little notice, but few in the country were far from a television or a radio when their emperor stepped to the podium.

Akihito leafed through his notes and waited for the senior technician to signal for him to begin. This was the first truly political address in his short reign. He correctly sensed it would be the most important Imperial address since his father had spoken to the nation by radio to announce the end of the war—not to surrender, for Japan had never officially admitted defeat—but a cessation of hostilities.

"Citizens of Japan," the emperor began, looking directly into the camera. "Today I will speak to you about recent events on a small Pacific island halfway between Japan and the United States of America. Two days ago on December 8th, a small band of Japanese rightists took control of Johnston Atoll. The atoll is the property of the United States and the location of an important military facility. The attackers have also taken nearly one thousand Americans as prisoners. I join the elected government of our nation in voicing my personal condemnation of this lawless action. Furthermore, this illegal act by a group of Japanese citizens and the continued threat to innocent, unarmed Americans has placed our nation in a most difficult position.

"Over the past several decades, the evolution of our modern society and the demands of global economic competition have placed great strains on traditional Japanese values and thought. True, it may seem that we are moving in a direction away from the spiritual and harmonious way of our ancestors, but is this really what has happened? Are we not free to pause and offer a prayer at a local shrine on our way home from the office or factory? Can we not still set aside a few hours each week to appreciate the splendid beauty of our land, for quiet meditation, and to seek that which is pure? We are a free and democratic people. Because we enjoy this freedom, there are many distractions in our cities and our homes. Many of these diversions have come to us from America and other Western nations. But Japan is rich in religious tradition and a land blessed with unsurpassed natural beauty. Each of us must choose. Politician, factory worker, farmer, student, laborer, government worker . . . emperor. Do we have to give ourselves over completely to these modern electronic devices or to a jaded Western lifestyle? Or are we not free to look within ourselves for our noble heritage, and around us for the natural beauty brought to life by the *kami*?

"The men who have captured the American island in the Pacific would like to make that decision for you. They, by their actions, would have us return to the Tokugawa Era of the seventeenth and eighteenth centuries—a time of isolation. But those were times of great repression and military domination. Today the people of Japan enjoy freedoms only the elite classes knew before the Meiji Restoration and the dawn of our modern state. The freedom to pray as we choose, whether Shinto, Confucian, Buddhist, or Christian, is the bequest of the honorable ancestors who precede us. So is the right to live with honor and in harmony as we choose. This is not the right of the men who have captured the American island.

"These men call themselves the New Shield Society. They demand that our Self Defense Force again become a national army, and that as emperor, I again acknowledge my direct lineage to the Sun Goddess." Akihito stared directly into the camera, but paused to measure his words. "Our constitution correctly forbids Japan to raise and maintain a national army. This can be altered only by a modification to our constitution; this is not an Imperial decision. As for my lineage, my family traces its origins back to the beginning of Japan. And are we all not the descendants of the Sun Goddess? And does the *kami* not dwell within each of us, just as it does the soil, air, and waters of our sacred land?''

Akihito again paused and carefully turned a page of his text. "The United States of America has been our friend and mentor for almost a half century. We have prospered together, and much that is good in both Japan and America is dependent on our continued cooperation. It is also true that our two nations have had their difficulties. Younger brother has grown, and there is bound to be a time of testing and friction with elder brother. This is to be expected. But let us not lose sight of that which has made this nation prosperous and a leader in the world community. Let us not allow this small band of *ronin* to destroy what we have accomplished this half century.

"To Commandant Tadao of the New Shield Society, I command you and those with you to release your hostages and present yourself to the American authorities on Johnston Atoll. No matter how noble your motives, you have dishonored us with your actions. Only the immediate repatriation of American property and those Americans held in captivity can cleanse this impurity which has stained our reputation as a responsible and trustworthy nation." Akihito was careful to avoid the word *surrender* in his remarks.

"To the American people, I ask your forgiveness and indulgence in this unfortunate incident. Please do not judge the nation of Japan by the actions of these few. To the people of Japan, I ask you to join me in prayer for a speedy resolution to this untimely event. Thank you."

Akihito inclined his head ever so slightly. He looked back into the camera for just a moment before the picture was cut away. Except for the two cameramen, everyone in the room bowed deeply from the waist. Then the emperor strode from the room with several attendants of the household staff hurrying after him.

A short while later, Akihito emerged from the Imperial suite dressed in a traditional kimono. He was immediately approached by a senior secretary.

"One-Under-Heaven, the prime minister is on the telephone. Mr. Mitsuzuka wishes to congratulate you on your address to the nation."

"Tell the prime minister that I have gone to pray."

With that, Akihito, normally a most courteous man, swept past the startled secretary, leaving him ashamed and bowing in his wake. He made his way to a private, immaculately tended courtyard garden. In the corner of the lawn, between two ancient pine bonsai, was the family shrine. Akihito approached with small, careful steps, head bowed. Then he knelt, head still bowed, and clapped his hands twice. At the center of the shrine was a picture of the emperor Hirohito.

"Honorable father, I humbly pray that my actions and words this day will reflect credit upon you and our illustrious ancestors who have gone before you. I also ask that you join me to beseech the *kami* that this danger will pass from our sacred land." He clapped twice more and bowed until his head touched the weathered stones at the base of the shrine.

Friday, 9 December, 8:43 P.M.
SIXTY-FIVE MILES EAST OF JOHNSTON ISLAND

The *Tarawa* had detached itself from the main body of the battle group and was steaming independently in a northeasterly direction. While the emperor of Japan was finishing his speech, the LHA was making eighteen knots to match the speed of the wind now coming out of the southwest at the stern. A quarter moon filtered through the thickening clouds. The *Tarawa* was at a darken-ship condition, and the only illumination coming from the ship was a soft red glow from the bridge windows, high on the starboard island superstructure. CH-53C and CH-46E helicopters crowded on the starboard side just aft of the island. Moody and Nakajima stood on the bow, looking aft down an otherwise deserted flight deck. Both men had their fingers in their ears.

Crack! A heavy .308 round ripped down the flight deck and found the ten-inch paper target propped up on the stern some eight hundred feet away. The shooter, lying prone on the deck behind a sinister-looking rifle, took his cheek from the weapon and spoke quietly into the Motorola transceiver. He made a single adjustment to the bulky sight on top of the rifle and again settled in behind it.

Crack!

After another consultation, he made no more adjustments but fired five rounds in quick succession. His was a semi-automatic rifle. Then he disengaged himself from the weapon and stood up, removing his clear shooting glasses and dropping the cupped ear protectors down around his neck. ''I reckon that's got it, sir,'' the shooter said to Moody. ''Both guns're sighted in. Course that's in a dead-air shoot. From what you been tellin' us, they's a purty good storm a-comin'.''

''That's what they tell me, Sly. If we can get you to the shooting position we want, you'll probably have the wind directly behind you, but there's no guarantees. You're ready to shoot night or day?''

''Yes, sir. I'll attend to the nighttime chores an' Darron will shoot in the light. Course, after sunup I'll take off the night-sight and give him a hand. Ah'm pretty fair with iron sights an' Darron ain't bad in the daylight—for a college boy.''

''I can whip your ass on a long-range course anytime, you fucking hillbilly,'' said the black SEAL standing behind Nakajima. The shooter turned around and they exchanged grins.

Moody had asked for the top SEAL sniper team in the Pacific Theater. Tom Slyfield and Darron Jackson were the best; they'd been shooting together for close to three years. There were certainly Marine sniper teams who could challenge them, but they were among the best in the U.S. military, perhaps the world. Petty Officers Slyfield and Jackson were attached to the Naval Special Warfare Unit in Guam, and they'd been on a training mission in one of the Gulf states when they were ordered to join the *Vinson* battle group. The twenty-four-hour delay in the operation had allowed them to re-sight their weapons after the long trip. Shooting in the desert was different from shooting in the tropics.

The two shooters were a study in contrast. Slyfield was a lean Texan and a fourteen-year SEAL veteran who'd been shooting all his life. There was a time his skill had kept venison on the family table when there was little else to eat. He'd quit high school to enlist and managed to complete his GED during his second hitch in the Navy. In spite of his time in service, he was still only a second-class petty officer.

Darron Jackson was a different man. His father was a prominent doctor in Baltimore, and Darron had a degree in physics from Penn State. He'd enlisted in the Navy to thwart his parents, who'd been pushing him to attend graduate school. Jackson had never fired a gun until basic training. Then, in a follow-on act of parental defiance, he'd volunteered for SEAL training. He was a solid six-footer who would have been fat had he chosen a profession that didn't require heavy exercise on a daily basis. Darron Jackson had been in the teams for five years and he was already a first-class petty officer. Jackson was a natural shooter, which meant he had the eye and a steady hand. He was a good sniper because he could put a round through a man's head or torso with the same detachment he would the ten rings of a paper target. He'd never hunted an animal besides man. Slyfield and Jackson were constantly putting each other down when they were together, but separately each would tell anyone who would listen what a great marksman and marvelous human being his partner was. Jackson held a senior rating, but he deferred to Slyfield, who acted as the sniper team leader.

Walker joined them having just walked the length of the flight deck. He carried a Motorola handset and two paper targets. He rolled the targets out on the deck and played a red-filtered flashlight across them. The five men knelt around them. They were small-bore, 1,000-inch targets with a 7-inch outer ring and a 2 ¼-inch black bull in the center. Both targets had a single round three or four inches off center and another just out of the black. The rest were in a tight group smaller than a quarter.

"Good thing we had time ta sight in," Slyfield droned. "We was all over the place."

Nakajima tested the perforations with his fingertips. He almost couldn't believe the accuracy. The men in the Counter Force were all very good marksmen, but nothing close to this, even with their sniper weapons. Perhaps, he reasoned, these men were so proficient because their primary duty was to perfect their long-range shooting skills.

He stepped over to the two weapons and dropped to one knee to inspect them more closely. One was a Heckler & Koch PSG-1 semiautomatic sniper rifle. Its barrel was supported by a lightweight collapsible tripod. Nakajima recognized the rifle but not the scope. A thick, short cylinder was perched on top of the weapon. The awkward-looking device was a Litton M845 night scope that allowed sniper accuracy under very low-light conditions. All the shooter needed was a sliver of a moon or starlight. The second rifle, the one the black SEAL had fired just before dark, was a McMillan M-86 with a Leupold Ultra 10X-M1 scope. It was by comparison a simple weapon, but deadly accurate. The M-86 was not a semiautomatic weapon, but a bolt action rifle that held four rounds in an internal magazine and one in the chamber.

"What are you shooting?" Walker asked respectfully, still staring at the targets. Both Slyfield and Jackson had won medals at the national Long Range Rifle Championships, achieving SEAL celebrity status in the process.

"That's probably th' only thing Junior an' me agrees on," said Slyfield. "We both fire a Federal Match 168-grain boat-tail hollow point. She flies purty well an'll kick the shit out of a man up to a thousand yards."

"You guys ready?" Moody said, glancing at his watch.

"Don't much know if we're ready or not," Slyfield replied evenly, "but we can shoot, 'ceptin' for that wind of course." Moody had told them of the dangers of the mission and held nothing back. They were accustomed to sniper missions where they could find a shooting perch in a safe area, well back and out of harm's way. Both understood this would be different.

"Do the best you can, Sly. This operation won't get canceled because of a little wind. You better get your rifles stowed and down to the Mike boat. We shove off for the sub in about an hour."

"Aye, sir. C'mon Darron, let's git packed up."

"Don," Moody asked, "the NODs being checked out?"

"Yes, sir. The chief and Sergeant Ozawa are doing that right now." Seeing at night was as critical as being able to shoot at night. Along with the other equipment airlifted in that day for the mission, the SEALs were equipped with sophisticated, goggle-like night observation devices, called NODs.

"Okay, let the OOD know we're all finished here. Then tell the chief I'll see him down on the well deck."

"Aye aye, sir."

While the two shooters tended to their weapons, Walker spoke into his Motorola. The *Tarawa* heeled to starboard in a port turn and headed back toward Johnston Island and the battle group.

"Taro, I need to speak with you." Moody motioned to Nakajima and they began to walk slowly aft. "Your people ready to leave the ship?"

"Yes. Your chief and my sergeant have spoken." Moody nodded. "Your snipers are amazing," Nakajima continued. "I have never seen shooting like that."

"We're lucky. Sly and Jackson are two of the best. I just hope we're able to get them into position, and the wind doesn't make it impossible for them to shoot." They walked in silence for several moments before Nakajima spoke.

"John-san, you seem troubled. Is it something more than the mission ahead of us?"

Moody forced a grin. "Isn't that enough?"

"Yes," Nakajima replied carefully, "but there is something else."

"Yes, there is something else." He hesitated, taking a deep breath before continuing. "We're going to have to work together pretty closely to have any chance of pulling this thing off, and uh, well, I understand that maybe some of your men are gay."

"Gay? You mean happy?"

"No, gay. You know, homosexual—queer."

"So," Nakajima replied with a look of understanding and relief, "you mean *okama*. Yes, homosexual; is that your meaning?"

"*Okama?*"

"That is our word for it, although the more common usage in Japan today is 'new half.' I think it is taken from your English expression when referring to a female mate as your 'better half.' As for my men, you must be referring to Hori and Mishizawa. Is this a problem?"

"Well, yeah, it could be. I guess we're not used to working with guys who are new half." For some reason, Moody found himself more comfortable with the Americanized Japanese term.

"You mean," Nakajima said with a show of surprise, "that you would reject a good soldier because he has personal feelings for another man?"

Moody thought about it for a moment. "Yeah, I think I probably would. I mean, doesn't this bother you? And wouldn't that affect their performance if the two of them were on a mission together?"

Americans! thought Nakajima. How can they shoot so well and be such masters of military technology, yet be so short-sighted? "Allow me to explain it," he said patiently. "We are samurai. The strict code that governs our lives, and even our thoughts, demands that we place duty and service above all else. The food we eat, the manner in which we dress, even our personal lives—all of this, is strictly controlled to allow us to become better warriors. A woman, or another man for that matter, is for companionship or sexual release—nothing more. This—'' Nakajima hesitated as he framed his words carefully, ''this diversion is useful as it contributes to our effectiveness as warriors. That Hori and Mishizawa have found comfort in each other does not affect their obligation as samurai. Both understand the role of such a liaison and its relationship to their duty. It harms nothing and perhaps makes each a better warrior. Do you understand, John-san?''

''I'm trying. It's just that we don't have queer—er, new-half men in our outfit, at least they're not openly new half.'' Moody smiled. ''Guess we're kind of American about that stuff. Will you take either of these men on the operation?''

''Only Hori. He is very comfortable in the water and he is most skilled at silent, close-range killing. Mishizawa is also capable, but his special skills are communications and parachuting, duties he would not be required to perform on this mission. Is there a problem with this?''

Moody considered it for a moment. ''Well, I guess not. It probably wouldn't do for one of my SEALs, but I suppose it's okay for your men.''

They walked in silence for a short time, then Nakajima said softly, ''Tell me, John-san, do you really think that as a warrior, you are so different from us?''

Moody didn't answer immediately. ''Look, Taro, I really don't know a lot about this samurai stuff, but your strict rules and your ideas about seeking an honorable death seem strange to us.''

''I see. Then you find it unusual that we think about death on a daily basis?'' Moody nodded. ''I can understand that most Americans would not grasp this. Today, few Japanese do. But you are a warrior, John-san. Surely you think about death and prepare for it?''

Moody considered this. ''Not really. It's always there, but I suppose in a lot of ways we try not to think about it. You see, we really try to get the job done without casualties. The idea is to hit the objective and not get anybody killed. When we plan a mission, we give a lot of thought to *not* dying.''

"I appreciate that, John-san; we too plan carefully, but it is more than that." Nakajima searched for the right words. "Each day a samurai thinks about his own death— that if his duty should require that he must die, he will embrace his fate and die well. We believe that only when a man has come to terms with his own death and no longer fears death, is he truly able to live freely. And in some ways, I believe you agree with this."

Moody gave him a sidelong, skeptical look. Nakajima smiled and continued. "You see, even though you Americans seldom talk about death or openly prepare for it, you expect men to die bravely. What is the most noble act a man in your army can perform? To give his life for his nation or his fellow soldier, is it not? A soldier who faces almost certain death to rescue his comrades is highly revered in your culture. You see, I have carefully studied the history of your military and it is abundant with such heroes. Men who fought and died to save others are among your most respected warriors. You give medals to men who fall on hand grenades and die to save those around them. I believe you encourage, even expect, your soldiers to die bravely, yet you seldom openly talk about death. I do not mean to criticize your ways, John-san, but *this* seems very strange to *us*."

"Well, I wouldn't look for any of my SEALs to go diving on any hand grenades," Moody said with a smile. "That's just not our style." Then he continued in a more serious tone. "So then, you're prepared to die?" He was not entirely comfortable talking about this, but he felt he needed to understand it. Nakajima and his men were critical to the success of the operation.

"Of course," Nakajima replied immediately. "It may be my fate to live long and die an old man, sick with disease. So be it. I will not end my life foolishly, nor will I leave this world seeking false glory. We all hope for a warrior's death, but duty comes first." Nakajima paused to face the taller American. "Don't you see, John-san? The probability of death on this mission is very strong. That is of no consequence, for I have already settled the matter; I will choose life or death as the mission requires." He gave a casual shrug. "Now I am free to focus totally on the work before us."

"And you are without fear?"

"Oh no, John-san; how I wish it were so." He chuckled softly and offered Moody one of his rare smiles. "I fear failure and I fear dishonor. I fear that if we are unable to stop Tadao my country will suffer terrible consequences. But I certainly do not fear dying."

Moody watched Nakajima closely, seeing nothing but sincerity and determination. And he envied him. During the few moments he had had to himself since they came aboard *Tarawa*, he had nearly been overwhelmed by fear—fear of the terrible responsibility of what he was being asked to do, but also of his own mortality. He managed these thoughts of death by keeping busy and crowding it from his mind with details of planning the mission. But if he were to peal back the responsibility and the planning and the operational details—all part of his intricate, personal self-defense apparatus—he had to admit that he was afraid to die. He had fought down these spasms of terror by telling himself that this was a normal reaction—that every man going into combat feels the same way. All men are afraid, he reminded himself, and a brave man is just one who can handle it—or conceal it.

But here was a man, a very capable and experienced warrior, who was serene and composed when talking of dying. Could their way be better? I'll do what I have to do, Moody thought now, and I'll do it my way. And God help me, I'll stand tall when the shit gets thick. In some ways, I wish I could be like Nakajima and be spared from the terror of it all, but that's not the way it is for me. I'm just not Japanese.

"I can't tell you that I'm not afraid, Taro. I just deal with it differently than you."

"I understand, John-san." There was a hint of compassion in his voice, almost pity. "I also sense that when the battle is joined, you too are a samurai. Until that time, let me know if I can be of assistance. It is an excellent plan, and I believe that our prospects are good."

"Thank you," Moody replied. Then, changing the subject, "I have to speak with the general before we shove off. I'll see you in the well deck."

General Sheppard was sitting in the commander's chair, flipping through a clipboard well stocked with message traffic. From time to time he scribbled instructions at the bottom of a page. Like most crisis situations requiring any kind of a military response, this one was largely a matter of bureaucracy. Only those few who would have to engage the enemy at close quarters would be spared the paperwork and the continuous exchange of message traffic and situation reports. The hum of conversation changed slightly as Moody made his way across flag plot to Sheppard.

"All set, Lieutenant?"

"Yes, sir. The equipment and weapons we requested are aboard and are being loaded onto the Mike boat." Moody looked at his watch. "We'll be shoving off in about twenty minutes. Preparations aboard the La Jolla will continue tonight and most of tomorrow morning. The sub will begin to maneuver close to Johnston Island late tomorrow afternoon. I'm glad we have the extra time. We're scheduled to launch in the SDVs at 2300 tomorrow night or perhaps later, depending on how close the La Jolla can get to the island."

"Very well," Sheppard replied. "Still plan to cross the beach at 0400?"

"Yes, sir."

Sheppard nodded. "We'll be in communication with the sub. We'll keep you posted of any changes in the situation on the island, and of course, if there's a decision to abort the mission. For now you have to assume it's a green light all the way. Nonetheless, once you're ashore you'll have to wait for authorization before making the final assault." Moody gave him a pained look. "I understand, Lieutenant, believe me I do. You have my sympathies, but those are my instructions from the national command authority, understood?"

"Yes, sir."

Sheppard slipped from the high padded chair to his feet. "I want you to understand one thing, Lieutenant. This staff and this battle group are here for one reason and one reason only—to support you while you do your job. It's your plan and your mission; all we can do here is stand ready to lend a hand. If there's anything you need, and I can get it, you'll have it. Fair enough?"

"Fair enough, sir, and thanks. I appreciate that."

"Any questions?"

"No, sir."

"Very well, sailor. I don't have to tell you how much we're counting on you. Good luck and God bless you." Sheppard reached for his billed fatigue hat and pulled it on. Then he came to attention and saluted *him*. "Take care of your men, Lieutenant."

"Aye aye, sir." Moody was uncovered but he returned the salute anyway.

Thirty minutes later Moody was in the Mike boat and clear of the LHA's well deck. The wind was beginning to lash at the sea, causing an occasional white-cap to tumble from one of the swells. The landing craft wallowed away from its mother ship, searching the dark sea for the even darker shape of the *La Jolla*, which had just surfaced about a thousand yards away on *Tarawa*'s port beam.

Friday, 9 December, 9:13 P.M.
JOHNSTON ISLAND

Takashi Tadao stood in the center of the carpeted reception area in the operations center, staring at the large color television. The speech of Emperor Akihito had been transmitted live to the Japanese people, but by an agreement with the major wire services, the broadcast was delayed two hours for international viewing. After a short introduction in English by a BBC anchor, the entire speech aired in Japanese with English subtitles parading across the bottom of the screen. Jim Bruso, Senator Blackman, and General Taggart sat watching from the corner of the room. Nearby, a small, dark stain on the carpet marked where Colonel Trafton had spewed blood with his last gasps. That had happened only two days ago, but for the three captives it seemed much longer. Two Japanese stood with Tadao, off to one side and a step behind him.

The commandant's feet were apart and his arms folded tightly across his chest. His face was a grim mask and the corners of his mouth drooped with contempt. During the portion of the speech where the emperor commanded him to relinquish his control of the island—in essence to surrender—Tadao stiffened and his eyes blazed. The two soldiers behind him glanced at each other and moved uneasily. The emperor had also commanded them to lay down their arms.

"What are your instructions, Commandant?" said one of the men following the telecast.

Tadao wheeled on him fiercely. "They are as before. This . . . this charade changes nothing. What we have seen is the puppet Akihito whose strings are controlled by the commercial and bureaucratic factions in Tokyo. His words are those of the bankers and merchants who hold him captive in the Imperial Palace. We and the people of Japan must free our emperor from this bondage. What we have begun here is the first step of the Akihito Restoration—a return of imperial power and the rule of the emperor by decree. We are here to free our emperor! Our mission will not be complete until the Son of Heaven has full and absolute authority, and he has returned us to the imperial way.''

Bruso and the others had watched the broadcast. They had not been able to follow the exchange between Tadao and his lieutenant, but it was obvious he would ignore the emperor's directive to relinquish the island. Tadao barked an order and the two subordinates quickly left the room. Then he turned to the Americans.

"The stupid politicians in Tokyo and Washington cannot deter us from our mission." A religious fervor was upon him, and his eyes glistened with maniacal conviction. "We are not afraid to die, nor are we afraid to spill the blood of those we hold captive. If they test my resolve, they will regret it. My terms are nonnegotiable, and they ignore them at *your* peril."

Tadao stormed from the room, leaving a single guard to watch the three Americans.

Friday, 9 December, 11:15 P.M.
FIFTY-SIX MILES EAST OF JOHNSTON ISLAND

The submarine was very crowded. The crew of the *La Jolla* had done their best to make room for the new arrivals, but space was always at a premium aboard a 688-class boat. Gear bags and weapons boxes that had been brought through the hatch that mated with the dry deck shelter now were stacked high on the bulkheads in the access trunk. Some of the equipment flowed out into the crew's mess, just forward of the trunk. It was much less chaotic now that the boat had dived; while on the surface it had rolled badly, sometimes flinging equipment and bodies across the deck.

Senior Chief Stockton and the leading boatswain on the *Tarawa* had come up with the idea of using a small landing craft to make the transfer, rather than lowering men and equipment onto the *La Jolla* by helo. They had lashed canvas-covered mattresses to the bow ramp of a Mike boat. The boat's coxswain was then able to jockey the craft alongside the submarine from leeward and drop the padded ramp onto the curved deck of the sub, just aft of the DDS. Twice he'd had to bear off as the waves became too rough, but while fast alongside, they'd been able to bring men and equipment aboard quickly. As soon as the transfer was complete, the *La Jolla* wasted no time in slipping below the surface.

As soon as the sub was under and trim, Chief Stockton took charge and began directing traffic. Other members of the platoon swarmed over the equipment and carried it away from the escape trunk area for storage around the boat. Walker, along with the other lead pilot, Chief Petty Officer Jim Berta, crawled back into the DDS to check out their SDVs. Slyfield and Jackson carried their rifle cases forward to the enlisted berthing compartment. They opened them carefully to check the contents, like a pair of traveling surgeons unpacking their instruments. The platoon SEALs were dressed in camouflage trousers, blue T-shirts, fatigue hats, and running shoes. The crewmen of the *La Jolla* wore blue zippered jumpsuits and baseball caps. Everyone was busy.

Stockton deposited Captain Nakajima and his men at a table in the forward part of the crew's mess. Here they waited while Stockton conferred with the chief of the boat, or COB, the senior enlisted rating on the *La Jolla*.

This was the Japanese contingent's third Navy ship in less than twenty-four hours. The *Vinson* and the *Tarawa* were large, and in its own way, so was the *La Jolla*, but the submarine was a thirty-three-foot-diameter steel cylinder that gave priority to piping, electronics, torpedoes, and machinery. Though it was a large attack submarine, fully half of the boat was devoted to reactor and engineering spaces. Habitability and room for the crew had been fitted around operational equipment, almost as an afterthought. One of the cooks, a Japanese-American, brought them a pot of tea. He welcomed them in poorly accented Japanese. Nakajima thanked him profusely in English. The Naginata Counter Force had worked from small Japanese coastal submarines for lock-in/lock-out training, but even these smaller subs had seemed more spacious and less crowded than the American boat. This was a *serious* submarine, not a shallow-water, conventional boat—one designed to prowl the open oceans for extended periods of time. Once again, Nakajima was impressed by American military technology. There was nothing frivolous about this craft or the American sailors who manned it.

Nakajima sipped the tea to be polite; it was quite awful. Suddenly he again began to feel isolated and vulnerable— aboard yet another *gai-jin* vessel, under the sea, and a long way from his home islands. Here there would be little privacy, no secluded place where he could be alone to pray and gather his spirit. Crewmen of the submarine and an occasional SEAL came through the compartment, moving quickly as if late for an appointment. A few nodded a greeting, but most ignored the small group of Japanese.

Now that they were submerged, Nakajima was aware that the submarine had become very stable—and very quiet. The air was clean and dry, but with a faint antiseptic quality to it, and unlike the larger surface ships, there was absolutely no sensation of movement through the water. While the others talked quietly, Nakajima silently prayed that the water spirits who bathed the *kami* of his homeland would find him here beneath the sea and give him strength. A hand on his shoulder interrupted his meditation.

"Hey, Taro, can you come with me for a few minutes? The captain would like to meet you."

"Of course, John-san." Nakajima stood and straightened his blouse. He said a few words to his sergeant and fol-

lowed Moody up a steel ladder to the next deck. They made
their way through a short passageway to a large room lined
with TV monitors and lime-green visual displays. A half
dozen crewmen manned a series of consoles that looked
like video games. Forward on the port side, two men sat
behind aircraft-like yokes, staring at a panel of complex
instrumentation. A senior petty officer hovered over them,
watching their every move. The control room of the *La
Jolla* had the feel of a spaceship, or of a spaceship attraction
at a large theme park. And unlike the combat information
center of the *Tarawa*, which was gloomy and bathed in red
light, the control room of the *La Jolla* was well lit.

Moody and Nakajima made their way around the raised
platform in the center of the room that served the two main
periscopes, now lowered in their wells. Little notice was
taken of their presence. Those on watch seemed not to care
or were more intent on their duties. They approached a tall
black man huddled with another officer over an automated
plotting table. The two were studying a small-scale chart
of the approaches to Johnston Island.

"Captain Kemp, I'd like you to meet Captain Nakajima
of the Naginata Counter Force. Cap'n Nakajima, Cap'n
Kemp." Moody felt like he was doing a Bill Cosby
monologue. "Sir, I think my friend Taro here may be able
to help us with our problem at the chemical storage facility
once we get ashore."

Nakajima snapped to attention and saluted. Kemp hesitated a moment before touching his right hand to the bill
of his ball cap. Then he extended his hand.

"Stand easy, Captain. Welcome aboard my boat. This is
Lieutenant Commander Bill Sisson, my executive officer—
and my navigator. We've just been working on the problem
you've given us, Mister Moody. There's a lot of shallow
water around Johnston Atoll, right Bill?"

Sisson was a bland-looking man, with thick, unruly
brown hair and serious, intelligent eyes. He wore a pinched
expression and his lips formed a grim line. He shook Nakajima's hand and shot Moody a troubled look. Then he

turned back to the chart. "Skipper, the book says to launch SDVs we need at least four hundred feet of water and an extended area free of obstacles. That's moving with minimum steerageway of about three knots while we make the launch. That restriction will keep us nine miles from Johnston Atoll. Normally, we could cheat a little and run at periscope depth, but not the way these seas are building. We'd be into the surge from the storm and a launch would be real chancy." At this, Moody nodded. "The ocean bottom around most of these Pacific atolls is poorly suited for submarine operations. Johnston Atoll's no different."

"How about it, Mr. Moody," said Kemp. "Can you make your approach from nine miles out?"

"Yes, sir, and that's about what we figured on, but my SDV pilots tell me our chances for success go up dramatically if you can get us closer. You see, sir, until we get into the channel, the bottom topography doesn't lend itself to our Doppler navigation systems. Essentially, we take a fix from the launch point and follow a compass heading until we find the entrance to the channel. From there we'll try to get a positive fix and move on to the staging area. Nine miles is a long way to run on a compass without datum. That's close to a two-hour run for us, all on dead reckoning. As you can see from the chart, the atoll sits on a broad shelf, which is why you can't get any closer. There's not much tide change at this latitude, but the shelf amplifies the tidal change. We could see as much as a two-knot current, and it varies with time and distance to the island. We can run the nine miles to the island, but it'll be tricky finding the entrance to the channel." Moody rubbed his jaw and stared at the chart. "If we launch that far out, it'll mean we have to allow extra time in case we get lost and have to pick our way along the coast."

Walker had cautioned Moody that it wouldn't be easy to get an SDV to an exact location off the coast of Johnston Island. The problem wasn't that difficult, but there had been time neither to gather adequate current and topographical data nor to rehearse this specific mission profile. SDVs were like cruise missiles; they could be incredibly precise, but a great deal of information had to be gathered and programmed into the flight plan, and that took time. Commander Kemp studied the chart for several minutes, seemingly oblivious to the others. Then he pointed to a spot on the map four miles from the entry to the Johnston Island harbor channel.

"What if we dropped you off right there?"

Moody started to answer, but Sisson spoke first. "You can't be serious, skipper. There's barely a hundred feet of water there. We can't launch SDVs in that kind of water."

Kemp never took his eyes from the chart. "Yes we can."

"Sir?"

"We can if we're sitting on the bottom."

A look of horror flashed across Sisson's face. "Jesus, skipper, you can't be serious. We'll risk damage to the bottom sensors, not to mention a chance of fouling the intakes."

Nuclear submarines were not designed to sit on the bottom like the old diesel boats. In addition to external fittings on the hull, the intakes that drew in seawater to cool the reactor were on the bottom of the boat. If they became fouled, *La Jolla* risked an overheated reactor.

Kemp ignored his exec. "How about it Lieutenant? What if you were able to launch from here?"

Moody studied the chart and the tip of Kemp's finger. "We couldn't have it any sweeter, Captain. A bottom launch is a whole lot easier than being under way. And we'd have an exact fix to begin our run in to the target."

"Very well, let's plan on it. Bill, tell the engineer what we're going to do, and have him prepare the plant as best he can to deal with a cooling water casualty."

Sisson still looked troubled. He started to say something, but the stern look on Kemp's face overrode any objection. "Aye aye, sir," he replied, and headed aft from the control room.

"What's your time line, John?" Kemp asked.

Moody did a quick calculation. "I'll want to confirm this

with my pilots, but if we can get this close, we can delay the launch until about 0130. That'll give us plenty of time if we miss the channel and have to work our way along the coast, but we shouldn't, not this close.''

"Anything else you need?"

"No, sir. My platoon chief will give the final pre-launch warning order in about an hour. Then we'll begin to load out the SDVs and prep them for the mission. The boat crews are scheduled for a sleep period beginning at 1200 tomorrow. I'll give the final mission brief at 1900. There is one thing; I'd like permission to flood the DDS sometime this morning. I want to give Captain Nakajima and his men a wet orientation in the SDVs and a quick checkout on our Draeger scubas.''

Kemp nodded. "Okay, but let's get that done as soon as possible, while we're out here in deep water. Once we get up on that shelf around Johnston Atoll, I don't want any distractions.''

"Yes, sir, and Captain, uh . . . well, sir, I appreciate your taking your boat in this close and putting her on the bottom for us. I think I understand what it means for you to do that.''

"No, Lieutenant," Kemp replied evenly, "no, I don't think you do, but then I can't really appreciate what you'll have to do once you get ashore on Johnston Island." He gave Moody a grim smile. "I guess we'd both rather be back off Oahu playing launch and recovery games, wouldn't we?''

"You got that one right, Cap'n. But thanks anyway." Moody glanced at his watch. "Unless you have something else, sir, we have to see to our men and equipment.''

As Moody and Nakajima were about to leave the control room they were nearly run over by an officer in soiled coveralls. He was a lieutenant commander but young, no older than Moody, and he had a murderous look on his face.

"Well, hello there, Engineer," Kemp said in a pleasant, synthetic voice. "I'll bet you want to talk to me, right?''

Saturday, 10 December, 7:30 A.M.
THE WHITE HOUSE

Gates Carlton and Armand Grummell sat across the desk from Robert Garrison. Tadao's ultimatum and the decision to delay any action against Johnston Island for a day allowed the president a few uninterrupted hours of sleep. He appeared refreshed in his trademark blue oxford-cloth shirt and striped tie, but there was a weariness in his eyes that said the tension was beginning to take its toll. He turned from the two men in front of him and concentrated on the speaker phone on the side of the desktop.

"Doctor Sunaga, we again want to thank you for joining us. I know it's very early out there on the West Coast."

"You are quite welcome, Mr. President," came the voice from the speaker phone on the desk. "I only hope I can be of some assistance."

"Doctor, I have with me Secretary Carlton and someone I understand you know well, Director Armand Grummell."

"Good morning, Doctor Sunaga," said the older gentleman seated next to Carlton. "I was delighted to learn that you've agreed to help us with this matter."

"Well, good morning, Mr. Grummell." There was a new warmth in the voice. "And I'm happy to again be working with you."

Armand Grummell had the distinguished look of a senior university administrator. He still clung to three-piece suits and spoke with a heavy Boston accent. Robert Garrison had been quick to appoint his own people to the top positions, and his administration had a much younger and more liberal texture than the previous one. Initially, many thought the president had only retained Armand Grummell as director of Central Intelligence until he could find a suitable replacement. This was not the case. Garrison had asked Grummell to stay on because he was capable, honest, and without a political agenda. Grummell was also a gentleman of the old school. There was money in his family, a lot of it, and he would not have agreed to stay on were he not able to honorably transfer his loyalty to the new president. The workings of government had changed dramatically under Robert Garrison, but Grummell continued to run the CIA with the same integrity he had for the last decade.

"Gentlemen," the president said, leaning across the desk on his elbows, "what more do we tell this guy, or do we tell him anything? We've got about nine hours until it's high noon on Johnston Island. And what will he do when the deadline passes and we haven't agreed to his terms?" Garrison was looking at Grummell.

The DCI carefully removed his wire-rimmed glasses and began to polish them with a handkerchief. "Since there is agreement on our inability to meet his demands, I'd like to hear Doctor Sunaga's opinion as to what might be the best way to tell Mr. Tadao his terms are unacceptable."

The three in the Oval Office had to wait a moment for the reply. "I have given this some thought, but I believe there is nothing that will appease Tadao other than total and unconditional acquiescence. And I believe he fully understands that what he is asking may be impossible."

"So he has orchestrated this impasse," Grummell continued, "one whose conditions we cannot meet and from which he cannot retreat?"

"Exactly," Sunaga replied. "He has placed himself in what he feels is an honorable, if hopeless, position. From a Japanese perspective, it is both elegant and tragic, and very compelling."

"So we come to the question of what he will do," Robert Garrison said. "Can you comment on that, Doctor?"

"From Tadao's perspective," Sunaga continued, "he has few alternatives, and he probably understands, Mr. President, that the same is true of you. So I believe he will continue to kill hostages until you meet his demands or move against him."

No one spoke for close to a full minute, then: "Doctor

Sunaga, Gates Carlton here. Short of capitulation, is there anything that we might say or do that could delay Tadao or that would serve to postpone the deadline he has imposed?''

"Perhaps," Sunaga replied, "but only if you show him respect and offer him at least the appearance that there may be a realistic chance to satisfy his demands. However, I believe there is little room for negotiation or meaningful compromise."

"Will a flat refusal along with the threat of force change his thinking in any way?"

"No, Mr. President, it will not, although you may let him know that he will be held accountable for the deaths of any more hostages. It will have little impact on Tadao, but I have no way to gauge the commitment of his followers. Perhaps some of those with him are not so committed."

"I see," Garrison replied. "Do you have any other advice for us, Doctor?"

"No, sir, I am afraid I do not."

Garrison looked across the desk and saw no takers. "Very well, Doctor. Thank you for your observations." Garrison reached over to the speaker and broke the connection.

"Gates, Director Grummell . . . your comments?"

Garrison called all his civilian top advisers by their first names, except for Grummell. It somehow just didn't seem proper to address him as Armand. Carlton gave a slight shrug of his shoulders. Grummell carefully replaced his spectacles.

"Sam Sunaga's assessment is much the same as the one I received from my Japanese desk," Grummell said. "They recommend that in keeping with your first address, you don't issue an outright rejection—perhaps a statement which again suggests a national apology is beyond your authority. This would show a measure of respect without agreement. And I agree with Doctor Sunaga that you have to go on record about any future killing of Americans on Johnston Island."

Garrison nodded. "Anything else?"

"Yes, Mr. President," the director said quietly, "I assume there is still a B-52 with an armed weapon in position over Johnston Island?"

For a moment, the president said nothing. The B-52 launch had been ordered through the most discreet military command channels and should have remained a secret, even from the CIA. Garrison had briefed a small and very select group of senators and congressmen less than twelve hours ago.

"I see," Garrison said, almost to himself. "Tell me, Director, was it the meeting with the congressmen?"

"No, sir," Grummell said gently, "although I would be concerned of a leak once this gets to their staffers. The information was a deduction from our satellite analysis section. B-52s are hard to miss, and since there was only a single aircraft, the inference was not difficult. The clincher was the tanker activity out of Hickam. And some of our people work closely with the FBI's counter-intelligence section that keeps an eye on our military bases. They're starting to hear things. I'm afraid the downsizing of the military has created, well, a condition where morale is not as it once was, or let us say, as it should be. Fortunately, while soldiers and airmen tend to gripe, few in the military are disloyal or disposed to talk with the press. I don't have the same conviction with congressional staffers." Grummell again removed his glasses and swabbed them unconsciously. "I guess what I'm saying, Mr. President, is that I don't think we have too much more time before the press is going to begin asking difficult questions—questions for which they may already have the answers."

"Will we have until tomorrow morning?"

"Perhaps, Mr. President, but I wouldn't count on it."

Saturday, 10 December, 11:50 A.M.
JOHNSTON ISLAND

Bruso and Nancy Blackman sat in the operations center watching Tadao move quietly around the room. They were both exhausted from lack of sleep and the constant effort required to maintain even a measure of personal dignity. A three-day growth hugged Bruso's face. His shirt and trousers were wrinkled from sleeping in them, but he still wore a tie. Senator Blackman's hair was now matted and limply outlined her tired features. She carried herself erect, but the continual strain was beginning to make her look drawn. Tadao had just returned in yet another freshly pressed uniform and there was an air of anticipation about him. Occasionally he would walk into the radio room for a few moments and return. He was not exactly pacing, more like prowling.

An hour ago, they had watched a televised statement delivered by Linda Gonzales, President Garrison's press secretary. The short speech was carefully prepared and worded so as to invite further dialogue, but it suggested the United States and Japan simply could not comply with the demands, at least not in the time frame allowed. And while the official used no aggressive language, she made it clear that the United States would hold those who had "illegally occupied" Johnston Island fully accountable for their actions. Tadao had watched impassively and then walked briskly from the room, taking General Taggart with him.

"What time do you have, Bruso?" he asked as he paused on one of his circuits.

"Two minutes after twelve."

"Then I believe it is safe to conclude that your government, and mine, will do none of what I have asked."

Bruso stared at him a moment. "Forgive me," he offered, "but I believe that's what they said in the televised statement."

"I understand that, Bruso. I only wish to fairly observe the conditions under which my terms were presented. Now it is time for my statement. Perhaps you and the senator will accompany me."

A deadly calm had now claimed Tadao and his eyelids had drooped slightly to give him a sleepy, sinister look. He walked out of the room without another word. Two heavily armed men motioned for them to follow.

The main entrance of the administration building was served by a small, well-tended grass plot and a scattering of young palm trees that heeled drunkenly in the gusting wind. Johnston Islanders called it Central Park. It was the only substantial vegetation on the island. The sun dodged behind a small cloud, and the air had a moist smell to it. Bruso noted the change in the sky and then the unusually large number of Tadao's men in the area. He knew something was happening as he quickly counted no less than twenty camouflaged figures. They waited as a group, their weapons slung. A single figure stood away from the others. He wore a cotton *gi* and had a long sword belted to his side by a wide cloth sash. His chest was quite deep and his tightly muscled arms hung away from his hips. Bruso and Senator Blackman followed Tadao onto the grass and waited.

Then a thought struck Bruso like a slap in the face. *Good Christ, they're going to execute us!* His mind flashed back to Tadao's wielding of the long sword on the morning he'd boarded the *Sea of Fertility*. A bolt of fear ripped through his stomach and into his bowel. Blackman gave him a questioning look; she could clearly see he was distressed. He met her eye and managed a half-smile, but he was having difficulty breathing.

Then he saw five figures being slowly led toward them from the building. They wore blindfolds and had their hands tied behind their backs. Each had two guards, one on either side. One was a woman and another, a man, was in uniform—a general's uniform. The guards herded them to the center of the grassy area.

Bruso felt a serge of relief as he suddenly realized that whatever was about to happen did not include him. Then he was washed with a sense of shame at his own cowardice. His remorse was short-lived. He watched as the five bound and blindfolded prisoners were forced to kneel on the grass in a line. In a flash of anger, he turned to Tadao and took a step toward him, then froze. The two guards behind Tadao brought their rifles up to their shoulders and aimed at his chest.

"Their instructions are to kill you if you take another step, Bruso. And what would that accomplish? I clearly stated there would be bloodshed. Today it will not be yours, unless of course, you do something foolish." Tadao tilted his head and smiled cruelly. "Perhaps Bruso, that you must watch is, for you, a harsher punishment."

Bruso turned back to the five who kneeled. One of the men began to moan softly; another tried to get up but was rammed back to his knees by the guards standing to either side. There was a soft, quick hiss as the swordsman unsheathed his blade. He swung the gleaming sword about his head as if to test the blade and himself. Satisfied, he checked the placement of his hands on the *tsuka* or haft, much as a baseball player, with one foot in the batter's box, would inspect his grip on his bat. Then he moved to the side of the first kneeling prisoner.

He looked to Tadao who inclined his head slightly. The two guards bent the first captive forward, using the victim's arms to lever its torso almost horizontal. What followed was almost a blur with the grunt of the swordsman masking any sound his blade may have made in the beheading. The body jerked once and went limp. The soldiers released it and allowed the torso to topple forward to join its severed head.

Nancy Blackman reached over and took one of Bruso's manacled hands in hers and squeezed fiercely. He was aware that she had made a muffled, inhuman sound as the executioner struck his blow, but he could not take his eyes from the spectacle before him. When he did look at her, she was white and a thin trickle of blood had started down her chin from where she had bit into her lip. Otherwise, she stood motionless and buried her nails into the palm of his hand.

The second victim, the man who was moaning, continued his lament right up to the instant his head fell to the grass. As the swordsman addressed the third man, a rich baritone suddenly replaced the slain man's silenced wail.

O-Oh say can you see, by the dawn's ear-ly light,
What so proud-ly we hailed, by the twi-light's last
gleam-ing,

Last in the line, General Taggart knelt upright and his clear voice rang over the windswept grass. It must have unnerved the executioner as he required two strokes to dispatch the third hostage. He took the fourth, a woman, cleanly. Taggart's voice wavered only slightly when his turn came as the two guards bent him forward to take the blow.

O'er the la-and of the free, and the home of the . . .

In the hush that followed, no one moved except the swordsman. He wiped his blade with a soft cloth, inspecting it carefully as he did. Then he reverently righted each of the severed heads, setting them in a line. Finally, he moved back along the row, bowing respectfully to each. At the third one, he apologized sincerely for his clumsiness.

Bruso wanted to protest this atrocity, but he could neither find the words to express his rage nor trust his voice if he had. So he just stood there, gripping Senator Nancy Blackman's hand and etching the brutal spectacle in his mind for the time when he could vent his anger. Finally he tore his eyes from the scene and looked at Blackman. She too had seen enough. Her head was bowed and the freshening wind blew her dark hair across her face. Then a movement to Bruso's right caught his attention. A Japanese in camouflaged utilities lifted a video camcorder down from his shoulder and walked toward the administration building.

"You have an excellent video transmission facility here, Bruso," said Tadao, smiling. "Perhaps when your Mr. Garrison sees the results of his inaction, he will think better of my simple request."

Saturday, 10 December, 10:34 P.M.
THE WHITE HOUSE

They were again gathered around the big desk in the Oval Office. The president, along with Gates Carlton and Armand Grummell, was now joined by General McKenzie and Linda Gonzales. Two NSA technicians busily worked at a wheeled rack of electronic components. No one spoke.

Finally one of the techs stepped back. "It's ready to go, sir. The quality's not quite so good as if we had the original tape, but we've been able to enhance it some with our equipment. Would you like me to stay and run it?" The man spoke quietly, as if he were addressing a bereaved family. He had seen the tape.

"Thanks, Tom. If it's just a fancy VCR, I think we can handle it, but stay close by."

"Yes, sir." He placed the hand control on the desk and led the other technician from the room.

"And you say we've plugged all the leaks?"

Linda Gonzales shifted in her seat. "There are no absolutes in this business, Mr. President, but I think we have. Two networks recorded the broadcast. I've made a few legal threats if they go public with it and some not-so-legal ones I'd rather not discuss." Gonzales was one of Garrison's more successful appointees. She had worked her way from weather girl to news anchor to senior network executive—a politically savvy operator with the knowledge of a media insider. The White House press corps called her *La Tigressa*. "I promised them an advance on the story if we do go public with it. And from what I'm told, the tape itself is not especially suitable for general release."

"So you've not seen it?"

"No, sir."

"Well then," Garrison said as he picked up the remote control, "I guess we'll all watch it together."

The picture rolled a few times before it caught, and the grassy scene in front of the administration building on Johnston Island came into focus. Its color and quality were quite good except for a thin line of static that periodically drifted down the screen. The president and his advisers watched quietly, except for a collective gasp at the first beheading. There was little sound from the recording, only a dull roar caused by the wind across the cameraman's microphone. But General Taggart's singing of the national anthem came through clearly, along with the emotion and dignity of his final moments. Then the camera panned around to Senator Blackman, who clutched the left hand of a solid-looking man with a rumpled white shirt and tie. The screen filled with snow as the video clip ended.

Secretary Carlton got up without a word and left the room, his hand over his mouth. Armand Grummell sat upright and unashamedly wiped the tears from his eyes. General McKenzie and Linda Gonzales were motionless. The president fumbled with the remote control and the screen went blank.

"I . . . I, uh . . . you'll have to give me a moment," Garrison said, and dropped his head into his hands.

A few moments later, Carlton returned, wiping his face with a damp towel. He took his seat and apologized, saying he was all right, but his face was still ashen.

Finally, McKenzie spoke. "It's never pleasant to watch good people die," he said quietly, speaking as the only one in the room with anything close to firsthand experience. "To have to see it like this, in this context, is . . . well, it's perhaps even more difficult than actually being there.''

"Those animals," the president said hoarsely, "those fucking animals—sorry Linda—" Gonzales shrugged; she was a newswoman. Garrison straightened in his chair and turned to McKenzie. "Do we have that link ready to Admiral Harrington?"

"Yes, sir. I think you just need to let your aide know and he'll patch it through to your telephone."

Garrison fumbled with the phone and the connection was made to the desk speaker. "Admiral Harrington, can you hear me?" There was a pause while the scrambler engaged.

"Yes, Mr. President, I hear you just fine, sir."

"Admiral, I just watched the videotape of what happened on Johnston Island a few hours ago. I assume you've seen it too?"

"Yes, sir. The signal was picked up by the comm center here. We've strictly controlled the distribution of that tape, but I can tell you that those few who have seen it are most disturbed by it. And that includes me, sir."

"That includes all of us, Admiral. Tell me, are your people in position to take action in the morning?" Even now, after what he had just seen, the president found it hard to say "attack Johnston Island."

"Yes, sir. The submarine *La Jolla* will move into position just before midnight Johnston Island time. The swimmers and their mini-subs are scheduled to launch at 0130. If all goes well, they will attempt to neutralize the chemical-weapons storage facility at 0530—just before dawn. Pending their success, the Marines will make a vertical assault at first light."

"I'm sorry Admiral, but it's been a long day. What is a vertical assault?"

"They'll attack with helicopters, Mr. President, weather permitting. The winds are gusting up to forty knots around Johnston Atoll right now, and stronger winds are expected." Harrington waited for a response but the president said nothing. "Are you still there, sir?"

"Yes, I'm here." Garrison sat with his elbows on the

desk, hands interlaced in front of his mouth. He stared at the telephone speaker as if looking for some encouragement. After a moment he continued, "Admiral, are you aware of my order that, once ashore, the team is not to move against the facility without further authorization?"

"Yes, sir. My task unit commander, General Sheppard, registered a rather strong objection to that order, but he understands it and your instructions will be strictly observed."

"I wish to countermand that order. My instructions now are to proceed with the mission, and to do everything in your power to ensure its success. In the unlikely event the Japanese on Johnston Island surrender unconditionally, you may then recall your forces as you see fit." How ironic, thought Garrison, unconditional surrender. Can we really be here again? "Do you understand these instructions, Admiral?"

"Yes, Mr. President. We will proceed with the mission unless the terrorists on Johnston Island surrender."

"That is correct. Do you have any questions about your mission?"

"No, sir."

"Very well, Admiral. Good luck and please pass my personal best wishes and prayers to the men who will be going ashore. God bless all of you."

"Thank you, sir."

Garrison tapped the disconnect button on the speaker and looked across the desk to his military chief. "Is that satisfactory, General?"

"Very much so, Mr. President. It will be one less thing the task group commander and assault team leader will have to contend with. Now they're free to concentrate totally on the objective."

"Good. And now, unless there's something else, I'm going to need some time to myself. Tomorrow will be a very long day." Garrison pushed himself to his feet and the others rose with him. As they made their way to the door, the two technicians returned to retrieve the video setup. "Just leave it," the president told them, "I'm going to have to watch it one more time."

Out in the hall, Carlton pulled Linda Gonzales aside. "Any rumblings from the press?"

"I don't think they have anything yet, but they're out turning over stones. I got a call from the *Post*. They wanted to know if there was any truth to the rumor that we're going to bomb Johnston Atoll. Nothing was said about an atomic bomb, so we assume that hasn't come out. We're pretty sure they got it from the Hill."

"Damn," Carlton said softly. "If they do get something concrete, think they'll come out with it?"

"I think they'll come to us first; they know how delicate this situation is. And they like the guy. The Garrison White House has pretty much played ball with the press. They owe him, and they don't want to go back to the way it was before he took office."

Carlton nodded. "What's the mood across the country?"

"A lot better than I thought it would be," Gonzales replied. "Incidents of violence directed at Japanese-Americans are really quite isolated, but the networks are giving them air time. As a whole, the nation sees this as a terrorist attack without a racial agenda. I don't anticipate any major upheavals, but if that tape gets out, things could change in a hurry."

Saturday, 10 December, 6:35 P.M.
TWENTY-ONE MILES SOUTHEAST OF JOHNSTON
ISLAND

John Moody lay in the middle berth of the three-tier stack. A soft glow from the passageway invaded the small cubicle from a part in the curtains. He'd slept fitfully and been fully awake for well over an hour, staring at the bunk above him just eighteen inches from his face. For the first time in a long while he really wanted a cigarette, but smoking was not allowed on the *La Jolla*. He took in a deep breath and let it out slowly. Soon it would begin—a chain of events that would put them on the beach at Johnston Island. And it would all begin with the mission briefing at 1900.

Before they'd left the *Tarawa*, Moody had given a briefing for his support-element commanders. Ships, naval gunfire, tactical air, and a battalion of Marines—all would be available to him, but only after he'd disarmed the chemical weapons. Medical teams and HASMAT—hazardous material—teams were standing by on the *Vinson* to come ashore, but again, not until it was safe. Senior Chief Stockton had given the mission warning order just after midnight. The warning order was a briefing that covered the final equipment preparation and weapons load-out for the assault team.

The balance of the morning hours was spent with the individual preparation. Moody and Stockton inspected each American team member and his gear while Captain Nakajima and his sergeant inspected the Japanese. After the assault team had gone down for their sleep period, Stockton assembled the remaining men and began the pre-mission preparation of the SEAL delivery vehicles. The extra day they'd been given had made all the difference. Had they rushed and gone in early this morning, they would have been far less prepared, but the issue would have been settled—one way or another.

As he lay there, Moody began to rehearse his briefing. A successful mission always began with a well-organized, concise mission briefing. He had mentally gone through the mission many times. Now he was beginning to live the sequence of events, projecting himself and his team into each critical aspect of the operation. He knew exactly how things were supposed to happen, and that would form the basis for his briefing. But what if things didn't go as planned? What if Kemp couldn't get them as close as he said he could? What if there were additional guards along the section of beach they'd planned to cross? And if they did manage to gain control of the storage area, what if they couldn't defeat the explosives that were attached to the chemical weapons? It was the what-ifs that had kept him tossing in the coffin-size bunk for the last six hours.

"Mr. Moody, you awake?"

"Yeah, Chief." Moody pulled back the curtain and looked at his watch. Stockton was fifteen minutes early. They were now on a rigid schedule, and even an early reveille was of concern.

"What's up?"

"We're twenty miles from the SDV launch point and on the way in at four knots. The approach looks good. We also got a solid green light, sir. Seems the Japs on Johnston Island have started killing hostages. It's a go all the way."

"That's helpful, I guess," Moody replied as he rolled out of the bunk and stepped into his flip-flops. He was dressed in sweat bottoms and a T-shirt. "What else?"

Stockton pursed his lips. "It's the EOD officer, sir. He ain't going to be able to do this mission."

"What!"

"He's coming apart, sir. I'd have woke you sooner, but there's nothing to be done about it. He's just gone over the edge."

"Jesus H. Christ! Where is he?"

"In the wardroom, sir. I told him you'd probably want to talk to him."

"Damn right I do. That son of a bitch'll do his job, or I'll wring his goddamn neck."

Moody started aft for the officer's wardroom, but Stockton held him up. "He's in pretty bad shape, sir. Captain Nakajima an' I been talkin,' and we figure you may be able to get along without him."

"We'll see about that," Moody replied. He pushed past Stockton and headed aft.

Explosive-ordnance-disposal technicians were specially trained to disarm both conventional and unconventional ordnance. They were also qualified parachutists and divers. Moody had asked for the best EOD man available, one with current diving qualifications and comfortable in the water. Lieutenant Commander Kenneth Rogers had arrived on the *Tarawa* midday yesterday, a quiet man with a great deal of experience in improvised explosive devices. Rogers, Moody had been told, was the best. He pushed aside the curtain to the wardroom. A slightly built, pale officer with a wisp of a mustache sat at the table. The man looked up with red eyes underscored by dark circles. Moody could easily have pitied the man, except he hadn't the time. He took a chair across the small table from him.

"What the hell's going on? Don't you know we're ready for the final mission briefing?"

Rogers continued to stare at the table. Then a single tear ran from one eye as he slowly shook his head.

"Hey, I'm talking to you, man," Moody said, more gently this time. "What the hell's the matter?"

He gave Moody a desperate, haunted look. "I just can't do it. God help me, but I can't face those chemicals." He started to pick up his coffee cup, but his hand was shaking badly and he set it back down. "If . . . if it were just explosives or conventional ordnance, but the chemicals . . . these particular chemicals . . . I'm . . . I'm so ashamed." Rogers bowed his head and made a choking sound.

"Then why are you here? Why not someone else?"

Rogers did not look up. "We weren't given any details. I thought it would be an administrative, render-safe procedure after the island was secure—that we'd be working with protective suits. I thought I could do that."

Moody sat back and looked at the ceiling. Fucking Navy and their security—never tell anyone anything! The whole mission was to get this man safely to the explosives that threatened the chemical weapons so he could do his thing. And it's my fault too, he thought. I should have insisted on a backup!

Moody stared at him. He wanted to reach across the table and slap the man, but what good would it do? A sickly, helpless feeling began to settle over him. All those lives on the line and it comes down to this!

"Excuse me, John-san, may I have a word with you?"

Moody pushed himself from the table and stepped into the passageway, holding onto the bulkhead. For a moment he thought he was going to throw up.

"You know about this, Taro?" he said weakly.

"Yes. It is most unfortunate, but as you can see, the man is in no condition to be of help to us. This is Sergeant Kodansha. Perhaps he can be of service."

Sunday, 11 December, 3:16 P.M.
TOKYO, JAPAN

Prime Minister Mitsuzuka sat at his desk and considered the range of difficult decisions before him. Among others, he had just met with his ministers for finance and for trade and industry. They had presented a very troubled picture. Along with the other senior members of the bureaucracy, all recommended that the exchanges and banks remain closed on Monday. Masayoshi Oka advised otherwise. He counseled business as usual, as if by observing the normal Monday business rituals, the gravity of the situation on Johnston Island would not be exaggerated. Mitsuzuka had yet to reach a decision. If we declare a banking and stock-market holiday on Monday, he reasoned, then what will happen on Tuesday? An aide entered the room and bowed.

"Minister Uno is here to see you, sir."

He had forgotten. Uno telephoned an hour ago and asked for a private audience. Mitsuzuka had tried to put him off, but the head of the Defense Agency had quietly urged for the meeting.

"Please show the director general in."

Uno stepped inside the door and bowed low. "Forgive me for disturbing you at this late hour, Prime Minister." Mitsuzuka bowed slightly and motioned him to a chair, then took a seat behind the desk. No tea was served, which suggested he wished to begin the meeting immediately.

"Earlier this evening I had a very curious meeting with the senior American military attaché," Uno began. "He asked that no one else be present and that our conversation not be recorded."

"You say not recorded?" Mitsuzuka asked.

Uno inclined his head. "When he arrived at my headquarters at Ichigaya, he asked if we could speak in a room that was free of listening devices. I assured him that my office was such a place. He told me several interesting things. First of all, Commandant Tadao has executed five Americans yesterday by beheading them. Tadao sent President Garrison a videotaped record of the event. So far, the tape has been withheld from the American public, but this may be a temporary situation. Secondly, the Americans are preparing to move against Johnston Island, perhaps within the next twenty-four hours."

"What! Why has this not come through diplomatic channels?"

"With all respect, Prime Minister, I believe it is because the Americans do not completely trust diplomatic channels—such sensitive information, by the time it reached you through the layers of bureaucracy at the Foreign Ministry, could be compromised."

Mitsuzuka grunted, knowing this was so. "What do you make of this, Uno?"

"My military people strongly feel that if the Americans attack, they will do so at night as they did in the Gulf War—it is their way. The Americans are very proficient in fighting at night. It will be dark on Johnston Atoll in another hour, so it is reasonable to expect them to attack within the next ten hours, probably just before dawn."

Mitsuzuka considered this in silence, slowly pulling his palm across his bald head. If the Americans do attack at night as Uno suggests, we will know of their success or failure here in Tokyo shortly after midnight. If the attack is successful, the financial markets can open normally. Should such an assault fail and be accompanied by widespread loss of life, there would still be time to declare a holiday as a show of respect. Either course of action would be acceptable. Mitsuzuka felt no small measure of relief with this scenario, but his expression revealed nothing.

"Forgive my interruption, Prime Minister, but the American attaché also said that the failure of a military operation to recapture the island would result in an international incident of the gravest proportions."

"So. Did he give you an indication of what that might mean?"

"No, he did not. I pressed him on that question, but apparently his instructions did not allow him to say more." Uno lowered his head. "Forgive me, but I was unable to obtain additional information."

"I understand," Mitsuzuka said, rising from his chair. Uno too was quickly on his feet. "Please monitor the situation, and inform me immediately of any developments."

"Yes, Prime Minister." Uno bowed low and let himself out.

Mitsuzuka returned to his seat and sat, unmoving, for close to ten minutes. Then he touched the button on his intercom.

"Yes, Prime Minister," came the voice from the speaker.

"Please ask Minister Oka if he will speak to me by telephone." A few minutes later the desk phone rang. "Minister Oka," Mitsuzuka said smoothly, "I have decided to heed your advice about allowing the banks and exchanges to be open tomorrow." He said nothing of his conversation with Director General Uno.

Saturday, 10 December, 6:57 P.M.
TWELVE MILES SOUTH OF JOHNSTON ISLAND

Lieutenant John Moody stood by the hatchway that led into the enlisted messroom. He took a deep breath and tried to compose himself. The confrontation with Lieutenant Commander Rogers had shaken him badly. With Nakajima's help, Moody now felt they would be able to continue without Rogers, but this near-critical error underscored the haste of their preparations. Good Lord, what else is about to go wrong at the last minute! We need more time!

This was not a standard operation covered by one of their preplanned-mission profiles. It was a complex and dangerous tasking, one that under normal circumstances would have required meticulous preparation and rehearsal. Each member of the assault team would have carefully studied his assignment. Together, the team would have practiced each phase of the mission many times. But the Japanese who held Johnston Island had allowed no time for this. There was too much on the table. They had to go in, and they had to go in now.

Then he remembered the advice of an old chief in the training platoon at SEAL Team Two. "You got to be able to improvise, sir, or you're not going to make it in this business. We're paid to handle the unexpected. If things was guaranteed to go accordin' to plan, they'd get the Army to do the work." Moody took another deep breath and stepped inside.

The messroom was the largest compartment on the boat. Senior Chief Stockton had arranged the briefing materials at one end of the room. The assault-team members sat around the two nearest tables; Moody noted that each table held an SDV boat crew and that the men were arranged in the approximate order they would sit in the SDVs. Behind the assault team ranged the other members of the platoon and crewmen of the *La Jolla* who would help with the launch. A flip chart on an easel dominated the center of the briefing area. A small-scale chart of the approaches to Johnston Island and the sand model of the chemical-storage facility flanked the flip chart. The mockup had been sprayed with Varithane in an effort to transport it intact, but the target model had still been damaged during the transfer from the *Tarawa*. Moody took it in with a glance and nodded his thanks to the Army lieutenant who had worked nonstop to have it ready for the briefing.

He flipped over the first page to reveal a list of events and times. Then he pulled open a telescope pointer and tapped the first line: Final Mission Briefing—1900 hours.

"Okay, gentlemen," he said, holding his watch at eye level, "it's 1904 and 30 seconds on my mark . . . stand by . . . mark! 1904 and 30 seconds. This will be our final briefing before launching SDVs for the assault on Johnston Island." He turned a page of his notebook and began. He flipped the pages to keep pace with his briefing, but he seldom looked at them. For the next hour and a half, he carefully walked them through each phase of the mission, covering the latest intelligence reports and updated weather conditions. Periodically Moody paused, and there was a hushed, guttural undercurrent as Nakajima translated for the Japanese members of his team.

Saturday, 10 December, 11:53 P.M.
CAMP H. M. SMITH, HAWAII

"Sir, General Sheppard is on the secure line."

Admiral Joe Harrington pressed the key on his intercom. "Thanks, Julie. I'll take it in here."

For the last two days, Harrington had followed the military preparations aboard the *Tarawa* and *La Jolla*, as well as the political developments in Washington. He was the man in the middle. The big decisions were made above him and the tactical planning and preparation were being done below him, at the operational level. There was little for him to do. His staff logistics people had been kept busy responding to the needs of the *Vinson* battle group, and his public-affairs officer had been working around the clock to hold off the press corps. Of the two, managing the media and the flow of information to the public was the more demanding task. Harrington and his senior staff intelligence officer were the only two people on Oahu who knew of the potential danger to Hawaii.

Nonetheless, Harrington had his battles to fight, though they were internal, political skirmishes. There was an extensive array of forces available to deal with this kind of problem—Army Special Forces, Rangers, the FBI Hostage Rescue Team, the Delta Force, and others. All had been variously offered to him and imposed on him, but Harrington had backed his task-group commander. He had given Sheppard the job; now his job was to support him operationally and defend him politically. If Sheppard succeeded, he would get the credit. If the operation was a failure, Harrington would accept the blame. That was a theater commander's role. His only concession had been two companies of Rangers on standby at Hickam and a platoon of Special Forces on the *Vinson*. Still, there were two AC-130 gunships at Barbers Point and the FBI resident office in Honolulu was buzzing with activity.

Harrington slipped his code key into the STU III coded phone to activate the scrambler. "Harrington here."

"Admiral, this is General Sheppard. Can you hear me?"

"I hear you fine, Jack. What's the status?"

"The submarine has successfully reached the launch point. They're resting on the bottom and will launch the SDVs in about an hour."

"Understood," Harrington replied. "Any problem with the submarine?" The decision of the *La Jolla*'s captain to put his boat on the bottom had generated a personal visit from the Commander, Submarine Forces, Pacific. He'd strongly objected to the grounding of one of his nuclear submarines, but Harrington had gently reminded COM-SUBPAC that this particular submarine no longer belonged to him; it was now the property of the task-group commander. Any decision on the sub's tactical deployment would be left to General Sheppard and the captain of the *La Jolla*.

"Apparently not, sir," replied Sheppard. "The boat's in about a hundred and fifty feet of water. They've sent a comm buoy to the surface so we have real-time communications with them. It seems there was a problem with the EOD technician sent out from Pearl, but they've resolved it and are going forward."

Harrington started to question his general about the problem, but refrained. The matter was out of his control; if Sheppard or his SEAL lieutenant wanted or needed help, they'd ask for it.

"Then we're on schedule."

"Yes, sir."

He hesitated before continuing. "How do you feel about this, Jack? Do you think we can pull it off?"

The scrambler could not disguise the apprehension in Sheppard's voice. "I honestly don't know, sir. We've done what we can in the time allowed us. I feel we have a good operational plan and the best men available to carry it out. There's simply nothing more I can do."

Nor me, thought Harrington. It always comes down to that. We succeed or fail on the ability of the young men in the fight. And the size of the battle makes no difference, he mused. Eisenhower knew little of the events in Normandy after he gave the order to go forward with the D-Day landings. George Marshall, the Army Chief of Staff and Roosevelt's confidant, was home gardening—he knew the issue would be decided without him. Ike had almost a hundred thousand young men to take his beaches.

I will send less than a dozen, thought Harrington, led by a Navy lieutenant and a Japanese captain. And just as in

Normandy a half century ago, the skill and courage of these young warriors will decide the matter.

"Are you still there, Admiral?"

"Yes, Jack, I'm here. Keep me advised of any changes as you think best. And good luck."

"Thank you, sir."

Harrington placed a call to his chairman and to the White House Situation Room. When he had finished, he called for his executive assistant.

"Julie, I'll be in the Crisis Action Center until further notice. I'll want no calls or messages unless they concern Johnston Island."

"Aye aye, sir."

Then the CINC called his wife and told her he would not be home tonight, again, but that perhaps they might be able to have lunch together tomorrow afternoon.

Sunday, 11 December, 12:47 A.M.
FOUR AND A HALF MILES DUE SOUTH OF
JOHNSTON ISLAND

"Just remember, Chief, once you're outside the door, hang a left and go straight north for about four miles or so. You can't miss it. It's the only atoll in the area." Moody had been the last member of the assault team to climb up through the access trunk into the dry deck shelter. Now he stood at the side of the Two boat talking with its pilot, Jim Berta. Berta was a short, wiry chief petty officer with over fifteen years in the teams, half of that in SDVs. Many in the platoon thought he was better than Walker, but there was a lot of that in the teams—who was the best marksman, the best swimmer.

Moody was just glad he had two good men at the controls. Berta had been with SEAL Team Four during the Panama invasion and had a purple heart to show for it. He was steady and Moody liked that. He trusted him.

"An' if I get lost, just stop at the nearest filling station and ask directions, right?"

"You got it, Chief. Any problems?"

"No, sir. All systems are up. I got the coordinates in my nav computer, but I shouldn't have any trouble following you. Unless there's a helluva current out there, we should be able to just drive right on over there and find a good spot to park."

After the *La Jolla* had bottomed, the sub's plotting team had met with the two SDV pilots. They had been able to give them a precise location, within just a few feet. Their relative proximity to the target would reduce any navigational errors on the run in; the current was the only variable.

"You all set there, Glasser." Don Glasser was new to the SDV teams, but an experienced SEAL. He was good in the water and he was big. He would have to swim with the biggest load and carry it ashore.

"Yes, sir." He sat next to Berta and fidgeted with his face mask.

"See you on the beach, guys."

Moody squeezed Berta's shoulder and stepped to the aft cockpit, which was loaded with equipment and snipers. Slyfield and Jackson lounged in the rear compartment with their legs fitted around gear bags and gun cases that were strapped to the floor of the boat. They were talking ballistics and wind conditions.

"Got everything?" Moody asked conversationally, inspecting their crowded quarters.

"Ah reckon', boss. Anythin' more on the weather?"

"The chief quartermaster on the boat says its forty-five to fifty knots, maybe gusting up to sixty by daylight."

Slyfield scowled. "That don't sound too encouragin' but we'll do what we can—that right Darron?"

"That's right, Sly," Jackson said quietly. He looked worried.

"Don't worry 'bout Darron," Slyfield said. "He jest don' like bein' made to sit in the back of the bus. He'll be all right once we get ashore." Jackson looked over and forced a grin.

"Good luck, guys." Moody shook both of their hands and turned to the Number Seven boat.

"Hey, Berta," Slyfield called behind Moody, "soon as we're airborne, how 'bout sendin' that gorilla you got for a stewardess back here with a couple of whiskeys for me an' my main man."

"Hey, fuck you guys," said Glasser.

Moody grinned. It was as it should be—the troops were trying to stay loose.

"Do you or your men have any questions, Taro?"

"No John-san. We are ready to proceed when you are."

Nakajima and three of his men filled the rear compartment of the Seven boat. Their weapons and light packs had been stored around the main ballast tank between the two compartments, and behind them around the engine housing. As did the Americans, they had Draeger oxygen scubas strapped to their chests. They wore camouflaged utilities like the Japanese who had captured Johnston Island, only their uniforms were made of nylon. They appeared calm and relaxed. Moody scanned their faces, noting that if they were at all afraid, they hid it well.

"We're almost ready. Just remember, when we get up close to thirty feet, shift to your Draegers. If for some reason we should go back below sixty feet, go back to the air regulators, okay?"

"We understand, John-san. You and Walker just take us to the water's edge, and we'll take you the rest of the way to the target."

"That's a deal." Moody started to offer his hand but instead bowed to them. All four lowered their heads as one. He clamped Nakajima on the shoulder and moved to the forward compartment. Walker was busy going through his pre-flight checklist.

"All set?"

"Piece o' cake, boss."

Moody lifted the Draeger from the seat and strapped it

to his chest. He quickly inspected the scuba to make sure the unit had a fully charged oxygen cylinder. Senior Chief Stockton had set the rig up for him, so he knew it was functioning properly. Then he climbed into the Seven boat cockpit beside Walker. He checked that his gear bag and weapon were stowed properly in the nose of the boat and clipped the seat belt across his lap. Moody, Walker, and the other Americans all wore lightweight black cordura coveralls. Some of them had a thin neoprene shorty under the coveralls to ward off the mild chill of the water.

He pulled his mission commander's pre-launch checklist from the console and began ticking off the items. There was refuge in routine tasks. You don't have to face chemical weapons and terrorists, his subconscious told him. For now, you just have to follow standard operating procedure.

For the last two days he'd played the mission through in his mind, with all the permutations and variations he could imagine. Now it was time to focus on each immediate task and let the future take care of itself.

"Ready to launch?" said the man standing by the SDV.

Moody quickly looked to Walker, who gave him a thumbs-up. "Yes, sir. You going to wait around for us?"

Commander Robbie Kemp gave him a twisted smile. "We'll give you two hours in case you have an equipment failure or have to abort. Then I'm taking this boat out to deep water where it belongs."

"Will you be okay?"

"You mean will I be able to get off the bottom or will I be relieved for cause when we get back to Pearl?" Both men knew he was asking if the sub would be safe from a nuclear blast if the mission failed. Kemp smiled broadly and held out his hand. "I'm sure we'll get off the bottom just fine. Good luck, Lieutenant."

"Thanks, Captain. I'll buy you a beer when we get back to Pearl."

"You're on. Anything I can pass on to the task-group commander for you?"

"Yes, sir. Tell him that when I call for the Marines, I want to see green rain."

"You got it, John," and with that, Kemp headed for the access hatch.

"Okay, people, we begin the launch sequence in five minutes. That's five minutes to launch sequence." Stockton spoke in a normal tone, but his deep voice filled the small, crowded cylinder. "All unnecessary personnel lay below."

The lights in the DDS were switched to red to ready the crews for a night launch. Senior Chief Stockton took his position between the Two and the Seven boats at the forward end of the DDS. He had a hand on the nose of each craft. Two SEALs also stood by each, and two more waited at the aft end of the DDS. All wore open-circuit scuba. Normally, with the parent submarine under way at low speed, the SDVs were backed out on trolleys and towed on a tether, like a glider. The mini-subs were tended as they bore off to one side, well clear of the big submarine's propeller, and released. With the *La Jolla* on the bottom, though, they would be guided out onto the deck and hand launched, like hot-air balloons.

And they didn't have much time. The DDS was in 115 feet of water, and the SDV crews and the deck handlers were breathing air. That gave them less than twenty minutes before they became susceptible to decompression sickness.

"Okay, gentlemen, here we go," said Stockton in a steady voice. The DDS fell silent and all eyes were on him. "On the *La Jolla*, commence flooding the shelter, over."

A speaker in the ceiling answered, "In the shelter, commence flooding, aye." Water began to swirl about the deck plates and rose to meet the keel of the SDVs.

"Passing thirty feet. Face masks in place, check your regulators. Raise your hand if you have a problem."

There was a bustle of activity as the crews donned face masks and stuffed the scuba regulators into their mouths. Each man tapped his regulator purge button to check that it was functioning properly. They would breathe air from the SDV storage flasks until they were in shallow-enough

water to use their Draegers. Moody looked up to see the
large depth gauge on the rounded end of the shelter pass
sixty feet. Water began to crawl over the gunwale of his
Seven boat; the level was now up to his chest, causing him
to shiver, not entirely from cool water. There was something threatening about having water rise up around you—it
was much easier to just jump in. Moody was the last man
to pull on his face mask. Then he strapped the communications regulator to his mouth.

The water climbed over the canopy of the SDV, and he
was in a different world. Moody closed his eyes a moment,
breathing deeply as he adjusted to the new environment.
Like most SEALs, he felt an odd sense of comfort being
underwater. This was a place he belonged—he felt safe and
protected. As his eyes adjusted to the dim light, he looked
over to Walker, who was absorbed with the task of trimming the boat. Now that they were fully submerged, he
worked to bring the boat to a near-neutral buoyancy. The
SDV was still strapped to its cradle, but a skilled pilot could
sense when the boat became light.

The depth gauge on the dash read 113 feet. As the pressure inside the shelter equaled that outside, the air trapped
in the top of the DDS was pumped into the mother submarine's storage flasks. Satisfied with this trim, Walker signaled one of the deck hands that he was ready to launch.
Then he looked over to Moody. "Let's bust out of this puke
hole," he said into the comm mouthpiece.

Moody grinned. It was their favorite Marlon Brando line
from *One Eyed Jacks*, reserved for special moments like
this. An attending deck SEAL gave them a thumbs-up, indicating both boats were ready. He slid the canopy closed
and then did the same with the rear-compartment canopy.
They were now sealed in their fiberglass glass cocoons.

The main buoyancy tank and several equipment canisters
separated the two compartments in the SDV. They had no
voice communications with the men in the rear compartment, but there was a low-light TV camera with a fish-eye
lens that allowed those forward to monitor the passengers

in back. Nakajima and his men were packed like subway commuters, each issuing an occasional stream of exhaust bubbles. Moody noted their breathing was regular and steady, and again he marveled at their courage. For them, this could be little different from boarding a spaceship for a dangerous voyage.

The underwater speaker crackled, "Stand by to open the DDS outer door . . . stand by to open outer door." An alarm buzzer began to pulse. Moody felt more than heard a soft clang as the latching dogs slid free and the big door yawned open. Beyond the large opening there was nothing. Then the deck lighting came on and outlined the rounded hull of the submarine. From Moody's vantage point, it could have as easily been the curved surface of some alien planet.

The Seven boat was backed partway from the hangar on its sliding trolley and the tie-downs released. A SEAL deck-hand tending the bow line waggled his index finger as if he was directing an aircraft. Walker nudged the electric motor into reverse, dead slow. The stern of the Seven boat rose slightly. Walker cut his power and cranked on the wheel that drew his ballast trim weight aft. The boat leveled, allowing the two deck SEALs to lead it docilely from the hangar like a giant manatee.

Once the Seven boat was cleated securely to the after deck of the *La Jolla*, the Two boat was eased from its shelter. Following a final check of boats and crews, the tethers were cast off. Walker left first in a shallow climbing turn, coming back along the port side of the mother sub. Lime-green Chemlites tied to the boat's bow planes and rudder marked its passage through the clear, dark water as it pushed slowly through the warm water like some prowling, deep-ocean phosphorescent creature. Walker headed north at low speed until Berta and the Two boat took station on his starboard quarter.

"Okay, Don," Moody said, struggling to look over his right shoulder, "I have the lights on the Two boat."

"Roger," Walker replied without looking up. He was now totally absorbed with the operation and navigation of the SDV. Slowly he brought the boat up to five knots and eased into shallower water. At twenty-five feet they began to feel wave action, so Walker settled for a depth of thirty-three feet. He didn't need a depth gauge; his ears told him how deep they were.

In both boats, the attackers began to shift to their Draeger scubas. Each man carefully purged his rig to rid the scuba and his lungs of nitrogen from the boat air, and soon all were breathing pure oxygen. The trail of bubbles, which would have been difficult to pick out in the wind-driven waves above, now ceased. The two craft, flying silently in formation, bore through the darkness toward Johnston Island.

Sunday, 11 December, 9:10 A.M.
THE WHITE HOUSE

The president sat across the table from Gates Carlton. In the center of the Situation Room was a luxurious captain's chair with soft leather upholstery and comfortable armrests. Several small TV screens and telephones attended the chair. This was the place of the commander-in-chief. Its occupant had an unobstructed view of the large rear-projection screen on the main display wall, now filled with a medium-scale chart of Johnston Atoll. A small blinking light at the bottom marked the position of the *La Jolla*.

Periodically Garrison spent a few minutes in the chair, but he was more comfortable at the table off to one side. The big chair made him feel less presidential and more like a military commander, not a natural feeling for Robert Garrison. Coffee cups, a plate of fruit, opinion polls, and message traffic littered the Formica. The president had not loosened his tie, but his oxford-cloth sleeves were rolled up two turns.

"Mister President," said an Army colonel who stepped away from one of the consoles, "the task-group commander reports that the two mini-subs are in the water. They experienced no problems or delays during their launch from the parent submarine. We project that they are now about three and a half miles from Johnston Island, sir.''

"Thank you, Colonel.''

Garrison sipped his coffee and tried to imagine how it was for them. Young men, most in their twenties, racing along through a dark, windswept sea to an appointment with what could very well be an agonizing death from chemicals or searing nuclear heat—or a Japanese madman. Except for what he had seen in films, Garrison could not identify with such a world. Nonetheless, the notion of what they were going through caused him to shudder. But the ultimate responsibility for what those young men were about to do, or not do, was something he knew all too well, and it caused the knot in his stomach to burn. Would I trade places with him, he wondered, this Lieutenant Moody, whose success or failure will define the future relationship of the world's two economic superpowers?

Garrison moved a section of cantaloupe into position with his fork and stabbed it. No fucking way!

"Hey, Bob,'' Carlton said quietly, "take a look at this.''

He handed Garrison a clipping from the Sunday edition of the *Los Angeles Times*. It was a second-page story about super-secret chemicals considered so deadly they had the killing power of a nuclear blast. According to "reliable sources'' at Lawrence Livermore Laboratories, these chemicals were being stored on Johnston Atoll. There had been a series of articles nationwide on chemical weapons stored at the eight domestic storage facilities; for decades, the American public had all but ignored the storage of chemicals in their midst. Now, all that had changed.

Garrison grunted. "Nobody gave a damn about the nuclear power plant next door either until Three Mile Island. If we can get through this, we'll have no problem finding the appropriations to do something about our chemical weapons.'' He set the clipping down and forced a smile, but the burning in his stomach increased slightly. "Gates, I guess we'd better be prepared to take action in case those fellows heading for Johnston Island are unable to complete their mission."

"I understand, Mr. President."

Sunday, 11 December, 2:34 A.M.
TEN MILES WEST OF JOHNSTON ISLAND

Colonel Anthony Fortino sat in the left seat of the B-52H with his hands in his lap. They had just separated from the tanker about fifteen minutes ago and he had given the controls to the automatic pilot. The computer had the aircraft in a lazy, fuel-efficient orbit at forty-three thousand feet. Since aircraft from the *Vinson* were unable to operate in the storm, the bomber flew closer to the atoll to serve as an airborne radio-relay station. They were well above most of the storm activity, but an occasional pocket of turbulence buffeted them, causing the old bird's wings to flap gently. There was little for them to do, so Fortino found a classical station in Honolulu, one that played Italian opera. He found it soothing, while the other members of the crew endured.

This was Fortino's third trip to Johnston Atoll. A B-52 they had just relieved over the island had found his tanker and a final drink before heading back to Guam. These were familiar procedures, but there was nothing routine about the missions. The 512th had often carried nuclear weapons on training sorties, but never with the immediate prospect for an actual drop. Fortino scowled under his oxygen mask. The crisis had been devastating for his squadron's morale. They were all on full alert, but only three crews flew the long missions out over the mid-Pacific. His idle crews appeared to resent this grounding, but most were secretly glad they were not involved. To hell with them, Fortino thought. This squadron has a mission to fly!

But that was not how he really felt. He loved his pilots,

and he loved the close-knit camaraderie of squadron life. And he loved the tired, reliable B-52s. Fortino and the big bombers had grown old together. He became maudlin at the notion that both of them were at the end of their service lives and would soon be retired. His eyes flicked across the cockpit instrumentation, quickly ensuring that all systems were functioning properly. The plastic Blessed Virgin watched silently from the dash panel. He raised a gloved hand and gently moved it over the plane's padded combing. We've had a long career together, old girl, he thought. Maybe it is time for us to step aside.

Major Dan Sprinkle, his bombardier, broke his reverie, stepping onto the flight deck and squatting between Fortino and his copilot, Major Ed O'Connor. Fortino took the slip of paper from his hand and read it aloud. "Foxtrot Delta India Yankee."

He looked to Sprinkle and then to O'Connor. Both men's eyes showed surprise—and fear. Fortino unhooked his mask and held it to one side so as not to transmit over the aircraft intercom. He leaned close to Sprinkle.

"Did you authenticate this?"

"Yes, sir."

"And you've acknowledged the transmission."

"Yes, sir."

Fortino believed him, but procedure did not allow him to take his word for it. He replaced his mask and tapped his personal code into a dash console, a black metal box that looked not unlike a bank ATM machine. The small display began flashing: Foxtrot Delta India Yankee. There was no mistake; they had been directed to arm one of their nuclear weapons and await further instructions.

"What do we do, skipper?" Sprinkle asked.

"We follow orders," Fortino replied, trying not to show his irritation at the question. "Let's get to it."

Fortino then opened his weapons-arming console and set a red-tabbed key into place. A few moments later, back at the bombardier's station, Major Sprinkle did the same at a similar console. "Sir, I'm ready to arm."

"Roger," Fortino said into his mask. "Stand by ... mark!" Both men turned their arming keys and flipped a toggle next to their key. On both console panels, a single red light replaced the yellow one. One of the two nuclear weapons they carried was now fully armed.

So what's changed? Fortino tried to tell himself. One little light that's changed color. But everything had changed and he knew it. He thought of the tens of thousands of hours that he and hundreds of men like him had flown in B-52s during the Cold War, all in the name of nuclear deterrence. And now it comes down to this! Again he reached up and placed his hand on the dash combing, as if to reassure himself and his old bomber that they were going to be all right.

Below and to the east of the B-52H, Master Sergeant Andrew Pierce sat in the pilot's seat of the C-141 Starlifter. The big transport creaked and groaned as the gusting wind flexed its long, drooping wings. Periodically it seemed to shift its 250,000-pound bulk on the main gear, and every so often it bobbed up and down on its nose wheel.

"Sergeant Pierce, this is Barndance Control, can you read me, over?"

Pierce quickly snatched up the transceiver. "This is Pierce, I hear you fine, over."

"What's the weather like there, Sergeant?"

"Rain off and on, but the wind has really picked up in the last hour or so. Must be over forty knots, maybe more, over."

"Understood. Are you ready, over?"

"Hey, man, I been living like a fugitive for the last four days, eatin' survival rations and shittin' mouse turds. Hell yes, I'm ready."

Walker slowly eased the Seven boat back to four knots, optimum speed for the Doppler navigation system. He tapped Moody three times on the thigh. Moody squirmed around to look over his right shoulder. He spotted the

fuzzy, lime-green glow that said the Two boat was still with
them. If they became separated Berta would probably be
able to find them at the rallying point, but the plan called
for them to go in together. Moody returned the three taps
telling Walker the other boat was still with them.

Walker concentrated on his gyro compass and the Doppler sonar presentation. He was steering the boat in shallow
S turns, searching the bottom ahead of the boat. They continued in near-silence as there were no bubbles from the
Draeger scubas. Their only audible reference was a soft
whine of the electric motor. Five minutes later Walker
pointed to the scope.

Moody wrote on the dully lighted dash slate with a
grease pen: "Left side?" Walker nodded without taking his
eyes from his instruments.

They could both see it now. The computer scope with
its enhanced graphics clearly marked an emerging cut in
the bottom—shallower to port, deeper to starboard. Walker
carefully flew over the left-hand wall of the dredged channel and slowly came right ten degrees. A few minutes later
they picked the right side of the channel and swung back
north and Walker brought their speed down to three knots.
As they continued, the channel walls became more defined.
Berta and Walker had carefully planned their approach and
the Seven boat easily maintained station. They were now
getting into the surface effect, and the SDV crews were
being mildly pushed about the cockpits.

Walker suddenly scribbled "cable" on his slate and cut
his speed to bare steerageway. He was totally absorbed with
his compass and sonar scope. Then he held up one hand as
if asking for silence. After what seemed like an eternity, he
quickly drew a hand across his throat several times. He cut
the power, then reversed the motor for a few seconds and
vented the main buoyancy tank. Moody pointed a red-
lensed flashlight toward the Two boat and blinked it twice.
Berta brought the other SDV abreast of them as the two
craft nudged into the bottom.

There were no reference points except for the Chemlites

on the boats and the dull glow from the instrument panels. Otherwise, it was very dark and very quiet. The surface swells rocked them ever so slightly. Moody glanced at the depth gauge—twenty-three feet. Walker clipped on the cockpit lighting, and a warm red bloom bathed the inside of the boat. The Two boat also came alive. Moody slid the canopy back and pushed to free himself from the cockpit. Nothing happened. Then he remembered and reached down to unsnap his seat belt. He slipped up and over the side, pausing to pull on a pair of swim fins over his thin-soled boots.

Walker was also out, busily twisting an auger into the bottom to anchor the boat. The wave action and current of a knot and a half were starting to push it in an easterly direction. Meanwhile, Moody eased himself back to the aft compartment and slid back the hatch. The Japanese tilted up their face masks in unison, like a nest of baby robins. Moody gave them an okay sign and all four returned the gesture.

One strong kick with the fins brought him to the other SDV. Glasser had already tied off the boat and was back in the cockpit. Berta signaled that all was well with the Two boat, and Moody paddled back to the other craft. Walker handed him a light nylon line and compass board. Moody clipped the line to a D-ring on his scuba harness and looked at the board, on which Walker had written, "Try 330 and don't get lost."

Cute, Moody thought. He spun the bezel of the compass to set in his course and headed off in a northwesterly direction. His progress over the bottom was slow as he tacked into the current. After no more than twenty-five yards of travel, he stopped and switched on his flashlight. The water was becoming cloudy as wave action stirred the sediment on the bottom. Moody swung the light in a thirty-degree arc—and there it was! A concrete cube, four feet on a side, with a chain leading up to the surface. He tied the line to a metal eye embedded in the concrete and tugged twice on the line to let Walker know he'd found it. Then he started toward the surface, staying well clear of the chain as it writhed in a deadly dance, slacking loosely one moment and snapping taut the next.

Moody broke the surface to find the storm howling over him, knocking the tops off the waves. Clouds were scattered and racing across the sky. The moon busted free for an instant, only to be smothered by another dark shadow. As Moody rode the crest of a wave, he could clearly see the lights of Johnston Island to the north. He kicked fiercely against the current to stay abreast of a black shape straining against its anchor chain. Swimming in a rough sea was far easier than being in a small craft. He closed easily on the dark clump and played a small, hooded penlight on it. There on the side of the red nun buoy was the objective of his search—a white block number, 4. They now had a positive fix.

Moody took another quick look around while the wind drove salt spray into the side of his face. Then he retraced his route to the SDV, grateful to be back underwater where it was quiet and he felt safe.

He handed the compass board back to Walker and pointed to where he had written, "Channel marker Red No. 4—seas 6 ft +, broken clouds. Blowing like hell."

Walker nodded. He took one of his plasticized map sections and a straight edge and marked their course with a grease pencil. Then he made some additional notes on the compass board and handed it to Moody, who kicked over to the Two boat and showed it to Berta. They read it together: "Confirmed at Red 4—Rally point bears 294, 1100 yds—Follow me at 3 kts."

Berta copied the data on his dash slate and gave Moody an animated thumbs-up. Moody returned to the Seven boat and eased back in beside Walker, carefully restowing his fins.

Slipping back into the SDV was reassuring, like climbing up onto your mom's lap. After sitting idle for more than an hour on the ride in, Moody had welcomed the activity. Checking the buoy and serving as messenger had also given

him a break from thinking about the chemicals ashore and
the difficult men guarding them. He was the mission commander, but while they were in the SDVs, Walker would
make all the decisions. He felt like a fugitive from responsibility, but that didn't keep him from worrying. Also, he
knew his time for decision making and leadership was not
far off. Moody reached under the dash for the reassuring
touch of his submachine gun. He found that he was starting
to breathe more rapidly. Take it easy, he told himself,
you've got another fifteen minutes at least before you really
have anything to do.

He found his slate and a grease pen and went to work
while Walker carefully brought the SDV to near-neutral
buoyancy. Then he slipped the line on the anchoring auger
and swung the boat around to a northwesterly heading.
Twenty minutes later, he again nosed the Seven boat into
the sand and coral bottom. The wave action was no worse
than when they had stopped at the channel buoy, but it was
more of a choppy, washing-machine action. The red cockpit
lighting revealed a great deal more sediment in the water,
cutting visibility down to less than fifteen feet. They were
now in eighteen feet of water, as close as Walker dared
take them in this kind of seaway.

Moody looked around, carefully peering into the silted
water, but there was no sign of Berta and the Two boat. A
mild panic grabbed him as he followed Walker out of the
boat and helped him auger it to the bottom. After the boat
was made fast, they stood by their craft and waited. A few
minutes later, following the acoustic beacon Walker had
activated on the Seven boat, a pair of Chemlites appeared
out of the gloom. Berta carefully approached them, moving
against the current, and set his SDV down a few yards
away. Moody gave a sigh of relief that sent bubbles out
from the sides of his face mask.

It took the men about ten minutes to pull their gear bags
and weapons from the SDVs and prepare for the swim to

the beach. Moody went from man to man, flashing a pen-light to his slate:

Conduct assault according to plan.
Course to beach entry point 330, approx 500 yds.
Steer 315 due to current.
Check your gear, move to position when ready.
Be prepared for surf and high winds.
Good luck.

As soon as they were ready, the men formed up on the Seven boat. Berta headed one file with Slyfield, Jackson, Glasser, and one of the Japanese in his line. Moody would have Walker, Nakajima, and the other two Japanese in his group. Berta's men lined up behind him along the port side of the boat and attached themselves with buddy lines in a daisy chain. Moody's element did the same on the starboard side. He looked at his watch—0334. Right on schedule!

Moody broke several new Chemlites and banded them to his compass board to serve as a guidon. This was also the signal for the others to partially inflate their vests to make themselves neutrally buoyant for the swim in. Glasser's large pack had a special bladder that allowed him to tow it underwater. The sniper weapons were sealed in special waterproof cases that were near-neutral buoyancy. Slyfield and Jackson would hold them like flutter boards. Signals were passed along the line; they were ready to swim.

Moody set off at a steady pace, hugging the bottom and concentrating on his compass needle. Berta swam alongside, one hand on his shoulder. The others streamed to the side and behind like an echelon of migrating geese. Occasionally the moon broke free, allowing them a few feet of visibility. At times the surge sped them forward, then pulled them back, but the line of swimmers steadily advanced on Johnston Island.

Sunday, 11 December, 3:45 A.M.
JOHNSTON ISLAND

Jim Bruso lay on the floor of the office, staring at the white acoustical tile in the false ceiling and listening to the wind moan. From time to time a brief squall line swept past, rattling the windows with rain. He was exhausted, almost physically past the point of sleep, and might have been able to drop off had the images of executions that day not been with him. Every detail of the ordeal—his fear, his shame, and General Taggart's death song, were quite clear. These images were in color and as crystalline as if they had happened only moments ago. Strange, he reflected. Before, he had thought of him only as Taggart; now it was again General Taggart.

Bruso had seen men die in Vietnam. He had not actually seen them die, but he had been near them, heard them cry out. When the attack was over, he'd watched as they were borne away on litters—some crying in pain, some unconscious, some in rubber body bags. It had happened often at Khe Sanh and had left him feeling angry and empty.

He'd also felt relieved, though. Some of them had to die and again it had been someone else—not him. In combat, the living immediately draw strength from the dead. He and his fellow Marines had been brave, but it was a collective brand of courage. If a man was afraid while in the field with his unit, he was careful how he showed it, if at all. What would his buddies think? And there was the combat soldier's ultimate crutch—it may happen to someone else, but it can't happen to me. Even the most fatalistic among them had lived with that hope—not to me! So Bruso and the others in his company who'd lived through Khe Sanh had been brave. But what if a man knew—really knew beyond any doubt—that he was about to die?

Bruso concluded that a man who knew he was about to

die, and yet was still brave, was truly a man. Those who banded together in combat units and clung to their individual hopes of survival were, by comparison, scared little boys. He thought of General Taggart and shivered. The man was Joan of Arc, Nathan Hale, the Hebrew Zealots, and all the martyred Christians embodied in a single noble figure. Bruso had been with the general almost constantly for three days. Now he probed his memory for a shred of evidence, some small indication, that he'd been a man of such courage. There was nothing. Perhaps, thought Bruso, a man never knows for sure until it's his time. He doubted General Taggart had known.

That afternoon, the realization that his time might soon come, perhaps within hours, had nearly caused Bruso to lose control in front of Nancy Blackman, but he'd managed to excuse himself and get to the toilet before vomiting. Dying badly frightened him almost as much as dying.

At moments he pictured himself kneeling in the grass with a bag over his head, wetting his pants and begging for mercy. He quickly chased the thought from his mind, for he knew if he continued to dwell on it, he would become sick again.

Bruso carefully moved his left hand, the bandaged one. Blackman's nails had dug deeply into the meat of his palm. The bandage was coming loose, and he gently tugged it into place with his right hand, careful not to disturb her. She had curled up beside him and was sleeping with her head on his shoulder. His wrists were still cuffed, but she'd pulled his forearm close and nuzzled it. She had finally drifted off just before midnight but had slept fitfully, jerking and making mewing sounds like a hungry kitten. Now she was sound asleep, hardly breathing.

If the executions were traumatic for Bruso, they had been a near out-of-body experience for Senator Nancy Blackman. For several hours after they returned to their office-cell, she was unable to speak. They sat on the floor, and she simply clutched his hand. She didn't cry, not at first, but she was racked by a periodic sob that nearly choked

her. Bruso stroked her hair and spoke quietly to her, but
there was no response. Finally she noticed the dried blood
on his forearm and traced it back to slash marks on his
hand.

"Good God, what happened to you?" she murmured in
a bewildered voice.

Then she saw his blood on her hands and under her fin-
gernails. And she remembered. A moment later she crumpled in his arms and began to weep uncontrollably. It took
almost a half hour to cry herself out. After that she rose
and left the room without a word. A short time later she
returned, face washed and hair brushed. She had a first-aid
kit and went to work on his hand. Bruso marveled at her;
the strong, defiant Nancy Blackman had returned. She apologized once for her actions, simply and sincerely, and said
nothing more of it, other than to periodically check his
dressing.

Suddenly she cried out softly, but did not wake. She
snuggled closer to him and settled down. Apparently, Bruso
thought, that remarkable self-control does not extend to her
subconscious.

He knew they would be coming and he thought he knew
when, although the storm could change that. He'd half-
expected them the night before; but after the beheadings,
he knew they would have no choice. Years ago in Vietnam,
the Viet Cong would have attacked by now, since they
needed to retreat in darkness. Americans too liked to attack
at night, but closer to dawn. Guards were the least vigilant
just before sunrise, and the coming daylight allowed full
use of air power and helicopters. He did not know who
would come—Rangers, the Marines, maybe the Delta
Force—or how they would deal with the wind. But he felt
sure they would come.

While he lay awake, he thought about what he and
Blackman could do when it began. Tadao had promised to
kill all the hostages if an attempt was made to recapture
the island. Gradually, he began to develop a plan. It wasn't
much, but it might give them a chance.

"Nancy, wake up," he said gently.

"Ummm . . . no, don't!"

"Shhh—shhh, it's okay Nancy," he whispered. "Wake up."

"No, please . . . huh? Jim!"

"It's okay, I'm right here. It's okay."

She clutched fiercely at him for a moment. Then she relaxed, and he felt her take control of herself.

"What is it? Is it morning?" She started to sit up but he held her back.

"Stay here for now. We have to talk; are you awake?"

"I'm awake," she said evenly. "What is it?"

Moody held his center position in the ragged line of swimmers and waited, but not without difficulty. The big swells coming in from the southwest were partially broken up by the shallow coral reef that girded Johnston Island. Nonetheless, each of them hugged the bottom and fought to hold his place. They were in eight feet of water and forty yards from the beach. Moody glanced at his watch—only two more minutes. Since they'd left the *La Jolla*, he had thought only of what lay ahead. Now, for a brief moment, he considered just how far they had come. Except for losing contact with the Two boat for a short time, everything had gone perfectly. He knew this had been the easy part, but he still felt a ray of optimism. The swim from the SDVs in had taken less than twenty-five minutes. Now they waited while the scouts went on ahead. Normal procedure called for scout swimmers to cross the beach and signal for the others to come ashore when the way was clear. But this was not a normal mission, and there was a typhoon raging across the surface just a few feet above their heads. They would wait five minutes, then follow the scouts in. He looked at his watch once more. One minute.

Moments earlier Nakajima and Hori had ditched their masks, fins, and Draegers in the surf and scurried across the beach. They'd quickly cached their equipment bags and broken out their weapons. The wind lashed them as they hid just below the beach scarp, but the rain that had greeted them when they'd come from the sea had almost stopped.

Then, without speaking, they stood and began calmly walking on the beach. Nakajima walked in an easterly direction, with the wind at his back, and Hori walked west. They pulled the hoods of their lightweight jackets about their heads and walked with the hunched stiffness of a sentry who is tired and cold. Each was to walk a hundred yards along the shore to clear it from any roving guards. Nakajima found nothing, but Hori encountered a man walking toward him not fifty yards from where they had come ashore.

"Halt. Who is there?" the man called in broken English. The moon shone through for a moment, dully lighting both men. There were thirty yards between them. Hori felt he could take him from that distance, but he wanted to be closer.

"It is Toshiro Mifune," Hori yelled into the wind, "and I've come to challenge you." Mifune was a famous actor who starred in Japanese samurai movies.

The sentry continued toward him, but Hori was still wary. They closed to within fifteen yards.

"Kimbashi, is that you?" the guard said uncertainly, clutching his weapon.

Suddenly Hori leveled his suppressed MP-5 and centered the laser dot on the man's chest, guiding two three-round bursts into his chest. The rounds destroyed the man's heart and one of his lungs. He crumpled to the sand, groaned once, and died. Hori was quickly beside him, making sure the man was dead. Then he continued up the beach. On the way back he dragged the corpse into the angry breakers and left it. There was no time to better conceal the body.

When he returned, the others were just coming out of the water. They huddled along the berm and began to prepare their equipment for travel on land. The SEALs, dressed in black coveralls, pulled on dark watch caps and carefully smeared black paint on their faces and hands. The other two Japanese were dressed as Nakajima and Hori, with camouflage fatigues and headbands. Finally, each of them fitted a single earphone from the individual squad radio each man carried and strapped on a neck band that held the throat microphone in place. Now Moody could communicate with his men, but he would do so carefully. The squad radios were MX-3000s—ruggedized, waterproof versions of the Motorola Saber II. They were compact, short-range, line-of-sight transceivers that broadcasted in the clear, but each set had a frequency-hopping device that made interception difficult—not impossible.

Moody pushed a magazine into his weapon and cycled a round into the chamber. He carried several extra magazines and would have carried more, but his night-vision goggles and radios completed his load. As the last man signaled he was ready to move, Moody flicked the transmit key of his AN/PRC-113.

"This is Sierra Juliet, over."

"This is Tradewind Three-seven. Go ahead, over."

"This is Sierra Juliet. Whiskey delta mike, I say again, whiskey delta mike, over."

Moody listened carefully and heard two pauses in the static of his handset. The aircraft overhead had acknowledged his report. The 113 was a reliable UHF radio, but Moody had elected to carry it without the heavy crypto adapter to save weight. For the time being, transmissions would be short and in voice code. The men were now dark clumps, squatting to stay below the berm line and shield themselves from the wind. Moody moved back to the last clump, bending close to talk above the wind.

"Ready to move out?"

"Yessir."

"Time." Both men studied their digital chronometers: "0412 and 30 seconds . . . and, mark."

In the moonlight, Moody saw a grin cut Berta's blackened face. "I'll wait to hear from you; then we'll start the party."

"Good luck, Jim."

"Same to you, sir." Berta began to move westerly along

the beach with Hori and Glasser. Their objective was the air terminal. Moody watched him go for a moment, then turned to the others. He worked his way back along the line, briefly checking each man as he went and dropping to one knee by the last one.

"Ready?"

"Yes, John-san."

Moody set the night observation goggles to his face and studied the beach and backshore areas to the east. He saw no movement. The lights of the chemical-storage facility, some six hundred yards up the beach, flared in the sensitive NOD goggles like mini-novas. When he removed the goggles, the lights were fuzzy but visible. The gusting wind delivered a steady curtain of mist in from the ocean, while the moon found an occasional break in the clouds. Good, Moody thought as he again studied the beach with his goggles, we can probably see them better than they can see us.

But the beach sentries still worried him. He startled slightly as Nakajima placed a hand on his shoulder. "So far, your plan has worked to perfection." The Japanese warrior's voice was calm and reassuring. "Shall we continue up the beach?"

Moody forced a grin. "Let's do it."

Sunday, 11 December, 4:11 A.M.
SIXTY MILES SOUTHWEST OF JOHNSTON ISLAND

The *Tarawa* pushed through the growing swells, heeling as much from the wind as from the seas. Going directly into or away from the wind and waves, the LHA rode reasonably well. On any other heading, with its extensive freeboard and rounded hull, it wallowed like a fat, drunk duck.

In flag plot, General Sheppard sat with his staff and waited. They were high enough in the superstructure that the ship's roll was quite noticeable. Most of the men on watch were Army personnel and several were quite pale. Sheppard was too concerned to be seasick. He studied the backlighted presentation of Johnston Island, one nearly identical to the display at the Crisis Management Center at Camp Smith and the Situation Room at the White House. He tried to mentally place himself with his assault team, working their way along a dark, tropical beach, lashed by a typhoon. This was hard for a general officer in a comfortable command post, and he knew it. He crushed out his cigarette and immediately lit another one. One of the watch officers quietly set a fresh thermos of coffee within reach.

Suddenly a tech sergeant at a communications console jerked his headset down around his neck and turned to Sheppard. "They just called in, sir. They're on the beach."

The general bounded from his command chair and was at the operator's side. "Did they have a report?"

"Whiskey delta mike, sir—they're on schedule and moving ahead as planned."

"Thank you, Sergeant." He turned to his operations officer. "Bill, what about the Marines? Are they ready?"

"They're loaded and waiting in the helos, General, but there's no way they can fly in this weather. It's marginal on the deck and even worse at altitude. The front of the storm has passed, but we have to contend with rain and low clouds as well as the wind."

"Damn," Sheppard said softly. The task group was now steaming southwest of Johnston Island. He wanted to be upwind in case of a chemical or, God forbid, a nuclear incident, but he also wanted the helos to have the benefit of a tailwind so Colonel Lister's Marines could get there quickly. But that was only if they could fly.

"How about the *Kearsarge*?"

"She's ninety miles northwest of Johnston Island and beating into the storm at flank speed. ETA on station is 0600."

Sheppard slumped back into his seat and scowled. There was nothing he could do but wait. "Okay, Bill. See that

CINCPAC is advised of the message from the team ashore and the status of our grounded helos.''

"Yes, sir.''

The information would be passed through normal channels, but Sheppard knew his boss would want to hear from him personally. He reached for the handset with the dedicated line to Admiral Harrington.

Sunday, 11 December, 4:34 A.M.
JOHNSTON ISLAND

Moody crawled up beside Nakajima. The nearest tank was about thirty yards from their position on the berm line. There were two of them; they contained the island's water supply. The seven-man squad had just covered the six hundred yards along the beach in a little over twenty minutes. Nakajima walked well out in front, posing as a sentry. Moody led the others, carefully monitoring Nakajima through his night-vision goggles. Twice already he'd halted the squad file and watched as Nakajima had hailed a roving sentry and killed him at close range.

Apparently it had never occurred to the enemy that an opposition force could have Japanese soldiers. But Moody knew these were costly victories. The dead sentries had radios and would no longer call in to report that conditions were normal.

They watched for a few moments but saw no one around the tanks. Then Moody bent close to the other man beside him. "You ready, Sly?''

"Yes, sir.''

"Get going. We can cover you for a minute or so, and then we gotta move.''

"Understood, boss. Y'all go kick some ass. Me an' Darron'll do what we can.''

"Thanks, Sly. We'll check in before we go through the wire.''

Slyfield and Jackson scurried across the open space and took refuge at the base of the easternmost tank. The steel cylinder was perhaps sixty feet in diameter and fifty feet high. Moody watched as one of them mounted the rungs on the side of the tank and began to climb.

Then he signaled the others to move on down the beach in the direction of the chemical-storage facility; they were less than two hundred yards from their objective. Moody looked at his watch: 0440. Twenty minutes to get through the fence and into position. He pulled on his night goggles and watched Nakajima casually walk up the beach, leaning to his right into the wind. Then he, Walker, and the two Japanese followed.

A little more than a half mile to the west, Berta, Glasser, and Hori crouched near one of the outbuildings of an abandoned power plant. They had encountered no more guards on the beach. From their current vantage point they could observe the air terminal some hundred and fifty yards away and the C-141 Starlifter crouched in the shadows nearby. They also had some protection from the wind. Glasser used his night goggles to scan the aircraft while Berta peered through a small pair of binoculars to survey the terminal, which was partially lighted. They had hoped the storm would take out the power, but Johnston Island was used to periodic storms and had too many vital functions that required a dependable source of electricity.

"See anything?" Berta asked.

"No one moving around the aircraft. How 'bout the terminal?"

"Nothing. Near as I can tell, there's no one in the tower. They must be down in the terminal building."

Berta watched a few seconds longer, then pulled a small Air Force survival radio from his pack. "This is Rescue One calling Sergeant Pierce, over."

The reply was instantaneous. "This is Pierce; where are you, uh, over?"

"We're nearby, Sergeant. Now, listen up; when's the last

time you saw the guards in the terminal, over?''

"About two hours ago. When the wind really kicked up, they left the tower and went down into the terminal building. I seen 'em once or twice in the operations office.'' Pierce knew the facility well, as he did all the terminals on the Circuit Riders' route. "There's a small kitchen and crew lounge off to the back. I'd guess they were in there, over.''

"Okay, Sergeant. Stand by the belly hatch and someone will be there in five minutes or so. Don't try to leave the aircraft until we get there, understood?''

"I understand, but hurry.''

"Just hang in there, Sarge; we won't be long. Rescue One, clear.''

Berta pulled out a schematic of the terminal and laid it between his legs. He held the red penlight in his teeth and pointed to the crew lounge area. "Two men. Two men here. Maybe more—understand?'' He gestured with two fingers.

"Hai." Hori took his weapon off safe and motioned to the terminal.

Berta showed him a clenched fist, the signal to hold, and turned to Glasser. "We'll give you a head start. Wait under the plane until we've finished our business. Remember, if something goes wrong, set the charges, grab Pierce, and clear out; you got that?''

Glasser nodded. He shouldered a light pack and his weapon and headed out. Most of their equipment would be left there in their hiding place at the power station for their return. Berta watched to make sure Glasser was working his way downwind and to the east so he could make his approach from the east, keeping the Starlifter between himself and the terminal. Berta liked Glasser well enough, but he felt uneasy about him. He was young and he hadn't had that much experience. But he was a horse. Few men, even few SEALs, could have swum that load ashore and carried it through the surf. Berta turned to Hori. "Okay, we *hi-a-ko* now, *dozo.*''

Hori grinned at Bert's pidgin Japanese for *hayaku*, "to

hurry." He headed out in a low jog-trot, leaning into the wind. There was little cover, so their best option was to cross the open area quickly. The terminal building was exactly 140 yards from their hiding area. They paused at the perimeter road in a shallow ditch, just outside the reach of the external terminal lighting. Lights burned in every room, which told Berta the defenders were not expecting trouble, or if so, were very inexperienced. The interior lights would make it difficult for them to see outside without standing with their face to the window, and they would have no night vision.

Moments later the two men were alongside the terminal. The wind made listening for activity inside impossible. They paused a moment to catch their breath, then moved to the entrance, flanking the door to either side. Berta nodded to Hori, who opened the door and casually walked in. Berta followed at a discreet distance, crouched and ready.

"Comrades," Hori called pleasantly as he strolled through the passengers' waiting area to the flight-operations office. He carried his submachine gun by the pistol grip, down along his leg. "Can you find a cup of tea for a tired and wet sentry?"

"Are you mad?" came the reply from around the corner. "If Tadao finds that you are here we'll all feel his wrath." Hori moved steadily through the office toward the lounge. The speaker stood up to greet him and suddenly noticed he was not armed with an Uzi—it was something else. "What's that rifle that you have? Wait a minute, just who are you . . ."

It was over in seconds; the man speaking died instantly. The other scrambled for his weapon, causing Hori to wound him with his first burst. He finished him with the second.

Berta was right behind him. They checked the two dead terrorists quickly. "*Dai jobu*—nice work brother," Berta yelled. "Now let's get the hell out of here." Hori gave him a thumbs-up, a gesture he'd learned from the SEALs, and followed him back through the operations office.

Glasser had taken cover under the belly of the Starlifter.

The giant metal bird struggled with the wind, groaning in protest as it rocked gently on its chocked main gear. He had watched Hori and Berta come around the corner of the terminal and go inside. He was downwind, but still he could hear nothing. Since both had suppressed weapons, he didn't expect to. A few moments later they reappeared from the building. Suddenly a figure moved from the shadows and dropped to one knee.

"Look out!" Glasser screamed, but the wind hurled his words back into his face. Berta and Hori walked into a point-blank stream of 9mm rounds. The kneeling gunman emptied the Uzi's full magazine into them. This time Glasser clearly heard the long, staccato burst. He fumbled with the M-14, bringing it quickly to his shoulder. His first round caught the Japanese sentry in the shoulder and shoved him against the terminal, exposing his chest. Then he center-shot him three more times, momentarily pinning him to the building. After that the young SEAL slowly looked up over the top of his rifle. "Dear Lord God, now what do I do."

A quarter of a mile to the northwest, a lone sentry, whose miserable duty it was to patrol along the runway, huddled away from the wind behind a pickup truck. The truck was one of many vehicles parked on the runway so aircraft couldn't land. For the last five hours he had worked his way from one end of the runway to the other, moving from vehicle to vehicle to hide from the storm.

The wind shrieked around the truck, but he was directly downwind of the terminal. He heard a muffled burst of static followed by four distinct pops. Puzzled, he stood and squinted over the hood of the pickup into the blowing rain. Like many of the New Shield Society, he was a martial artist and not a soldier, so he didn't recognize the distant sound of gunfire. And he was numb from long hours with the howling wind. Wisps of salt spray skittered across the concrete strip, mixing with the intermittent curtains of rain. The outline of the terminal was blurred under white cones of the outdoor lighting.

It was an eerie setting, but nothing looked out of place. He started to call them on his radio but decided to wait. The storm had all of them on edge. Since he was heading in that direction, he would walk over and see that everything was in order. It would be a good pretext to get out of the wind for a few moments and perhaps have a cup of tea. He put his head down and leaned into the wind toward the next vehicle.

Moody and his team covered the two hundred yards to the chemical-weapons facility without incident. Part of the way, Nakajima continued his masquerade, walking down the beach ahead of them. The last few yards, from the beach to the chain-link fence, they crawled. Moody marveled just how much the facility looked like the sand model. It was familiar, and but for the noise of the wind and the surf crashing just behind them, like somewhere he had been in a dream.

The lighting around the chemical-storage facility had been designed for maintenance personnel, not as an anti-intruder measure. The satellite photos had found a section of the fence on the southern end of the complex where one of the floodlights had burned out. Moody smiled to himself as he worked his way toward it.

Up until now, he had been totally absorbed in leading his men to the target and keeping to the planned schedule. Aboard the *La Jolla* and even in the SDV, he had been consumed with the details of the mission before him. Since coming ashore, his concerns had become more immediate. Was Berta successful at the terminal? When will the dead sentries be missed? Did Slyfield and Jackson find a good perch and are they ready to shoot?

Small things that happened as they should, like an expected missing floodlight that darkened a section of fence, were a huge boost to his confidence. It was almost as if it was now a game, one they just might possibly win. All this had almost made him forget the nuclear weapon overhead and the chemical death before them—almost.

There was no movement from inside the fence, but from their position, Moody could see the lighted windows of the storage control office. He nodded to Walker, who pulled a pair of wire cutters and began to slice a seam in the chain link. The lanky SEAL made quick work of it, springing back a four-foot mesh flap to test the access. Then he dropped back to the ground along with the others and keyed his squad radio.

After he had killed the guard, Glasser laid there for a full minute trying to decide what to do next. He knew what he wanted to do; he wanted to rush to Berta to see if there was something he could do for him. But those were not his chief's orders. Finally he banged on the belly of the Star-lifter. A moment later a hatch swung down, about three feet from him.

"Hello. Someone there?" a voice from inside called down.

"I'm right here," Glasser said. Pierce started to lower himself through the hatch, but Glasser roughly pushed him back inside and climbed up into the aircraft. Without a word he pulled off his pack and took out a ten-pound block of thermite with a detonator taped to the side of it.

"Where's the CG of this aircraft?"

"What!"

"The center of gravity, goddamn it," Glasser growled, "where is it?"

Pierce sensed that the man beside him in the dark was not to be argued with. "Right over there."

"Show me!" Pierce held the light while Glasser placed the thermite on the deck of the transport and tested the circuit of the remote firing device. Satisfied, he turned to him. "All right, let's get out of here."

They dropped to the tarmac and Pierce closed the hatch behind them. They lay there a moment, squinting into the wind at the terminal. "Where are we going? Where are the others?"

In the light from the terminal, Pierce could see the blackened face of his rescuer. Jesus, he thought, he's just a kid!

Finally, Glasser turned to him. "Okay, Sergeant, here's what we're gonna do."

He spoke quickly and Pierce's eyes grew large. "Jesus, I don't know if I can do that!"

"Then you can stay right here an' burn with your god-damn airplane. Right now, I just don't give a shit." Then he was up and running toward the terminal. Pierce staggered after him, leaning into the storm.

Berta was lying face up, his eyes already dilated and glazed; Hori lay face down in a pool of blood, but he was still breathing. Glasser grabbed them both by the collar and dragged them around to the west side of the building, away from the lighted area. Then he went back to help Pierce with the dead sentry and collect the weapons. The only evidence of a struggle was the dark red stains on the walkway to the terminal entrance.

"Here, take these." He handed Pierce the two MP-5s and took his knife to cut free their ammunition pouches.

"What are we going to do?" Pierce yelled over the wind that was now tearing into their backs. Glasser ignored him and shined his penlight into Hori's face. He was still alive, choking on the blood that now filled his lungs, but Glasser knew there was nothing he could do. He took a last look at Berta. For an instant, he thought of closing his eyes, like they do in the movies. Finally he turned away, shouldering the extra weapons and ammunition.

"All right, let's go."

Pierce again started to protest, but fell silent as he saw the tear stains on the big SEAL's blackened cheeks. Glasser turned and headed back toward the old power station, crouching low as he jogged. Pierce followed and tried to imitate him.

Slyfield and Jackson pressed close to the flat steel top of the big cylinder; their only protection was the rim of the tank. They had carefully removed the sniper rifles from their waterproof aluminum cases, and, after attaching the bipods, had wiped the weapons with a soft dry cloth and loaded them.

If they laid very flat, most of the wind was deflected over them by the rim of the tank. But when Slyfield raised a small hand-held anemometer up over his head, it was almost torn from his grasp. "Fifty fuckin' knots," he yelled in Jackson's ear, "an' gustin' higher."

His friend shrugged and began to set up his scope. They'd known all along it would be tough shooting. Their first job would be to cover Moody's assault on the chemical-weapons facility. For this they would be shooting with a ninety-degree crosswind at two hundred yards. Much of their training had involved windage, but never this much. It was like shooting from a moving car—or at one. Both worked on their rifles for several minutes.

"You ready, Sly?"

"Ah reckon."

They swept the area looking for activity—Jackson looking in the lighted areas with his scope, Slyfield into the shadows with his night optic.

"You got anything?"

"Nothin' in the immediate area," Slyfield replied. "Let me see if'n I can find the boys." He searched the dark area between the beach and the fence, where the shoreline angled in a southeasterly direction. "There they are, just to the right of th' third floodlight on the right side. See 'em?"

Jackson had a more difficult time with his daylight scope, but as the team moved closer to the fence and the lighted area, he picked them up. "Yeah, I see them. Good thing I'm not a Jap sniper; I'd start knocking them off."

"Are you kiddin'—in this wind? Get serious. And yer a shitty shot anyway."

"Sly, this is Moody. What's your traffic?"

"No one outside in the complex that we can see, boss. We seen movement inside th' office, but that's it. Ah think they're stayin' out of the wind."

That'd be a break, Moody thought. "Can you see anything of the explosives on the special-containment bunkers?"

"Not from where we are, but I think I see a wire leading from the office in that direction."

That seemed right, Moody thought. On the *Tarawa*, the rep from the contractor who'd built the storage facility had showed them about where a saboteur would place his charges. It made sense that the firing circuit would lead into the office building. The specialists from EOD Headquarters at Indian Head, Maryland, had predicted they would probably have to defeat an electric firing circuit. Well, with a little luck, we may get a chance to do just that, Moody thought hopefully.

"Thanks, Sly," he said, "we'll proceed as planned; keep an eye on us. Break, Moody to Berta. You with us, Chief?" There was no response. "This is Moody, you there, Berta?"

"Uh, sir, this is Glasser, over."

"Glasser, where's Berta?"

"He's dead, sir. One of the Japs killed him an' Hori comin' out of th' terminal."

No, Moody thought, *we were doing so well!* "What happened? Do they know we're here?" Nakajima put a hand on his shoulder. He was shouting.

"I don't think so, sir. I shot the guy an' hid the bodies."

"Where are you now?" he heard himself say, trying not to think about the jovial, steady Berta.

"Where I'm supposed to be, where we were all supposed to be—at the power plant. I got th' Air Force guy with me."

"The explosives, Glasser—where are the explosives!" *Christ, do I have to interrogate him!*

"They're ready to go, anytime you're . . . uh, hold on a second, sir. We may have a problem here."

At the air terminal, a figure with his rifle slung staggered out of the shadows from the runway and made for the front door. He straightened up and began to walk more normally as he entered the lee of the building. Glasser picked up his M-14 and quickly sighted in. He guessed at the windage and squeezed off a round. His first shot missed completely, but the sentry stopped as if he'd heard the round ricochet off the cinderblock wall of the terminal. Puzzled, he turned, exposing his back to the shooter. Glasser fired again and the man went heavily to one knee, stumbling into the terminal as Glasser sent another round harmlessly into the door casing.

He dropped the rifle and pressed his transmit key. "Bad news, sir; another guard just showed up. I got a round into him but he's just wounded an' he's gone in the terminal."

Moody hesitated, only for an instant. "Now, Glasser— set it off now! Sly, we're going in!" Vaguely he heard them answer, but he was too busy following Nakajima and Sergeant Kodansha through the gap in the wire.

In the bowels of the Starlifter, the block of thermite flashed to life. A small, very hot fire began to burn and started to spread along the floor of the cargo bay.

There were three of them standing duty in the administration building operations center—four counting the guard out in the hall. One man sat at the radar scope and searched the windblown waters around Johnston Atoll for ship traffic; another monitored the radiotelephone and secure fax lines to Hawaii. He also watched CNN, taking notes from time to time so he could report the events to Commandant Tadao. The Johnston Island Crisis occupied most of the broadcast, but there was little new information to report. During the past several hours there had been talk of bombing Johnston Island, but no one in the government or at the Pentagon could be reached for comment. Tadao had been advised of this earlier but had dismissed it.

The third man served as a dispatcher for the security patrols around the island. He was the first to sense something was not right. First he heard someone intermittently keying the transmit button on their radio, but there was no voice transmission.

"Hello . . . hello. Station keying your radio please acknowledge, over." He repeated the call several times, but there was no reply.

"Problem?" asked one of the others.

"I doubt it," replied the dispatcher. "Someone is keying his radio but won't speak. He probably pushed his radio into a pocket with the transmit button partially depressed."

"Are the others up on the net?"

"Yes, but a few of the sentries have yet to report in, and I can't raise them. It's probably the storm. There's a great deal of static on the circuit, and these radios are not the best." He laughed. "They were made in America."

"Should we wake the commandant?" asked the man studying the radar scope. The dispatcher looked at his watch. "He asked to be called at 5:15—that's only twenty minutes from now. Let's wait." Again he tried to raise the man who was keying his radio, but there was no reply.

Across the island inside the air terminal, a sentry with a .308 round lodged deep in his chest tried desperately to speak. He moved his mouth, but no sound would come. The man knew he was bleeding to death. Still, he felt he could die with honor and in peace if only he could sound the alarm. The pain was excruciating, but the tears that streamed down his face were from frustration. He simply could not speak. It took all the strength he had just to squeeze the transmission button on his Motorola transceiver.

Nakajima led them through the fence. Walker and a Japanese named Hattori were the last two through the chain link. They immediately took positions where they could cover the entrance to the lighted office building. Walker moved as well on land as he did in the water, but Hattori was like a cat. Walker crouched near one of the bunkers directly across the road from the entrance, while Hattori positioned himself parallel to the front of the office, at a ninety-degree angle from Walker's line of fire. Theirs was a classic two-man setup. The area was well lighted from lamps on the surrounding storage buildings. No one could enter or leave the office and escape their field of fire.

Moody, Nakajima, and Sergeant Kodansha headed for the VX storage vaults. They were set apart from the other storage bunkers across the main roadway from the office complex, like a line of circular metal pillboxes. Concrete wainscoting rose five feet from the ground, whitewashed like the metal upper portions to reflect the sun. The vaults were partially dug into the coral and served by a short flight of steps that led down to a heavy, airtight door. Valves, gauges, and air-monitoring equipment flanked the entrance. As they approached the first vault, they found the locks had been broken and the door was partially open. Kodansha carefully followed the two firing leads inside. Moody pulled the door behind them, careful not to crimp the leads. Their lights revealed rows of gray metal cylinders; it was as if they had entered the larva chamber of some giant insect. An eighty-pound pack of C-4, enough high explosive to easily shred the chemical containers and blow the roof off the containment bunker, was strapped to a pallet of the gray canisters. There was a wicked-looking detonator attached to the explosives. Kodansha squatted to inspect the device.

Moody touched his throat mike to make sure it was still in place. "Hey Don, what you got?"

"Me an' Hattori are set. Bad guys are still inside, but I can't tell how many. Two or three for sure—maybe more."

"Understood. Now listen Don, how many wires do you see leading into that office?"

"One . . . hold on a sec." Walker pulled out a small pair of waterproof binoculars. "Got the one, and, uh . . . got another. Hang on . . . no, that's it—just two wires."

"Roger, Moody clear."

That meant they'd set the explosives in series—at least some of them, maybe all of them. This was encouraging, but they'd have to check them all. He dropped to one knee to join Nakajima and Kodansha, who were carefully studying the electrical detonator assembly on the C-4. A tool pouch and several small pieces of metered test equipment rested on the metal floor near the explosives. Kodansha made several low guttural sounds and sucked noisily through his teeth. He checked the leads and several wires on the detonator with a clamp-on ammeter. Finally there was a rapid exchange between the two Japanese, and Nakajima looked up.

"He says there is a slight current, which means there is an anti-disturbance device in place, so he cannot simply cut the firing leads. The detonator is of a North Korean design. Sergeant Kodansha is not sure of the procedure to disarm it."

Jesus H. Christ! Moody thought. Here I am in Samurai Land with a North Korean bomb and a Japanese bomb expert. It'd be funny except I'll probably die laughing. "Tell him to pretend he's an American; tell him to improvise!" Moody looked at his watch. "And tell him to hurry."

Nakajima spoke a few words to his sergeant. Kodansha sighed and went back to work. Moody closed his eyes for a long second, trying not to think of the tons of chemicals that surrounded him.

"Do not worry, John-san," Nakajima said in his calm voice. "If my sergeant is unsuccessful, you and I at least, will have the benefit of a quick death from the explosives."

Moody was not sure his legs were going to hold him so he put a hand on a pallet of cylinders to steady himself. He'd about had it with Nakajima and his cool-ass samurai crap and was about to tell him so. Then there was a crackle in his earpiece.

"This is Slyfield, over." He heard him but didn't respond. "Hey, boss, you there?"

"Go ahead, Sly."

"You got company. There's a guard comin' in from th' beach on th' east side of th' facility. He's jes' about to th' gate. There . . . he's inside now. Oh yeah, an' th' plane is startin' to burn real good now. It'll go quick in this wind."

"Uh, thanks, Sly." He had to concentrate—it was hard

standing next to eighty pounds of C-4 with a live detonator and all the chemicals in the world. "Uh, Walker, you got him."

"Just picked him up. He's got to walk past Hattori, wait one."

The guard shuffled down the road that led to the office, head down and one shoulder hunched against the wind. The burning C-141 was a bright red ball in the west, but the sentry shielded his face from the wind and did not see it. Hattori hugged the shadows, allowing the man to walk within a few feet of him. Walker was waiting for him to take him with a knife or some cute karate move, but Hattori simply shot him with his suppressed 9mm pistol. He stepped out, caught the man before he hit the ground, and dragged him back out of the light, silently and quickly like in the movies.

"He tapped him, boss," said Walker, "and very neatly too."

"Understood," Moody replied, looking at his watch and then down at Kodansha. He started to say something, but thought better of prodding a man who was working on a bomb.

Tadao stood in front of the mirror, adjusting the high collar on his tunic. He had just pinned a fresh white, starched insert to the stiff, cotton fabric. Tadao had taken over the duty officer's quarters on the third floor of the administration building. They were small but quite adequate, and there was an adjoining bath. Normally Tadao would have been up much earlier, but the storm had afforded him an extra hour or so of sleep. He had laughingly called it the return of the kamikaze or Divine Wind, sent by the *kami* of the home islands to help them defend their conquest. He felt good and took a few extra minutes to dress carefully.

"Commandant!" The man broke into his room from the hall, but the stern look on Tadao's features caused him to halt and bow. Tadao returned the gesture with unhurried precision.

"Now," he commanded, "what is it?"

"The airplane by the terminal. It is on fire."

"Show me!" He followed the man back down the hall at a brisk walk, forgetting his collar for the moment.

"They're comin' out, boss!"

Inside the storage-facility office, one of the men saw the red glow coming from the direction of the terminal. Two men ran out to get a better look at the burning aircraft, almost a mile away but visible through the blowing mist. A third man came to the window and cupped his hands around his eyes, shielding his vision from the inside lighting. Walker had the shot he wanted and took it. First he sent two rounds into the man at the window, then he shifted his fire to the two outside, but they were already going down under a long burst from Hattori's MP-5. His weapon was suppressed, and the only sound to rise above the wind was the bark of Walker's M-14.

The two shooters then advanced quickly across the lighted area to the entrance of the building. Hattori briefly checked the two forms near the door, then slipped through the entryway with Walker covering him. An unarmed man came rushing into the room from one of the back offices. In the split second before Hattori killed him, he wondered why another Japanese, one dressed like himself but whose face he did not recognize, was pointing a submachine gun at him. Walker and Hattori quickly cleared the back-office spaces.

"Okay, boss, we're clear. Four bad guys down."

"Understood. Follow the firing leads to the blasting machine, but don't touch it. Just guard it and don't let anyone near it." In the storage bunker, Nakajima looked up to Moody. "Do you still want the explosives removed from the chemicals, John-san?"

It was a critical question. Should they just leave the armed explosives on the chemicals and concentrate on defending the facility from counterattack, holding out until help arrived, or should they take the additional risk and disarm them now? There was good cause to leave well enough alone, except for the chance that Tadao had a remote-control detonator keyed to the explosives.

"Yes," Moody replied in a strained voice, "unless the sergeant feels there's no way he can do it."

Nakajima spoke a few words and Kodansha went back to work. Moody knew he should leave the bunker and help Walker and Hattori with security, for there was nothing he could do here. But he could not move. It was as if the demolition package were a treacherous dog, and to turn his back on it would be to invite an attack, or in this case an explosion.

Kodansha probed carefully at the detonator. He again checked the circuitry and, with only a moment's hesitation, cut two of the many wires. His shoulders seemed to sag slightly. Then he cut the straps and carefully lifted the explosives away from the chemical cylinders. He looked up and smiled.

Moody swallowed. "That's it?"

"For this one charge," Nakajima said. "This detonator had an internal anti-disturbance circuit but Sergeant Kodansha has defeated it. It would seem that the charges are wired in a series circuit, and this circuit too has an anti-disturbance feature. So we will have to disarm each of them. That should not take long, now that he understands the procedure."

Relief flooded over Moody and he felt light-headed. "You and the sergeant keep working along the circuit. Let me know when they're all disarmed. And Sergeant Kodansha," Moody said, bowing to him, *"Domo arigatoh."*

Kodansha and Nakajima both bowed, then hurried out, following the firing lead to the next bunker. Moody was right behind them. He paused outside to speak on the squad radio. "Walker?"

"Walker, aye."

"Slyfield?"

"Right here, boss."

"You there, Glasser?"

"Yes, sir."

"Okay guys, phase one will soon be complete. They'll be coming after us now, so stay alert. Glasser, you going to be okay down there?"

"I'll do what I can, sir."

"Fair enough. It's hold-the-fort time, guys. Sing out when you see something."

Moody pulled the AN/PRC-113 handset from its Velcro carrier on his harness and began to transmit.

The administration building was the tallest building on the island. From the window at the end of the hall, Tadao could see the burning transport and, by contrast, the dimly lit terminal. So, they have come! he thought. Now the final struggle will begin.

He turned and headed for the operations center, the soldier on duty trailing in his wake. "What have you learned from the sentries around the island?"

The dispatcher pointed to a chart of Johnston Atoll. "I have been unable to raise any of the beach guards along the southeast beaches or the men at the terminal."

"And what of the chemical-storage area or the disposal facility?"

Tadao's manner was accusatory and the dispatcher lowered his head as he spoke. "The men at the disposal facility have been alerted, as have the guards along the harbor waterfront. We have not been able to raise the men at the storage complex."

Tadao gave the man a stern look and turned to study the map on the wall. Somehow they've managed to come ashore along the southwest portion of the island, he reasoned; they now occupy the terminal or perhaps the storage facility, or both. They must have swum ashore or come in a very small, low-profile boat. The surface-search radar was excellent, even in these conditions. He stepped over to the scope. "Have you detected anything?"

The radar antenna, located atop a tower on the eastern end of the island, guarded the approaches to the harbor.

The operator had manually tuned out most of the sea clutter, leaving only a sprinkle of phosphorescence around the base of the sweep. Computer filters and enhancement functions did the rest. All three smaller islands to the east were clearly visible, as well as the approach buoys marking the shipping channel from the south, around the eastern end of Johnston Island.

"No, Commandant," the operator replied. "Nor has the alarm sounded." In addition to the visible presentation, the surveillance radar was programmed to sound an alarm when it detected the approach of a surface contact.

Tadao concluded that a small American special-operations team had managed to sneak ashore and surprise the men at the terminal and the storage facility. Had they come ashore in larger numbers, they would have attacked the administration building and tried to free the hostages. He assumed they now controlled the explosives on the chemicals, although he knew the booby-trapped firing circuits could be tricky. But the Americans were clever; they would probably know this and not attempt to remove them.

Then he smiled. If a small group of Americans think they can intimidate us because they now have control of the chemical-storage complex, they are mistaken. They may have the chemicals, for now, but we still have hostages. And above all, we are samurai warriors.

There was a sound of running feet in the hallway. Taiyo stepped into the office and bowed curtly. Since Araki's death during the assault on the island, he had assumed the role of Tadao's first assistant. He had been resting with the group scheduled to relieve the watch-standers later that morning.

"Have the off-duty men been alerted?"

"Yes, Commandant."

"Good. Have them assemble in the auditorium. That includes all the beach sentries and the men at the disposal facility. Assign an additional man here and leave the hostage guards in place; all others are to prepare to fight."

"*Hai*, Commandant!"

Taiyo left as Tadao turned to the dispatcher. "You are to remain here and keep me informed of any ships approaching the island." As he turned to leave, he heard a door slam followed by several muffled crashes. Puzzled, he stepped into the hall to investigate.

Jim Bruso had waited as long as he dared. He didn't know what was happening, but something had captured everyone's attention. He knew it was a gamble but sensed if they didn't move now, they might never have another chance.

"Ready?" he whispered in the senator's ear.

"Ready," she replied.

They slowly rose. As Bruso had instructed, she moved quietly to the door and he to the large metal desk. When he was behind it and ready, he nodded. She slammed the door and locked it, then jumped to one side as he pushed the desk across the room and rammed it into the door. Together they pushed a four-drawer file cabinet over and scooted it behind the desk. Then another and finally the third. The last two cabinets were laid lengthwise and fitted neatly behind the first that held the desk to the door. The third rested against the cinderblock wall and completed the chain. The door, which opened inward, was now firmly blocked.

In the hall, Tadao turned the handle and found it locked. He called for the two guards, who came on the run. Together they tried to force the door, but it held. It was a sturdy metal door in a metal casing.

"Shoot the lock!" he commanded.

One of the men pulled his Uzi from his shoulder, stepping back and to one side. The staccato of the Uzi on full automatic filled the hallway. The lock absorbed almost a full twenty-round magazine before it yielded. There was a crack, but the desk held the door from opening further. The two guards and a man from the watch team crashed into it without success. Tadao watched and turned crimson.

"Leave it for now, but guard them closely," he said loud

enough for those inside to hear. "If they try to leave the room, shoot them on sight."

Inside, Bruso held Nancy Blackman as they crouched in the corner, shielding her from the few ricocheted rounds that whined about the room.

Moody keyed the 113. "This is Sierra Juliet. Whiskey bravo hotel—whiskey bravo hotel. Please acknowledge, over."

This time when the signal reached the aircraft overhead, Colonel Anthony Fortino depressed the transmit key on his control yoke and replied, "Sierra Juliet, this is Tradewind Three-seven. Understand whiskey bravo hotel, over."

"Sierra Juliet, roger, out."

Fortino knew this was the voice code that reported the team ashore on Johnston Island had secured the chemical weapons and disarmed them. He closed his eyes a moment and crossed himself, then relayed the message by secure radio to the task-group commander.

Aboard the *Tarawa*, there was a huge cheer from flag plot as the report came in. But the joy was short-lived as the air operations officer informed General Sheppard that the wind was gusting to sixty-five knots—too strong for helicopter operations. Furthermore, the main body of the storm would soon be moving across Johnston Island, bringing a series of thunderstorms in its wake.

Moody stood by the entrance to the storage facility flanked by Walker and Hattori. The abandoned guard shack served as a good windbreak. It was still dark, but the eastern sky had started to turn a dull gray. Down the runway to their left, flames licked at the hulk of the C-141 as the giant transport gradually became a lumpy puddle of aluminum. The storm had driven a squall across the island, lashing them with rain. It passed quickly, but another soon followed. Moody considered their position.

Any counterattack would have to come from the north

across the east end of the runway, or along the southern beaches. His two snipers had a commanding view of the eastern approaches, weather permitting, and Glasser covered their western flank. He winced as he thought of Glasser. He had almost called him back from his position near the terminal, but as long as someone was there, the attackers would have to assume the terminal was occupied, which could split the counterattacking forces. This strategy would favor the defense of the chemical-storage complex, but it abandoned Glasser.

The mission came first, always the mission. Tactically, it was the right decision and Moody knew this, but that didn't make it easier. He had lost Berta and Hori and now he had to cut Glasser loose. Finally, Nakajima and Kodansha joined them.

"Have you disarmed all the explosives?"

"Yes, John-san, and the firing leads and blasting machine have been destroyed."

"Good work, Taro—Sergeant. Okay everyone, listen up." They all bent close to hear over the wind. "We have to hold this place until help arrives. There's too much wind right now so we can't count on the Marines from the *Tarawa*. There'll be a destroyer in the channel in about three hours, but we're on our own till then. Everyone know where your defensive positions are?" They all nodded. "Good. Captain Nakajima and I will stand guard. Between us and the guys on the tank, there's no way they can surprise us. Walker, I want you, Hattori, and Kodansha to start humping C-4. Take it back behind the office building and set it on fire—just in case."

What Moody didn't have to add, but they all understood, was that just in case Tadao and his men overwhelmed them, they wouldn't be able to use the explosives. C-4 was a powerful explosive but highly flammable, and it burned easily without detonating. "We'll let you know if we see them coming, and you can get back to your positions."

"They are making preparations now, so it should not be too much longer."

"You know this for sure?"

Nakajima held up a radio he had taken from one of the sentries.

"And they're speaking plainly in the open on the radio?" Moody couldn't believe it.

Nakajima smiled. "They are not true soldiers, John-san. And Japanese is a difficult language, too difficult for a *gaijin* special-operations team. Please remember, Tadao has yet to learn that I am with you. Perhaps if they use this circuit for tactical messages when they attack, I can redirect some of their efforts."

Christ, Moody thought as he found himself grinning, and to think we considered trying this without these guys. He was on an adrenaline high and felt marvelous. They were still in grave danger, but with the immediate threat of a chemical-agent release behind them, even a firefight was something to look forward to.

"Questions?" There were none. "Okay, let's get to work, but before you do anything, all faces black."

They expected fighting at close quarters, and this was to tell Nakajima and his men from the Japanese terrorists. Moody and Walker dabbed on some additional paint just to be safe.

Slyfield and Jackson watched the approach of dawn with apprehension. Like most snipers they were shy and introverted, and they disliked attention. Neither was particularly anxious to be on top of the tank in the daylight. The wind that now threatened to blow them off the top of the tank was both a curse and a comfort. It would affect their shooting, but they'd been trained to deal with windage. But this wind would make them very difficult targets from the ground.

There were metal padeyes along the rim of the tank, welded there to assist workmen in painting and maintaining the tank. They had brought along fifty-foot sections of quarter-inch climbing rope and had been able to anchor themselves to the tank. The wind was bad, but there was another problem. The surface was caked with sea-gull droppings that, when wet, were more than treacherous. Slyfield and Jackson now lay on the eastern rim of the tank, clutching their weapons and the section of line between them.

"Bet you wished you'd listened to your daddy an' stayed in school, huh, Darron. You could be in some laboratory, wearin' a white coat an' all. Now you'll be white aw-right, 'cept it'll be from ally-gatorin' around in sea-gull shit."

"Least I wouldn't have to listen to your jive-ass cracker lip." Jackson looked at his watch. "Guess it's about time to go to work. Five bucks says I get it in three."

"Two," Slyfield shot back.

"Two it is." Jackson grinned. He had figured he could do it with two, but he knew Slyfield wouldn't buy it unless he lobbied for three.

The radar tower stood two hundred yards almost due east and was now backlighted by a dawn the color of wet concrete. The antenna tower was exactly twenty-one feet lower than the top of the tank. Jackson settled in behind his reticle and centered the cross hairs on the rotating antenna's mounting. It would have been an easy shot except for the wind, which was blowing from behind him and to his right. The scope was zeroed for a hundred yards. Jackson compensated precisely for the longer distance and drop in elevation, but he had to guess at the correction for the quartering wind. He squeezed off the first round, and the antenna continued to turn.

"Granny's drawers, ya bum," said Slyfield, watching through binoculars. "Git out yer wallet."

Jackson shifted his aiming point twelve inches to the left and fired again. The antenna still turned.

"Haw, missed again. Pay up, pilgrim."

Then the radar stopped for a few seconds, made one more revolution, and stopped again. Jackson chuckled and sent another round into the mount for good measure.

"You was lucky," said Slyfield.

"I'll put it on your tab," Jackson replied.

* * *

Tadao strode into the auditorium. There were close to sixty fighting men, all in full combat gear, much as they had been when they'd first come ashore four days ago. Tadao, also in camouflage battle dress, stepped purposely to the raised stage. A ripple of apprehension passed through those assembled as Tadao stood fully before them. He wore a headband, but it was the headband of a kamikaze warrior—one who anticipated a fight to the death.

"Brother samurai, the Americans have finally come to our island, and they have recaptured a portion of it. They now occupy the air terminal and the chemical-storage facility. We believe this to be a small element, sent ahead of the main attacking force. The storm that now blows over our island will keep the Americans from reinforcing those few who have come ashore. We must strike now while the kamikaze winds act as our shield. Once we again control the chemical weapons, any reinforcements will face certain death, something for which the Americans have no stomach." He took a step forward and held his sheathed long sword over his head. "For us samurai, every fight is a fight to the death."

"To the death!" they echoed, raising their swords and automatic weapons.

"Now listen carefully to my plan, for we haven't much time."

Moments later, they were filing out of the auditorium and into vehicles parked in front of the building.

Moody sat in the guard shack and squinted into the blowing mist. A leaden cast now claimed most of the sky, slightly lighter in the east, favoring the position of the defenders if the attack came from where he expected. The sun above the clouds had done what it could, but the wind-driven sea spray, now mixed with rain and fog, promised the visibility along the ground would get no better. They'll have to attack across the airfield or along the perimeter road from either direction, Moody reasoned. But it was still seven of them, eight counting Glasser, against fifty or more. Nakajima slipped into the guard shack beside him.

"They will be coming soon, all of them, and they will be in trucks and jeeps."

"Will they attack the terminal?"

"I don't think so. From what I've been able to learn, they will send a small group around the airstrip and come in from the west, but they'll have to pass the terminal en route. This attack is more of a diversionary thrust. The main attack will be around the airfield from the east."

Moody nodded. "Anything else?"

"No, John-san. I will continue to listen and remain silent until such time as I am able to disrupt their tactical plans. And here, I thought you might need this." Nakajima handed him an H&K PS-1 assault rifle he had taken from the dead occupants of the storage-facility office, along with several magazines of ammunition. Moody set aside his MP-5, one similar to Nakajima's. The 9mm submachine gun was an excellent weapon in close quarters, but the PS-1, with its heavier 7.62 rounds, had much greater range and accuracy. If they attacked across the open space along the access road, it would prove useful. He would have preferred an M-14, the American 7.62 assault rifle, even though the German weapon was superior. How ironic, Moody thought—an American fighting Japanese with German guns. Heckler & Koch made both the PS-1 and the MP-5.

"What about yourself?"

Nakajima patted his own MP-5. "My friend and I have shared a few experiences together. We will be just fine. And now, I must find my sergeant and get to our position. I am a little disappointed, John-san, that we cannot fight side by side."

"Let's hope it doesn't come down to that," Moody replied evenly.

In the event that Tadao's men were able to overrun the chemical-weapons facility, the plan was to fall back to the special-weapons containment area and make their final stand. The two men bowed, then Nakajima disappeared along the perimeter fence into the storm.

Sunday, 11 December, 7:45 A.M.
CAMP H. M. SMITH, HAWAII

Admiral Harrington sat in the Tactical Operations Center with a handset pressed up against his ear and a sour expression on his face. He listened for several minutes before speaking.

"I see, Jack, but just when do you think you *can* get something into the air . . . I see . . . certainly it's a risk either way . . . understood." Harrington took the receiver and held it to his chest for a moment before bringing it back to his ear. "Okay, Jack, proceed with your plan. And good luck."

He pushed himself from the commander's chair and walked over to the large, lighted display of Johnston Atoll and the surrounding area. Up in the corner some sixty miles northwest of the atoll was a blip marked *Kearsarge*. Harrington stared at it for several minutes, then returned to his chair and picked up the secure line to the Situation Room in the White House.

The USS *Kearsarge* (LHD-3) was a newer class, but essentially the same type of ship as the *Tarawa*. The main body of the storm was south of it and the wind, while strengthening, had not yet had time to work their part of the Pacific past sea state three. Nonetheless, with the wind and eight-foot swells building on the starboard beam, the *Kearsarge* rolled badly as it made for Johnston Island at flank speed.

Down in the well deck, Major Tom Lenze stood braced against the small pilothouse on the starboard side of the LCAC. Lenze was a stocky man with a round face and an impatient manner. The "El-Kack," as the Marines called them, was short for landing craft, air cushion. It was a ninety-ton hovercraft that could carry a tank or a company of men across the water at forty knots. The landing craft was large enough to handle rough water, but the seas that were building around the *Kearsarge* were approaching its limit. There were two LCACs in the belly of the ship, each with a half company of Lenze's Rangers aboard. One LCAC could carry them all, but they had been ordered on to two of them in case one had mechanical problems or broached in the storm. The well deck was stuffy and damp, and there was a stench of fresh vomit in the air.

Christ Almighty! Lenze thought. This is Marine work; they should have a company of Marines here instead of us! But Major Tom Lenze knew why he and his men were there. The Marines were a fine naval infantry and very proficient in over-the-beach operations. But when it came to the business of armed assault in company and platoon-size units, the U.S. Army Rangers were the best light infantry in the world.

But armed assault was not on Major Lenze's mind right now. He leaned over the rail of the LCAC and retched, but nothing came. After several minutes of this unsuccessful effort, he leaned back against the pilothouse and dragged a camouflaged sleeve across his mouth. Christ, I can't wait to get off this metal coffin and onto stable ground!

He looked at his men huddled on the deck of the LCAC with their equipment. None of them looked well, but these were hard young men. If the damn Navy can get us ashore, Lenze told himself again, we'll get the fuckin' job done; we'll handle these hot-shit, super-ninja Japanese.

The *Kearsarge* had been halfway to Okinawa from Hawaii with no embarked troops or air group—just two LCACs. Then it had been turned around and headed for Johnston Atoll at top speed. The Rangers had been taken aboard when the ship had come within range of the extended-range CH-53 helicopters, flying out from Hawaii. Data-link transmission had been able to provide them with considerable information on the physical layout of Johnston Island, but Lenze had been told little of the mission before him other than to prepare to fight a lightly armed but entrenched, determined foe. We can do that, he thought, if we can ever get off this god-awful rolling steel box. He was thinking about trying to puke again when a loudspeaker boomed across the well deck.

"Now hear this; now hear this! Prepare to launch hovercraft from the well deck. All deck department personnel, stand by your launching stations. Now, prepare to launch hovercraft!"

Lenze stepped into the pilothouse where the LCAC's coxswain, a first-class petty officer, had just finished stuffing his mouth with a cold burrito. Grease ran down his chin. Lenze hurried back out and flashed all over the side of the LCAC. He soon returned, patting his face with a gauze pad wetted from his canteen. His face had gone from white to gray.

"We get orders to launch?" Lenze asked hoarsely.

"Yep," said the coxswain, wiping his chin with an oily rag. He closed the throttles and spooled up the four Avco-Lycoming gas turbines. "An' sir, tell your troops to secure any loose equipment—an' themselves. It's gonna be wet out there and rough as a cob." Then he looked at Lenze with some compassion. "The well deck's the shits, sir. It'll be a lot better when we're out in the open ocean."

The LCAC rose up on its skirts and the jet engines shrieked in the confines of the metal hangar. The *Kearsarge* had swung around to a southwesterly heading. Steaming into the swells, it traded its roll for a gentle pitching motion. Both LCACs, now fully cushion-borne, were sliding around the steel floor of the well deck like two air-hockey pucks. Finally the stern gate opened, offering them a way out. First one LCAC, then the other, caromed off the side rails and down the ramp into the wake of the mother ship.

At first the two hovercraft turned and roared along in its wake. Clouds of spray billowed from the skirts of the two hovercraft as they howled along in the flat water behind the helicopter carrier. Then they turned in unison to port and headed southeast toward Johnston Island. Gradually they came up to forty knots. The swells were almost directly on their beam, and they slid over most of them, but every so often the top of a wave broke over the bow and sent a wall of gray foam into the men huddled in the cargo bay.

"Jesus," said the coxswain, "I ain't never seen it like this!" The LCAC slid off a swell and dug into the next one, sending another surge of sea water into the bay. One of the jet engines hesitated as it ingested a dose of spray, then screamed back up to full power.

"We gonna make it?"

"Maybe, sir." The sailor squinted into the blowing sea head. His knuckles were white as they gripped the control yoke. "I ain't never seen it like this."

Lenze lurched through the watertight door and made his way down to the cargo bay. A tall black non-com, looking like a giant drowned rat, leaned into the wind and spray as he turned to meet him. "Jus', sir, what the fuck you got us into?"

"Here." Lenze gave him a cold look and jammed a thermos of hot coffee into his ribs. "Check the first platoon, First Sergeant, and I'll check the second."

The two men moved from one helmeted, camouflaged lump on the wet deck to the next as the LCAC pounded its way toward Johnston Island.

Petty Officer Darron Jackson was the first to see them coming. The fog and blowing sea spray had lowered their visibility, making everything fuzzy. They could see along the south edge of the eastern end of the runway, but sheets of gray cotton had claimed the buildings north of the runway and the eastern shoreline. The first vehicle, a six-by-six truck, charged out of the mist along the perimeter road toward the storage complex. An assortment of vans and light trucks followed.

"This is Jackson. I got a small convoy headed your way on the eastern approach. Looks like a six-by, three vans and couple of pickups, over."

"Get on 'em!" Moody shouted into his radio. From his

position at the gate to the storage complex, he could neither see nor hear them.

"Sir?"

"Engage them—shoot to kill!"

"Understand shoot to kill," he replied calmly. "Jackson, out."

Even though they were ready and fully expecting it, it was a strange order. Snipers are patient animals by training, used to waiting long periods for their quarry, and even longer for an actual order to shoot. On those rare occasions when they did fire, it was a single round—one bullet, one kill. Now they were asked to stop a convoy and slaughter as many people as they could. Jackson and Slyfield had talked about this and knew what they wanted to do. Without a word, they settled in behind their rifles and went to work.

Hitting a vehicle is much easier than hitting a man, but killing one is more difficult. Wind and movement were enemies of the sniper. If they could stop the convoy, half their problem would be solved. The two shooters concentrated on the six-by-six, a five-ton Army truck leading the procession around the eastern end of the runway. Slyfield went for the tires while his partner worked on the cab. Jackson worked the bolt of the McMillan quickly, never taking his eyes from the scope. Slyfield had removed the night scope and was now squinting over his sights. Every three seconds the big rifle jumped. Both men wished they had one of the big .50 caliber sniper rifles for this job. The large-caliber weapon was lethal against vehicles, but both gun and ammo were heavy. They'd have to do the job with their .308 weapons. The snipers had expended eight rounds between them before the lead trunk lurched to a stop near the end of the runway.

As the other vehicles in the column came to a stop behind the six-by-six, they began to work their way down the line, pumping shells into the windshields and front wheels. Only the driver of the last pickup reacted, jerking his vehicle out of line and moving to the front along the stationary column. He paused for a moment on the protected side of the six-by-six, then accelerated along the perimeter road for a short distance before bounding off the road toward the shoreline, away from the water tanks. Slyfield and Jackson chased the pickup until it was lost in the fog bank.

"Son of a bitch," yelled Slyfield into the storm.

"Forget the truck," Jackson called back as he deftly pushed a speed loader clip of ammunition into the action of the McMillan. "Concentrate on the Japs."

As if on command, close to thirty men burst from the vehicles and began to sprint along the road and toward the beach. With the wind mostly behind them they moved swiftly, making them difficult targets. On average, every third round from each barrel caused a running man to pitch forward into the coral sand. They harvested well over a dozen, but the rest escaped.

Both SEALs looked up from their shooting positions at the same time. Slyfield keyed his radio. "Hey, boss, we stopped some of them, but a lot of 'em got away into the fog. There's probably twenty of the bastards headed your way, maybe more."

"They on the road, Sly?"

"No sir. Looks like they're comin' along the beach, an' they got a pick-up truck."

"Okay, hang in there; shoot when you can see them. You guys all right?"

"Yes sir, we're fine—Slyfield clear."

He and Jackson exchanged a painful look and settled back in behind their rifles. Several of the downed men were still crawling in the sand toward the beach and safety; one had even regained his feet and was staggering forward. They then began the grim task of nailing the wounded into the sand with 7.62mm 168-grain boat-tail hollow points.

Tadao had been sitting on the passenger's seat of the six-by-six when one of the first rounds spider-webbed the windshield in front of him. He dove under the dash just as another round splattered his driver's brains across the side window. The truck continued to idle along for a short distance until the front tires were shot out.

"Morita!" Tadao shouted into his Motorola as the truck coasted to a halt. More bullets tore into the side of the vehicle. "Come up here alongside the lead truck—stay to the left side and come quickly!"

Tadao reached over and opened the driver's door, pushing him from the truck. Then he quickly tumbled out to the ground beside the dead man and took stock of the situation. In the lee of the truck, he watched as the windows of the truck immediately behind him were punched out, then the one behind it.

"Get out!" he shouted into the transceiver. "Take cover behind the trucks—they're shooting from the airfield!"

Most of the men escaped, but not all. The side doors of the vans opened into the line of fire and the two snipers took full advantage. All but one of the men in the back of the six-by-six were able to get to the ground and take cover behind the big truck. Tadao watched and pounded his fist on the rear wheel in frustration. He'd planned on using the truck to smash the gates of the weapons-storage area.

Then a pickup slid to a stop behind the big truck, well hidden from the snipers. Tadao tapped six men on the shoulder and each bounded into the back of it while he snatched a kit bag from the cab of the six-by-six. "We will draw their fire and try to get to the cover of the beach dunes," he shouted to the men crouched behind the vehicles. "When we are gone, you must follow us on the run. Spread out and move quickly. Banzai!"

"Banzai!" they yelled back, but, as Tadao noted, not with the enthusiasm they'd had just a short time ago when they'd gathered in the auditorium.

We can still do this, he told himself, but we must somehow make this a close-quarters fight! He leapt into the passenger's seat of the pickup and sped into the wind and rain.

Petty Officer Don Glasser peered into the mist with his binoculars. A squall line marched past and there they were, moving along the perimeter road, a hundred meters from the terminal access-road turnoff.

"Hey, sir, I got two vehicles approaching from the west toward my position, over. Looks like a van and a stake truck, over."

Moody sat in his bunker, squinting into the blowing sand and rain in search of the survivors of the sniper ambush. He hated to ask it of Glasser, but he had no choice.

He keyed his radio, "Don, I want you to try and stop them. You have your AT-4s ready?"

"Yes, sir, but it won't be an easy shot."

"I understand that. We're gonna have our hands full here so I need you to try and hold them up."

"Aye, sir. I'll do what I can."

"Keep me posted, Don, and good luck—Moody clear." He bowed his head, knowing that he had probably just sent Glasser to his death. There would be twelve to fourteen armed men in those two vehicles. Again he thought of Berta, and a sense of sadness and frustration gripped him. Then an idea burned through the despair. He fumbled for his transmit key.

"Taro, you there, over."

"Yes, John-san."

"Tell the men in the trucks coming from the west to stop at the airport access road; tell them to wait there for further instructions!"

"I understand, John-san."

Nakajima had been listening carefully to Tadao and his men on the captured Motorola. They spoke often and from the manner of their communication, he knew they had no idea that someone else might be on the net.

"Taiyo," Nakajima said gruffly into the Motorola, forcing an imperial tone into his voice, "halt at the turn to the airport terminal. Wait there for further instructions."

"Wait at the terminal, Commandant?" replied a tentative voice on the transceiver—tentative but respectful.

"Yes, those are my orders, out." Nakajima listened carefully, but there was no further traffic. He could hear distant sounds of gunfire over the noise of the wind, and rightly guessed that Tadao was too busy with the snipers to monitor his radio.

Forty yards south of the perimeter road, Glasser held the van in the sights of his AT-4 rocket launcher and waited for them to pass abreast of him. Even at this close range, it would be a chancy shot—his lead angle would have to be the difference between the speed of the vehicle and the speed of the wind. Glasser guessed the lead truck was probably traveling twenty miles an hour slower than the wind.

"You ready?" Glasser said to Sergeant Pierce.

Pierce had wanted to let them go past. He had said as much to Glasser, but the big SEAL just gave him a cold look and readied his rocket launcher.

"I guess," Pierce replied. If I ever again get back on a C-141 Circuit Rider, he vowed silently once more, I'll never again complain about the long, routine, boring flights.

Glasser put the lead van in the center of his sights, then aimed for a point about ten yards behind it. He had begun his trigger squeeze when Taiyo told his driver to halt the van at the access road turnoff. Then the terrorist climbed from the front passenger's seat and hurried back to the stake truck to brief the driver on the delay.

Glasser couldn't believe his good fortune. He increased the lag of his aim to a point twenty yards behind the van, and squeezed. The rocket leapt from his shoulder and streaked for the van. His aim did not lag the vehicle by enough, but the warhead still caught the van a foot behind the right headlight. The four-and-a-half pound shaped charge destroyed the front portion of the chassis and tore the engine from its mounts. Shrapnel and blast fragments from the floorboards and dash shredded four of the six men in the van, blowing the two in the back out the doors. The van didn't burn.

Sergeant Pierce was supposed to hand Glasser a second rocket for the other vehicle, but he sat staring at the wounded van that was now nose down on its fore-axle with the front wheels blown off. Glasser growled something, snatched the AT-4 from Pierce, and sighted in on the truck. He centered the round better this time, and the rocket tore through the middle of the door. And this one did burn. A few of the men in back were able to scramble off the bed of the truck, but several more were caught in the fireball as the gas tank exploded. Glasser tossed aside the launcher and took up his M-14.

He jammed an open palm into Pierce's shoulder that almost knocked the Air Force sergeant down. "Start shooting, goddamn it!"

Pierce took up an MP-5 and began spraying the area like he was watering the garden. Glasser searched the twisted metal with his scope for individual targets. He worked with deadly efficiency. Any compassion he may have felt was quickly extinguished when he thought of his dead chief lying out behind the terminal. Every few seconds, the M-14 barked. For those burning and still alive, it was a merciful end.

The wind carried the sounds of rocket detonations and firing to Moody at the gate of the chemical-storage complex. He continued to search the area in front of the facility and to his right along the beach. Pockets of mist again raced before him over the island, but visibility seemed to be improving.

"Walker, Moody—anything?"

"Negative."

"How about you, Taro?"

"Nothing yet, John-san, but it won't be long."

Moody looked at his watch and cursed softly. It would be another hour or more before they saw a ship on the horizon, long after the issue had been settled. He desperately wanted to call Glasser, but refrained. He knew Glasser would call him when he had the opportunity. Moody also feared that if he called, he would get no answer. The storm made the firing sounds indistinct, but he thought he could distinguish the crack of a heavier-caliber weapon from the popping of 9mm submachine guns.

There, he thought as he saw a figure emerge from the haze near the beach. By the time he swung the barrel of the PS-1, a band of mist blanketed the area. When it cleared, there was nothing.

"Christ!" he said aloud. He gritted his teeth and stared into the blowing fog, wanting to be involved, but the action seemed to be moving around him.

Moody was experiencing the timeless battlefield apprehension of military field commanders. Events were taking place, but he had no idea what they were. With the exception of losing Berta and Hori, luck had been with them. To this point, they'd beat the computer odds that said they wouldn't get this far. Now their plan called for Walker and Hattori to take a defensive position on the eastern perimeter of the facility and to watch along the beach access from the north and east. Nakajima and Kodansha were dug in along the western perimeter and covering the beach access from the southern shore. Moody held the sandbagged guard shack at the main gate—all according to plan. Now he had to wait, but it was not easy.

It looks like they may come from the south or east, he thought. If that's the threat axis, maybe Nakajima or I should move over there to support Walker. But they still have a vehicle—will they try the front gate? There's still shooting at the terminal—was I right to leave Glasser on his own? And when the fuck are those choppers gonna get here?

"Hey, boss!" It was Walker, and his voice was hushed and tense. "I got something here."

Moody was anxious and scared, but he was also busy. General Jack Sheppard was just anxious and scared. He had nothing to fear personally, although the atomic bomb was still an option if the VX agents were somehow released. His was a powerless fear, well spiced with frustration, that gnawed at all rear-echelon commanders with men in the field. The matter was out of Sheppard's hands and he knew it. Those were *his* men out there; it would be their victory, but he would share in any losses. He was like a mother waiting for her children to come home from school, knowing they had to walk through a particularly nasty neighborhood. There was little he could do but wait, and General Jack Sheppard was not good at that.

He prowled flag plot like a caged animal, unable to remain seated for more than a few minutes. Every few laps about the room, he walked to the porthole and looked down on the rain-swept flight deck, then to the anemometer that surged between fifty and sixty knots. The wind had leveled off but the seas were still building, causing the *Tarawa* to buck and shudder as it shouldered its way through the swells.

Several times he'd been on the verge of ordering the helicopters, with their embarked Marines, into the air. He could do that; it was his prerogative, but that would mean he'd have to overrule the *Tarawa*'s air boss. The CH-46s were old birds. Crashed helicopters and dead Marines would be of no help to the men ashore. And those Marines were also *his* men.

Sheppard had sent two destroyers ahead to Johnston Island. Since the use of the bomb could not yet be ruled out, the rest of the task group would close only to within thirty miles of the island, still far enough away to veer off if Moody were to lose his battle for control of the chemicals. And Moody didn't need a task force right now; he just needed a few platoons of Marines. Sheppard desperately wanted to radio him for an update, but he knew his SEAL lieutenant would call him when and if he was able. Sheppard stalked back to his chair and lit another cigarette. Then he angrily punched a button on the comm box. "Air ops, this is Sheppard."

"Yes, General?"

"What's the latest on the storm?"

The Crisis Action Center at Camp Smith was much like flag plot on *Tarawa*. Operations officers and communicators manned desks and consoles, waiting for word from

Johnston Island. The atmosphere was tense but the man wasn't, at least not on the surface. Admiral Joe Harrington sat in the padded armchair reserved for the Commander-in-Chief, Pacific, like a man in a theater box. The white hair, solemn manner, and all those stars on his collar made him appear confident and invulnerable. Only the small bottle of antacid pills at his elbow suggested he might not be immune to the tension. As on the *Tarawa*, a spontaneous cheer erupted when Moody reported they had captured the chemical-storage area. Harrington allowed himself a brief smile, then began asking questions. How soon can we get more men in there? What further opposition do they expect? Are the special weapons completely disarmed? Did the assault team take any casualties?

Harrington had a growing temptation to pick up his direct line to General Sheppard, but he knew that would accomplish little. Sheppard would notify him immediately of any changes, and in reality, it was unnecessary. Any word from the SEAL assault element on Johnston Island would be relayed by the orbiting B-52 and received at Camp Smith as well as by the *Vinson* battle group. Sheppard might have something new on the weather there, but the real-time satellite imagery on the screen in front of him showed the blotch of storm clouds just passing over the island. No, he thought, I'll have to wait, just like my task unit commander, for word from Moody.

This disciplined patience along the military chain of command did not, however, extend to the commander-in-chief. The green phone at Harrington's elbow trilled loudly. He sighed heavily and picked it up before the third ring. "Harrington, speaking . . . no Colonel, there has been no change and we have heard nothing further from the element on the ground . . . Colonel, it is just as it was ten minutes ago; we will not initiate contact for a reasonable time and that determination will be made by my task unit commander with the battle group . . . no, there is no word as to when we will be able to reinforce our people now in control of the chemical-weapons facility . . . of course, Colonel, the very minute we know.''

Near a white board in the corner of the CAC, an Air Force master sergeant punched the stem of a stopwatch and began to time the interval to the next call. He noted the intervals posted on the board were becoming shorter.

Sunday, 11 December, 11:52 A.M.
THE WHITE HOUSE

Colonel Tom Pelsiring was a senior military aide to the president. He was a handsome man in his mid-forties, a Military Academy man, tall and with only a hint of gray in his thick dark hair. Pelsiring was one of the few men around the president in uniform, and the large bank of ribbons on his left breast identified him as a highly experienced combat veteran. Right now he would much rather have been shot at than carry out his next duty. But Pelsiring was a brave man. He hung up the phone and strode purposely across the Situation Room to the commander-in-chief.

''Sir, there has been no change. The men ashore are still holding the chemical-weapons area and the prevailing weather conditions prevent us from getting additional forces ashore. The storm front has crossed Johnston Island, but it could be several hours before conditions permit air operations on the island.''

President Garrison and Secretary Carlton sat at the table in their shirt sleeves, ties loosened, amid a scattering of coffee cups, messages, press clippings, and uneaten sandwiches. Pelsiring assumed it had probably been much like this on Garrison's election night as they sweated out the returns.

Garrison tossed a photo of Johnston Island onto the table in a show of frustration. ''What the hell's taking so long? There just has to be some way to get more troops ashore.

Maybe parachute them in? And you say there's no way we can contact them?''

"Sir, our forces in the Pacific are doing everything they can to relieve our men on Johnston Island. But the typhoon severely restricts our options. We are in communication with the team on Johnston Island, but they will only break radio silence for tactical reasons.''

"Jesus Christ, Colonel, we need to know what's happening there. Call them for a status report; it can't be that hard, can it? I mean the guy does have a radio, doesn't he?''

This was not the first time the president had pressed him for information, but there were only so many ways an Army colonel could tell the commander-in-chief to keep his pants on. Pelsiring was a hot-running officer headed for early selection to general. He had been chosen by the Army brass to serve in the White House for a number of reasons; he had good combat experience, he was very smart, and he was politically savvy. And perhaps as important, he *looked* like he was smart and politically savvy—the kind of guy Bob Garrison would have on his team. The president had met him just after he'd taken office and had immediately confirmed his appointment as senior military aide.

Now Pelsiring was again faced with having to say no to the president. He almost withdrew to again call Admiral Harrington with a presidential order to contact the Johnston Island team. But Pelsiring instinctively knew what Harrington, General Sheppard, and everyone else close to the operation knew; Moody would hold on or he would not. He would be relieved on Johnston Island as quickly as weather conditions and resources allowed, and nothing could change that.

"I asked you a question, Colonel. Does he have a radio or not?'' The politician in Pelsiring screamed at him to be accommodating, but four years of duty, honor, and country at West Point won out.

"Mr. President, those men on Johnston Island are very busy right now; they're engaged in combat. They'll hold on and defend those chemical weapons until help arrives, or they'll die trying. That's their mission and they know it. If we force them to take time to give us a situation report, we risk their lives and the mission. I strongly recommend you wait and allow them to call in when they're able."

Pelsiring held the president's gaze, mentally seeing his career and his general's stars slipping away from him. Finally Garrison gave him a tired smile. "You military guys stick together, don't you?"

"When lives are at stake, yes, sir." Neither man spoke for a moment. "Thank you, sir," Pelsiring said quietly and withdrew.

Sunday, 11 December, 6:10 A.M.
JOHNSTON ISLAND

Lieutenant John Moody held his hand against his earpiece waiting for more from Walker, then there were several sharp explosions followed by a furious round of automatic-weapons fire—all coming from the eastern perimeter. Shit, he thought, we go! The pace of the firing slacked as the fight settled into an intense exchange. There was nothing in front of him along the access road to the facility, only the firefight off to his right.

"Taro, do you have anything?"

"No, John-san, nothing from the west or along the beach to the south."

"Sly, Jackson—you guys see anything?"

"Not much, boss. We caught some muzzle flashes through the mist just east of you, but that's it."

The perimeter's too big, Moody thought quickly. They come through the wire and get between us and the game's over!

"Everyone pull back to defend the special-weapons facility! Pull back; everyone pull back. Acknowledge!"

"Understood, John-san. Kodansha and I are moving."

Moody listened, but he heard nothing from Walker. Either he was too busy to talk, or worse, and he didn't want to think about that. Moody took up his submachine gun, deciding to abandon the heavier H&K PS-1. From here on it would be close-range shooting.

"Hey, sir. What do you want me to do, over?"

He was so concerned with pulling back to support Walker, it took Moody a moment to recognize Glasser's voice.

"What's your status?" he said, recovering quickly. In his preoccupation with events around the storage facility, he'd mentally discarded Glasser and, time permitting, would have been ashamed for having done so.

"We were able to take out two vehicles and maybe a dozen guys. A few got away but not many."

"Still got the sergeant?"

"Yes, sir."

"Okay, double-time along the beach to fifty yards or so of the storage area. Take a position there and guard beach approaches. Shoot anything you see that moves along the western perimeter or along the beach, you copy this, Sly?" Snipers always had to know where the friendlies were.

"Slyfield, aye."

"Glasser?"

"Understood, sir."

"Roger up when you're in place. Moody clear."

Already he was on the move, working his way back toward the VX-agent storage area. Each man had been assigned a fallback position for the final defense of the special weapons. With Glasser guarding their rear from an attack from the west, they could concentrate on the attack from the east—the attack on Walker.

Firing along the eastern side of the facility had settled down to a sporadic, ammunition-conserving pace and told Moody that Walker and Hattori were holding, or at least still engaged. He found his place, a shallow revetment that protected the door of one of the VX-agent storage vaults.

From there he watched Nakajima break cover and sprint to a similar position at a nearby vault. Nakajima set up behind a berm that led down to the door of the vault. This would have been Walker and Hattori's position. Anticipating, Nakajima took their place, leaving Kodansha near the fence toward the south. He waved to Moody, then concentrated on the open area in front of him. If Tadao and his men got through, they would have to cross almost twenty yards of open space to get to the VX agents and to them.

"Hey, boss, you there."

"Walker!" Moody almost yelled, "what's happening— are you okay?"

Fifty yards from where Moody, Nakajima, and Kodansha had established their final perimeter, Petty Officer Don Walker had just rolled onto one side and pushed his last magazine into the M-14. The terrorists had come through the fence about thirty yards south of his defensive position, almost directly in front of Hattori. Following a blast from several grenades tossed against the fence, the pickup truck had burst over the rise from the beach and into the gap in the chain link.

Two men were in the back firing over the cab, while several others pushed from behind as the truck dug its way across the packed coral sand. Hattori quickly shot out the windshield and exploded the radiator in a cloud of steam, but the vehicle still forced its way on through the wire mesh. Walker had a good angle and knocked several of them down as they poured through the hole in the fence; as the attackers sought cover from Hattori's field of fire, they were exposed to him.

Walker thought they could hold them, and they may have if Hattori hadn't been killed. He shot the man right after he threw the grenade, but it landed beside Hattori, the force of the explosion flipping him onto his back and killing him instantly. With Hattori out of action, they became bolder and raced from the protection of the pickup into the complex. Walker was again able to thin their ranks, but many made it to safety.

"Walker, you okay?" Moody repeated.

"Hattori's dead, sir, and a half dozen or so of them got past us."

"Get the hell back here, Don, now!"

"On my way, boss."

Walker lay in a slight depression, partly shielded by the foundation corner of a building. He knew he had probably stayed too long and was about to push himself back from his shooting position when he spotted a man in desert camouflage trying to crawl forward from the pickup. Nine-millimeter rounds splashed nearby as men still outside the fence with Uzis tried to cover their comrade. Walker aimed carefully, going for a head shot, and got it, shattering the man's skull. But just as he turned to leave, a well-aimed 7.62 round from a PS-1 glanced off the concrete above his head. The jacketed bullet distended into an ugly piece of shrapnel, tearing into his side. The fragment shattered two ribs, carrying bone fragments and metal into his lung. Walker bit into his lip to keep from screaming—it was like he had been lanced with a hot poker.

Stayed too long, he thought. Christ, what a dumb shit! The rangy SEAL tried to push himself back to safety using the butt of his rifle as a paddle.

"Walker! Talk to me Walker!" screamed the voice in his ear.

The pain rose an octave when he moved, but Walker knew his only chance was to try and link up with the others. Now using the M-14 as a crutch, he forced himself to one knee. He paused to catch his breath, but even the act of breathing stoked the fire in his side. Move! You have to move! Once on his feet he staggered back, face twisted in pain and dragging his rifle by the sling, but he was moving. After a few steps he stumbled, and the pain of the fall almost caused him to pass out. But he kept moving, now crawling back to safety, still dragging the M-14.

The wind continued to scrub the island with sea mist and low clouds. At best it was a dirty-gray day, with no hint of the sun. Yet through a curtain of pain, Walker felt a shadow pass over him. He looked up into a face bound with a headband and twisted with hate. There was rapid movement and a hiss that cut through the wind, and Petty Officer Don Walker felt no more pain in his side.

Tom Lenze and his first sergeant stood in the crowded pilothouse on the starboard side of the LCAC. They had covered just over half the distance to their objective, but time-wise they were still much closer to the *Kearsarge* that followed in their wake. They were alone now. The other LCAC had lost two of its jet engines and was now wallowing back to the mother ship. Lenze's coxswain had just slowed their craft to twenty knots. Occasionally he looked out at the building seas, but mostly he studied the instruments and circuit breakers on his panel.

"Sir, the electrical system's all shorted out. We got no radios, an' no radar. The GPS and SATNAV are down. We're blind; we got no choice but to turn back. We can head back the way we came, and the *Kearsarge*'ll find us on their radar." Lenze said nothing. "We got no choice, sir."

Lenze squinted through the windows at the angry, gray-green sea. Even the wipers had quit. The swells were only slightly larger than when they'd left the mother ship, but now they appeared to come from more than one direction. They were more confused—less disciplined and irregular. It was tempting. The big ship represented sanctuary, but it was still a ship in a typhoon and Lenze wanted to be on land.

More than that, he remembered a terrifying afternoon on the outskirts of Mogadishu when his helicopter was shot down. He and his men survived the crash but were attacked by swarms of Somali technicals. They were no match for the Rangers, but there were more Somalis than they had bullets, and he and his men were about to be overrun. Then a squad of Navy SEALs broke through and helped them hold on until the helicopter gunships arrived.

Later, Lenze had seen the news clips of those animals dragging American corpses through the streets of the city.

The SEALs had saved him from that. Now there were SEALs trapped on this island, and they needed his help.

"Keep going."

"But Cap'n, we got no electronics, no communications, no nav gear. Hell, we'll be lucky to find th' carrier in this, let alone an island."

"Keep going," Lenze repeated.

"Sir, you ain't listenin'; we got no electronics. Even the gyro compass has gone tits up."

"You got a magnetic compass, don't you?"

"Well, yessir, but we still—"

"All right. Steer by your magnetic compass and keep going."

The coxswain straightened at the helm. "Look, sir, an' with all due respect, I'm the craft master and th' decision to turn back is mine, not yours."

He began to turn the wheel to change course when the first sergeant's hand, one the size of a baseball glove, gripped the helm. "You best be doing what the cap'n said." His voice was a low rumble.

The Navy man looked to the hard features of the first sergeant, then to Lenze, and back to the sergeant. He started to say something but steadied down on a magnetic heading for Johnston Island. Gradually he brought the LCAC back up to forty knots. After the two Rangers were gone, he thought of making a log entry that his decision to turn back had been forcibly overruled, but he was afraid to let go of the wheel.

Back out in the cargo deck, Lenze and his sergeant leaned into the wind and rain. "Thought you weren't too keen on this mission, First Sergeant."

"I ain't, sir. I just weren't gonna let no squid tell us what to do. It's quittin' time when you say it's quittin' time."

Lenze nodded. "Better have one of the radiomen see if he can raise our controller—let them know we're having problems."

"Airborne!" growled the first sergeant as he moved off across the wet deck to the huddled mass of Rangers.

In the administration building on Johnston Island, Jim Bruso and Nancy Blackman huddled in the corner and waited. Periodically Bruso crawled over to the window and looked for activity, insisting that Senator Blackman remain well away from the entrance in case they again fired through the crack in the door. All he could see were the buildings along Main Street and, when the clouds lifted, the northern edge of a portion of the runway. The wind continued to lash the building, but it was a solid, modern structure and up to the task.

"See anything?" she asked as Bruso returned from the window. She spoke softly and laid her hand on his arm.

"Nothing. With the exception of our friends next door, I think they've all gone."

"What do you think they'll do with the hostages in the gym?"

"I don't know, Nancy. They can't all be as fanatical as Tadao. If the Marines get ashore and gain control of the chemicals, maybe the ones guarding the hostages'll give up."

"So you think it'll be the Marines, huh?" She knew he had been in the Corps.

"Who else?" He smiled and put his arm around her shoulders. Both knew the ordeal would soon be over, one way or another, and that they could well be living their last few hours. The days of tension and fear had spawned a lassitude that allowed for a near-indifference to their fate; they were now almost blasé about it. Bravery and exhaustion had become indistinguishable, and they were simply weary of being sick with worry. The elation that had followed barricading themselves in the office and reasserting some control over their destiny had come and gone, like eating a sugar cookie on an empty stomach. Events were once more out of their hands, and near-indifference and apathy had again claimed them.

But something else was happening. Over the past several days, and especially the last few hours, they had become as intimate as lovers, driven by a compelling need to be close to someone—someone of the opposite sex—and yet it was not a sexual thing. There was the need to touch, but it was not sensual—it was more mutual tenderness and assurance. If one had a moment of weakness, the other immediately grew stronger. They were each holding on for the other.

Their office-cell was four floors from the ground and there was a concrete pad below the window. If the terrorists came with tools or explosives and tried to force the door, they planned to jump, Blackman first followed by Bruso.

Suddenly there was a commotion outside and the sound of boots racing down the hallway, then silence. Bruso was immediately on his feet, moving near the door to listen.

"Have they gone?" Blackman asked.

"I don't know. Sounds like it, but it may be a trick. I think we should wait a while."

They both went to the window this time and watched, but they still clung to each other.

"Sir, there's another problem on the LCACs from the *Kearsarge*." On the *Tarawa*, Colonel Bill Simms stood at General Sheppard's elbow. They were now thirty miles southwest of Johnston Island and still unable to launch their helos.

"Christ, what now?"

"The lead craft is still moving at full speed, but they've lost their electronics—no radios or radars. We're only able to talk to them because of the radio carried by the embarked Rangers. They're blind out there, sir, and in this weather there's a good chance they'll miss the atoll. They could be within a mile of it and not see it."

"Shit, Bill! Those guys can't hold on forever." Sheppard pounded the arm of his chair in frustration. "We've got to find a way to relieve them."

"Sir, I talked with the CAG on the *Vinson* and he had

an idea. He thinks they can get an E-2 Hawkeye airborne. The E-2 should be able to find them out there and guide them in." Simms was a Special Forces colonel and Sheppard's operations officer, but the CAG, or commander, air group, on *Vinson* was the senior naval aviator in the battle group. "It's worth a shot."

When Sheppard had ordered the two destroyers to make for Johnston Island at flank speed, he had also sent the *Vinson* southeast at a right angle to the path of the storm, hoping to get it into calmer weather where it could launch and recover aircraft. Or at least launch them.

"Do it," snapped Sheppard.

"John-san?"

"Go ahead, Taro."

"They are through the fence. Tadao has ordered additional men from their command post to join the fight here. They have been told to come along the beach to avoid the snipers on the water tanks. Only the hostage guards are to remain at their post."

"Understood, Taro," Moody replied. "You got that, Sly?"

"Yessir, we'll be looking for them."

"How's your visibility?"

"Comes and goes, sir, but if they come along the beach, we may not have a shot."

"Understood; do what you can."

Moody, Nakajima, and Kodansha formed an arc around the cluster of storage vaults that housed the VX agents. Their positions had been carefully selected during the mission workup. Each had an excellent field of fire to defend against an attack from the east and was well placed for mutual support. Moody could not see Kodansha from where he was on the southern rim of their defensive arc, but Nakajima, positioned in the center, could. The special-containment vaults were segregated from the rest of the complex by a road leading into the facility. The attackers would have to cross this open area to get to them.

"Glasser, where are you?"

"Down the beach about forty yards west of the fence. If they try to backdoor you, I'll be here."

Moody thought about ordering him to come through the fence and join them; then they would all be together, what was left of them. He wanted to protect Glasser, but his position outside gave him a better vantage to guard their rear. Again, Moody winced. The mission always came before the men.

"Let me know if you see anything, then shoot to kill."

"Aye aye, sir."

Moody again wanted to call Walker but refrained. If he had been able to use his radio, he'd have called in by now. Nothing you can do for Walker—forget him and concentrate on the mission.

Less than forty yards east of where the three defenders waited, Commandant Tadao marshaled the remnants of his force. Of those who had escaped the carnage from the snipers on the water tanks, almost a third had been killed coming through the fence. Now there fewer than twenty-five of them, including himself. Three of those had been wounded but could fight. Two others had survived the skirmish at the fence but were more seriously wounded. Tadao himself had relieved them of their suffering.

They gathered behind the main administration building. Tadao had put flankers out to alert them of a counterattack. The storm was still full upon them, and Tadao reasoned that help from helicopters or ships would not come soon, or not soon enough if they moved quickly. And since the two men who had fought them so well from the perimeter had not been reinforced, there could only be a handful still holding out. Tadao had considered breaking into one of the unguarded storage vaults and dispersing some of those chemicals in such a manner as to kill everyone on the island. But the challenge and the opportunity for a warrior's death was too appealing. And he wanted to recapture *his* island.

Then there was the body of the one defender who had

so gallantly fought them at the fence; he was Japanese. Perhaps a Japanese-American, but there was something about him, other than the fact he had dressed to look like one of his men. Few Japanese born in the United States or serving in their armed forces could speak Japanese well enough to pass as true Japanese. On impulse he pulled the Motorola transceiver from his belt and spoke in Japanese.

"Samurai! One who waits for me to attack; are you not fighting on the wrong side?" There was no response, but Tadao sensed his words had not gone unheard. "Hear me, samurai. One of us—perhaps both of us—is about to die. We are both favored to be permitted such a death, but may I have the honor of knowing your name?"

After a long pause: "I am Shintaro Nakajima of the Naginata Counter Force."

"So!" Tadao replied. "And you stand with the *gai-jin* against us?"

"Yes, Tadao-sama, for you have dishonored our nation with this unprovoked attack on the Americans."

"I think not, Nakajima-san. There is much we could discuss about honor and the rulers of our nation that you serve, but there is little time now for talk. May the gods be with you Nakajima-san. I honor you."

"*Domo-arigatoh gozaimasu*, Tadao-sama. I too honor you."

Tadao tossed the transceiver aside and dropped to one knee. The others crowded around. He noted with satisfaction that those who remained were still anxious for a fight. "We must rush them," he told his men. "Hand to hand, they are no match for a samurai!" Then he began to diagram his plan of attack in the sand.

Moody too had taken a radio from one of the dead Japanese. He couldn't understand what had been said between Nakajima and the man who wanted to kill them, but he easily grasped the respect Tadao showed for Nakajima and the deference Nakajima had for him. Moody almost asked if something was said that might be useful in their defense, but Nakajima would have said so if there had been, and

Moody didn't want to offend him. Finally, he just shrugged. Here I am scared shitless, he thought, and they're acting like a pair of fucking English knights at a jousting tournament!

He turned back to the serious business of preparing to fight. First he laid out his extra magazines and an Uzi submachine gun he had taken along with the captured Motorola. He also readied his two flash-bangs, small concussion grenades used to stun the enemy in room-to-room, close-quarter battle. They were of little use in the open except as a diversion. But he knew they had grenades—real fragmentation grenades. Moody briefly recalled stories from the Second World War about the surprise of the Japanese at just how far the Americans could throw grenades. Back then, only American kids grew up playing baseball. Today, Moody thought, a lot of Japanese kids probably play baseball. He looked at his watch and clicked on the AN/PRC-113.

"Tradewind Three-seven, this is Sierra Juliet, over."

"This is Three-seven; go ahead Sierra Juliet."

Moody hesitated a moment, knowing he was transmitting in the clear. Aw, what the hell!

"Tell the general we're holding on, but there's only six of us left. If we don't get some help soon, it won't make a hell of a lot of difference, at least not to us."

"Understood, Sierra Juliet. Good luck to you; this is Tradewind Three-seven, clear."

Eighty miles south of Johnston Island, Lieutenant Commander Darren Midieros again looked to see if the cabin heat in his E-2C Hawkeye was turned on. It wasn't, but he was still sweating. They had just passed through eight thousand feet and most of the severe turbulence.

"Everybody okay back there?" he said into the intercom as he exchanged a knowing look with his copilot.

The other four crew members of the Hawkeye rogered up; they were fine and the gear seemed to be okay. Midieros had close to three thousand hours in Hawkeyes and over four hundred carrier landings; he knew his business. But this launch, if that was the word for it, and the subsequent climb through the storm were the scariest things he'd known in nine years of flying. Midieros gave the controls to his copilot and pulled out a handkerchief, unabashedly wiping his face.

The *Vinson* had slowed to fifteen knots for the launch, but the wind over the deck was still close to seventy miles per hour. He'd elected to launch with no flaps, and that had probably saved them. His Hawkeye was straining for altitude halfway down the catapult run, and by the time they'd been released, their airspeed was close to 150. The aircraft had all but ripped itself from the cat and leapt into the air. After that they'd had to work their way up through the goo—gray-gauze layers of swirling clouds—hoping not to run into a thunderstorm spawned by the typhoon.

The Hawkeye was a carrier-based airborne warning-and-control system, or AWACS, aircraft. Like its big brother, the Air Force 707 AWACS, it was an airborne radar platform whose mission was to detect hostile aircraft and guide friendly flyers to the attack. A large saucer attached to the top of the fuselage housed a powerful and highly discriminatory radar. But it added weight and another airfoil to the Hawkeye, making their launch into the storm that much more terrifying. Now they were above most of it, and with the large tail-wind component, they were over Johnston Island in a matter of minutes. Midieros was anxious to complete their mission and head on into Barbers Point.

"Okay, Slick, what you got?" Lieutenant Sam "Slick" Snyder was Midieros's lead radar-intercept officer. Right now Snyder searched the sea north of Johnston Island for the lost LCAC. The Hawkeye's Rantron AN/APA-171 radar had been designed primarily for aircraft, but the system's ability to find and track low flyers allowed it to locate small surface craft as well.

"Pretty choppy down there, skipper. Might take a few minutes."

"Word is our guys down there may not have a few minutes."

"Doin' the best I can. Like I said, it's pretty . . . hold on . . . hello!"

Snyder's hands flicked over the controls like an accountant working a desk calculator, but his eyes never left the scope. "Got him!" Snyder yelled as he toggled his transmit key. "Tradewind Three-seven, this is Navy Five Niner Golf, over."

Colonel Anthony Fortino had been passing the time with some rough calculations on his remaining fuel, but he was right there. "Tradewind Three-seven here. Go ahead, Navy Five Niner Golf, over."

"We found your lost sheep. He bears three-three-five from the main island—range, six miles. Recommend he steer one-five-zero magnetic, over."

"Roger, Navy. Understand my sheep at three-three-five and six miles from the island; you recommend one-five-zero magnetic to target, over."

"That's affirmative, Three-seven. This is Navy Five Niner Golf standing by, out."

Fortino had to relay the LCAC's position to the hovercraft since the Hawkeye didn't have VHF capability. Below the two aircraft and a blowing mass of clouds, the lone LCAC came right and pounded through the furious sea toward Johnston Island. As they got closer they came into the lee of the atoll, and the seas became less turbulent. The Hawkeye had not yet been released from its mission, but Midieros was already calculating just how many scotch-and-waters it was going to take to blot out the terror of the launch.

"Grenade!" shouted Moody. At the same moment, Nakajima called out the same thing in Japanese. While the three defenders pressed themselves to the sand, several dark metal balls thudded into the packed coral roadway in front of them. Following the explosion, Moody heard the hiss of fragments quickly followed by the clatter of shrapnel on the metal vaults. He waited as long as he dared, then rolled up with his MP-5 looking for targets.

They're going for position, he thought, as he carefully brought one man down and got a piece of another as he sprinted for a storage vault on their side of the road. Another man trying to cross the road farther to the north was knocked to the coral, a victim of a break in the clouds and heavy .308 sniper round. Both Nakajima and Kodansha were now firing short, disciplined bursts. Then, more grenades. These were not lobbed into the street as had been the others, but thrown at them. One landed ten feet from Moody, but he was able to flatten himself in his shallow revetment to escape the scattering fragments. Jesus, he thought, they do play baseball! He changed magazines and came up shooting. They now knew where he was, and rounds began to spatter nearby.

From the corner of his eye, Moody saw something move quickly. He turned in time to see Nakajima swing his submachine gun toward him. For a split second he thought his Japanese friend was going to shoot him. A long burst sailed over his head, several rounds catching the side of the storage bin as Nakajima walked them up over the top. Then the body of one of the attackers dropped from the roof and landed just a few feet in front of him. The man jerked once and was still. Moody stared at it for a second, then grabbed the Uzi and began firing over top of the dead man.

The Rangers and their LCAC came ashore near the harbor where a small boat ramp breached a hole in the seawall. They crossed the east end of the runway and continued toward the chemical-weapons storage area. At first Moody thought it was a freak gust of wind or just the storm taking on a new ferocity. Then it became a distinct mechanical shriek, too loud for an act of nature. The firing slackened and Moody became aware of someone shouting in his ear.

"Hey, boss! You there, sir. Come in Lieutenant, over!"

It was Slyfield. "Go ahead, Sly."

"The cavalry's here, sir. There's a fuckin' hovercraft headin' right for the gate of the storage facility!"

Moody hesitated, trying to make sense of it. A hover-craft? Christ Almighty, they got through in an LCAC!

"Hey, sir, you copy?" said Slyfield, but Moody ignored him and was now yelling into the handset of the PRC-113.

"This is Sierra Juliet, I say again, Sierra Juliet! You my Marines, over?"

"Even better, Navy," came the reply. "Seventy-fifth Rangers at your disposal."

With the help of the orbiting Hawkeye, Lenze had been able to quickly guide the LCAC to Johnston Island and into the harbor. When they'd been told they were two miles out, his first sergeant had begun to kick the Rangers to life. They'd shed their ponchos and checked weapons, preparing to fight. Two of them had braved the wind and spray and manned the M-60 machine guns mounted forward on the port and starboard gunwales. The waves had abated con-siderably as they'd come into the lee of the island, and the LCAC had crawled awkwardly over the barrier reef that ringed the atoll.

Lenze stood in the pilothouse behind the coxswain. Both now wore helmets. The Ranger captain held a laminated map of Johnston Island. Target details and photos had been faxed to the *Kearsarge*, and Lenze had been able to brief his men in almost the same detail as had Moody. He'd been able to guide the LCAC past Akau Island and Sand Island, through the harbor to the small-craft ramp, and across the island to the chemical-storage facility. Down on the cargo bay, two dozen Rangers waited to charge across the bow ramp.

"You still there, Navy, over?"

"Moody here, go ahead."

"Where are you, exactly?"

"There're three of us in a defensive position in the spe-cial-weapons storage area—just west of the road from the storage-facility office. I also got a man outside the fence along the beach guarding our rear, east of our position, over."

"Understood. How many Japs?"

"As many as a dozen, maybe more, I'm not sure. Two of my guys are Japanese. They got black faces; they're good guys—friendlies—got that, over?"

"I got it, Moody. You and your men just stay where you are and don't do any firing unless you really have to. We'll sweep the area from the main gate south. Just keep down, okay?"

"No problem, Army," Moody shouted as another grenade bounced off the wall of the vault behind him and rolled into the street. The dead Japanese in front of him absorbed most of the blast, but a piece of shrapnel ripped through the top of Moody's ear.

"Fuckers!" he yelled into the wind. Dropping the radio handset, he took up one of the small concussion grenades and jerked the pin. Moody had spent six years behind the plate in high school and American Legion ball, and was a better-than-average catcher. He popped to his knees and made a snap-throw that sent the flash-bang through the window of the administration building window. *Played a little baseball myself, assholes!* He dove back for the ground as a spray of bullets rang off the vault behind him.

The LCAC barged into the main gate and sent the chain-link sections flying. Then the howling beast cut its engines and, very ladylike, settled down on its skirts. The bow ramp dropped and the Rangers poured out. Lenze had had only a moment to brief them on the current situation, but it was enough; these men knew their business. Dressed in wet green camouflage, flak vests, and kevlar helmets, they quickly moved out onto a skirmish line and through the complex.

The dramatic appearance of the LCAC and the Rangers broke the samurai attack. The Americans were armed with M-60s and SAWs—squad assault weapons—and they quickly gained fire superiority. Tadao's men fought bravely, but they now fought as individuals, not as a unit. A few of the Japanese charged their attackers armed only with a long sword. These were gallant individual efforts, but no way to deal with highly professional, well-armed light infantry. Moody watched as they worked past him, leapfrogging from building to building. The Rangers methodically sifted through the complex, killing the last of the Japanese raiders. Then, it was over.

Three of the Rangers had been wounded, one seriously. Lenze left his first sergeant to set up a perimeter while his corpsman tended to the wounded.

Moody pushed himself to his feet, feeling a little light-headed. He was exhausted and the adrenaline rush that had come with the firefight and the grenade exchange was quickly leaving him. But it was partially offset by the wonderful notion that he wasn't going to die.

"Lieutenant, I'm Captain Tom Lenze, First Battalion, Second Company, 75th Rangers." Moody took an uncertain step forward to meet him and almost fell down. "You okay, buddy?"

"I think so." Moody took his hand. "Thanks, Tom; I'm John Moody. You guys sure know how to make an entrance, don't you?"

"We try. Hey, corpsman! Get over and take a look at the lieutenant." There were several cuts on Moody's face and the tear in his ear was a bleeder.

Moody waved impatiently. "You have contact with General Sheppard?"

Lenze nodded and motioned to his radioman. "Same as you, by airborne relay."

"He know we're secure?"

"He's been informed, but I know he wants to hear from you."

"In a minute."

He stepped past Lenze and went to look for Nakajima. Moody was bloody and dirty and had the look of someone who had been in a bar fight. The Rangers eyed him with a measure of awe and respect. His Japanese captain was not there, so he hurried on to Kodansha's position.

"Taro, what're you doing, what's...."

Nakajima knelt in the sand with his buttocks on his heels. He'd apparently rolled Kodansha on his back, for the dead man lay with his arms at his sides, face straight up. They were all soaked, but the front of Kodansha's wet jacket was several shades darker. Nakajima clapped twice and slightly bowed. Moody looked from one to the other, blinking back the tears. How do they do it? How in the hell do they do it!

Both men's faces were composed and relaxed, as if they were in meditation or contemplating something pleasant. The big Ranger first sergeant approached Moody carefully, and he had anything but a calm look about him. Neither did the buck sergeant who stood beside him, staring at the ground.

"Lieutenant," he said softly, "we did this."

"Did what, First Sergeant?"

"Friendly fire, sir," he said, nodding to the dead Kodansha. "We took him for one of the bad guys. It was an accident, but God help us, it was our fault."

Moody understood exactly who had done the shooting, but the first sergeant was not about to give up his man. It was also clear to Nakajima. He rose quietly and joined them. Then he put a gentle hand on the dejected Ranger's shoulder.

"It is no one's fault. Kodansha followed a warrior's calling and he died a warrior's death. Can any of us ask for more? I suggest we leave it at that. Come, John-san. We must see to the others."

Moody started to follow Nakajima but instead went back to where Captain Lenze and several of his men stood guarding the special-weapons vaults. "What about the hostages? There's over a thousand civilians being held over on the other side of the island."

"I asked about that, John. My orders are to stay here and guard these chemicals. Your orders are the same. The task-force commander was very specific about that."

"We know there's only one or two guards watching them."

Lenze shrugged. "I'll pass it along, but our orders are to stay here until we're relieved, no matter what."

Moody started to object, then turned and set off to find Walker.

Jim Bruso and Senator Nancy Blackman watched the LCAC leave the perimeter road and head across the airfield toward the chemical-weapons storage area. The machine was downwind from them, and the scream of its jet engines was snatched away by the storm. It drifted along like a haze-gray ghost on dark skirts and disappeared into the blowing fog.

"Told you it'd be the Marines," he said to Blackman. He knew the Marines used LCACs, but was unaware that this one carried Army Rangers.

"Will they send someone for the people in the gymnasium?" she asked.

"Probably. If there's a ship close enough to get one landing craft ashore, there's got to be others. Maybe they already have."

"Do you think it's safe to leave?"

Bruso had vowed to remain barricaded in the office until an armed Marine knocked on the door. It was their best chance—her best chance. But his concern for the fate of his people in the gym was causing him to waver.

Moody quickly found Walker. One of the Rangers had covered him with a poncho liner so only his legs protruded. Walker's M-14 and several rocks anchored the light fabric against the wind. Moody could tell from the drape of the quilted nylon that his head was not attached to his torso. I have to see him, he thought. Lord help me, but I have to see him one more time.

Moody had known Don Walker since the two had come through SEAL training together. They'd been in the same team or the same platoon for more than six years. On duty and off, Moody led and Walker followed. SEAL officers and their enlisted men were often close, but he and Walker had been more like brothers. Now it was over. Moody knelt and carefully pulled back the shroud.

There was both shock and relief. Moody had seen dead men before—a few of them had been men he'd known. The shock of the severed head almost caused him to drop the shroud and flee, but it was not Walker. The hair was the same and the pale features were familiar, but the smiling, affable kid from Arkansas was gone. The drenched corpse was just an ugly reminder that he would never again see his friend. Moody replaced the poncho liner and anchored it.

"Rest easy, old buddy. I'll be back for you," he said to what used to be Walker, and he pushed himself to his feet.

"John-san!"

"What is it?"

"He is not here; I cannot find him."

"Find who?"

"Tadao—he is not among the dead."

They looked at each other for only a second, then both were racing back to the special-containment vaults. As Moody ran, he pulled the MP-5 from his back and clicked off the safety. Nakajima churned alongside, matching the tall American's strides two for one. Two patrolling Rangers just stared as they raced by the office complex.

"What is it?" Lenze asked as they rushed past him to the door of the main vault, the same one Kodansha had first disarmed earlier that morning. "What's going on?"

They ignored him and pressed close to either side of the door. Nakajima nodded and Moody returned the gesture. Nakajima led, knocking the door open with his shoulder, and dove through the opening, crossing right to left. He rolled and came up in a shooting crouch. Moody followed him in, stepping quickly to the right of the doorway and sweeping the room with his submachine gun. A small rear-access door to the vault was partly ajar, and there was a trail of blood leading inside.

Tadao sat on the concrete floor leaning against a pallet of VX-agent tanks. There was a dark stain on one pant leg of his tan camouflage utilities. Near him against the chemicals, a large block of C-4 explosives rested on a canvas kit bag. In the dim light of the vault Tadao glared at them, trying to hold them with his stare while he struggled with the pin to the grenade. The concussion of the grenade would be more than enough to detonate the C-4 and release the chemical agents.

Moody took him quickly with a three-round burst in the stomach. He had to aim carefully—under his chest, guiding the rounds squarely into Tadao's stomach—not to either side or higher, where there was a chance of hitting one of the cylinders. One of the bullets shattered Tadao's arm, allowing the grenade to roll away, scarcely a foot from the C-4. But Tadao still had the pin.

Moody knew the sound all too well—the snap of the percussion cap that initiated the timed delay, the ringing of the spoon as it clattered across the concrete. *Not now!* Moody's subconscious screamed. *Not after all we've been through!* No conscious process bound thought to action. Moody dove across the containment vault after the live grenade and, in a single motion, gathered it to his midsection and coiled himself around it, like a wide receiver who'd short-hopped a low-thrown ball and wanted the referee to believe he'd caught it cleanly.

He also gathered in most of the shrapnel when it exploded. That which escaped lightly peppered the vault walls, away from the explosives and the chemicals. One fragment caught Nakajima in the shoulder as he rushed to help his American friend, but he felt nothing. He reached the fetal form coiled on the concrete as the echo from the concussion died. Carefully, he rolled Moody face up.

His jaw worked several times before he spoke. "Walker . . . Walker . . ."

"I will see to him, John-san, as I will to you," Nakajima said, but he was not sure Moody heard him. Already his eyes were beginning to dilate. "Go on ahead, my friend, and go with honor. I will pray to you."

The first sergeant burst through the door, closely followed by Lenze and two more Rangers. "What th' hell . . . aw, man . . . aw, man, no!"

"Good God!" Lenze gasped as peered into the vault.

The room was thick with the acrid stench of cordite and death. The four men slowly gathered around the dead American and the Japanese who held him. No one spoke for a long moment.

"All right, let's get him out of here," Lenze said quietly.

They gently pushed Nakajima aside. One of the Rangers surrendered his poncho, and they used it as a makeshift litter to carry Moody away. After they had gone, Nakajima stepped over to Tadao. He squatted beside him and watched for several minutes. Then Tadao's eyes fluttered open.

"What happened?" he said through clenched teeth. Tadao was in a great deal of pain and very surprised that he was still alive.

"The American. He took the force of the grenade with his body and his life. He beat you, Tadao-san. The chemicals are safely contained."

Tadao closed his eyes for a moment to hide his shame. Then, marshaling his strength to speak clearly and make himself understood, he continued. "Then he died well. Perhaps he is a better warrior than you or I, Nakajima-san?"

"Perhaps. He is a *gai-jin*, but he is also a samurai."

Tadao nodded and, with great effort, swallowed. "My sword?"

"It is here; I have it."

"My wounds are serious, but there is always the possibility that I could recover. You must finish what the American started. You have served him well, now serve me . . . as my second."

Nakajima considered this. If Tadao lived the Americans would hold him, and there would be a public trial. They would brand him a criminal. Worse yet, they could fail to execute him and imprison him for life. This would embarrass his nation and humiliate a noble warrior. He rose and unsheathed the long blade.

"*Arigatoh,*" Tadao managed. Then he pushed himself

away from the pallet of chemicals and bowed his head to give Nakajima a clean stroke.

When he left the vault, Nakajima found Moody just outside the door, lying in the lee of the containment building. Glasser knelt beside him, leaning on his rifle. Nakajima squatted and gently rested a hand on the big SEAL's shoulder.

"Jesus Christ, sir. I lost my chief an' now I lost my officer." The tears streamed down his face and he made no attempt to hide them.

"And I have lost a brother." Nakajima rose and turned to Slyfield and Jackson, who waited with the Ranger first sergeant.

"Will you help me go for Walker-san? I think they should be together."

Jim Bruso carefully worked his way down the first-floor hallway of the deserted administration building. They had finally decided to chance leaving their barricaded office. Actually, Senator Nancy Blackman had decided they should leave and Bruso had finally agreed. He'd made her promise to follow him no closer than thirty feet with the idea that if he ran into trouble, she might be able to escape. But each time Bruso had turned his back on her, she'd closed the distance. Finally they stood at the rear door, looking out into the storm. Bruso had slipped by his office, where he'd found a pair of bolt cutters and severed his handcuff chain. He'd also found his passkey and opened the small-arms locker. Now he carried a Mossberg 12-gauge riot gun.

"What do you think?"

"I think they're all over at the storage area. Our people in the gymnasium must still be under guard or we'd have seen some of them by now." Or they've been killed, he thought, but didn't say it. "There's a separate, outside entrance to the weight room that joins the main gymnasium. Perhaps we can slip in there and at least see what's going on." Bruso had studied the position of the two guards when he and the senator had visited the hostages there. He felt they could sneak inside and see without being seen.

They began to work their way toward the gym, like a pair of drug agents approaching a crack house. Then they heard the helicopters. It was still too rough for the big CH-46s, but two MH-60K special-operations Pave Hawks from the *Vinson* came through the overcast near the terminal. They too had been guided to the island by an E-2 Hawkeye from the *Vinson* and had managed to ride their radar altimeters down through the clouds. The two machines bobbed in the gusting wind like a pair of angry hummingbirds, then crabbed across the airstrip toward the administration building. Bruso and Blackman waved frantically.

The Pave Hawks held their noses into the wind and carefully set down. Men poured from them. They swarmed into the cover and protection of the buildings along the northern edge of the runway and quickly made their way to the gymnasium. Two of them detached themselves from the group. One was a Marine in battle dress; the other wore black coveralls and baseball cap. He had body armor, several radios, and a megaphone. They moved past Bruso to where Nancy Blackman waited in the lee of a warehouse.

"Senator, I'm Special Agent Sisk with the FBI Hostage Rescue Team," said the man in black. The Marine officer saluted. "Happy to see that you're safe, ma'am. My instructions are to see you to a safe place until we can secure the island."

"I'll be just fine here with Mister Bruso."

"Beg your pardon, Senator?"

"I'm with Jim Bruso; talk to him."

"Bruso," the FBI man said, "you're the facility manager, correct?"

"That's right, and there's about a thousand of my people being held over in the gymnasium. Now, what about the chemical weapons?"

Sisk looked from Bruso to Nancy Blackman and back. "Your storage facility and the chemical weapons are being guarded by Army Rangers. Our mission is to see that the senator is safe and then to release the hostages."

"Okay. As you can see, the senator's just fine. Now, are you familiar with the gymnasium?"

"Just in general terms. Our standard procedure calls for us to seal off the area and open negotiations."

"Agent Sisk, I'm sure you know your stuff, but you don't negotiate with these people. Now, let me tell you how things are—where my people are and where the guards are. I think you'll find there are only two of them." Bruso dropped to one knee and began to diagram the layout of the gymnasium in the sand.

A few moments later Bruso repeated his sand drawing, this time ringed by the other members of the HRT contingent. While the Marines provided area security, he led the FBI men through the weight-room door and, unobserved, to the main entrance to the gym floor. Nancy Blackman followed. Several of the team members noiselessly slipped away to their assigned positions. As they approached the door, Sisk paused.

"I tell you, Bruso," he whispered. "I don't like having her here. It's still too dangerous."

Bruso gave him a tired look. "She doesn't listen when I try and tell her what to do, and I don't think you'll have much luck either. She's a U.S. senator."

One of the HRT men moved to the door, and with his ball cap reversed, carefully peeked through the window in the door. After a few seconds he turned back to Sisk. "It's just like Bruso said. Two guards, about ten meters apart over by the exit to the heads."

Sisk now wore a small headset and padded lip mike. He looked like he was ready to do Monday Night Football. Quietly, he flicked the transmit button and whispered into the mike.

"Okay, Frank, what do you have . . . how about you, Billy . . . and you Tony?" He listened a moment and then turned to Bruso and Blackman. The senator hovered close to and slightly behind Bruso. "Okay, we can see no more than two of them, but that doesn't mean there aren't more.

And my guys have them bore-sighted. You ready?'' Bruso nodded. ''And, Senator, *please* stay back behind the door.''

Sisk nodded to his man at the door. He opened it and Sisk stepped through, the battery-powered megaphone at the ready.

''Stand where you are—do not move—F.B.I. Do not move!''

One man hesitated, then leveled his weapon. For the HRT sniper a hundred and fifty feet across the gym, it was a point-blank shot. The man's head snapped back and he crumpled to the hardwood. A sharp crack from the high-powered round ricocheted around the concrete walls and died quickly. The second guard saw this, hesitated, then slowly raised his hands above his head. A murmur of excitement and apprehension rippled across the mass of humanity on the basketball courts.

''You people on the floor: Are there any more guards?''

After a few nerve-wracking seconds, a man called out, ''Them's the only two we seen in a couple hours or more.''

Bruso stepped out. Sisk offered him the megaphone but he pushed it away. Instead he jumped up onto a nearby chair as two black-clad HRT men rushed to the Japanese guard. They quickly stripped him of his weapon and took him roughly to the floor.

''Okay, folks,'' Bruso called out, ''it's over. The Marines and the FBI are here, and they've taken control of the island. All the chemicals at the storage facility are safely contained.'' He held up his arms and tried to calm the rising din. It was like trying to lay hands on a volcano. ''We've all been through hell,'' he said speaking louder, ''and as you all know, some good people, good friends and co-workers, have been killed.'' The growing roar abated. ''Before we leave here and go about the business of taking back our island, will you please join me in a moment of prayer for those who are no longer with us.''

The moment of silence lasted about fifteen seconds, then dissolved in a melee of cheering, crying, hugging, and a few angry shouts. A pair of FBI men quickly hustled the sole survivor of Commandant Tadao's attacking force out of the gym. Two men went over and kicked the corpse of the dead guard, but one of the agents easily turned them away.

"People . . . people, listen to me." Bruso was now using the megaphone and regained a measure of control. "I want you to return to your quarters, get cleaned up, and get some sleep. I'm going to ask the food-service crew to keep the cafeteria and snack bar open for about an hour. The Tiki will also be open; drinks are on the Emerson Management Corporation." This brought a weak cheer. "I'd also like the chaplains and the medical staff to be available for as long as needed. Department heads, I'll want to see you in my office in a half hour for a short meeting." He looked down on a sea of faces that had suddenly gone quiet. "That's it, people. God bless every one of you."

A strangely quiet, emotionally drained stream of weary Johnston Islanders filed out of the gymnasium. Bruso and Blackman tried to shake hands or have a quick word with as many as possible. All had questions but they were also tired, dirty, and they wanted to go home—at least to their Johnston Island home.

Outside, the storm was beginning to blow itself out. A heavy rain squall had just swept across the island, but it was followed by a brief sun break. The wind had slackened noticeably. A Spruance-class destroyer eased its way up the channel and more helicopters were dropping through the overcast.

"Could you hold on for just a second, Doctor?" A man with long stringy hair pulled back into a ponytail stepped off to one side. Bruso greeted the last of the ex-hostages as they filed out of the gymnasium. He gathered Rosie, his secretary, in his arms for a long, tearful hug. After the last of them had left, he turned to the man with long hair wearing a dirty white lab coat and hit him just as hard as he could. It was not a particularly well-aimed blow, but it broke Dr. Gary Demming's jaw and several bones in Bruso's hand. Demming's legs buckled and he went down hard, dazed but conscious. The whole side of his face went numb. Bruso stood over him ready to hit him again if he moved.

"Damn it, man, what are you doing?" Sisk pushed Bruso aside, forcing himself between him and the man on the floor.

"Tell him, you rotten little cocksucker! Tell him what you did! It's going to come out—you may as well own up to it!"

Demming closed his eyes. "I'm sorry—God, I'm so sorry. It wasn't supposed to be like this." The tears came and he thought he was going to be sick.

Nancy Blackman kneeled by his side, brushing his cheek with her handkerchief. "What wasn't supposed to be like this?" Her voice was soothing, but when her eyes looked up and met Bruso's, they were alive with rage. "Tell me about it," she said in a motherly tone.

"They were supposed to come ashore and hold a demonstration," Demming managed between sobs. "It was to show that chemical weapons were vulnerable to terrorists— even here on Johnston Island. That if they could sneak ashore here in the middle of the Pacific, they could easily break into storage sites on the mainland. It . . ." He again broke down and covered his face with his hands. Blackman now held his head in her lap, making reassuring sounds. "It was to make people see how important the security and destruction of these chemicals are. It . . . it wasn't supposed to be like this; it was supposed to be a demonstration."

As his voice trailed off Nancy Blackman rose quickly, allowing Demming's head to bang on the floor. He looked up to her with a puzzled expression, then turned away when he saw the look of disgust on her face. She took Bruso's arm and led him from the building.

BATSUBUN: "THAT WHICH FOLLOWS"

Sunday, 11 December, 11:17 A.M.
EIGHTEEN MILES EAST OF JOHNSTON ISLAND

By switching between command and tactical frequencies, Colonel Anthony Fortino had been able to follow the developments on Johnston Island, and when the Marine commander announced that the hostages were free and all hostile forces neutralized, he knew it wouldn't be long. Still, he was carrying armed nuclear weapons and anything was possible. But then it came.

"Tradewind Three-seven, this is Magnum Two-five. You are directed to go immediately to Condition Delta; I repeat, go to Condition Delta. Please acknowledge this transmission and when Condition Delta has been achieved, over."

Fortino hadn't realized he'd been holding his breath. Now he closed his eyes and exhaled forcefully and, unconsciously, he again crossed himself.

"Tradewind Three-seven, please acknowledge." Even through the scrambled transmission, Fortino could detect the urgency and insistence in the voice.

"Magnum Two-five, this is Tradewind Three-seven. Understand we are directed to Condition Delta. Please stand by."

Fortino was ready and immediately keyed his weapons–arming console and flipped the toggle from "arm" to "safe." Behind him in the aircraft, his bombardier did the same. Then he watched the lights on the arming panel in the cockpit blink from yellow to green. A moment later the bombardier came up on the intercom.

"Sir, I verbally certify that both weapons on board are now unarmed and safe."

"So noted, Major," Fortino replied with a forced casualness, as he jotted the exact time on his knee pad.

"Magnum Two-five—Tradewind Three-seven. We are at Condition Delta, time 1128 Juliet, over."

"Roger Tradewind Three-seven; understand Condition Delta at 1128 Juliet. You are released from station—mission complete. Return to base, how copy, Three-seven?"

Fortino acknowledged and turned to his copilot. "Okay, Eddie, you got her. Let's find that tanker, get a drink, and head for the barn."

"Yessir!"

They were both smiling broadly now. Fortino's eyes fell to the small Blessed Virgin statue on the dash console. He thought about it for a moment, then began to tune one of the radios in his communications console. He quickly found the squadron frequency on Guam.

"Tradewind Three-seven to Home Plate, over."

The response was immediate: "This is Home Plate, Three-seven. Go ahead, over."

"That you, Frank? Got the duty again, huh, over?"

"Yessir, Colonel. Understand you've gone to Condition Delta, sir. Congratulations, over."

"That's affirm; we are Condition Delta. Listen, Frank, I want you to contact the chaplain's office. Ask Father Coughlin if he'll say a special Sunday mass for us just as soon as we get on the ground and parked at the ramp."

"You mean for you and your crew, sir? The executive officer was wondering if he could stand the squadron down and start sending people home, over."

"Negative, Home Plate. I want everyone in church for mass, you copy?"

"Uh, yes, sir, but ah, begging the colonel's pardon, can you do that—I mean, hold the squadron on alert for Catholic services."

"Who's the Charlie Oscar of the 512th, Frank?"

"You are, sir. You're the CO."

"Then when I get on the ground, I want everyone not on duty in church with me and that's an order, you got that, over?"

"Understood, sir. Home Plate out."

His copilot gave him a questioning look that said, You sure you want to do this, skipper?

Fortino read his thoughts and laughed. "What're they gonna do, Eddie? Send me to Vietnam? Retire me as a colonel?"

Major Ed O'Connor just smiled tightly and shook his head. Fortino was sure to be called on the carpet by the wing commander for this—he was exceeding his authority. Fortino was not unaware of what might happen, but he was more concerned with putting his squadron back together. There were bound to be some lingering hurts over who had flown the missions to Johnston Atoll and who hadn't, and Fortino was a calculating man. This'll give 'em something else to talk about, he thought. On a personal level, though, there was more to it. He wanted to thank his God for sparing him the fate of being the third pilot to drop an atomic bomb on civilians.

While O'Connor guided the B-52 neatly up behind the KC-10 tanker, Fortino again smiled and patted the plastic BVM on the dash.

Sunday, 11 December, 12:30 P.M.
FORTY-THREE MILES SOUTH OF JOHNSTON ISLAND

The *Tarawa* steamed leisurely to the west, seeking a comfortable heading to ride out the last of the storm. Most of the helicopters were gone. Unlike the *Vinson*, the *Tarawa* had turned downwind to launch them, and they'd been able to fly off the stern into thirty-five knots of relative wind.

Following the capture of the chemical-storage facility and release of the hostages, there had been a brief, spontaneous celebration in flag plot. Sheppard's command sergeant major had moved carefully about the room with a stack of small paper cups and a bottle of Wild Turkey. But the revelry had been short-lived; many of the staff had been without any real sleep for forty-eight hours. Fatigue and the horror of what might have been suppressed any extended festivity. General Sheppard quietly lounged in his command chair, one leg thrown casually over a padded armrest. He'd been on the phone almost constantly for the last two hours, to either Camp Smith or the Situation Room in the White House, but that too was over now. Colonel Lister was ashore and firmly in command of the atoll. Sheppard knew that Lister would clamp a tight security on the island and begin to sort things out in typical Marine-like fashion. The communications center on Johnston Island was now manned by a team of radiomen from the *Tarawa*. The men in flag plot would continue to monitor the activity on Johnston Atoll, but Colonel Lister would report directly to CINCPAC headquarters in Hawaii. Sheppard's group was a special-operations battle staff, and their work was done.

"Sir, would the general care for some more medicinal beverage?"

The soldier who had just appeared near the chair held a thermos of coffee in one hand and a bottle, discreetly at his side, in the other. Sheppard held out his cup. He filled it two-thirds with coffee and topped it off from the bottle.

"Thank you, Command Sergeant Major."

"Sir," he replied and moved away.

Sheppard sniffed appreciatively and took a small sip. He knew Navy regulations concerning drinking aboard ship. Fuck 'em, he thought. Given the job they'd done, a little celebration was in order. Four days ago they had received word of the capture of Johnston Island. During that time, Sheppard had not had two hours of uninterrupted sleep. Time enough for that, he mused as he drew heavily on the bourbon-laced coffee. A dry heat burned in his stomach and radiated outward. He sat a little straighter in the chair as his operations officer approached with a clipboard.

"Whatcha got, Bill?"

"Latest from the atoll, sir. The HASMAT and medical teams from the *Vinson* have arrived by helo. The USS *Elliot* is now in Johnston Island harbor and tied up pier-side. Looks like they may have scraped the sonar dome getting in there, but they made it." Sheppard shrugged. He knew the Navy was fussy about those things, but at this point he really didn't care. Fuck 'em. "We now have the ship's medical and food-service capabilities there," Simms continued. "The team of Air Force combat controllers that landed earlier report they'll have the runway cleared and operational by 1500. Additional relief teams at Hickam are loaded aboard C-130s and waiting for the go-ahead."

"How about the sub?"

Colonel Simms flipped through his message file. "Nothing serious but it seems the intakes have been partially fouled. They're heading back to Pearl at low speed; looks like she'll have to be dry-docked." He looked up. "The commander of the Pacific Submarine Force is going to be hot about that."

"Fuck him too," Sheppard said aloud. "What about that other matter I asked you to check on?"

Simms looked back to his clipboard and pursed his lips. "Colonel Lister confirmed it personally, sir. Lieutenant Moody's dead. Of the ten men who went ashore, only four made it—Captain Nakajima and three of the SEALs."

Sheppard didn't reply. Absentmindedly, he lit a cigarette, snapping the battered Zippo closed in a mechanical motion. For a long moment he just stared into space as if trying to bring the features of the SEAL officer into focus.

Sheppard recalled the cocky Navy lieutenant he'd met just a few days ago. News of the VX agents and the nuclear bomb waiting overhead had taken some of the starch out of him, but he'd sucked it up and got the job done. So did I, Sheppard reflected dispassionately.

For close to thirty years he'd trained, advised, planned, staffed, commanded, and waited—waited for the chance to do it for real. Now he had. All things considered, the operation had been a success, and given the odds they had faced going in, the result was far better than anyone would have imagined. He knew he would be commended for his role as commander, and this would make his second star a certainty.

But Sheppard felt anything but elated. He'd lost men under his command in training accidents, but never operationally; this too was a first for him. *That cocky Navy lieutenant made me look good,* he thought—*made all of us look good. Now some assholes up the line will probably consider the deaths of those boys, Japanese and American, as acceptable losses. Well, fuck them too.* The general smiled sadly as he studied the ash of his cigarette. In the twisted smoke that rose to the ceiling of the crowded room, he could almost see the faces of the two tall, lean, grinning SEALs who looked like brothers and the blocky, serious Japanese captain. *Nakajima made it and thank God for that,* he thought, *but I'd trade all the credit they're gonna give me to have them all back here alive.*

"General . . . sir, are you all right?"

"Huh, yeah sure, Bill. Just a little tired." He took a quick drag on the cigarette and dropped it into his coffee cup. "I'll be in my quarters; think I'll try for a little sleep. Wake me if there're any new developments."

"Yes, sir."

"And send Colonel Lister my compliments. Tell him I'd like to visit him on Johnston Island later this afternoon at his convenience."

Sunday, 11 December, 4:42 P.M.
JOHNSTON ISLAND

Jim Bruso sat in his office with the phone wedged between his shoulder and his ear. Paperwork and an endless string of inquiries from corporate headquarters had pinned him to the desk for the last two hours. He knew he should get some rest, but there always seemed to be just one more thing to do. Bruso had ordered Rosie to leave and get some rest, but she continued to shuttle in and out of the office— bringing in files, delivering messages, maintaining a steady stream of coffee for him, Blackman, and herself. In truth, Bruso would have had to rely on the senator for assistance had Rosie gone home, as both of his hands were now bandaged. His left hand, the one gouged by Senator Blackman, was loosely bound and healing nicely, but his right was tightly wrapped in a temporary splint and would have to be properly set and cast. He looked like a weary prizefighter in street clothes.

While Rosie hovered over Bruso, Nancy Blackman occupied her desk, making a series of short, self-assured calls back to the Capital. She'd dismissed the extremely persistent and stubborn FBI man, but she needed to explain it all to her assistant in Washington. She'd be back soon, she assured the nervous young man, she just needed to stay on for a few days. Yes, meetings would have to be rescheduled, and yes, she knew the president wanted to see her as soon as possible. But this had been a life-and-death tragedy, which all concerned would understand. It would be fine. She would talk to the president on the phone, if he insisted.

Aircraft had been arriving for about two hours now. At first just C-130s, but Bruso had seen a few of the larger C-141s. There were medical teams, engineers, MPs, and an Army graves-registration team that set up a temporary morgue to handle the dead. Most of those killed had been military personnel, but not all. There was a short stack of personnel files on the edge of the desk that accounted for deceased Emerson Management Corporation employees— his people. Corporate headquarters would make most of the arrangements with next of kin, but he wanted to write each family a personal letter, or dictate it to Rosie since he wouldn't be writing for a while.

Outside, the sun breaks were more frequent and longer in duration. The waterfront was busy, mostly with people in uniform. The sleek gray lines of the USS *Elliot* were in sharp contrast to the rust-streaked, battered hull of the *Sea of Fertility*, moored nearby. Bruso and Blackman seemed to be taking turns looking out the window, checking to make sure the destroyer was still there and the stars and stripes still snapping in the wind on the stern. They both needed that now.

Blackman was in with Bruso when Rosie buzzed him from the outer office. "Jim, Colonel Lister is here to see you."

Bruso clubbed the intercom button. "Thanks, Rosie. Ask him to come in."

Bruso had met with Lister shortly after he'd arrived. The colonel was ready with a list of questions and quickly set about taking command of the island. Bruso liked him immediately, thinking that it might not be a bad idea to make a Marine the permanent atoll commander. He rose from the desk just as Lister came through the door. The tall Marine colonel wore battle dress—desert cammies, web harness, and helmet—just as the Marines had in Somalia and Kuwait. He nodded politely to Bruso, then snapped to attention and saluted Senator Blackman.

"Mr. Bruso; ma'am." Lister took out a notebook and continued. "We've established routine security patrols on the island and I've established a guard rotation at the chemical-storage site and destruction facility. The Army and Air Force are providing just about anything we ask for. They've even set up a dozen extra phone lines with dedicated operators. Your folks can make all the calls they want, anywhere they want."

One of Bruso's priorities had been to make sure that his people could contact their families as soon as possible. He had also asked that the families of those Emerson employees who'd died be notified in person through military channels, rather than by a phone call from the head office. The military was practiced at telling families their loved one overseas would arrive home in a casket. Lister had taken that request up the chain of command, but as yet had had no reply.

The colonel methodically worked through a list of house-keeping, security, and medical issues. Finally he turned to Senator Blackman. "Ma'am, there's a VIP aircraft due here within the hour that will take you back to Hawaii and to a connecting flight to the mainland—compliments, I understand, of the commander-in-chief."

"Thank you, Colonel, but I'm staying."

Lister frowned slightly. "Ma'am?"

"I said I'm staying."

"I see, ma'am," he replied, now looking nonplussed. "Begging the senator's pardon, ma'am, but don't you want to get out of here, I mean after what you've been through?"

"In a few days, but as you've pointed out, I've been through a lot with these people. I feel I need to be here with them for a while."

Lister started to say something, but then he shrugged imperceptibly and made an entry in his canvas-covered notepad. "Yes, ma'am. I'll see that your wishes are conveyed up the line. And now, if you'll excuse me, I have to attend to my duties."

Lister saluted and left, joining another senior Marine officer and an NCO waiting for him in the outer office. Bruso didn't move for a moment, then turned to Nancy Blackman.

"So, uh, how long are you going to be with us?" Bruso was still trying to get used to the idea of Blackman's continued presence on the island.

She gave him an easy smile. "Maybe a day or two, if that's not going to be a problem."

"No, no problem at all. I'll have Rosie make sure one of the transient suites is cleaned up for you." He reached over the desk for the intercom but she gently caught his hand.

"If you don't mind, I'll just stay with you."

Bruso just stared at her. He started to reply but could think of nothing to say.

"That is," she continued, "if you don't mind."

"Why, no, I don't actually mind . . . but, uh, why—why with me?"

She wrapped both her arms around his left one and smiled again. "Jim, these past few days I wouldn't have made it if you hadn't been there. Sometimes I was so scared I almost couldn't breathe. The only time I could sleep at all was when you were holding me. Now I'm almost afraid to be alone. And," she leaned forward and kissed him lightly on the cheek, "I'm not sure I'll be able to sleep comfortably unless you're willing to hold me again."

He looked at her closely. Her expression was calm and warm, but there was a hint of anxiety in the clear green eyes. He smiled. "I think I probably need to hold someone tonight about as much as you need to be held."

Monday, 12 December, 4:15 P.M.
TOKYO, JAPAN

Prime Minister Mitsuzuka sat in one of the two brocade armchairs and carefully sipped his tea. It had been a difficult and emotional day. Initially news of the success on Johnston Atoll had been qualified and, after much debate, Mitsuzuka had decided to delay the opening of the Japanese stock market by two hours. Nonetheless the Neikke average had plunged by more than 10 percent before the institutions, responding to some not-so-subtle government pressure, had waded back into the market and led a modest recovery. When the yen finally closed virtually unchanged against the dollar, they knew the crisis was over.

"It could have been a great deal worse."

Mitsuzuka lowered his head in acknowledgment. Masayoshi Oka had worked tirelessly behind the scenes, particularly within the ponderous and near-autonomous bureaucracy that, in reality, governed Japan. The wounds made by Tadao, and opened further by the debate that had followed, had deeply scarred the fabric of Japanese society.

It was now being openly debated: Was Japan precipitously abandoning centuries of culture and tradition in a headlong rush to beat the West? If they won, would it be enough? And what share of the blame should the United States accept for the war and the nuclear weapons that had so dramatically ended it? Tadao's gallant, misguided, and noble gamble had touched them all. He had awakened some dormant yearning in the Japanese soul that longed for the past, however irrational and destructive the reality of that craving might be. And it was a genie not easily lured back into its ancient lamp.

"How do you recommend that we proceed from here, Oka-san?"

The old man folded his hands across his lap and spoke softly. "We must move slowly. Everything can and should be done to ensure that Tadao and his men are not idolized. If necessary, we must mount a carefully crafted disinformation program. They must be branded as criminals and shameless glory-seekers." Oka paused and considered his words carefully. "This will not be easy, for I feel they will become as famous as the Forty-seven *Ronin* and take their place in a modern version of that feudal legend."

Mitsuzuka lowered his eyes to signal his concurrence. "And what of the one survivor at Johnston Island, the man who surrendered?"

Oka shrugged. "Let the Americans keep him. Their jails are places of violence; perhaps he will die there, either by his own hand or by that of one of his fellow criminals. I am more concerned about the men we sent to help the Americans. I understand they did well?"

"Very well indeed." Mitsuzuka slipped a pair of half-moon reading glasses from his jacket pocket and took up a message from the lamp table by his chair. "This was conveyed from Secretary of State Carlton to our embassy in Washington through coded channels." He slid on the glasses and began to read. "The unfortunate incident at Johnston Atoll could not have been resolved without the gallant efforts of Captain Shintaro Nakajima and his men. Their professionalism and courage were an inspiration to members of the United States armed forces who served with them. The President of the United States wishes to extend his sincere condolences to the families of those who perished in the recapture of the atoll.'' Mitsuzuka refolded the message.

"Their work on Johnston Atoll," Oka said leaning forward in his chair, "this gallant service Mr. Carlton speaks of—is it public knowledge?"

"I am told that it is not."

Oka nodded at this. "I see. And do you plan to keep it so?"

Mitsuzuka slowly inhaled through his lower teeth. "I believe so. Now that Tadao is dead and the Americans have their island, I see little to be gained by admitting that we had a hand in the matter. It is enough that President Garrison and his senior advisers know that we helped. And there is the matter of Article Nine in our constitution. We would be inviting trouble from the left as well as the right."

Oka nodded. "And the men from the Naginata Counter Force who died at Johnston Atoll? How will that be explained?"

"Minister Uno was here earlier this afternoon and we discussed the matter. We have yet to learn the identity of those killed, but the men of the Counter Force are mostly from poorer families with a history of military service. They are, if you will, samurai. And as you know, the death of a retainer in the service of his liege is not an event that is questioned—certainly not if the retainer's wages are brought current and the death benefit is promptly paid."

Oka made no reply, and both men sipped their tea in silence. Then the prime minister continued. "But I will tell you one thing, Oka-san. At some future time, I will find a way to bring this Captain Nakajima to Tokyo and privately convey to him my gratitude."

Once again, Oka nodded.

Monday, 12 December, 7:15 A.M.
THE WHITE HOUSE

The Starbucks coffee, bran muffins, and plate of fruit were at the desk in the Oval Office by 6:45 that morning, but President Robert Garrison was a half hour late. It had been Garrison's intention to return to his normal schedule, but Gates Carlton had rapped at the door to his study just before midnight with half a fifth of Glenfiddich scotch. It was on to 1:30 A.M. before they finished it. Once in the office, he made straight for the coffee, then tackled the papers.

As expected, there was a blend of indignation and analysis along with high praise for the military. The bipartisan support he'd enjoyed during the crisis had dissolved into ringing endorsements by members of his party and accusations of neglect by the opposition. Politics as usual, Garrison mused, as he tossed aside the *New York Times* and took up the *Post*. Both papers had front-page articles on the domestic chemical-weapons storage facilities and the need to take action.

Garrison smiled and shook his head. Two weeks ago, getting Congress to authorize funding for the destruction of chemical weapons would have been a long and painful process. And *if* the funding had been approved, there would have been monumental local issues and environmental considerations. Now they'll be throwing money at the problem and the people living near those storage sites will want it done yesterday. Nothing like a near-catastrophe to get people off their butts, thought the president, especially congressional butts.

"Good morning Mr. President!" Gates Carlton poked his head around the door, having again slipped past his receptionist. "Got a second?"

"Only if you're not armed with a bottle of scotch."

Carlton advanced on the desk with his hands in a show of surrender. Garrison smiled and poured him a cup of coffee. "How're they treating us?"

"Pretty much as we expected," Garrison replied. "It's too early for any polling data, but it looks like we're getting good marks for the handling of the crisis." He grinned. "And Congress will take a bath for the delays in chemical-weapons destruction."

Carlton dropped into one of the padded cane chairs in front of the desk. "Ready for this morning?"

Garrison took up a set of notes he'd prepared earlier the previous evening. "The press conference is set for 10:30. I'll announce a day of mourning for those killed on Johnston Atoll—flags at half mast, the whole bit—urgent call for the security and destruction of all weapons of mass destruction." Garrison rose and started to pace, mentally reviewing his delivery. "I'll make an appeal for understanding on behalf of the nation of Japan, that this was a terrorist act and not one with national intent. And, of course, kind words for our men in uniform." He flipped a page over, then back. "That's about it. Not a lot different from what Linda Gonzales gave them yesterday at her scheduled press conference. Of course, I'll want General McKenzie and you there for any questions concerning the military operation or the diplomatic side. Anything else?"

Carlton sipped his coffee and leaned forward with his forearms on his knees. He was suddenly serious. "As you suggested, I met with McKenzie earlier for a detailed account of exactly what happened. He says we almost lost the whole ball game right at the end. Somehow this Tadao guy managed to get to the chemicals and was about to blow them up. The Navy lieutenant died stopping him or those special VX agents would have been released." He pursed his lips and looked up at the president. "We dodged a bullet, Bob. This thing almost got away from us."

Garrison returned to his desk and sat down heavily. "Yeah, I know." Both men were silent for a while. But not too long; neither of them wanted to dwell on the disaster that might have been. "You're not suggesting we say anything about these super-VX agents, are you?"

"No, of course not. I just thought you ought to know. It may come out and again it may not. Security is pretty tight on Johnston Atoll and the press has had to cover the story from Hawaii."

"What about Nancy Blackman? She still there?"

"Word is she'll stay on a day or two." Carlton shrugged. He set his cup on the desk and rose to leave. "Beats me why. You'd think she'd be on the first plane out of there. I know I would."

After Carlton had gone, Garrison hurried through the other papers and his intelligence reports, then tackled the bran muffin and another cup of coffee. When Martin Sizemore and Rita Breamer arrived for their 8:00 A.M. appointment to brief him on options for chemical-weapons disposal, they had to wait. The president was in the Oval Office water closet with his economic summary.

Monday, 12 December, 6:53 A.M.
HICKAM AIR FORCE BASE, HAWAII

A single olive-drab C-141 crouched on the hardstand at the southern end of the landing strip. The gently drooping wings seemed to mark its sadness at being segregated from the other aircraft parked at the terminal and around the hangars across the field. The big transport had no markings, which positively identified it as a special-operations aircraft.

The main portion of the storm had passed south of the islands, but a stiff morning breeze ushered a steady procession of low, ugly clouds across the approaches to Pearl Harbor. They hurried inland, only to be gathered into the dirty cotton curtain that had formed at the base of the Koolau range. Rain had spattered Oahu on and off throughout the night. None fell now, but the gray dawn promised more.

A blue club-cab pickup and a nine-passenger van waited near the SPECOPS 141. Under the wing a small group of men milled about, talking quietly. All conversation stopped when they spotted the ambulance that approached along the service road. It was an Air Force military vehicle, boxy and more like a delivery van than an ambulance. As it backed up to the massive doors at the tail of the aircraft, those under the wing filed back to meet it.

Two Air Force corpsmen opened the rear doors. They then stood aside as the men—some Japanese, some American—took one of the caskets from the ambulance and up the ramp into the belly of the aircraft. They returned for two more. No words were spoken, but the driver presented Captain Nakajima with a clipboard, indicating where he should sign. Nakajima made no move but the man insisted. Finally, a tall American jerked it from his hand and scribbled roughly across the bottom.

"Hey, look man," he said, "I need an officer's signature."

"You're gonna need a ride in the back of that rig yourself if you don't get the fuck out of here. Now beat it."

The driver started to say something, but the look on the big man's face froze him. He quickly realized he'd rather deal with some administrative unpleasantness at the other end than force the issue here. He left without another word.

"Excuse me, Glasser-san, but I believe he was just carrying out his assignment."

"I know, sir, but we don't have to take that shit off these Air Force pukes."

"Are the men flying us home not, ah, Air Force pukes?"

"Oh, no, sir. They're special-ops guys; they're our people."

"I see," Nakajima replied dubiously. Just then an enlisted crewman stepped down from the ramp, saluted, and announced that those making the trip should be on board. Nakajima thanked the crewman and turned to Glasser.

He bowed. "It has been an honor to serve with you Glasser-san. And with both of you." He bowed in turn to Slyfield and Jackson. The three Americans bowed awkwardly. Had their efforts not been so sincere, they would have been comical. "If your duties ever bring you to Okinawa, you must come for a visit."

"Thank you, sir."

They exchanged salutes and Nakajima led his men to the aircraft, but before they could board, a black staff car roared off the service road and screeched to a halt. The driver was out immediately to open the rear door. Admiral Harrington emerged with a small attaché case under his arm, pushing his hat firmly on his head in deference to the wind. He walked quickly over to the men at the bottom of the ramp; they snapped to attention.

"Please, stand easy," he said, briskly returning their salutes. "I wanted to thank each one of you personally for what you were able to accomplish on Johnston Island. The people of the United States and Japan are in your debt." Harrington shook each man's hand, beginning with the Americans. Then he motioned to Nakajima. "Captain, may I have a word with you."

While the others waited, the Japanese captain and the Commander-in-Chief, Pacific Theater, walked out past the wingtip of the C-141. "Captain," Harrington began, "General Sheppard briefed me on your role in the success of the operation. I'm also told that your role in this matter will not be made public, either in this country or your own." Nakajima nodded impassively. "I just wanted to let you know how grateful I am for what you've done. And I speak for the president and the American people; thank you very much. Your sacrifice and those of your dead comrades will not soon be forgotten by those of us who were privileged to know of your contribution."

Nakajima lowered his head. "You honor me, Admiral, but it is not necessary. It was my duty, one that I was privileged to carry out. My men," he paused, looking toward the aircraft, "they were warriors and died properly, as did your men, in particular Lieutenant Moody. He was a great warrior, Moody-sama, perhaps the greatest I will ever know.''

Harrington nodded his agreement. ''Nonetheless, we owe you a great deal.'' He looked at Nakajima for a long moment. Then, as if coming to a decision, he pulled a faded blue leather box from the attaché case and handed it to the Japanese. ''Captain, I want you to have this.''

Nakajima took the box in both hands, Japanese fashion, and opened it. He stared at the contents and quickly bowed very low—to show respect and to hide his face. ''Admiral,'' he finally replied in a husky, emotionally charged voice as he rose, ''I have read a great deal of your history; I know what this is and I know how it came to you. I . . . I am honored beyond words, but how can you give this to me?''

It was Harrington's turn to search for words. ''I'm not entirely sure, but I know that I want you to have it. Perhaps,'' he continued in a firm voice, ''I want you to have this so that your son and my grandson will not have to meet like this at some future time.''

Nakajima again bowed low, and the Commander-in-Chief, Pacific Theater, holding onto his hat, returned the gesture.

Later that morning, high over the Pacific Ocean, Captain Nakajima took out the leather case and carefully opened it. Reverently he touched the sky-blue ribbon that was spattered with white stars and the five-pointed, wreathed medallion that hung from it. The ribbon was slightly faded and one of the star points tarnished, but that was understandable. This Congressional Medal of Honor was more than a half century old.

Dick Couch graduated from the U.S. Naval Academy in 1967. He was a platoon commander with Underwater Demolition Team 22 and SEAL Team 1, serving two tours of duty in Vietnam. He holds the rank of captain in the Naval Reserve and serves as a senior staff officer with the naval special warfare community in Coronado, California.